EDEN

C. J. Singh

This is a work of fiction. Names, characters, places, and incidents either are the product of the author's imagination or are used fictitiously. Any resemblance to actual persons, living or dead, events, or locales is entirely coincidental.

Copyright © 2020 by Christina J. Singh

All rights reserved. No part of this book may be reproduced or used in any manner without written permission of the copyright owner except for the use of quotations in a book review. For more information, address: christinasingh28@gmail.com.

First paperback edition February 2020

ISBN 978-1-7366354-1-4 (paperback)
ISBN 978-1-7366354-0-7 (ebook)

www.worldofcjsingh.com

For my Grandma, my first reader

Chapter 1

Eden

Slapping the mosquito biting my arm, I stretched my stiff neck and smiled down to Ash, my wolf, who sat patiently at my feet panting. He looked at me expectantly with his bright gold eyes. "Ah, you lush." I reached down and stroked his beautiful, thick black coat with brown undertones, relishing the moment. But it was short-lived as another mosquito penetrated my arm. "How much longer do you want to sit here? I'm getting eaten alive."

"Just a few more minutes. My feet are killing me," Tate, my brother, replied. He was resting against a tree, his ice-blue eyes looking pathetically exhausted as he gave me a dimpled grin.

Tristan, my brother's best friend, nudged Tate. "You're such a baby. You need to get out more. All that fishing is making you weak."

I laughed but stiffened at the echo of a snap. Then another. Only something big would make twigs snap like that. After motioning the boys to be quiet, I scanned the woods for predators, seeing only oak trees and brush. My shoulders relaxed a little. Nothing in the immediate area. Ash stood, hackles up, letting out a low growl. I put my hand on his head to quiet him. If it was a bear, I didn't want it to hear us. Tate and Tristan both took their daggers from the sheaths on their legs as I slowly pulled an arrow from my pack, knocking it into my bow. If it was something big, my arrows would keep us alive better than their daggers would.

"You idiot!" A man's voice echoed from the bottom of the mound.

People? There weren't any people this west of the cabin. We crept toward the edge to get a better look. Ash stayed glued to my calf, ready to attack on command. We had the advantage of being on higher ground, but I continued to scan our surrounding area in case there were others.

"I'm sorry," a tall young man said. He moved his long black hair from his face as he turned toward two other men.

A man with sandy hair squared off. "You're sorry? That doesn't do us any good out here! We're going to die! Die!"

"We might as well have been killed inside the walls. It would have been quicker than out here. Less painful too," the third man said. He seemed like the oldest, but I couldn't get a good look at any of them from our distance.

"Jim is right. We had a plan. Get in, free my sister, and get out. But that wasn't enough for you. You had to go and be Mr. Salvation. Well, look where it got us!" the sandy-haired man snapped.

"I know! It's just that once we got there, I saw all the other rooms. I just couldn't leave them all. So many children! It's just not right!" Mr. Salvation dropped his head.

"I get it. I do, but Jace... we weren't prepared for that. You should have known it would be suicide to try and save them all!"

"Well, at least I tried!" Jace's voice cracked. "I couldn't live with myself if I hadn't even tried."

"At least you tried? Are you kidding me? You got us banished to die! How is that a good outcome?"

Jim moved between the other two. "OK, guys. Cool it. We need to figure out what's out here and where we'll spend the night. I don't plan on just giving up."

"You only think of yourself, Jace. You should have stuck with the plan." The sandy-haired man pushed him to the side.

"Landon... Jace." Jim inched between them.

"Seriously? I wasn't thinking of myself. I was thinking of all those people in cages, with needles stuck in their arms. I was trying to free them. Give them a chance at life!"

"Free them? Where the hell would they go once you freed them? Did you think about that? You know everyone dies once infected. No one survives."

"Well..."

"That's what I thought. Idiot."

Pursing his lips, Jace swung his fist and met the side of Landon's jaw, filling the trees with a loud grunt.

"What the hell!" He wiped his lip, and when he looked down, there was a smear of red on his finger. Jace never took his eyes off him as he shook out his punching hand.

"You're going to regret that." Landon tackled Jace onto the leaf speckled ground. Their grunts filled the clearing, and I cringed at what kind of animals they might attract.

Still hidden within the shadows of the trees, all three of us watched the chaos below. "What the?... We can't let them kill each other," I whispered. Jace had Landon pinned on his stomach, but with one swift swing of his head, Landon was on top.

"Why not? We don't know who they are or what they want. They are from the city. If they kill each other, it saves us the dirty work." Tate turned and walked away.

I looked back at the fighting men. Landon's knuckles met Jace's face over and over, causing blood to spray the surrounding grass. The breeze brought the hint of metal to my nose and I winced. That had to hurt. Jace looked like he may have passed out, but his eyes were open, and I'm pretty sure he was trying to push Landon away with weak arms. Jim grabbed Landon's shoulder, pulling him, but Landon pushed him away where he fell onto his back.

How could we just let them kill each other? We had never met anyone from the city and the possibility of learning about life within the walls sounded exciting. I didn't want to just sit back and watch. "I can't, Tate. He'll kill him."

"Eden, leave it."

I tapped my foot, watching the men. Jace put his hands on Landon's shoulders in an attempt to push him off. Landon didn't budge.

"Eden," Tristan echoed in warning.

I turned and took a step over the top off the mound, but Tristan grabbed my arm, pulling me back into the shade of the trees. Ash stood, moving between us, and Tristan dropped his hold. He tried not to look intimidated by Ash, but his rigid shoulders said otherwise. Clearing his throat, he looked back at me. "Tate's right. You know how people in the city feel about us. Why should we care if some of them were banished?"

I hesitated. "OK, but have you ever heard of anyone being banished before? If we leave them, they are bound to come across someone out here. We just let them jeopardize others' lives?"

Tate nodded. "We have no choice. We go back to Old Bob and let him know. He will know what to do."

Kicking up some leaves on the ground, I rolled my eyes. "All right. Let's go."

I gave the three men one last look. Landon was slumped on top of Jace, whose face was unrecognizable through the blood and swelling. Oh yeah, that had to hurt. Turning, I followed my brother and Tristan back to our cabin with Ash trotting at my heels.

࿇

We approached our old cabin just before dinner. Ellie, our adoptive mother, was lugging two full buckets of fresh creek water up the small hill the cabin was built on.

"Here, let me help." Tristan jogged over, grabbing the buckets.

"Thank you," Ellie gasped out, shaking out her arms. "You would think I would be stronger doing that for eighteen years."

"You're just getting old." I nudged her side playfully. "Where's Old Bob?"

"Inside. He just got back with a rabbit."

My mouth watered at the thought of juicy rabbit stew. Our garden had been doing well with plump potatoes and carrots.

"Come. We better get everything on the fire before it gets dark," Ellie grumbled. She tried not to complain about the lack of luxuries she had since the quarantine of the city, but one escaped her daily.

"Hey, just be happy we have four walls and a roof for the rain and nasty winters," Tate said, emerging from the outhouse.

Ellie smiled, giving his shoulder a squeeze. "Always the voice of reason."

The porch door screeched as we entered and our feet created heavy thuds along the wood floor. You couldn't move about without someone hearing you. Ash's nails clinked his way to the fire where he curled up on his favorite blanket.

I helped Ellie with the stew, and as it simmered over the fire, we all relaxed in the living area. I watched Ash's side move up and down in the slow rhythm of his breaths as the firelight glowed against the brown in his coat. It'd been three years since I found him, a tiny pup in the burnt ashes of a cabin. He imprinted on me, and since then, we have been inseparable.

We told Old Bob about what we saw in the woods as he clutched his cup of tea, the firelight hitting the small crow's feet on his weather-worn skin. He wasn't old, but we teased him that he was.

"How many were there?"

"Three," Tate replied.

"They mentioned being banished. Why would the city banish people now? No one leaves. They are all scared of us," I said.

Old Bob gave Ellie a quick look before focusing back on his fingers moving through the grooves of the table. Looking away, Ellie went to the kitchen without a word, her long brown hair swinging in a high ponytail down her back.

"Not sure, but if they were banished, we should stay away." He took a long sip of his tea, narrowing his eyes at me over the top of the mug.

I fought the urge to roll my eyes. Why was I always the one who was considered reckless? "What should we do then?"

"We?" Old Bob chuckled. "*We* do nothing. They won't find us, and in the small chance that they do, I will handle it." He was always so confident about his abilities. Yeah, he was a good fighter and trained all three of us, but he couldn't take on the world alone.

"Seriously? We just let them wander the woods? They could come across others." Our closest neighbor, Ms. Lydia, lived alone. Thinking of her rickety, old body coming in contact with some strangers from the city made my head light.

Old Bob stood. "Seriously." He softened his gaze. "It's fine. Nothing will happen. The woods are large. I am more concerned with their survival than them hurting us or anyone else." He moved through the room toward the kitchen. "If they are from the city, they won't last long out here alone."

I looked out the window at the glowing sky. The sun was almost down, leaving the fire as the only light left. Old Bob was probably right, between the virus and scorched land from the war, not even a hundred miles from here, they wouldn't survive.

"I will set up watch tonight," Tristan said.

Old Bob looked over his shoulder as he washed his mug in the sink. "If that makes you feel better, feel free. I don't think it is necessary though."

"It does."

Old Bob rubbed his faded scars that marred his tan face. "Very well." He walked out the back door. I followed his dark shape through the windows as he trudged toward the boathouse and a pit in my stomach formed.

"Do you guys think Old Bob is hiding something?"

"Why would he? He has no reason to lie," Tate said.

"Yeah. You always think the worst. We'll sit up, so you don't worry about a thing," Tristan said, giving me a grin.

I glared at him. I was not scared and didn't need them to keep me safe. It was crap and they knew it. I could handle myself as well as they could, probably better. Plus, I had Ash. "If that makes you feel better." I stomped out of the cabin, their laughs following me.

∽

"The blueberries are plump this year." Tate put a large spoonful into his mouth, smiling as a drip of blue juice rolled down his chin.

"Are you going to go or not?" Tristan rapped his fingers on the table, giving Tate his best game face. Cards were the nightly routine for them making for a good show of entertainment for everyone else. The fun jabs and jokes toward each other filled the cabin with laughter, often pulling Old Bob's eyes out from behind his books.

"Your hair is so beautiful." I closed my eyes as the gentle scrape of the brush massaged my scalp. Ellie's delicate hands worked through my long, thick hair as she braided it in our nightly routine. When I was younger, we would sit back and read stories together, but now we just chatted quietly. I savored our time together, wondering if it would have been the same with my own mother.

She reached down and touched the silver butterfly necklace that hung around my neck with a smile. She had given it to me on my tenth birthday saying, *Butterflies represent change and hope*, as she slipped it around my neck. I haven't taken it off since.

"What the... really?" Tate yelled.

A blueberry flew across the room, and I batted it away. "Hey!"

"All right you two. I just swept!" Ellie laughed. "I'll make you two tea if you're planning on keeping watch tonight."

"I'll do it." Old Bob put his book down and headed to the kitchen.

Resting my head on Ellie's shoulder, I smiled at the warm moment of firelight, laughs, and love. I squeezed her arm, pulling her warmth into my heart as she kissed the top of my head. I never wanted this to change.

∽

I awoke with a start in the night. Staring up at the wood rafters in the moonlight, I held my breath to hear what woke me. The quiet steady breaths that filled the cabin from the others were washed out by something large slithering across the grass. Ash's head lifted from his warm sleeping spot at my feet. I sat up and slid out of bed, pulling in a long breath. Dust and old wood filled my nose, and I stifled a sneeze. Sliding my bare feet on the wood floor, I moved through the cabin. Ash's paws clicked as he followed and I furrowed my brow at him. "Could you be any louder?" He cocked his head at me, and I smiled.

I worked my way to the back bedroom where Tate was sleeping in his bed. I pushed his shoulder lightly. "Tate." He didn't stir. "Tate," I said a little louder. Still no response. He didn't usually sleep this deep.

The slithering neared and a knot formed in my stomach. I leaned down and sniffed his mouth, which had the hint of sweetness. Valerian root? Or maybe the blueberries?

I got up and slid my feet to the porch where Tristan was on watch. My movements were quick as my heart rate increased. When I got to the porch, Tristan was asleep upright in the chair. A rush of air left me. Ash sniffed his hand, giving it a little lick as I shook him lightly, but he didn't stir. When I leaned in, I smelled the same sweet smell. That was definitely valerian root.

"Tristan?" I whispered. Nothing.

Ash whined quietly as the slithering sounded almost right outside the door. Scanning the dark yard, I saw a large, dark figure moving in the dark. Crouching down to get a better view through the porch door, I watched the shadows move through the brush. When the figure hit the clearing in front of the boathouse, my heart dropped as the moon shone on Old Bob's figure dragging something very large. White puffs of air left his mouth with each pant he made as he lugged the large object. I squinted, trying to get a better look at what he was pulling, but it was too dark. What was he doing?

He moved down the small hill and disappeared into the boathouse. I felt every pump of my heart as I waited, eyes pinned to the boathouse door until he reappeared a few moments later. As he slowly approached the cabin, hunched over, watching the dark ground, Ash licked my hand in an urgent plea to move. I crawled back to the main cabin door careful not to scratch the wood, then tiptoed back to my bed. Ash and I cuddled into our usual positions, but I held my blanket a little tighter to keep my hands from shaking. I kept my eyes closed as I listened to Old Bob creep into his room and shut the door. I let out a breath I didn't know I was holding.

The rest of the night I lay awake tossing and turning as I wondered what Old Bob had been doing. Hunting? No, that would be stupid.

When the pink of the sunrise peeked through the trees, I couldn't contain my curiosity anymore. With the cabin still quiet, Ash and I crept outside, past Tristan still sleeping in the chair. Once outside, we jogged down the small hill toward the boathouse. As the cool air tickled my lungs, I slowed my pace so I didn't slip on the dew-covered grass. My mind raced with the possibilities of what could be in the boathouse.

When I reached the wooden door, I moved the bolt slowly and cracked it to peek inside. Taking a minute for my eyes to adjust to the darkness, I breathed in the smell of fresh-cut wood with a hint of sweat and blood that permeated the air. On the far back wall, in front of a pile of cut wood, lay a bruised, dirty, blood-covered body. Long, dark hair covered half of his face, but I still recognized it. He was the boy from the clearing, Jace. His hands were tied behind his back and his ankles tied together in front of him. He was sleeping or passed out, I'm not sure, but his stomach was moving with steady breaths, so he was alive. The sun streamed through the crack of the door, and I quickly shut it and slid the bolt over. I needed to get back inside before the others woke. My heart hurt as I worked my way up the small hill to the cabin.

Chapter 2

Eden

Sitting quietly curled up on the cushy couch, I clutched my tea. Ash was snuggled at my feet, sleeping soundly. My mind raced with every possible reason why Old Bob would have dragged Jace to our boathouse.

Tristan walked into the room, stretching. "I must have been more tired than I thought." No one replied as he sat down next to me, disappointment written on his furrowed brow. His bulky arm rubbed mine as he scooted over to leave room for Tate.

"Me too." Tate rubbed his tired blue eyes, squishing in next to him. I scooted over to give them both more room. This couch was not meant for three adults and a wolf. Poor Ash jumped off and trotted to his favorite blanket, so I didn't get squished into the arm of the couch.

While the boys discussed their confusion, I stared ahead, not moving other than to bring the tea to my lips. I watched Old Bob drink his tea slowly as he read a book. Not a worry showed on his face, no sign of his doings from the night before anywhere on him.

"You OK?" Tristan asked, pushing a hand through his golden curls. Tate stood and walked over to the table.

I gave a sad smile, not taking my eyes off Old Bob. "Yeah. Of course."

Sucking in his breath, he hesitated for a moment, then with one finger he gently tilted my head toward him. "Eden. You know better than to try and lie. I can read you like a book."

I gazed into Tristan's kind emerald eyes and gulped. Momentarily lost, forgetting about the events from last night, I thought of how pretty they were. My one blue eye never could compare.

"Eden," Tristan said, snapping me from my reverie. I glanced over at the table where Old Bob sat with his tea. Tristan noticed my gaze. He furrowed his brow and leaned a little closer, making our conversation more private. "I need you to tell me what's wrong. I'm getting concerned."

I stared down at my tea and whispered, "Last night, I heard something."

"What did you hear?"

I looked up into Tristan's handsome face. His eyes were fixed on mine and my cheeks warmed. I ducked down at the intensity of his gaze. He was basically my brother, but these looks had become more frequent the past year, and I wasn't sure how I felt about them.

"I don't know, but when I got up to find out what it was, I found you and Tate, out cold. I tried to wake you, but you wouldn't wake up. Then I saw Old Bob…" I paused and glanced at Old Bob who was now eating some fruit and nuts. "He put something in the boathouse."

"Did you see what?"

I nodded. "I went out after he came inside. I am warning you. You aren't going to like it."

"Eden, I am already pissed that somehow he may have drugged me and Tate. Whatever you have to say isn't going to make too much difference."

I let out a breath. "It was Jace. One of the guys we saw yesterday. The one that got beat on."

"You mean he is in the boathouse right now?"

"Tied up, but yeah. He was unconscious when I saw him."

"Stay right here." Tristan stood, but I grabbed his hand to stop him from doing anything rash. He clenched his jaw and fists. Ash woke up and gave his hand a lick for comfort.

"No, wait. Please, Tristan, don't make a big deal about this. We don't know everything."

He looked down at me, squeezing my hand. "Eden, he lied to us. He said to leave them, but he obviously didn't. What is he planning on doing with this guy?"

I didn't respond. I had no idea; I don't think I wanted to know what his plans were.

"See? I have to confront him." He pulled his hand from my grip and walked toward Old Bob.

At least he wasn't explosive about the situation. I give him props for that. He quietly sat in the chair between Old Bob and Tate, staying silent for a few moments before he addressed Old Bob.

"Were you planning on telling us that you have a hostage in the boathouse?"

Old Bob stopped mid-sip of tea, then slowly set it down. He eyed Tristan before he glanced back at me, and I dropped my eyes.

"Wait. What?" Tate scratched his dirty blond hair, still groggy.

Old Bob sat back in his chair, eyes locked with Tristan's. "So, what if I do? There could be many reasons, but I am getting the feeling you are accusing me of something. Are you?"

My stomach lurched. I hadn't thought about how this conversation might go, but this definitely wasn't the way I imagined. This never happened; we didn't fight. Flashes from the night before streamed through me, the card game, blueberries, and laughter. That was us, not this.

"I just want you to tell us the truth."

Old Bob cleared his throat. "No. I wasn't planning on telling you."

"So, there is a hostage in the boathouse?" Tate asked.

"Yeah. Old Bob here managed to drug us so we would sleep last night. Then he proceeded to capture one of the three men we told him about."

Tate leaned forward. "Why would you do that?"

Old Bob picked up a blueberry. "To protect all of you." He popped the blueberry in his mouth.

"Protect us? From what?" Tristan snapped.

"Look. I have raised you all since you were very young. I think of you as my own children. When something happens that may threaten my family, I'll do whatever it takes to protect them."

My heart squeezed at his words. I understood his feelings. I feel the same way; I just didn't understand why he would lie to us. If we are family, we should be working together.

"I understand that, but why tell us yesterday not to worry about it, then go out and capture one?" Tate asked.

Old Bob rubbed a hand over his tired face. "I didn't want to worry you, and I didn't want to put you all in danger, so I decided I would deal with it myself. I underestimated them and was only able to capture one safely. I thought I would track the other two today and take care of them."

Everyone was silent, letting the words register. Standing, I walked toward the table with Ash following closely at my ankles. "So, why do you foresee them as a threat?"

Old Bob turned to look at me. He didn't look as angry as I expected, which I was grateful for. "They are from the city. Anything from the city I see as a threat."

I sat down next to my brother. Ash walked out to the porch, curling up on the fuzzy rug in the sun. He loved that rug. "What is so threatening about the city? We haven't had any issues before."

Ellie leaned on the kitchen doorway. "They fear us. When people are scared, they do irrational things."

"Ahhh, right. The *virus*," I mocked.

"Right." She chuckled. "So, we don't know what they may try and do."

"So my strategy is to take them out before they can hurt us." Old Bob lifted his mug back to his lips and took a long sip, scanning all our faces before putting his mug back on the table.

"What did you mean that you will take them out?" Tristan asked.

"What do you think I mean?" Old Bob shook his head expectantly at Tristan.

I leaned forward. "Wait. You mean you want to *kill* them?"

"Yes, but before you scold me, listen. The virus will most likely kill them if it hasn't already, now that they are in the woods. So, if we take care of them first, it will be doing them a favor. Trust me. The one in the boathouse—"

"Jace," I snapped. "He has a name."

Old Bob's eyes widened. "Jace," he said carefully. "Yes, well we have limited time with him. He may not last more than a few days."

"Is he already sick?"

"No, but when he does show symptoms, it won't take long. Two, maybe three days, and trust me, I remember what it was like to be sick with the virus. Killing him would be a mercy."

My stomach tightened, and I pushed my tea away. If I drank one more sip, it would just come back up. "These are humans. People's sons! How can we so easily plan on killing them?" Tate squeezed my shoulder in reassurance, but I shrugged his hand away.

"You all know we love you so much. We would do nothing to hurt you or put you in danger, but we would do anything to protect you," Ellie said.

"Just remember, everything we do is for your safety. But from now on, I will tell you everything needed, even if it is against my better judgment. Deal?" Old Bob held out his hand to shake with us.

While I watched uneasily to see what Tate and Tristan did, Jace's words from the day before came to me. Kids in cages, needles in arms. If we just kill him, then we will never know what's happening in the city. Tate reached out and shook Old Bob's hand; Tristan followed. When Old Bob reached his hand out toward me, I stared at it, worn and cracked from hard work. I couldn't shake it.

I stood. "I'm sorry. I can't make that deal."

"Eden," Old Bob said quietly.

"Don't get me wrong. You're the only dad I've known, and I love you, but you can't just keep information from us like that. We aren't kids anymore. I just... need time."

Old Bob started to respond, but Ellie's hand on his arm stopped him. She smiled. "We understand. Please just know that we do love you, Eden. We will always do what we feel is right to protect you."

"Yeah, sure." I took my cup to the kitchen and set it in the sink. I could still feel the tea sloshing in my empty stomach, but I knew eating anything would only make it worse.

Old Bob leaned closer to the boys speaking quietly, "Can I talk to you both outside a moment?" They stood, brushing past me as they left the cabin, all trying not to meet my gaze. Clenching my jaw, I took a step forward, watching them meet in the yard, the breeze blowing their hair about.

"Come." Ellie touched my elbow leading me back to the table. She put a plate of fruit and nuts in front of me chatting about the plans for the day, but my mind buzzed with what Old Bob could be saying so that I didn't hear anything she said. I moved the berries around the plate, but not one made it to my mouth. I pushed my plate away. A heavy stream of footsteps on the porch brought my eyes up as all three men walked back inside.

"We better leave within the hour. I don't want them to get much of a head start." Old Bob leaned on the kitchen counter. "Eden." I looked at him. "I need you to stay behind with Ellie. I don't want to leave her alone with the man... um Jace."

"What was that?" I motioned to the door.

"Just planning." He pushed off the counter and strode into his room.

I started to say something but stopped when Tate gave me a small head shake. I didn't want to stay, but if I wasn't wanted, then I didn't want to go, especially if they were going to murder two people. My eyes stung as tears of betrayal filled them, but I squeezed them back. "All right. But for the record, Ellie doesn't need my protection. Don't insult her with your attempts."

Old Bob chuckled. "I agree."

I grabbed some first aid supplies from the cupboard. "Speaking of our hostage, I'm going to clean his wounds and offer him food."

"No, you're not," Tate snapped.

Grabbing my uneaten plate of food, I turned and glared at him. "If I am strong enough to stay behind to help *protect* Ellie, then I am strong enough to handle myself while I clean a beaten and tied up man. I don't think he can do much."

"It's all right," Old Bob said. "Go on, Eden. If we don't see you before we leave, then we will tonight or tomorrow for sure."

Leaving the cabin, I let the rickety wood porch door slam behind me and stomped toward the boathouse with Ash following closely at my heels.

Chapter 3

Eden

I closed the wood-paneled door behind me and looked at Jace. He was so bruised and cut, I sputtered at the thought that I needed protection from him. I cracked the door to let in some fresh air as the musty, sweat-filled room made me gag. Ash stood at guard next to me, and I smiled down at him. He was the only protection I would ever accept.

Jace's eyes fluttered open and he scooted back to the wall of piled logs. His hands and feet were still tied, and he didn't look comfortable.

"Who are you?" he rasped.

He looked thirsty, his lips were chapped, and I heard his belly grumble when his eyes flicked to the plate in my hand. Without responding, I stepped forward, but he jerked back, making Ash give a quiet growl.

"Don't come near me. Don't think about touching me." His eyes darted between my large furry companion and me.

I stopped, surprised. "What?"

"You do speak then. I said, 'Don't come near me.'"

I studied him. His thick, black hair was matted with blood and dirt as it framed his strong jaw. His eye that wasn't swollen shut was bright blue, which had a striking contrast from his dark hair. He didn't seem much older than me, nineteen maybe. I am not sure how someone got the better of him since he looked like he could handle himself with that muscular built body.

"Why don't you want me to come near you exactly?" I crouched and slid the plate of food toward him. A peace offering. He just stared at it, but he licked his lips at the sight of the berries.

"Because I don't want to get infected, duh."

"Infected?"

He furrowed his brows. "Yeah. Infected with the Fever."

"Fever? I don't have the Fever. If I did, I wouldn't be here, right? All I want to do is clean you up."

"You mean you don't have the Fever... the Ferine Fever? The virus?" He pronounced the name like I didn't know what it was and shook his head with confusion.

I put down the bag and held up my hands, turning in a circle. "Do I look like I have the Fever or the virus?"

He scanned me from top to bottom. "Well, no." He paused a moment calculating his next question. Trying to lean away from me again, he licked his chapped lips. "How is it you live here? I was told no one lived outside the walls."

"Seriously? How hard did your head get hit?"

"No, really." He turned his neck, and I heard it crack. "I mean, you have a home here. I can smell firewood burning. How many are there with you?"

Scanning his eyes, I thought of Old Bob's words about not trusting anyone from the city. "None of your business. Where does it hurt?" I started shuffling through my supplies.

"The crazy guy who tried to kill us all can throw a punch, that's for sure. Is he your dad?"

"Sort of." The fear from before must have passed since he didn't protest when I kneeled next to him. Before he could ask another question, I said, "If you are so chatty, then answer this. Why did you leave the city?"

The skin around his eyes tightened, and he set his mouth in a line. "It wasn't my choice."

I sat, quiet for a moment, watching him look everywhere but at me; his heart beat rapidly in my ears. "So, you were... banished?" I used the word that he said the day before.

His wide eyes shot to mine. "Something like that." I started to dab a cool cloth on his face. "So, your family is letting you in here alone, with me? A strange guy? What if I hurt you?"

"Hurt me?" I laughed. "They're probably more worried about you than me. I am fully capable of taking care of myself."

He smiled. "I'm sure you are." He flinched away when the cloth touched his arm. "Ow... Careful."

I smirk. "Plus, I have a wolf."

He glanced at Ash, leaning away slightly. "That you do."

Grabbing a bottle of water and a cloth from the bag, I said, "Put your head back." I wet the cloth more and blotted his cut eyebrow and lip. His one eye was so puffy and dark I couldn't do anything with it.

I felt his eyes on mine, and he cleared his throat. "So... how long have you lived out here?"

I put salve on his cuts. "My whole life."

He raised his eyebrows in disbelief. "You're telling me that you have lived out here for what, sixteen years?"

"Sixteen? You think I'm sixteen? I'm eighteen!" I stood and his laugh filled the small room, but he stopped and coughed.

"OK, eighteen. But, you're alive. How have you not gotten sick and died?"

I paused at his words. I was only a baby when we escaped the city, a group of fifty. Tate, Tristan, Old Bob, Ellie, and I were all that had survived.

I shrugged, putting my supplies back in my bag. "Just lucky, I guess." He watched me in silence, and I think of Old Bob and the boys heading out to find his friends. Jace didn't seem too bad, more confused than anything, so I can't imagine his friends being much worse. I turned to him. "Here's the deal. You are going to take me to where your friends are. If you do, I'll let you live."

"You haven't done much *dealing* before have you, Spunky. What you just offered isn't much of a deal. Why would I compromise my friends to you and your fist-happy father figure?"

"Did you just call me Spunky?" I watched his mouth twitch, but he quickly licked the cut on his lip.

"Well, you wouldn't tell me your real name. I needed to call you something."

"Yeah. Don't call me that again," I snapped as he smirked; he was going to be difficult I could feel it. "It's a deal for you. I am trying to help you and your friends."

He tried to scoot up more, but it looked painful with his hands and feet still tied. "Really? How so?" He sucked in a breath. "Can you call off your guard here? His breath stinks." Ash sat not two feet from him panting happily.

Rolling my eyes, I pulled out a small flip knife from my pocket. "Ash, leave him." Ash trotted back to the doorway and lay down with a groan. I took a few steps toward Jace when he flinched back, glancing at the knife.

"All right, all right, I won't call you Spunky anymore."

I stopped mid-step and smirked. "Just sit forward."

He hesitated a moment before giving in. Crouching in front of him, I pinned him with a stare. "If you try anything, I won't hesitate to kill you or let Ash have you. Understand?"

With a twinkle in his eye, he nodded. "Understood." Not believable, but I wasn't concerned, he was wounded.

Right as I finished sawing the rope from his hands, he added a soft, "Spunky."

I elbowed him in the side as I got up, and he coughed out a chuckle. "Wow. Aggressive much?"

"Are you going to help me find your friends or should I just kill you now?"

He reached down to his ankles and untied his feet. When he was fully free, he stood stretching his body. "Just tell me, how would you be helping us?" His tone turned serious.

"If we don't go find your friends, my fist-happy father figure and brothers are going to find your friends first and kill them." He dropped his arms slowly and opened his mouth like he was going to say something, the tip of his perfect white teeth showing, but instead he closed it into a tight line and nodded, and I gave a quiet sigh of relief.

Chapter 4

Jace

"OK. You have my attention. How do I know you aren't just trying to get me to show you where my friends are so you can kill us all together?" I couldn't believe I was here, saying this. I mean not too long ago, my dad had to pull some strings to get Jim, Landon, and me out of the city before we were executed, and now, I'm being held captive with a crazy woodland tribe that keeps wolves for pets. Like real wolves.

She sighed, dropping her head back. "If that was my plan, I wouldn't have come in, cleaned your wounds, and untied you. I would have beat the location out of you, then when I got it, I would have killed you and gone to kill your friends."

Did her eyes just glow? I think they did. I have never seen eyes like hers, one blue and one gold. It almost matched her wolf's gold-eyed stare. "OK." I paused and took a step from the wall, pushing my hair from my face. "So, what happens when we do find them? How will you convince your fist-happy father figure not to kill us?"

She fidgeted a few steps back and forth, avoiding my eyes. Her wolf nudged her. "Well, I haven't thought that far."

"You haven't thought that far." I gave her a dry stare.

"Yeah. My current problem is keeping you alive. Not what happens next. We can deal with that when it comes." Her upper cheeks flushed with frustration, her gold eye glowing again, or was that just the light?

"OK. Fine. At least tell me how you will get your family not to kill us?" I narrowed my eyes at her. I was making her nervous. It was fun seeing her squirm. There weren't many girls in the city this interesting, and if there were, they were heavily guarded by overprotective parents. They didn't want them to associate with a delinquent like me, even with my powerful father.

She stood a little straighter. "I don't really know, but I promise I will."

"Seriously?" I couldn't hold the laugh that escaped me. "You want me to blindly follow you, a girl whom I just met and know nothing about, but who *promises* me that she can talk her crazy family out of killing my friends and me. Not to mention that a day ago I thought there was no one living outside the city, and now I find myself among a group who have lived here for what... seventeen years?"

"Well... yeah." She tried to keep her composure, but I could feel her confidence waver. Her eyes darted everywhere but at mine as she shuffled her feet. Her wolf paced between her and the door, his eyes glued to me. Straightening my back, I lifted my chin at him, to make myself larger than I felt as his eyes calculated my movement. I had never been around a wild animal... or any animal for that matter.

Ah! What the hell. We all die sometime.

"All right."

Her eyes shot to mine, and she held her mouth open a moment.

"Really? Like... really?" Her wolf stopped, cocking his head at me. His mouth almost looked like it curled into a smile. Can we say creepy?

"Well, I was feeling pretty confident about my decision until now. You sure you're up for this?"

She cleared her throat. "Yeah! Yeah of course. Let's do this."

"OK then. Let's get going." I started toward the door, but an unnaturally strong grip on my arm pulled me back. "Ow! Whoa there, Spunky. That's my bad arm."

She quickly pulled away. "Sorry, but " – she paused, narrowing her eyes – "first off, I told you not to call me Spunky. Second, you can't just walk out there."

"Why not? I mean, we don't have any time to lose. Haven't they already left to find my friends?"

"Yeah, but there's still Ellie. If she learns that I untied you and am planning to run away with you, she will find some way to stop us. Probably by killing you herself."

"Wow." I held up my hands with an overdramatic look. "Nice family you have." Giving her a little wink, I continued, "I guess it isn't the first time someone tried to kill me for running away with a girl." My smirk faded when her expression was blank. "Never mind. OK then, what's your plan?"

She paced for a moment with her finger on her chin. The poster child for being lost in thought. Stopping, she turned to me. "Just hang tight. I'll figure something out."

"Uh, yeah, sure?" My stomach sank, and I did my best not to take my chances and bolt out the door. Maybe that would be better than leaving it up to her.

"OK, great. Just be ready. I'll be back." She left the boathouse with her wolf at her heels.

I started back toward the log piled wall when the door swung back open, scraping on the stone ground. She stuck her head inside. "And if you try and escape, Ash and I will track you down and kill you ourselves. If we don't, the fever or virus, or whatever you call it, will get you." The light behind her made her long, apricot hair glow as it framed her sculpted cheekbones. She was pretty, very pretty.

"Umm, I thought you said that there wasn't any fever."

"I said I didn't have it, not that there wasn't one."

Crap.

"Yeah, got it."

She stared at me, trying to gauge if I was being serious. "Good." She started to shut the door.

"Hey."

She stuck her head back in, eyebrows raised.

"Um, when you come back, can you maybe bring me a hair tie or something? My hair is driving me crazy." I smiled sheepishly and held in a laugh when her mouth dropped open. Her response was the slam of the door.

"What the hell has happened to my life?" I muttered to myself sliding down the pile of logs to sit, the bark scratching my back. "Hang tight until the crazy-eyed girl comes to get me. Perfect." I closed my eyes and waited.

Chapter 5

Tristan

We had been walking a few hours when Old Bob slowed and crouched to examine the dirt and leaf litter on the ground. My gut still clenched at what he told us outside the house, and I didn't want to leave Eden alone with that guy, but he insisted that with Ellie and Ash, she would be fine. He *was* injured pretty badly, and he will be worse off if he tries anything stupid.

"This is where I found them. They went in that direction." Old Bob stood and pointed to the east through the thick brush and trees.

"OK, let's go then."

"Wait. I'm starving. Can we eat something?" Tate asked, rubbing his belly dramatically.

Old Bob chuckled. "Yeah, sure."

Walking to a few large trees, we sat down against the trunks. I slid my back around, trying to get comfortable, but the hard, jagged bark made it impossible. We each took out our sacks of food and I eyed mine, unsure if my nervous stomach would let me eat. Tate dug right into his food, not a worry on his face. How could he be so calm? Eden was special, Old Bob had said. I had always known she was different than us, but so special that people from the city may be coming for her? Old Bob was pretty adamant they could be coming, and it made me uneasy.

"Hey, man. You good?" Tate asked me.

I gave him and Old Bob a quick glance. "Yeah, I'm good. Just doing some thinking." Old Bob focused on his apple, but by the twitch of his eyebrow, I knew he was listening.

"Yeah, I get it."

Old Bob cleared his throat. "You don't like that I left Eden alone at the cabin with that guy."

"No." Our eyes met as he lowered his apple and took a long breath.

"You two are young. You were just babies when the Fever moved through what was left of our home. I have lived through much more, the war being the worst thing possible. If you knew what the world was like before it was wiped out by bombs, you may look at things differently. I know threats, and Jace, he's not an immediate threat to Eden or Ellie."

"But what you said—"

"I know what I said." He took a bite of his apple. "But that guy"—he pointed back toward our cabin—"that guy isn't able to do much. He's too beaten up."

My shoulders dropped at his words. Old Bob has spoken of the war before, but only briefly, and he avoided the topic whenever he could, especially if Ellie was around. "I'm sure you're right. I just... I just can't crack this feeling that something isn't right." I picked up a twig and snapped it in half.

Tate gave my shoulder a playful pat as he popped part of a boiled egg in his mouth. "Well, I can crack your head for you and see what's inside."

I punched his arm back. "I'd like to see you try!" I smiled, but it fell quickly.

Old Bob studied my face. "Well, you know what I always say about your gut feelings."

"To listen."

He nods. "Then listen. What is it telling you?"

Looking between them, I sighed. "It's telling me to go back."

Tate chewed slowly as he watched me carefully. "You really feel all this? Why don't I feel like this?"

Old Bob chuckled. "People are different, Tate." He stood and wiped off the dirt from his pants. "If your gut is telling you that, then I feel you should go back. Tate and I can handle this."

"You sure?" The knot in my stomach loosened a bit at the understanding in his eyes.

"I'm sure."

I wasted no time and stood, stuffing my food back into my bag. I can eat when I get back to the cabin, but until I am there and see that Eden and Ellie are safe, I can't put anything in my stomach. "All right. I'll see you both later."

Old Bob held out his hand to me. I looked at it a moment before taking it. He squeezed and pulled me forward into a hug. "I'm proud of you. You're beginning to think like a man." Pushing me back, he held my shoulders with a smile. The memory of green eyes crinkling at the corners flashed through my mind, and I stood taller with pride. My father always looked at me with this same look. My heart tightened at the last memory of him before he died. He had lain next to me, sick and holding my hand. I felt him slowly turn cold until someone slipped his hand from my grasp. Too many people died within those first few weeks in the woods, almost everyone. They have become my family, and I wasn't going to let some stranger from the woods take that away from me.

"Thanks."

I coughed as Tate slapped my back. "See ya later, buddy." I shrugged him off, trying to hide the redness in my cheeks from my memory.

"Right. See ya." I turned and headed back toward the cabin, but before I was too far, I turned, walking backward. "Don't be heroes! If it's too much, just come back!"

Their laughs echoed through the leaves, their feet crunching the twigs and leaves on the ground.

"Always!" Old Bob yelled back.

I turned, increasing to a jog back toward home.

Chapter 6

Jace

My head drooped down and my eyes fluttered shut when the door scraped open. Jolting to my feet, I hissed as pain shot through me, instinctively pulling my arm into myself.

"What?" I croaked.

"Let's go! We don't have a lot of time!"

I hobbled to the door behind her, nursing my bad arm. Man, it ached badly. She peered outside, then reached back to grab my shirt and tugged me forward.

"Let's go. Don't stop until I say. We have to get as far as we can."

"I will try, but—"

Yanking me forward until my nose touched hers, she locked her eyes to mine, and yes, her gold eye did glow. I gulped.

"There is no trying. You will run. I know you're sore, but just suck it up and deal with it. If you don't make it, I won't help you. Understand?"

I nodded. What had gotten into her? Straightening my back, I prepared to run through the pain.

She took one last glance outside before running straight ahead, toward the trees. I followed closely, limping, but my long legs helped me keep pace. At the top of the small hill, chaos erupted. A woman, I assume Ellie, was screaming with chickens squawking and goats and sheep running everywhere while the girl's wolf yipped excitedly chasing the animals to cause a frenzy. This was her brilliant plan?

"What..." –I bent over, breathing heavily— "did... you do?"

"Move, talk later!" she hollered at me.

We ran through the tree line on the far side of the yard. She kept running, jumping over logs, ducking under branches, not letting up one bit. I followed much less gracefully than her, tripping over the logs rather than jumping them, but I managed to keep up. My body screamed. When we finally slowed, I squeezed my eyes shut for a moment and leaned against the tree. After a minute of panting, I opened my eyes but immediately closed them while rubbing my temples. The world spun and it caused my head to ache. Seeing her up ahead, I took a step, but then leaned back against the tree, gripping my stomach. The hunger I had felt earlier changed to nausea. I didn't trust the food she gave me, so I had pushed it to the side, despite my growling belly.

"Can we... rest a moment?"

She turned back. "Just for a moment. We need to keep moving." She stopped and leaned against a large oak tree and dug in her pack, pulling out a water bottle.

I leaned next to her, but my legs gave way and I slid down to the ground. My head still throbbed, but at least the world stopped spinning. "I thought... you would never... stop."

"You're just out of shape." She smirked and handed me the bottle.

"Thanks." I took a long drink. Wiping spilled water off my chin, I said, "Just so we're clear, I'm not out of shape, just injured."

"Yeah, sure." She angled her body to face me. "I need you to tell me where your friends are now."

"Ah, yeah. About that." I pulled myself up to standing again with the support from the tree and fought the bile down that threatened to come up. "I don't really know *exactly* where they are." I lowered my head, avoiding her glare.

"What do you mean, you don't know *exactly* where they are?"

"Well, as you know, I come from the city. Never been out here before, so..." I took a few steps away from her. I didn't want to be within reach if she decided to attack, and by the narrowing of her eyes, she wasn't happy. "So, I'm not really sure where they are."

Her face flushed. "What? So, you don't have any idea where they are? Nothing?" She didn't yell but made more of a hiss. It was scary, really scary.

"Well, not nothing. I do know we found a cave. That's where we were planning on staying. Know any caves?" I shuffled my feet. Please, please, please know some caves.

"A cave. Was this cave near a cliff or woods?"

Tilting my head, I thought back. I had only seen it once, but I don't remember a cliff, only trees. "Woods," I said confidently.

"It's this way. Come on."

She didn't wait for me as she hiked on. I sighed and limped after her. "Where is your trusty sidekick?"

"He stayed behind to make sure Ellie would be safe." She kept her eyes forward. "If you don't mind, I really don't feel like talking. So just shut up and follow me."

I had been planning on asking fifty questions, but based on her edginess decided against it. "Yeah, no problem, Spunky."

She sucked in a breath and paused mid-step, but continued to face forward. I thought she would turn around to show her anger, at least yell at me, but she just shook her head and continued on. She had poise. I would give her that.

᙮

We walked in silence for about an hour. She was relentless, didn't care that I was huffing and groaning behind her. Even standing only to my shoulders, she was able to cover more ground than me. Her long, auburn braid swayed with her movements. She was so focused, she never looked back to check on me. She walked with confidence between trees, bushes, and over small creeks.

The only sound that I had heard for the past hour was our footsteps on the leaves and twigs, so it was hard to hear her when she started to mumble. I couldn't make out what she was saying, but she wasn't happy.

"Want to talk about it?" I asked her after a few minutes of her grumbling.

She quieted and replied after a moment of silence, "No."

"Can I ask a favor?"

"What?"

"Can we take a break?" I paused. "I'm just... well, exhausted." I looked at her when she turned to look at me, her face flushed from her steady pace.

"Can you last a few more minutes? We're almost there." She sounded understanding, but her tight jaw said otherwise.

"Well, since you asked so nicely, yeah. I can last a few more minutes, but when we're there, I can't promise I'll be able to get up once I'm down."

She chuckled as her shoulders relaxed a little and she slowed her pace. When we rounded a large group of birch trees, the ground dropped down a small hill. We moved down the dip, then around a few more trees to the opening of the cave.

"I'm impressed."

"Impressed by what?"

"Impressed that you found the cave so easily."

"Is it because I'm a girl? Because, apparently, people don't think girls can handle themselves. Just ask my family."

"Ummm, no. I'm impressed because I wouldn't have been able to find it. Probably at all."

"Right," she said, her cheeks turning rosy, and she looked away. "Well, you go in and see if your friends are here. Get comfortable. I will see if I can find any food." She walked back out into the trees.

I turned toward the cave opening and walked inside. It was dark and rocky. "Hey! Guys! It's me." My voice echoed, but I was met with nothing but silence.

I inched deeper into the cave, searching for any sign of my friends. There was nothing, only leaves and twigs strewn about. It didn't look as neat as I remembered when we found it.

Steps entered the cave and stopped behind me. I turned to see Eden surveying the cave, but her face had gone pale.

"Back so soon, Spunky?"

"Don't call me that," she snapped and walked past me to investigate the leaves and twigs. "I smell something. Where are your friends?"

"Uh, I don't know. They don't seem to be here. Maybe they left?"

She knelt down, picking up a twig to look at it. Bringing it to her nose, she smelled it. "They didn't leave. They were taken."

"Taken? Taken by whom?" I walked over and picked up the same twig she just held. "How do you know?" I asked, slowly bringing it to my nose like she did. I smelled nothing but dirt.

She was now feeling the sides of the cave, nose close. Was she sniffing the rock walls? "Here." She stopped to show me something. "Blood."

I inched as close to the wall as I could. There was a speck of something red, but I couldn't tell if it was blood. "Are you sure that's blood?" I tried to sniff it like she had, but again, I smelled nothing. It only made my nose itch... Should I know how to spot out bodily fluids with a sniff of my nose or was this a special talent she had?

"You can't smell it?"

"No... Can you?"

"Yeah. Of course." She turned and walked toward the cave entrance.

I stepped back. I could have questioned her more, but we had more important things to deal with. "So... can your nose tell us who took them? Was it your brother and makeshift father?"

She knelt down to inspect the ground at the entrance. "I don't know. There was more than one." She stood with her eyes fixed to the ground, and she moved out of the cave. Crouching again, she seemed to be calculating in her head, tipping it back and forth in thought. She looked up. "They went north. If it was my family, I don't know why they would have taken them north."

"Maybe to kill them? Take them further away from your cabin to do the deed?"

She closed her eyes and stood. "Maybe." Opening her eyes, she scanned the woods around us.

"What?"

She turned to look at me. "It's just... if they didn't take them, I don't know who else would have."

I stepped outside a little, looking into the woods where she had. "Is your family the only ones out here?"

"No, but I don't know what use they would have for taking two strangers." She continued to focus on the area surrounding the cave entrance. Her movements were swift and elegant, barely making any sound on the messy ground.

"Probably the same use your family has?" The thought raised panic. I wouldn't be safe anywhere out of the city... or in it, for that matter.

She turned to look at me, but stayed silent, then went back to inspecting our surrounding area.

"All right." I take a hobbling step toward her. "Then what?"

"Well, we need to track them and hope that whoever has them hasn't killed them... yet." She gave me an apologetic smile before looking back to the ground.

"Right. Can I have one request?"

She nodded.

"Can we not leave right now? We just got here, and I really need to rest."

"Yeah. We might as well spend the night here. It'll be too dark to track soon anyway."

I let out a breath of relief. "Thank you." Moving back into the cave, I found a nice spot with the best back support a cave could offer, and I sat. "I'm going to rest my eyes a bit." If Eden responded, I wasn't awake to hear it.

Chapter 7

Tristan

My legs were burned from jogging all the way back to the cabin. I had to pick my feet up higher to miss downed trees and push through bushes. The yard was in shambles with chicken feathers, twigs, and leaves scattering the ground. Ellie was sitting up against the goat fence with Ash panting at her feet.

"Hey! What happened?" I asked, searching the rest of the yard. "Where's Eden?"

Ellie's chest heaved as a laugh escaped her. "No idea. If you find her, let her know that she needs to get better control of her wolf or he'll become dinner."

My heart sped up. "What do you mean you have no idea? When was the last time you saw her?" I scanned the area for any sign of her. All I saw was an empty yard and garden.

"This morning. She was tending to the prisoner."

I took off running toward the boathouse. "Eden!" If that bastard hurt her, his bruised face would be the least of his worries. The door slammed against the wall when I threw it open. Small pieces of wood flew about the small room. "Eden!" My bellow was met with silence and the sawed-off ropes that once held the prisoner.

They were gone.

Ash trotted in behind me and surveyed the area. There was no sign of a struggle and Ash didn't seem upset. If I know one thing, Ash wouldn't let anything happen to Eden, so his lack of concern was oddly comforting.

Ellie came in behind me and sucked in her breath. "Where is the prisoner?" She put a hand over her mouth. "Oh, no."

"You're telling me that you didn't notice him take Eden?"

"Tristan, we don't know if he took her or if she took him."

I looked up from inspecting the ground. "She took him? Why on earth would she do that?" Eden was smarter than that and Ellie knew that, so for her to suggest that was outrageous.

"Well, yeah. She made it clear she wasn't happy about killing anyone. Maybe she wanted to... save him?"

I stood, towering over Ellie's small frame. "Old Bob told Tate and me something yesterday. I was hoping I would be able to protect her, but..." I couldn't finish my sentence. I didn't want to think about what could have happened and how I failed her.

"Eden is strong, Tristan. She can handle more than you think. When Old Bob and Tate return, we will go after her." She gave my arm a reassuring squeeze.

"I'm leaving now. You catch up with me when they arrive." I headed toward the door but was intercepted by Ash. His gold eyes glowed in the evening light that shined through the door. "Why is Ash here? He never leaves Eden's side."

"Ellie sighed. "He was too busy working up all the animals."

"And you don't think that is a little odd?"

"He is an animal. I don't think of him like a human who would think to protect Eden."

I could see her point, but it didn't feel right. I narrowed my eyes at Ash and squatted to his level. "Why didn't you protect her?" I scratched his ears gently, then put my mouth to them and whispered, "If anything happens to her, I will kill you."

Ash pulled his head back, baring his teeth rumbling a low, quiet growl.

"All right, all right. We will find her." Ellie tugged my shoulder.

Too angry to respond, I stormed out of the boathouse. I needed to prepare, so we could leave when the others returned.

೨

Tate and Old Bob returned just after dark with no prisoners.

"We lost the tracks," Tate said between gulps of water. He and Old Bob rested at the table. "Where's Eden?" He glanced around the cabin.

"Well..." Ellie started.

"She's gone and so is the prisoner," I said as I shoved some fruit into my sack.

"What?" Tate knocked over the chair as he stood. Old Bob looked to Ellie with wide eyes before turning to me.

"You heard me. You might want to start packing. We leave at first light."

"Do we know if he took her? Were there any signs of what happened?" Old Bob's face was ashen as he stood walking to the kitchen. He leaned on the counter, looking outside through the window over the sink.

I shook my head. "Only the cut ropes. Nothing else."

"Wait. The ropes were cut? How would he do that?" Tate paced the length of the cabin, focused on what could have happened to his sister.

"Maybe..." Old Bob hesitated as he turned back to us, leaning a hip on the counter. "Maybe while we were out tracking the others, they made it here first. They could have freed him and taken Eden."

I hadn't thought of that, but I clutched my pack tighter at the idea. My eyes fell to Ash sleeping on his favorite rug. "But, Ash." His ears perked at the sound of his name and he lifted his head. "He wouldn't have let her be taken."

"He's an animal," Ellie replied. "They are unpredictable."

"No, he's right," Tate said, walking to Ash. He crouched to scratch his ears. "Maybe he didn't know?"

I didn't have a response to that, but it wasn't wrong. I just didn't like it. Didn't like it at all. I pushed both hands through my hair and tugged. The feeling always helped to center me.

"We leave at first light. Get ready and get some sleep." Old Bob's voice returned to his typical fatherly tone.

Everyone nodded.

I went back to packing, trying not to think about what Eden was going through.

Chapter 8

Eden

The wind on my feathers felt like silk washing over me. I soared down through the crisp, cool air and let my claws glide through the icy water. Little specks of water splashed onto my beak. As I flew into the trees, something small and furry caught my eye. I dove down to snag the rodent, but before my claws could clasp the plump body, ropes surrounded me. Squawking in panic, I tried to fly back into the sky, but the ropes tightened their hold on me.

"Eden!"

I shot up, bumping my forehead onto Jace's. "Ow!" we both said in unison, rubbing our heads. He sat back down, letting out a whiff of air. His one eye was still swollen shut, and he nursed his right arm.

"What were you doing?" I scooted up and away from him.

Jace's wild hair blended in with the dark cave. "You were thrashing about, screaming. I wanted to wake you from your nightmare."

He sat back against the cave wall opposite me, his sapphire eyes glinting in the moonlight.

Embers from our fire still glowed, giving off some light, but the cool, dewy air breezed in through the cave opening. A shiver went through me, and I pulled my knees into my chest. Nightmares have plagued me since I was a young child, but it has been a long time since I have had one. I thought it was a phase done and over with. I felt my cheeks warm at my vulnerability being exposed.

"Sorry. I didn't mean to wake you."

"Not a big deal." He paused. "Want to talk about it?"

I looked away. "Talk about what?"

"Your dream." He grunted in pain as he worked to sit more upright against the wall.

"Why would you want to hear about my dream?"

"I was once told that if you tell your nightmares... I mean dreams, they won't come true."

"Who told you that load of crock?"

His smile faded. "My father."

Well, great. Now I hurt his feelings. "I'm sorry. That was rude."

We stared at each other a moment, then he chuckled. "It's all right. He's an ass."

"Smartass! I really felt bad!" Picking up a twig, I threw it across the darkness at him.

He blocked it with his good arm and laughed. "Hey! You don't have to get violent, Spunky!"

"How many times do I have to tell you not to call me that?"

His laugh grew louder. "Ow, ow, don't make me laugh. It hurts." He took a few slow breaths, getting himself composed. We sat in awkward silence, watching each other before he looked toward the opening of the cave. "Well, I'm going to go see if I can find something to eat."

"What? Seriously? It's the middle of the night."

He squeezed his good eye shut, clawed his fingers into the wall, and strained to pull himself up. Grunting, he fell back to the floor; his hand instinctively went to his bruised stomach. I raised my eyebrows at his determination. Ignoring me, he took three big breaths then heaved himself up. He leaned his forehead on the stone wall and coughed out the pain.

"Well... yeah... I'm hungry."

He turned, leaning his back on the wall, giving me a wince, which I'm pretty sure was his attempt at a smile. "Any requests?"

"Requests?"

"Yeah, like you tell me what you want, and I get it. A request."

His marred face looked so confident that I almost felt bad for him. Almost. He had no idea how to survive in the woods. He was going hunting in the middle of the night. Well, probably not hunting since I'm positive that was beyond his scope of abilities, even when he was in full form.

"Ummm, no, but if it would make your life easier, I left some food right there for you." I motioned toward a big leaf I placed next to him. "You can just eat that instead of going out and getting yourself killed."

He looked down at the leaf and stared a moment. "And what is that exactly?"

"Wild berries and bark."

He made a noise between a cough and clearing his throat. "I'm sorry, did you say bark?"

"Have you never had bark before?"

"Ummm, no, I can't say that I have."

I motioned back to the ground. "Just sit back down and eat. You're going to hurt yourself."

"Well, thank you very much for the offer. Don't take this the wrong way, but I can't eat that."

"Well, pretty boy, I'm sorry that it's not good enough for you, but good luck trying to find anything else around here right now." I reached into my pocket and pulled out the hair tie and flicked it at him. "Here, use this. Your hair is a mess."

I moved further into the cave and sat back down, hugging my arms close to fight off the damp cold. I missed Ash's warmth.

I glanced back at Jace, who hissed in breaths as he slid back to the ground. He picked up the bark, trying to examine it in the dark, then took a nibble. His body moved in an exaggerated gag, and I snorted. "Night."

His quiet mumbles and gags lulled me to sleep.

∽

Jace's cough echoed behind me as we walked deeper into the woods. It was deep and persistent. My eyes darted about on watch for any predators that may come lurking for the sick human. The last thing I needed was to defend us from a wild animal.

I looked back at him. He had pulled his hair back into a messy bun which showed his strong jaw and high cheekbones glossed with bruised, clammy skin. He staggered between trees with his eyes on the ground. His feet dragged heavily on the ground, picking up leaves and twigs. If he wasn't careful, he was going to snag them on a tree root and fall. He paused at a tree to hunch over coughing. The deep rattling in his chest startled a nest of birds, and they flew through the trees tweeting in protest.

I dug the water bottle out of my sack. "Here, drink this. It may help."

He raised a hand in thanks as he took the bottle, unable to speak. After taking a long drink, he looked at me. "Can we rest?" His voice cracked with exhaustion.

"We need to keep going. I'm sorry, but we have to find your friends before anything happens."

He nodded and pushed off the tree, dropping the water bottle back in my sack. "As you wish." He was unsteady, but I brushed that off to his injuries.

"No smart comments?" I asked, oddly missing his boyish humor.

"I'm sorry." He coughed. "I just don't feel... like myself." He took a few swaying steps toward me then collapsed. Lunging forward, I caught him before he hit the ground. His skin was hot to the touch, and he smelled of sweat and infection.

"You're burning up!" His damp shirt clung to him and moisture built on his brow.

Putting his arm over my shoulder, I half dragged him as we stumbled to a tree. "Sit down." I slowly lowered him to the ground. He gratefully took the water bottle again, drinking it down.

"I'm sorry. I didn't realize you were this bad." I felt his forehead. "Are you in pain?"

He coughed. "Honestly? I can't tell if the pain is new or from Landon's fists." He rested his head on the tree.

"Lie down. I'll see what I can do for the pain. You need rest."

"No, I can walk. We need to keep going; you said so yourself."

He moved to stand, but I gently put my hands on his damp shoulders. "You're in no condition to walk. I would end up carrying you, and one, I don't feel like carrying you, and two, I think it would hurt your ego to be carried. So, we might as well rest."

Jace looked at me, then gave a slight nod and closed his eyes.

I felt his damp, hot forehead again. What was causing this? I inspected his wounds, washing them with cool water from my second water bottle. None of my poking and prodding woke him. Digging in my pack, I pulled out some herbs that would hopefully help with his pain. Scanning the area for more water, I lifted my nose and sniffed in a long breath. The air was damp, and I heard a creek not too far. I double-checked his position, making sure he looked as comfortable as he could, then I left.

Jogging through the woods, I followed the smell of water. As I scanned the area, I picked up the pace so I wouldn't leave him alone too long. When I reached the creek, I carefully walked over the slippery rocky bank to the edge of the water and crouched to fill the bottle.

I smell someone.

A man's voice spoke in my head, and I dropped the water bottle. Scurrying back toward the bank, I surveyed the area around me but saw no one. Sniffing the air, I tried to catch a scent, but the water from the creek masked any other scent. I moved back to the water and grabbed the bottle. Filling it as quickly as I could, I kept my eyes moving around me.

He is alone. Sick.

I stilled and my blood froze. Jace. Shoving the full bottle in my sack, I turned and ran. My knees scraped against the small pebbles that rolled under my feet as I stumbled up the bank toward him. Please be OK, please.

I smell someone else.

Stopping mid-step, I dropped to the ground and surveyed the area again. No one. Who were these people? How could I hear them in my head? A tingling, starting at my feet, prickled its way up my body. What was wrong with me? Panic hit me. Did I have the virus?

Then I felt it, a presence. Turning frantically in a circle, I still saw no one, but yet I felt them.

Take the sick one, leave the other.

My stomach knotted at the thought of Jace, lying there helpless. I needed to get to him. I sprinted through the woods – leaves and twigs flew in my wake as I jumped over downed trees and pushed through the brush. When I arrived, falling to my knees out of breath, I found nothing. Jace was gone.

Chapter 9

Jace

I blinked awake and looked up at the sky. Wait, it wasn't the sky, but some kind of cloth. Moving my hands along my stomach, I felt a soft blanket. I blinked. I wasn't in the woods anymore. Jolting upright, I felt pain shoot through my entire body, and I screamed.

"Ah!"

"Relax, lie back down." A middle-aged man gently pushed my shoulder down.

"Where am I?"

He shined a light in my eyes before checking my pulse. "The Birches."

"The Birches?" What kind of name is that?

"Yeah, it's what we call our community. We are near a thick batch of birch trees. It was an obvious name." He chuckled. "You're lucky we found you."

How had I gotten here? The last thing I remember was lying on the ground while Eden went for more water. Eden!

I struggled to sit up again, searching the small room. There was nothing but three other empty cots and a small trolley covered with supplies. "There was a girl. I was with a girl. Is she here?" *Please be here, please be here.*

My struggle to get up was once again stopped by firm hands pushing me back down. "No, sorry. You were the only one brought in. Please, stay down. You need rest."

"Are you sure? She couldn't have been far from me."

"Like I said, you're the only one brought in. Let me get someone who may have more answers for you." He slipped out the tent door.

My arm stung where an IV was pumping liquid into me. I squeezed my eyes shut at the thought of the kids in the labs in the city. They had similar IVs in their arms. My stomach tightened; what was this place? I had to find Eden. I tugged on the IV tubes only to be stopped by a delicate hand.

"I wouldn't touch that. You don't want to burst your vein," a small woman said. "I'm Sarah, one of the healers here. What should we call you?"

I ignored her question. "I was traveling with a girl. Is she here?" I coughed. *Crap, the cough is returning.*

Sarah sat on the cot next to mine. "No, I'm sorry. We only found *you*."

"But she couldn't have gone far. If you go back, you may be able to find her. I can't just leave her out there all alone." I dropped my head back onto the pillow. It throbbed and all I wanted to do was close my eyes and sleep, but I had to try and find Eden.

"Was this girl sick?"

"No. What does that matter? She's alone!" I willed my body to sit, but it wouldn't budge. I felt like I had fifty pounds of bricks holding me down. My eyelids drooped.

"Well, she is in a much better position than you are. If she were sick, it would be harder for her to survive."

"Sick?"

She nodded as she checked my fluid bag. "The Fever, I'm afraid."

"The Fever? As in the Ferine Fever?"

"Yes. Fortunately, we have been working on some natural remedies that have been successful in slowing the progress of the virus. Unfortunately, we have not been able to fully cure it." She gave me a reassuring smile. "But there is always a first time." She looked at some notes written on a paper next to my cot. "We have given you something for your pain and to help you rest. You are showing the same reactions so far as the other two, but we would like to keep you under quarantine for a bit longer since the others' symptoms returned with a vengeance."

I widened my heavy eyes. "The other two?"

She nodded. "Two young men, about your age."

Jim and Landon. A laugh escaped me. "Where are they? Can I see them?"

Her eyes dropped a little. "I'm sorry. Like I said, their symptoms returned even worse. One died and the other is... well... we are keeping him comfortable. It shouldn't be long."

"Dead? One is dead? Which one?" I croaked.

"He said his name was Jace. Do you know them?"

Jace. They used my name. Crap. "No, I thought it may be someone else."

"What did you say your name was again?" She repeated her question.

"Jacob."

Sarah stood. "Well, Jacob, welcome to The Birches." She quietly left the tent.

I didn't like the feeling of this place. I had become exactly what I was fighting against in the city. A lab rat. Staring at the IV in my vein, I wondered if what was being pumped into me was actually going to help, or was it an experiment. I pushed my head deep into the pillow and let out a frustrated groan. I had to find Eden.

Chapter 10

Tristan

Old Bob kept his eyes on the ground, watching for any sign of Eden and Jace, but it was almost easier to just follow Ash. He trotted with his nose in the air and tail wagging. Old Bob bumped into his fourth tree.

"Careful, hun!" Ellie chuckled.

"Can't we just follow Ash? He seems to know where to go." I pushed my fingers through my hair.

"He has never been—"

Ash barked and Old Bob shut up. Turning his nose forward, Ash barked again and looked back to us.

"Ah, all right. Follow him, I guess." Old Bob scratched his head as he watched the wolf trot forward. Ellie gave his arm a reassuring squeeze as she passed him and followed Ash.

We picked up the pace and settled at a steady paced walk. My heart got pumping and my skin broke a sweat, but I didn't mind knowing that every step was closer to finding Eden and the bastard that took her.

Just as the sun started to set, Ash trotted down a small hill and around into the mouth of a cave. I spotted footprints scattered throughout the dirt and not too far inside there were the remains of an ash-filled fire pit.

"Well, someone was here," I said.

"Ash seems to be content," Tate said, watching the wolf sniff out a spot along the rock wall and curl up. "They were probably here."

"All right. It's almost dark. Let's get a fire going and rest." Old Bob looked up at the sky, grey clouds building. "Rain's coming. We should leave at first light."

Cool, damp winds picked up as the rumbling dark clouds neared us. Pulling a jacket from my pack, I shrugged it on, zipping it to my chin. I helped Ellie block the breeze to get the fire going, and when the crackling flames burned, I hung my hands over them, trying to pull the warmth into me.

Pulling food from our packs, we all gathered close to the fire. Rain poured down in sheets outside the cave and large gusts of wind brought speckles of cold water in toward us. Ash had moved closer to the fire once it was lit and slept snuggled to Tate's leg.

"This is the opposite direction of the city walls, so I may have been wrong about them taking her." Old Bob took a bite from his apple, staring out at the large raindrops, gathering into puddles on the mud.

"Maybe there are other cities?" Tate said.

I looked at him, tossing berries into his mouth. I closed my eyes. I knew what was coming.

"Tate!" Ellie yelled.

And, there it was.

Tate looked to her with both eyebrows raised. "Yeah?"

"Did you listen *at all* when I taught you history?" Ellie asked.

Tate gulped. "Ummm."

I laughed, giving his back a pat. "If he wasn't sleeping with his eyes open, then he listened."

Old Bob's laugh echoed in the cave, and Ellie playfully nudged his arm. "Sorry," he said, clearing his throat. "Right. Tate, you know there are other cities, but why is it difficult for us to communicate with them?"

"The war," Tate spoke so quietly the rain drowned out his words.

"And what happened in the war?"

Tate squeezed the bridge of his nose, quickly searching for the answers. "It started out as a dispute in a place called Eastern Europe, which quickly started to pull other countries into it, and ended up becoming a nuclear war with most of the world demolished."

"Right and what was the dispute about?" Ellie added, trying not to look too proud that her hard work had stuck in his brain somehow.

"Umm, religion." Ellie closed her eyes and let out a long sigh, and Tate quickly changed his answer. "No wait, I know this. Water... food—"

"Weapons!" I yelled out through a laugh.

"Yes, what started the war ended it," Old Bob said, giving Tate a very sympathetic look due to the wrath that will come to him for forgetting Ellie's lessons.

"Right. Sorry," he said, avoiding Ellie's gaze.

A loud bang of thunder made us cringe, turning our gazes outside. The ground was mucky; tomorrow's hike was going to be a mess.

"Our lack of communication and transportation has made travel hard, if not impossible. I highly doubt that she was taken to a city that could be fifty miles away," Old Bob continued. "We will find her." He smiled at us and stood. He held his hand out to Ellie, helping her up. "You two get some rest."

Tate stood, waking Ash, who turned with a quiet groan. He stretched out and went right back to sleep. "I will take first watch." He walked to the edge of the cave and sat along the wall, just out of the rain.

Old Bob and Ellie moved to the wall. She snuggled into the nook of his arm with her head on his shoulder. Sighing, I pushed at the fire with a stick, too worried to sleep. At least I could keep us warm through the storm.

∽

I sat on a large rock at the opening of the cave. The rain had calmed to a drizzle a few hours earlier, but the air was still crisp as it kissed my cheeks. White puffs of air left my mouth with every breath, and I began to make different shapes of clouds in my boredom. The sky began to glow its early morning light. Shivering, I tugged the sleeves of my jacket over my numb hands, blowing into them to thaw out my fingers. The cave was dark with only the coals left to light it. Ellie and Old Bob had curled into each other, and Ash had moved to snuggle with Tate. I shook my head, snuggling with a wolf?

The ground glistened with puddles of muddy water, and I dreaded our day of walking. All I could think of were heavy muddy shoes. The bushes ahead rustled, and I stiffened, holding my breath to keep the white puffs from giving me away. Sitting up straighter, I squinted toward the bush where the leaves shifted and a twig snapped. Whatever it was, it was large. Bear? We definitely didn't want to deal with a bear attack. I slowly reached for the dagger in my boot and stood, but stayed low behind a large rock at the entrance of the cave. Taking a step, I scanned the area for more movement, but in the dark with the drizzle, all I saw were shadows. My feet squished in the wet mud as I worked my way closer to the bush. The leaves rustled again and a shadow emerged.

"Holy crap," I whispered.

Crouching lower, I moved forward slowly to get a better look. Another twig snapped behind me and I spun, slipping in the wet mud and landing on my knees. "Crud." My pants were caked with mud. Holding my dagger out, I looked where the second twig snapped, but there was nothing except trees. My skin prickled and I turned back to the bush; the large dark shadow was still there.

The creature shifted and turned toward me. Squinting, I tried to make out the large shape. It stood slightly shorter than I and tilted its head as it inspected my movements. Clenching the handle of my dagger tighter, I let out a big white puff of air. Should I charge or stay put? I was big, but I could take it.

The sun grew over the horizon, giving the woods a bright orange glow, and the creature became more visible. It looked... human? My puffs of air disappeared, and I slowly stood, all sounds were drowned out by my heartbeat pounding in my ears.

A loud screech resounded through the trees and I jumped back, looking to the sky. I saw nothing but grey clouds and fog. When I dropped my gaze back to the bush, the creature was gone. I stood tall and stepped out further into the mud, scanning the area, and saw nothing. Pushing the wet hair from my face, I shook my head to calm my frayed nerves. What was that? Returning my dagger to its holster in my boot, I walked into the cave. The way the creature had watched me sent ice through my veins. Were there more of them stalking us, or worse, stalking Eden?

Chapter 11

Eden

My legs burned as I sprinted through the trees, holding on to any speck of Jace's scent left, but it was gone. I fell to my knees, pounding the ground with my fist, and screamed. My voice echoed and birds flushed away in a frenzy of tweets. Whoever took him moved fast, unusually fast for someone carrying a person. How could I lose him? He depended on me. I kicked the trunk of a tree and stomped on.

Thunder rumbled overhead and dark clouds built above me. A storm was coming, and by the looks of the whirling wind, it would be to me soon. Increasing to a jog, I worked my way forward, in the direction I thought Jace had been taken. If the rain came, I would have a harder chance of finding him. A loud clap of thunder shook the trees, and I ducked. Rain poured down on me like someone just tipped a bucket over the woods, and I was drenched within seconds. Pushing the sopping wet hair from my face, I tied it in a quick knot at the nape of my neck. Slowing my pace so as not to slip on the muddy ground, I adjusted my pack to cover my head. It didn't do much.

A tingle went up my spine and I stiffened but continued my forward motion, not wanting to give away that I knew something was near. Dropping my pack to my back, I put a hand on my dagger at my hip, just in case. I scanned the area as I walked, but saw no one. The feeling in the air was familiar, like when I was filling the water bottles. Maybe I was getting closer to Jace? I rolled my neck in a circle, rubbing each ear along my shoulders, trying to rub the prickling away as I continued forward.

I carefully climbed a mud-covered embankment but had to stop at the constant tingles moving through me. I shook my head and arms, trying to rid my body of the invasion. As I continued my way up, a sheen of sweat covered my skin, and the pumping in my heart became rapid. I pulled in long breaths to calm myself. The pressure was too much; I dropped my head to my knees so I wouldn't pass out. I growled low and shook my body again to rid the sensations that blanketed me and continued on. The rocks on the embankment in addition to the mud made my climb difficult. I slipped to my knees and crawled most of the way, wiping a muddy hand over my face to keep the rain out of my eyes. When I reached the top and scanned the area for what direction to go, I saw a large dark figure through the sheet of rain. Squinting my eyes, I craned my head to get a better look, taking a few steps forward. When I got twenty feet from the figure, I froze. It wasn't one thing, but three.

Three human-looking creatures were surrounding a dead, mauled deer carcass. The two males ripped bloody meat from the belly of the carcass, and the female gnawed on the poor animal's jugular.

I took a small step back, scanning the area. There was nothing but trees, bushes, and rain. Silently thanking the rain for masking the sounds of my feet and scent, I slowly backed up; the creatures continued their feast without noticing me. I swallowed hard, sliding my feet through the mud. I was almost to the embankment. I slowed my breath, closing my eyes a moment to calm my rapid heart. My foot slid back, and my heel got caught on a large, slippery rock. In an attempt to break my fall, I put my arms out, but they just slid in the oozy mud before my back hit the ground and mud splashed over me.

"Drat!" I wiped the mud from my face only to get more dirt on my face. "Ahhh, double drat."

"What's this?" A gravelly voice spoke through the buzzing rain.

I looked up to see two of those human-like creatures. The world was stagnant as I met their eyes. They each had one gold eye, just like me. I swallowed hard and took three deep breaths before jumping up and running. I ran toward the embankment, my feet slipping and sliding through the rocky wet ground. I could hear the thick, raspy breaths of the creatures behind me, and I picked up my pack, but when I reached the top of the embankment, my feet slipped out from under me and I slid down, the rocks scraping my behind and back. I reached the bottom and gulped down the bile that rose to my throat. They watched me from the top of the embankment with their slimy grey skin and yellow fangs. They looked human, but acted like... animals.

RUN!

I stood and ran toward the water, shaking out the echo of the voice in my head.

When you get to the river, go through it.

I squeezed my eyes, wondering if I would wake up from this nightmare, but no. I was being chased by violent creatures and was hearing a voice in my head. The rushing sound of the river was almost drowned out by the rain, but I managed to hear it. I pushed forward.

You can do it. Just go through it.
Wait, is this a voice or my conscience?

I reached the river, and the water was overflowing as it rushed quickly through the woods. This rain wasn't helping. Hesitating to enter, I glanced behind me and saw the quickly approaching creatures. Their eyes focused on their prey... me.

Go Now!

The voice rang with irritation, and I felt a ripple of impatience on my skin, almost pushing me forward. I half jumped, half slipped into the ice-cold river. The water washed over me, and the current pulled me downriver much faster than I anticipated. I sputtered water, quickly moving my arms and legs to keep my head from submerging. I could swim, but not in a rushing river during a rainstorm with mud-caked clothes. The wind made waves that were too strong for me to navigate and my head went under. I gulped a mouthful of water but kicked myself back to the surface, coughing as I sucked in a large breath of air; then I was pulled back under.

There is a large branch a little further down. Grab it.

Thrashing to the surface again, I spotted the branch. My legs burned from fatigue as I kicked to keep my head above water and reach my hands up so I didn't miss the branch.

You are getting closer now. Grab it!

It was thick and bent over half the distance of the river. Grabbing it, I held it with all my strength as the wet bark cut into my palms. I let out a scream. My fingers and arms threatened to give way when the current continued to pull my body then... smack! My vision blurred and my grip slipped from the branch. A hand gripped my wrist and I blacked out.

Chapter 12

Eden

My eyes fluttered open and I squinted, trying to focus my fuzzy surroundings. Moving my fingers, I felt a soft warm blanket. I was dry. Was it a dream? Squeezing my eyes shut, I pushed back into the pillow. Everything throbbed. I put my hand to my pounding head and felt a bandage over my forehead.

"How are you feeling?"

I turned toward the man's voice, but my sharp movement made my head spin more.

"Argh." I closed my eyes, pushing my fingers to the bridge of my nose. "Where am I?" My voice was stronger than I expected it to be, but the vibration from speaking caused my head to throb even more.

My eyes flew open as I heard a chair dragging across the floor. The man set the chair down next to me. I gulped. His eyes. One blue and one gold. My heart thumped and the room swayed; he had eyes like mine, like the creatures.

His gold hair sparkled in the light that melted through the walls of the tent. He smiled, and the crow's feet at the corner of his eyes reminded me of Old Bob. Why did I leave?

"You are safe."

I scoffed quietly, looking up at the bright cloth ceiling. What does safe mean exactly? I have no idea where I am.

"You're in a place called The Birches and no one here will hurt you."

I blinked. Drat. He can read my mind? Blood pounded through my veins, but I didn't look at him. I didn't want him to know how unnerved he made me feel.

So, instead, I thought nonchalant thoughts. *Red, green, blue...*

He chuckled. "Red, green, blue... I can hear you. Your thoughts." Double drat.

Just like I can speak to you like this.

I turned so fast toward him I hovered on the edge of the cot, grabbing the side so I didn't roll off. It was him! He was the one in the woods! Positioning myself securely in the middle of the cot, I groaned and moved my hand to my head. Squeezing my eyes shut, I slowly counted my breaths. One... two... I opened one eye and was met with my eyes and a smirk. He had my eyes and he could read my mind. I scooted away again, but the darn cot was so skinny I almost fell again.

"Easy." He reached forward to keep me from falling.

"Don't touch me!"

He calmly backed off and watched me struggle back onto the cot, grunting with each movement.

Sitting in silence, I focused on keeping my mind clear. He started to leave when I asked, "Why can't I hear your thoughts?"

He sat back down. "I have learned to control the flow of my thoughts."

I blinked.

He smiled. "I can teach you if you like."

Examining his eyes, I imagined this is what others feel when they look into mine. They were really cool.

Another man walked into the tent. "Brian—"

The man who I assumed was Brian held out his hand to stop the man. My eyes moved up the tall, bulky man to his face. One brown eye, one gold. Drat! I scooted back.

"It's all right," Brian said.

I pointed at the man. "He has them too."

"Yes."

I gulped. "How many others have..." I moved my finger back and forth between my eyes.

"Unsure," the man said carefully. I let out a small breath.

"Us... and the creatures," Brian added.

How could I forget? Wasted away, greying skin, crouching over a deer corpse... eating it raw. I stifled a shiver.

"Yes, they are similar to us, but we are definitely not like them," the man said. "We haven't been able to verify the big difference... yet."

My stomach turned. "So... I could become like them?"

"Don't scare the girl, Derek," Brian said.

Derek laughed. "No, no, like I said. They are different somehow. If you were like them, you would be like them now. It's all very complicated."

They locked eyes for a moment longer than was comfortable.

"Are you talking to each other?" They turned to me, their faces stone. "You are! Just like in the woods when... Jace! Where is Jace?!" I propped up on my arms to sit, but my body protested and I fell back.

I watched their eyes, still and focused on me, but the switch at the corner of Brian's eye told me he knew who I was talking about.

"Perceptive."

Drat. He could hear me analyzing them.

"Where is he? Is he alive?"

Derek sucked in a breath. "I'm sorry—"

"No."

"I'm sorry. He didn't make it."

I closed my eyes. I failed him. He trusted me to find his friends and keep him alive, but I failed him.

I didn't open my eyes when I heard them walk out of the tent.

Rest

∽

My mouth felt like sandpaper as I opened it and cleared my throat. The room didn't spin when I opened my eyes, but my head still throbbed.

"Here." A woman handed me a cup of tea. "It will help with your throat and the pain."

I slowly took the cup and examined its contents. It looked similar to the tea Ellie would give us when we were sick. I sniffed it. Yep, it was the same. I sighed at the thought of Ellie. I missed her. Taking a sip, I let the warm liquid soothe my mouth and throat.

"Better?" She smiled at me, and I nodded. "Good."

Scooting up, I sat with my back rested against a pile of pillows. My head was starting to clear from the fragrance and herbs of the tea. I quietly watched the woman move through the tent to work. When I finished my tea, I set the cup on the small table next to my cot.

"What's your name?" I asked.

"Sarah." She smiled at me. "And yours?"

"Eden." I coughed, and she brought me some more tea. I gratefully sipped it.

"Let me get Derek and Brian. They wanted to talk to you again when you woke."

I nodded and gulped half the cup down. It felt so good on my thorny throat.

I listened to the commotion outside, people talking and laughing, kids playing and crying. This wasn't an ordinary small camp. This was a colony. I hadn't met so many people in the same place before. It made me uneasy, needing Old Bob's expertise and advice. Now that Jace was gone, I ached to get home, but everything I could learn from Brian and Derek was... tempting.

"You're awake!" Brian walked into the tent with Sarah next to him. He squeezed her shoulder before walking over to me. The emotions that flowed between them were so thick it made my cheeks warm. Brian gave me a sheepish smile. "Sorry."

I cleared my throat. "It's fine." A tickle in my throat threatened to erupt a fit of coughs, so I quickly drained my tea. The tickle subsided.

He pulled up a chair next to my cot. "How are you feeling?" Clasping his hands together, he watched me intently.

"Fine," I spoke at almost a whisper, fearful my throat tickle would return.

"Good. We were wondering what your plans were?"

"My plans?" I put the empty cup on the small side table.

"Yes. Like if you are going to go on your way, or if you wanted to... stay?"

The word hung in the air, waiting for me to grab it. And I wanted to. Badly. But without Jace, what was the point? I missed my family, and I am sure they were worried about me... but... I could learn about myself.

Brian watched me patiently, not changing his expression and staying quiet as I thought through my options.

"What if I stay just for a few days? See what you have to offer... training wise."

Brian's smile grew, making small crinkles at the corners of his eyes. "That sounds perfect. But I have to warn you"—he narrowed his eyes—"I'm not an easy trainer."

I laughed. "You don't know Old Bob."

Chapter 13

Eden

"Again!" Brian yelled. He stood on the edge of a small grassy clearing, arms crossed and eyes glowing. He wasn't joking when he said he wasn't easy, but it still wasn't as bad as Old Bob's daily drills.

Panting, I slumped to the ground. "I'm sorry. I don't see the point of this."

"Again!" He walked toward me.

Once he was by my side, I pushed up and faced him. I straightened my back to stand as tall as I could. "Like I said before, I don't see the point in me running back and forth. How does this help with keeping you out of my mind?"

"Because you have to be strong in all areas. Mind and body. If you can't run a few times through a meadow, then you aren't ready to practice anything else." He turned and started back to the edge of the clearing. "Again!"

"What happened to the nice man I met earlier?"

He chuckled. "I warned you! He will come out once you are able to match me in a race. Right now, you can't even get two lengths before you're out of breath." He paused, smirking before he bellowed, "Again!"

"You do remember what just happened to me, right? Being chased by the creatures, almost drowning, my—"

"You think your enemies will wait until you heal? Again!"

"My enem—"

"Again!" He placed his hands behind his back, narrowing his eyes at me.

Rolling my eyes, I stood and started jogging. A smile formed as the breeze pushed my hair from my face and the smell of oak filled my nose. Ellie's necklace bounced softly on my chest, a reminder of her love, a reminder of family. I missed them. I could almost feel Ash bounding next to me, listening to the sound of the wind on the leaves and the song of the birds as we run. Looking down, my smile faltered at my empty side. With that, I started running. I didn't care if my lungs screamed and my side ached.

༄

I shoved food in my mouth as fast as I could.

"Easy." Derek chuckled. "You don't want to choke."

Swallowing my last bite, I looked between Derek and Brian. "Then tell this one to go easy on his *training.*" I nodded my head toward Brian.

"I told you before, you need to be strong in both mind and body."

"I know what you told me, but so far all we have been working on is the body strength. When do we start the mind?" I raised an eyebrow at them. "I said I would stay a few days. I would like to learn a little about my other... abilities." They were silent, too silent. "Ahh, you're doing it again, aren't you! You're talking to each other!"

"All right then, let's start now." Brian rested his forearms on the table. "Think something, anything."

Sitting up straight, I closed my eyes. *I miss Ash.*

"Who's Ash?" Brian asked.

I opened my eyes and mouth simultaneously. "He's... He's my—"

"Never mind." He waved his hand impatiently. "Now, think something else, only this time imagine there are walls around it. So strong nothing can penetrate it."

"All right." I closed my eyes again. *Green is my favorite color.* After my thought, I imagined a pile of stones circling my thought. There was no entrance, no way to break it down. Squinting my eyes tight, I focused until I felt a light nudge. *What was that?* Another nudge hit the stones and some rattled. My eyes flashed open.

Brian smirked. "Something green?"

"Aghh! How did you know?" I slammed my hand on the table. Our plates clanked and a fork fell, clunking on the grass.

Both their laughs filled the tent, and Brian spoke, "Well, it would help if your wall wasn't green."

I sat back, folding my arms. "Yeah, whatever."

"Not bad for a first try though. We'll work on some more tomorrow."

"Here." Derek slid me a bowl of blueberries.

Looking at them, I remembered the last night at the cabin. Tristan and Tate playing cards, throwing their berries around. Ellie's gentle hands brushing through my hair. Instinctively I moved my hands to the necklace, my rock.

"Thanks." I popped a small blueberry into my mouth. The tarty sweet juice covered my tongue. I loved berries. "So, tomorrow then?" I stood and popped another berry into my mouth.

"Bright and early," Brian said.

"All right. I need sleep. Night." I left Derek's tent and slowly walked down the row of tents to mine. They had me in the last tent of the middle row, closest to the training clearing. The night air had a cool breeze as the sky turned pink. The smell of roasted vegetables and meat filled the air through the tents, ripping the hole in my heart a little larger. I missed home, missed my family, but I needed to learn about myself. Just a few more days; then I would leave.

Chapter 14

Jace

My overheated body writhed as the tent filled with my moans. The fever came back, and much worse. My body was too weak to do anything but breathe and even that was difficult. Every time I sucked in air, it was like trying to pull it through a clogged straw. I wanted to give up, but something was keeping me here.

Pain erupted over every portion of my body, from the hairs on my head to the nails on my toes. There was no part of me that didn't hurt.

"His fever spiked again," a woman said.

"Do the best you can," a man responded.

"Of course, sir, but... have you thought of trying..."

"Sarah, we don't know if that will work. It was just a speculation."

"I understand, but it could save him."

"It could also kill him."

"He may die anyway."

"But he may not. It's a no, Sarah. Just do the best you can and keep him comfortable."

After cracking my fifty-pound eyelids, I moved my eyes, unable to move my head. I saw a blurry picture of a tent. No one was in it except them and me. They were speaking about me. The sound of tools moving and cupboard doors opening and closing increased the throb in my head. I moaned. I needed the pain to stop. Please stop. I needed to get out of here.

"Eden," I moaned.

I needed to find her.

"What did he say?" the man asked.

"He has been mumbling that name on and off. Eden."

"Eden. Are you sure?"

"Yes. That and moans are all that comes out of him. Why?"

"Never mind. Just take care of him." His footsteps disappeared, leaving nothing but silence and my whimpers.

My whole body radiated heat, so when a cool wet cloth rested on my face, I leaned into the sweet relief. If only it would move over my whole body. Release me from the fire on my skin.

"Shhhh. Relax. We need to get you better. You are strong. Stronger than the others. You must survive. For your Eden," the woman soothed.

Eden. Yes, I must survive for Eden. As the cool wet cloth sizzled along my skin, I let sleep take me.

Chapter 15

Tristan

We tracked Eden in silence. No one had been alarmed at my early morning interaction, saying it was most likely due to lack of sleep and stress. Probably just a rabbit, Tate had said.

That was until we saw the carcass.

"What in the world is that?" Tate said, approaching the mutilated deer.

"I think it's a deer," Ellie responded.

We inspected the bloody ripped flesh that was once a deer. Its entrails scattered the ground around it, torn to shreds. The dirt had soaked so much blood that it became dark burgundy mud. Quickly looking away, I heaved and put a hand to my nose, attempting to block the wretched smell.

"What kind of animal would do this?" I asked.

Old Bob knelt. "Bear, wolf..."

Tate shook his head. "Are animal attacks always this... messy?"

Spotting something in the dirt near the carcass, I moved closer to get a better look. "Are those... " Kneeling down, I examined the familiar imprint in the ground. "What the? No. Are those feet?"

Ash trotted over and sniffed the prints, letting out a growl. Old Bob and Tate knelt down next to me.

"Yeah, that sure does look like a footprint. Bare feet," Old Bob said.

"Why on earth would anyone be running around in bare feet?" I asked.

Old Bob shrugged. "I don't know." He stood surveying the area again. "We should keep moving. Whatever did this may still be close, and I don't think we want to meet them."

Nodding, we followed him with Ash at the lead. As we walked, I trailed behind everyone, scanning the area looking for any sign of Eden. We had to find her. My eyes were on Tate's pack when I heard Ash growl. Looking at him, I saw he was frozen with his eyes fixed on the trees. The others passed him, paying no attention, but I stopped, looking with him to the trees. Crap.

"Tate, Old Bob, Ellie... run." I was still, eyes glued to the beasts that watched us. What I saw this morning definitely wasn't a rabbit.

"What?" Tate looked back at me, then followed my eyes. "What the..."

"Run!" I yelled pushing him forward. He stumbled, bumping into Old Bob, who took Ellie by the hand and all three took off toward the river.

A twig snapped and Ash snarled. We sprinted through the trees, jumping over logs toward the river. I didn't dare look behind us. Reaching the embankment, we slid down the rocks toward the river. The cold stones cut into my back, and I grunted. Ellie's scream echoed through the woods.

She sat, clutching her ankle at the edge of the river. Her face scrunched in pain. Old Bob pulled her arms. "Get up!" She put her foot down to take a step but crumpled back onto the rocks. I could hear the beasts grow closer.

"Get up, Ellie!" I yelled at her.

"I can't! I think it's broken."

Crap.

Rocks toppled down the embankment. Looking to the top, I saw the beasts—greyish skin, sharp teeth, ragged clothes, and bare feet. Human, but not quite. Sucking in a breath, I stared at the four sets of eyes, each had one gold. My heart sunk. Just like Eden.

Turning back to Old Bob and Ellie, I screamed. "Get her out of here!"

The beasts snarled and bounded toward us, stones spraying in every direction. Old Bob picked Ellie up and ran as quickly as he could downstream. Grabbing my dagger from my boot, Tate, Ash, and I charged.

Wham!

I took one down onto the rocks. Grunting at the beast's unnatural strength, I was flipped on my back. My shirt and hair soaked up the cool water, weighing me down. Holding the snarling beast above me, the sounds of battle filled the air. The loudest being Ash, his snarls matching the beasts.

I kicked the beast over my head. It landed on its back. Jumping to my feet, I spun toward it. When it came back at me, I sliced its arm with my dagger. Throwing its head back, it let out a high screech, showing its yellow fangs. Instinctively, I moved my hands to my ears, but quickly recovered and lunged toward it. My dagger sliced into its chest. Thick, black blood dribbled out onto my hands. Take that, sucker.

I turned back to Tate and Ash who were fighting off the remaining three beasts. Old Bob still carried Ellie downstream, much slower than expected.

"Run, Old Bob!" I screamed.

The stones were slippery from the rushing waters. Old Bob's face scrunched in concentration, struggling with her weight as he tried to stay upright despite the slick stones.

"Tristan! Watch out!" Tate yelled.

Whack!

My head hit the rocks. I tried to push up, but the pebbles split in two. Squinting, I brought my hand to my eyes when a sharp pain stabbed me in the shoulder.

"Aaaah!"

I shook my body, but the weight of the beast and pain made it hard to move. It held tight with its claw-like nails and fangs digging into my shoulder. Clutching my dagger, I sucked in a few breaths and swung the beast over my shoulder. A loud pop rang as the blade penetrated its skull. As I released its jaw, more thick, black blood sprayed my face, and it fell to the ground.

Ellie's scream jerked me to my feet; the world spun. Resting my hands on my knees, I watched Old Bob fight off two creatures in the shallow waters of the river. Tate and Ash continued to fight them as they came.

Shit. They keep coming.

"Watch out!" Ellie screamed, scurrying deeper into the water.

I ran toward them, but my uneven sight made the world tilt. Sharp stones dug into my knees when I fell. I brought my eyes up. Crap! I was facing the wrong direction. Everything spun, and darkness sat just on the edge of my vision, threatening to take over. My shoulder ached and my stomach threatened to expel my meager breakfast.

Slowly turning around, I spotted Old Bob fighting two beasts. He used two daggers, blocking and ducking away from their claws and dripping fangs. His twists and twirls looked like a dance, but the sprays of blood from each cut he made brought me back to reality. Flipping one creature over his shoulder, he lunged forward toward the other. His front foot hit a large stone, and it slid out from under him. His knee hit the ground and he caught himself with his elbow. The splash from the water muffled his cry. The beast was on him again.

"No!" Ellie screamed, trying to stand, but the stones were too slippery, and she fell back into the shallow water.

Everything slowed. The beast was in the air. No, no, no. I stood and ran, only to end up back on the stones. Ellie's arms reached up and a beast was on her. Her arms flexed from the strain. No, no, no. Snarling, it snapped its fangs inches from her face, drool dripping onto her cheek.

"Ahhh! I can't... hold it!" she screamed.

"Hold it, Ellie!" I yelled, crawling toward her.

"No!" Old Bob pushed the creature off him. He crawled toward her too, but the beast jumped on his back. Its shriek rang through the trees as it pulled Old Bob's head back.

Ash yipped and snarled. Tate grunted.

"Fight, Old Bob!" I yelled.

A beast jumped at me. I flipped to my back and kicked it right into the water. The fast river took it downstream.

Ellie's arms were slightly bent. She was growing weak. "Hold on, Ellie!"

Old Bob twisted and turned, trying to get out of the beast's hold, his eyes never leaving Ellie.

Standing, I stumbled toward Ellie, clutching my dagger. My vision zoned in on her. Her exhaustion came through her screams and grunts.

I had to get to her.

My foot caught a rock. Flying forward, I threw my hands down to catch myself. My palms cut on the rocks as I watched my dagger disappear into the rushing white waters.

"Shit!" I slammed my hand onto the rocks. Water splashed onto my face.

I had nothing to defend Ellie. Helpless, I watched her struggle. She screamed and the beast pushed harder. Her arms weakened. She squeezed her eyes shut, pushing all her strength out, but she was done, too tired. Her arms gave way with a snap, and the beast's fangs were in her throat.

"NO!" Old Bob and I screamed in unison.

My jaw dropped. No, no, no, no. This wasn't happening. Ellie batted at the beast gnawing on her neck. I ignored the stones cutting into my knees and hands as I tried to crawl faster toward her.

Old Bob got a second surge of energy. He pulled the beast off his back, swinging it forward. The beast landed with a thud. Taking a stone, Old Bob smashed its head and rushed to Ellie.

But I reached Ellie first. I grabbed a stone and beat at the beast's head. Its hold didn't budge from her throat.

"Get off her!" I screamed.

Tate and Ash slid down the embankment to us. Tate's dagger shone in the light. Without hesitation, he dug the dagger in the side of the beast's neck, and it released Ellie. Her blood dripped from its mouth, and Old Bob threw it into the river.

"Ellie, God, Ellie. My love." He pulled her to him. A pool of her blood forming on the wet rocks below her. "My love, my love." He pushed his hands to her throat, blood pulsed between his fingers. Using his free hand, he worked to pull off his shirt. His eyes turned to me filled with tears. He was saying something, but all I heard was the rush of the water. The water that was washing Ellie's blood away. A lot of blood.

Ellie's mouth gaped open and shut as she tried to speak. Old Bob moved the fingers of his free hand along her cheek. He gave up on taking off his shirt. When he looked at me, my heart sank. I never wanted to see that face again. Ever.

"Get something! We need something to patch her up!"

I stared at him, my mouth moved, but nothing came out. How could I tell him it was no use?

"Get something!"

"There is nothing," I whispered.

"Get my bag!" He pushed harder on her throat as her face grew paler, eyes drooping.

Tate put his hand on his shoulder. "I'm sorry. There is nothing we can do." His eyes were soggy.

I looked down at Ellie's wide eyes. The same eyes that watched me run, swim, dance, sing, laugh. The eyes that were always kind, always loving. I would never see them again.

I put my hand on her arm. I needed to feel her warmth, just one more time.

Old Bob let out a sob. "No! I can't let her go." Pressing his forehead to hers, he said, "Ellie, Ellie. I love you."

A tear escaped her eye and she reached out her hand. It was a silent plea. Tate took her hand and knelt next to her. My grip tightened on her arm. "It's all right," I managed to whisper.

My chest cracked. A wound so painful and deep I didn't know if it would ever heal. My mother. Gone.

We watched the light fade from her eyes. Saying a silent prayer, I embraced Tate in a brotherly hug. I buried my face in his shoulder and we both shook. A piece of my heart was gone and would never be full again.

"Ellie?" Old Bob choked, moving his hands over her cheeks. "Ellie? No, no, no." His tears mixed with her blood as he kissed her nose, eyes, and cheeks. I put my hand on his back, letting him know I was there. She was everything to him.

The woods were silent, except for the sobs of a heartbroken man who lost the love of his life and the howls of a wolf.

∽

We buried Ellie near a large oak tree close to the bank of the river. I carved her initials in the trunk, so we would always know which tree it was when we visited.

Old Bob moved methodically, not speaking, barely breathing. Sitting around her freshly covered grave in silence, we listened to the leaves rustle in the trees. Ash nuzzled his nose in the dirt, letting out quiet, pitiful whines. The smell of fresh flowers filled the air as we laid them along the top. Ellie loved fresh flowers.

"I know this is hard, but we have to keep moving. We still need to find Eden. With these beasts, or whatever they are, we need to make sure she's safe." I spoke quietly.

"Those beasts won't take anyone else I love," Old Bob said.

"What were they?" Tate asked.

Old Bob shook his head. "I don't know. They were human, but they sure didn't act like it. It was almost like they were... infected."

"The virus?" I asked.

"No. We all had the virus, but none of us changed to... that. " Old Bob stood. "It's like they were all scourged." He took a silent moment to gaze down at Ellie's grave, tears welled in his eyes.

"I'm going to miss her too." I placed a gentle hand on his shoulder.

"We all will," Tate said. "She was the heart of our home."

Old Bob wiped his swollen eyes. "Come, we need to find Eden."

Ash barked and sniffed the area. He took off back toward the trees with intent. Quickly gathering our belongings, we followed Eden's wolf into the woods.

Chapter 16

Eden

Panting, I dropped to the ground. "I'm getting faster." Lying on the lush grass, I looked up at the bright blue sky. The light breeze moving through the leaves created a soothing sound that drowned out the daily life within the camp. It almost reminded me of home. Almost.

Most people here were very welcoming, only a few wary eyes. Thankfully those few keep their distance. I enjoyed walking through the camp, talking with people. I had never met so many new people, and I loved learning about their lives. But every time I saw a mother brushing her daughter's hair, I thought of Ellie, and every time I saw a father with their son, I thought of Old Bob and the boys. Guilt built within me. I chose to leave. I chose to stay here.

"How many people live here?" I asked, watching two girls walk hand in hand between two rows of tents.

"We have thirty tents. Families living in each. I don't know the exact amount, but it's a good number," Brian said.

"And you just let anyone in?"

"Wouldn't you?" He looked at me and I blinked. Sighing, he continued. "Of course, we make sure they don't mean harm, but it was hard... in the beginning." He lay back onto the grass, linking his hands behind his head. "When people are scared, they turn... violent."

"So, you have been here the whole time? Since the outbreak?"

He turned to me. "No. Since the rebel bombing."

His eyes watched me. I looked back to the blue sky, following the flow of a white puffy cloud. The bombing. The same bombing that opened the door for my family and me to run from the city before the virus killed almost everyone in our group. Why had we run? Given the fear of the virus outside the city walls, I don't know.

"No one here gets sick then?"

His eyes roamed my face. "Not anymore. Most people who left the city during the bombing died, and anyone who was still living outside the walls had already survived."

Brian watched me as he played with a blade of grass. "No more talk. Back to work." He jumped up. "Drop and give me twenty push-ups."

He narrowed his eyes at me, taking a step forward when I gave him a defiant look.

"Why am I not sick?" I asked. "I came from the city... a long time ago, but why didn't I get sick?"

"Drop now, little one."

Continuing to glare at him, I stood, taking a step toward him. "Tell me why. Then I will continue my training."

Brian took another step toward me, mouth open to scold when Derek chimed in from behind him. "You will continue your training." He walked toward us, and the thick wave of dominance had me stepping back. I fought the urge to bow my head, but I wouldn't. I couldn't. I don't bow to anyone. He stopped in front of me. "You will get information, but let's finish one thing at a time."

I stiffened my body. I wanted to stomp my foot in frustration, but I had a feeling that wouldn't have the same effect on these two, like it did with Old Bob. "Just tell me why I haven't got it? That's all I want to know."

Derek's lips tightened when he met my eyes. The sounds of the camp drowned out, and I focused all my attention on him, trying to pull any information I could from his head. He blinked and shook his head. "Interesting." He looked back at me and sighed. "You're immune. We're immune."

I took a step back. "What? How?"

"We don't have all the information, but when we were in the city we were... prisoners." He watched my face a moment before continuing. "As prisoners, we were given the virus and then a doctor gave us something else. We are unsure of what it was, but we survived and became what we are."

I blinked at him a moment; a breath caught in my throat. Shaking my head to clear it, I spoke. "So, I was a prisoner as well?"

Brian furrowed his brow. "Did you come from the city?"

I nodded. "Yeah. I was a baby when the bombing happened, but my family escaped." I paused a moment watching them. "Both my parents died. Most of them died. Only five of us survived."

They watched me solemnly; no one sure of what to say.

Breaking the silence, Derek walked away. His back a signal that the conversation was over. Still, I took a step toward him, opening my mouth to ask more, but Brian grabbed my arm. "Drop down and give me twenty." I turned and saw Brian's determined face. He wouldn't give me any more information either. He smirked at my snarl, knowing he won. "Your enemy won't wait for you to mourn. You need to be prepared to fight at any moment in your life, good or bad."

I dropped down grumbling, but after I finished my twenty push-ups, I sat back on my knees. I wasn't a prisoner. I was here voluntarily. "You know what?"

"What?"

"I think I'm done for the day." I stood and walked toward my tent.

"Eden!" Brian's voice attracted the eyes of others who worked outside their tents. They watched me, curious who would defy Brian, one of their leaders. Giving a few a sweet smile, I kept walking until I arrived at my tent. I could feel eyes burning into my shoulder blades, but I never turned.

Eden

Brian's voice moved through me, and I smiled at his desperation. I couldn't leave him hanging, so I responded.

We can resume when you're ready to talk. Right now, I need a nap.

He didn't reply, so I went to my cot and slept.

∽

Wake up!

Brian's voice boomed inside my head, and I jumped off the cot, landing on my feet. Eyes wide, I scanned the room only to land on his smirk. He stood near the tent door with his arms crossed.

"Come." He didn't wait for my reply and walked out of my tent.

Rubbing my eyes, I pushed my fingers through my tossed hair and followed, jogging slightly to catch up. "Where we going?" He didn't reply. We passed a tent with a crying child, and I caught a glimpse of a young mother rocking it, singing a sweet song. My fingers touched the butterfly on my chest and I sighed at the empty feeling. Ellie's warm hold on me a distant feeling. Looking forward, I met Brian's eyes as he looked back at me with an eyebrow raised. "What?" He ignored me again, gesturing for me to enter Derek's tent.

"Come sit." Derek motioned to me upon entering. He sat at the head of a well-worn wood table, smiling. I sat in the chair next to him and watched Brian choose the chair across from me. "You want some answers. I understand that, so let's talk."

I looked between them. Both harboring serious faces as they waited expectantly for my questions. "All right. Where does the virus come from?"

"We don't know exactly." Derek sat forward, linking his fingers together. "It could be us carrying it, the animals, maybe it's in the soil. There are many possibilities."

"So since we have already had it or have already had some kind of cure, we don't get it, but people like… my friend Jace from the city get sick and…"—my throat restricted at the word—"die?"

Derek nodded slowly. "Yes. There is only a one percent survival rate. So, chances of anyone from the city surviving are very, *very* low"

I squeezed my hands together, thinking of Jace. I may not have been his biggest fan, but I wouldn't wish for anyone to die in such a manner. "Do you have any idea what was given to you to… possibly to me, to survive?"

The look between them was quick and fleeting, but I didn't miss it. "No." Derek's voice was thick, and I ground my teeth together. I could taste his lie in the air, but I could see I would get nowhere.

Three arguing men barged into the tent. Their faces red from heat and anger as they stopped short at the sight of us sitting around the table.

"So, she a leader now too?" a tall, dark-haired man snapped.

Derek stood. "No Jon. We were just having a conversation." He sighed, taking a few steps toward the men.

Jon's eyes narrowed on mine, and I fought the urge to growl. He was challenging me, and I don't back down from challenges.

Easy

I turned to Brian's warning stare.

That won't give you props with the citizens.

Looking back at Jon, I let out a huff, disappointed that Brian's words were right. If I started fighting with the people, they would never fully accept me, and I needed to be accepted. I craved it. I missed my family, my sense of belonging.

I stood and took a few steps toward him, extending my hand. "Hello, Jon. I'm Eden."

Jon looked at my hand, scoffing. "Is this a joke?"

I kept my hand extended and a smile plastered to my face.

"No joke," Derek replied.

Jon inspected me as I stood there, hand outstretched, waiting for him to accept me. "Drop your hand, girl. I'm not going to shake it."

His words stung, but I dropped my hand and stepped back. Brian moved to my other side. I could taste the tension in the room, and every hair in my body tingled.

"Why are you here, Jon?" Derek asked.

Jon looked at me a moment, then took another step closer to Derek. The two men behind him still red faced and panting stood like statues. No one was leaving this tent before they allowed it.

"Why is there a sick boy in the medic tent? Not just a cold sick but with the virus." He pointed a clenched, white-knuckled hand in the direction of the medic tent. "He has the Fever, Derek!"

My stomach tightened and I looked to Derek as well, curiosity brewing. They said Jace had died, but yet there was a sick boy still here.

"And what would you have us do, Jon? Put him out in the woods and leave him for dead?"

"He's going to die anyway! Why put us all at risk?" He squared off in front of Derek and his two henchmen stood a little taller, fisting their hands. I could feel Brian stiffen, and he put a soft hand on my shoulder, pulling me slightly behind him and Derek.

"That's not how things work here, Jon, and you know it. We don't just throw people out."

"He has the Ferine Fever!" one of the men behind Jon yelled.

"Yes, and he is quarantined. Sarah is making sure no one goes in other than us."

Jon scoffed again. "Sarah, what does she know?"

"She's was a doct—" Derek focused on keeping his composure, and I had to give him props; even I was clenching my jaw in frustration.

"She's a beauty queen! One good for cuts and bruises, nothing as serious as the Fever!"

"Careful." Brian growled taking a step toward Jon, but Derek's hand clutched his forearm in warning.

"Why are you so worried? None of you have gotten sick yet." All eyes turned to me, and I fought the urge to step back.

"Yes, girl, we all survived the virus, but we haven't forgotten the feel of it. How every breath felt like it was our last. We don't know enough about it to know for sure we can't get it again, and I will do everything I can never to get it again." Jon narrowed his shoulders at me and Brian tensed.

"All right, stop!" Derek moved in front of Brian. "You all know we don't just dispose of people. We could learn something from this boy. Sarah, who is a doctor"—he narrowed his eyes at Jon—"is trying different remedies, to see what she can do with what we have, to prolong it, which she has been able to do, by days, and if we are lucky, she may save him." Jon opened his mouth, but Derek cut him off. "And you know that we have never had a second case. So if you have had it and survived, which everyone here has, the likelihood is low, so stop your bellowing and deal with it!"

Jon's shoulders tightened and his face grew red. "Very well. I'll follow *your* rules then." He gave us all a stern look before exiting the tent, his henchmen following.

I let out a long breath. "What did he mean? *Your* rules."

"He meant he is going to get enough people to argue on his behalf, and then I'll have no choice but to throw the boy out." Derek's shoulders slumped. He rolled his head to relieve the tension in his neck.

I swallowed the large lump in my throat at the thought of a helpless person being sent in the woods to die, or even worse, to be ripped apart by the beasts.

Chapter 17

Eden

The next day I trained hard, barely breaking a sweat. In such a short time, I had built stamina and become faster and stronger. Derek and Brian were pleased with how quickly I was strengthening, but not surprised, almost like they suspected it.

The tension within the camp was thick. Jon and his thugs had started spreading rumors among the people, causing fear. Derek had spent most of the day calming worried people.

Since my physical training has been such a success, Brian decided to increase my skills and start training my senses. Apparently, I had heightened senses. They did too. And it was time I learned how to use them in combat. Blindfolded, I stood in the middle of the clearing with Brian stalking around me.

Tune out all the distractions, he says. *Fight me with only your hearing and smell.*

Groaning, I leaned down and rubbed my sore knee. The start has been rough.

Clutching the long staff, I turned in a circle slowly.

Snap! A twig.

I whipped around, but it was too late. Brian swiped my legs out from under me, and I landed on my back. "Oof." I coughed, gasping for breath.

"Up!"

"Just... give me a—"

"Your opponent won't wait for you, so you need to get back up on your feet. Now!" He gave my leg a nudge with his foot.

Leaning on the staff, I pulled myself up. Listening carefully, I turned my head until I heard his steps, soft and slow. He was circling me. A child's scream pulled my attention in the opposite direction.

Wham!

I folded forward coughing, gasping for more breath. Grinding my teeth together, I thought, *he's going to pay for that.*

"You have to tune everything out. Don't let little things distract you. That one second could be your life."

I pulled off the blindfold, piercing my eyes on him. He smirked.

"All right, little one. I think we'll call it a night."

I lowered my staff, still clutching it tightly as I scanned the camp. Everyone was quietly retiring to their tents for the evening. The pink horizon glowed over the top of the trees. After sunset, not many, if any, people wandered the camp.

"Fine."

Brian walked toward Derek's tent, and I looked down at my wood staff. Right when his muscled back disappeared through the tent flap, I snapped the staff on my knee and dug the sharp end into my palm, creating a three-inch cut. Stifling a grunt, I watched the dark red liquid seep from me, painting the grass at my feet.

Fisting my hand, I entered the tent. "Uh, so I tripped, broke my staff, and my hand got cut." I gave them the sheepiest smile I could muster. *Clear head, clear head, clear head...*

Brian's gaze narrowed on me as he snatched my hand to examine the cut. He didn't say anything, but I felt his distrust. I would be surprised if Derek didn't feel it too. It took all my strength not to pull away and lower my eyes in submission. He fixed his mouth into a straight line as he held my eyes.

Chuckling, I tried to lighten the thickened air. "Too bad all this training can't fix my clumsiness."

"Indeed," Brian said.

"That's unfortunate," Derek said, looking over Brian's shoulder at my hand. "Brian, escort her to the medic tent. Sarah should be able to patch it up."

"Yeah. Sure." He pulled me from the tent by my arm.

When he got outside, I pulled my arm back. "I cut my hand, not my legs. I can walk without you holding me."

He spun around. "I don't know what game you're playing, but you better be careful."

My stomach sank; maybe I didn't think through my plan very well. I was never a good liar. "I don't know what you're talking about." I fought the instinct to turn away.

"Don't be coy with me, little one. You may be getting stronger and learning fast, but we don't need a troublemaking little *girl* around here."

The blood drained from my face. Not wanting to let Brian know how much his words affected me, I cleared my throat. "Yeah, all right, but just so you know, I'm not a little girl."

He scoffed before leading me down the middle row of tents. Halfway, there was a tent that was slightly larger than the others.

"Sarah?" Brian moved the tent's flap to the side.

Sarah turned from a small desk, giving Brian a blushing smile. Warmth flowed through the air as he approached her.

"Eden cut her hand." Brian motioned to me with disinterest. He tried to keep his back to me, but it didn't keep me from seeing his cheeks flush. Obviously, the feeling was mutual.

Standing awkwardly near the entrance, I kept my hand away from my clothes, so as not to stain them. I only had one extra pair. Sarah floated to me, her eyes fixed on my hand.

"Let me see." Her grasp was gentle with skin so smooth I wondered what her secret was. "Here, come sit. I will clean the cut and patch it up."

I sat on a cot as she rummaged through a small cabinet, grabbing all the items she needed. Brian stood gawkily at the entrance of the tent, and when I looked at him, he was conveniently very interested in a small snag in the tent's fabric.

"You don't have to stay, Brian. I remember the way back to my tent."

As he turned to us, I could read his struggle between feelings and duties.

Sarah smiled down at the cotton pad she was disinfecting. "Yes, Brian. I am sure she is capable of getting back on her own. It *is* just her hand that's injured." Her tone was teasing. I liked her immediately.

"All right then"—Brian cleared his throat—"you know where to find me." He briskly left the tent. For the second the flap had opened, I spotted the twilight sky, the sun was almost down, exactly what I planned.

Sarah worked in silence cleaning and bandaging my hand. If she felt my eyes roaming her face, she didn't show it.

"How long have you lived here?" I asked.

She didn't look up. "Since the beginning. Since we built the walls fifteen years ago."

"Where did you live before?"

She put the supplies in the cabinet next to the cot. "I had a home, cabin type near the water. My husband..." – she paused – "he worked in the city. He would commute."

"You gave up a home for tents? To follow Derek and Brian?" What could these two men have that would make someone leave the comfort of a home?

She smiled at me. "We only live in the tents in the summer. We have a group of log cabins closer to the water we move to when it's colder. Protects us better from the cold." Playing with a piece of fabric wrap in her lap, she stopped smiling for a moment, but then she tightened her face, trying to keep the mask of constant happiness. "You're young. You don't know what we went through when the virus hit. When we were banned entrance into the city. When they built the walls, keeping us out." Her smile now disappeared to what looked like disdain. "We had to learn survival, which many of us didn't know how to do. People went crazy, violent. It became fight and kill for survival. When Derek and Brian showed up, they offered a safe haven. The structure and security we all craved."

I sat quietly as her face grew soft, thinking of the memories. "You are safe now. Derek and Brian will take good care of you." She stroked her hand through my hair. I had to fight the instinct to turn into her touch. It was a very motherly action, and it reminded me of Ellie. Watching her dark hazel eyes disappear into thoughts, I wondered if she had any children.

"Have you met many others living in the woods?" I asked, pulling her from her memories.

"Yes. Some have created groups like this, but many still live on their own, surviving by any means possible. We get stragglers that come, many due to the creatures that are becoming rampant. Those creatures go through camps and homes killing anyone in their sight."

My stomach rolled at the thought of the creatures in the woods. "Do we know what these creatures are? Where they come from?"

"No. Years ago, we may have seen one or two infrequently, but they have been growing in numbers. They are aggressive and bolder in their attacks."

Their squeaky, gravely voices had been spine-chilling. Clutching my necklace, I sent a quiet prayer that they hadn't found my home and hurt my family.

"Anyway"—she cleared her throat and smiled—"you must be tired from all that training. Come see me tomorrow, and I'll clean and rebandage it."

"I will. Thank you, Sarah." I smiled at her as I left the tent.

The cool night breeze kissed my skin as I started my walk down the row of tents toward my own. Each tent was lit within by lanterns, shaping the paths through the camp. Stopping a few tents down, I hid around the corner to wait and watch. Sarah was the lead healer in the camp, so chances are she was the one caring for the sick boy. I needed to find where he was. If Jace was dead, maybe I could help one of his friends.

I hugged my arms around me to keep in the warmth from the chilly night and shuffled my feet so my blood continued to pump. Just as I was about to give up and leave, Sarah stepped out of the tent. I followed her brisk walk down the row, staying within the shadows of the tents. She topped at the largest tent in the camp, the tent at the end of the row. As she went inside, the flap stuck open giving me a glance inside. Hanging over the back of a chair was a familiar set of clothes. Blue pants and a white shirt. They were the same clothes that I last saw Jace in.

"Jace," I whispered to myself. Was there a mistake? Was he still alive? My stomach bottomed out. If he was alive, why did Derek and Brian tell me he died? I needed Sarah to leave. I needed to see who was in that tent.

Chapter 18

Eden

My hands ached from the tightness as I wrung them together. My feet wouldn't stay still. I needed Sarah to leave, needed to see who was in that tent. Sarah finally left, disposing a mask into her pocket and walking down the row to her tent. Without thinking that someone else could be inside, I charged in. Luckily, the only person inside was a patient. Their head was turned away, but I skipped a step at the long dark hair. It had to be Jace; it had to be. Slowly, I approached the cot, putting a soft hand on his shoulder and turned him onto his back. Letting out a sigh, I smiled at the sleeping, handsome face.

"Jace."

I knelt next to his cot. "Jace," I repeated, feeling his hot damp cheek. He turned his pale, clammy face toward me, cracking his eyes.

"Eden?" he croaked, his lips white and chapped. I put my hand on his chest to still him when he tried to move and felt his slow, steady heartbeat; he was alive. I let out a relieved sigh.

"Hi." I leaned closer, smiling. "I thought you were dead. They said you were dead." I didn't realize I was crying until the wet tear slid down my cheek. Wait, why was I crying? I quickly wiped them away.

"Eden," he repeated, closing his eyes.

I surveyed the tubes and needles in his arms. "What did they do to you?"

He let out what I assume was supposed to be a laugh, but it came out as a coughing croak. "Nothing," he managed in a dry whisper. "They're helping." He cracked his eyes again to look at me. "Are you crying?"

My cheeks warmed. Ignoring him, I touched his forehead again. "Helping? Then why are you still hot with fever?" Scanning the room, I grabbed a small bowl with cool water and a cloth, placing it on his forehead.

He tried moving again and his face grimaced. Grunting, he gave up. "You... OK?"

"Me? You're worried about me? Have you looked in a mirror?" I chuckled, continuing to gently rub the cloth over his face and neck.

His cheek twitched in an attempt to smile. "Fever" was all he was able to get out.

"Yes. I know, but how do we cure it?"

"Can't."

I took a cup of water from the small table next to us. Holding his head up, I brought the cup to his mouth and he drank. More water spilled down his chin than actually made it into his mouth. I hated seeing him like this, would hate to see anyone like this.

"Procedure," he rasped.

"Procedure?"

His eyes pleaded with mine. He wanted to say more, but he was too weak. "It's OK," I said. How about I ask yes or no questions, and you blink to respond. Blink once for yes, twice for no. Good?"

He blinked once. Yes.

"Good. Do you know this procedure?"

Two blinks. No.

"Did Sarah say something about it?"

One blink. Yes.

"Does anyone else know about it?"

One blink. Yes.

"Is it another woman?"

Two blinks. No. My heart sank.

"A man. Do you know his name?"

Two blinks.

I wasn't sure if I was happy or frustrated. As much as I didn't want to hear if Derek or Brian knew more than what they had told me, I wanted to learn more and help Jace. There weren't many men here that would be talking to Sarah about such a vital thing.

"I'm sorry to keep asking questions, but did they give any information about it? What it was or how to do it?"

Two blinks. No.

I sighed, pursing my lips.

Jace closed his eyes and his breath turned deep and steady. He had fallen asleep. I returned the bowl and rag back where I found it and watched him a moment, unsure of when he had become someone I had to help, but he had. He had become my friend, and if what he just told me was true, he may be the only person I now trusted within this camp.

Chapter 19

Tristan

Ash's tail wagged slightly as he led us through the woods. He was focused, never stopping, even to check the scent. He knew exactly where to go. The only sounds around us were from our shoes crunching the dry fallen leaves.

No one spoke. Ellie's death still lingered between us. It was still hard to believe that she had been gone for four days now, that she wasn't just walking slightly behind the group. Our backs were taut and we clutched our knives, ready if another scourge attacked. I agreed with Old Bob; no one else I cared about would be taken by them. Not if I had a say about it.

"Stop," Old Bob hissed. He slowly moved in front of us, keeping his eyes fixed on the trees ahead. "We aren't alone."

I scanned the area where Old Bob's eyes moved. Nothing.

"I don't see anything," Tate whispered.

"Same."

Old Bob motioned us to follow him. Careful not to make too much noise, we moved through the trees, placing our feet carefully to not snap any twigs. Coming to a clearing, we stayed back within the tree line. Ash started to whimper quietly, wagging his tail.

From the top of the small hill within the trees, we stared down at a large wooden fence surrounding a camp. Small watch towers stood near the entrance with four people holding weapons. Inside people moved about freely, happily going about their day.

"There must be about a hundred people in there," I whispered.

Neither of them looked at me as they continued to search our surrounding area.

"We have been practically living in solitude with one neighbor miles away for our whole lives when there are places like this?" Tate whispered.

I nodded in agreement.

Old Bob sighed. "We have lived in solitude for your protection. You don't understand what life was like when the Fever happened."

I turned to face him. "No. We wouldn't since I can count on two hands how many people we have met in the last sixteen years, and with three of them, before we could learn anything from them, you scared them away." I turned back to the camp. "I say we go in. They may have information about Eden. Maybe even about the scourges."

"Everything we did for you was to protect you. You were young, not old enough to remember or comprehend the chaos that happened when the virus, the Fever, came." He sucked in a breath and let it out slowly. "We can't just go in. When everything happened, people changed. They became more violent, unsafe. We can't trust them." He motioned to the men standing at the entrance. "Plus, they have guns. Our daggers are no match for guns."

"I understand what you're saying, and I appreciate everything you have done for us, but we have to take a chance at some point. Right now, we have to think about Eden. These people may have some answers; we have to try," Tate said. I nodded in agreement and fought the urge to give Tate an atta-boy pat on the back.

Old Bob sighed, closing his eyes in defeat. "Fine."

A loud clanking rebounded from inside the walls. We moved to a better vantage point to see inside.

"What is that?" I asked.

"Come," Old Bob whispered, moving toward the sound.

In a clearing near the edge of the camp, between the tents and the wall, two people fought. They moved gracefully, almost like a dance, holding wooden staffs that clanked together. The movements reminded me of Old Bob fighting earlier. I moved to the edge of the tree line to get a better view. A tall blonde, muscular man barked orders at a girl. Her long apricot hair flowed through the breeze with her movements. She was strong, nimble, quick, and... blindfolded. Eden.

"Tate! It's Eden."

"What?" He moved to my side. "What is she doing in there and why is she fighting blindfolded?"

"I don't know, but I'm going in there." I started toward the entrance only to be halted by Old Bob grabbing my arm.

"Wait. We can't just go in. We have to have a plan."

"A plan?" I scowled at him. "Eden is in there."

"More of a reason that we need a plan. We can't just go barging in knowing nothing about the situation." He let go of my arm. "I care about Eden, too, you know that, but if we want to do her any justice, we have to think about what to do first." He looked toward Eden and the man. "Anyway, she doesn't look like she is any immediate danger at the moment. Remember, I did teach her to fight. I know she can handle herself."

"She's blindfolded." I motioned toward her and the man. They still moved smoothly. He attacked her from all directions, but she blocked him with ease. It was a dance. A dance that turns bloody. Ellie's wide, scared eyes flashed before me, and I turned away, squeezing my eyes shut.

"I think he's right, Tristan. We have to be smart about this." Tate's hand gently folds over my shoulder and I slump.

Turning back to watch Eden, I saw her swing the staff with confidence. Her cheeks flushed with heat, and her hair flowed around her like golden water. She was beautiful. I sighed. "All right. What's the plan then?"

"Plan for what?" a man said.

We turned to see a man behind us. Five more men walked into view behind him from the trees, all pointing guns at us. Guns. I hadn't seen guns since I was a small child living in the city. Even then it was only the guards who had them. Crap.

"Easy, easy," Old Bob said, putting his hands up. "We mean no harm." He put his knife in his sheath, and his earlier comment about knives and guns had Tate and I doing the same.

"Sure. Let's go," one of the men said, motioning for us to move forward. One pushed the head of his gun into Tate's back, and he stumbled forward.

"I'm walking! I'm walking!" Tate yelled.

Another man started toward me, but I dodged him so his gun missed me. We marched toward the open gates, open and ready for us, where more people with guns waited. What had Eden gotten into?

Chapter 20

Eden

The sky was clear and the sun beat down on us, sizzling away the coolness of the morning. Sweat formed on my brow as Brian and I sparred. The clanking of our staffs ringing through the clearing was much more prominent to my ears since I was blindfolded... again. Today, however, I wasn't taking a beating. I was focused and tuned in to my hearing and sense of smell, blocking Brian's attack. My bandaged hand clutched the staff, but the ache in my palm didn't show in my swift movements.

Letting my senses run on autopilot for a moment, I allowed my mind to wander to earlier when I had met with Sarah to have my cut checked and bandage changed. She wasn't as sweet and talkative as the day before due to a run-in with Jon and his thugs. He had done just what Derek said he would: gathered more people. They had shown up to her tent demanding Jace be thrown out. Derek and Brian ended the small protest, but Derek wasn't sure for how long he could keep them away. Sarah insisted she was doing the best she could, but she wasn't positive Jace would survive.

I had pushed her about the procedure. She didn't even seem too surprised when I brought it up, but she didn't have much information.

Frustration fueled my training.

Derek walked from his tent to the edge of the clearing and sat on the shaded grass. He hollered corrections or praise to me. I'm sure Brian and he were chatting in their heads, but since I was blindfolded, I couldn't be sure. I had to practice more on building my interior wall.

"Focus!" Brian bellowed at me.

I shook out my body, rolling my head to stretch my neck. Focus, focus, focus. I moved in for an attack that was easily avoided, but it felt good not to be on the defensive all the time.

After an hour of nonstop work, my muscles ached and sweat dampened the back of my shirt. A guard from the camp entrance approached, stopping our session.

"Derek, there's something you need to see."

I pulled off my blindfold. The guard's face was stone, but by the way he rubbed a hand along one pant leg, I would say he was nervous. His eyes flicked to me, then quickly back to Derek.

Derek stood with a sigh, brushing off his pants. The relaxation he had shown on the grass transitioned to dominance. The hairs on my neck spiked and my whole body stiffened. I would not bow. I repeated the mantra in my mind.

Come.

Derek's voice rang in our minds. The pull was too strong to ignore. My foot took an almost involuntary step forward, but I shook my head and arms out, fighting the instinct to follow. This may be the only time to find any information. I bent over to fix my shoe, letting Brian walk ahead.

"Little one! Come on!"

"Yeah! I'll be right there. Just need a drink."

Nodding, he followed Derek toward the gate.

With no time to lose, I slipped into Derek's tent and fixed my eyes on his desk. If there really was a procedure, then Derek was the best person to hold that kind of information. Papers littered the top, and I quickly shuffled through them, but nothing caught my eye. I opened the top drawer, nothing but pens. Moving to the top right, I didn't find anything important. Frustration built and I pinched my lips together. There had to be something. I pulled out the bottom right drawer and spotted a dark leather-bound folder. Opening it, I discovered three loose pages, wrinkled and soft at the edges. Whatever they were, they had been looked at a lot.

I scratched my head, inspecting each page. I had never seen anything like it before, even in all of Ellie's lessons. One page had a picture, hand drawn, of what looked like two twisted ladders mending together. Bonding the ladders was an odd spider-like symbol. There was a sketched picture of a human and a few sketches of different animals. Bear, deer, dog, and bird on the outside of the ladders. While skimming the few journal entries that accompanied it, I was interrupted by yelling outside. Almost dropping the pages, I shoved them back into the folder and back into the drawer. I peeked out the flap before rushing outside.

The feeling hit me like a gust of air. I stiffly walked toward the entrance of the camp, shaking out my trembling hands. This feeling, it was like when the bear attacked Ash in the creek a few years back. He had been terrified, as was I. It took a long few weeks to rid ourselves of the ripples of feelings that continued to plague us, but we got through it... together. As I neared the growing crowd, the sensation was so strong my breaths started puffing through my nose. What was happening?

My ear twitched at the low growl. Not just any growl, that was Ash's growl. A rush of blood pumped into my head and I quickly pushed through the crowd. Ash, Ash was here. My fingertips ached in anticipation of feeling his thick, soft fur. When I reached the front of the crowd, my elation quickly transformed to rage. My family stood in a row, tied up with guns pointed at their backs. I looked at Old Bob, then Tate, then Tristan before my eyes dropped down to Ash at the end of the row; he had a rope tied around his muzzle. How they got that on him, I have no idea.

My lips pulled back, baring my teeth, and a guttural roar filled the air as I charged.

Chapter 21

Eden

The first man I tackled had his gun pointed at Tate. His eyes were wide and terrified as his back hit the ground. After pulling the gun from his weak grip, I knocked him unconscious. Jumping up, I pivoted to the next guard. His gun was pointed at Tristan. He tried to run but fell forward at the swipe of my foot. His scream was silenced by the blow to his head.

"Eden!" Derek bellowed.

I blocked him out, my rapid heartbeats thundered in my ears. My vision, rimmed with red, focused in on the third man. A growl in my throat grew loud as I stalked him. His shaking gun was pointed at Old Bob. He licked his lips, shuffling his feet as I slowly neared him. The whites of Old Bob's wide eyes drowned out the hazel. Just two steps before I reached him, the guard set the gun on the ground, backing away. Closing my eyes, I put my nose in the air, pulling in the thick smell of fear. It rang through my nerves, exciting me.

WHAM!

My back hit the ground and all the air left my lungs. I widened my eyes and opened my mouth, willing myself to pull in air.

Derek.

Pulling in a deep breath, I curled my lips and flipped him off me. Jumping to a crouch, I spun, swiping his feet out from under him. He fell with a grunt. Standing tall, I looked down at him over my nose. I would bow to no one. He locked eyes on mine, the skin around them taut, and he slowly stood.

"Back off, Eden." His voice was firm, strong, and... dominant.

I will not bow. I will not back down.

"That's my family!" I snarled. "If you threaten them, I will rip you to shreds."

Derek stilled, tilting his head as he observed me. "Back off. Release them," he said to the guards.

"Derek..." Brian protested.

"Don't argue! They're Eden's family. That makes them guests." He inclined his head toward me, a peace offering. Letting my shoulders drop, I stepped back.

The remaining three guards gratefully lowered their guns and moved away quickly; one wiped the sweat from his brow.

The moment I turned, Ash's paws hit my chest and we fell back. Happiness twinkled in his gold eyes.

"Ash!"

I wrapped my arms around him, burying my face in the soft fur of his ruff. All the tension in me disappeared. I held him back and untied the rope from around his muzzle. Whoever did that will have a word with me later. The roughness of his warm tongue scratched my nose and my smile returned.

"Is that a wolf?" Jon said in disgust from the growing crowd behind us. "We're letting wild animals in now too, Derek?"

Standing, I turned to face him. "This is my wolf. If you have an issue with him, you can take it up with me." Ash stood at my side, my fingertips grazing his soft head.

"That's enough!" Derek's voice rumbled, causing everyone to go silent. He turned to me "You need to cool off. Take your family back to your tent. I will be there shortly."

Breaking away from Jon's gaze, I turned toward Derek. The dominance in his eyes told me not to mess with him. Letting out a small snort, I turned to Tate, Tristan, and Old Bob, who regarded me with wide eyes, almost scared.

"Follow me."

My lack of control prohibited me from giving them the greeting I would like. The only one who understood was Ash. Feeling the tickle of his coat on my legs brought a sigh to my chest. Without speaking, I escorted my family and focused on maintaining my temper the entire walk to my tent. Brian followed, for what I suspect was protection. Not to protect us, but to protect others from me.

∽

"Sooo, you look good," Tate finally said.

I looked up from my cot at him standing in front of me, his sweet face soft and smiling. We had been standing in a thick silence for a few minutes. No one seemed to know what to say to me, or I to them. Their uneasy fear was obvious in their shuffling feet as they avoided staring at me, giving me only fleeting glances.

With his words, I jumped forward into his arms, burying my face in his shoulder and letting the tears come. I held him tightly, imagining we were back at the cabin. That we never saw Jace and his friends. That I hadn't decided to rebel and go off on my own. When I saw them, on their knees in danger, I realized that my life would be incomplete without them. It would mean nothing.

"Are you crying? What happened to the brave, warrior girl we just saw?" He gave me a quick squeeze before pushing me back to inspect my face. He chuckled, wiping the tears away. His dimples made him look much younger than his twenty-two years.

"Hey." Tristan moved to me, squeezing my arm, still not fully meeting my eyes.

He smiled slightly when I turned to him. When he finally did meet them, the look he gave me did not say brother; it showed more. I pushed down the knot in my stomach and stepped forward, and he pulled me into a hug. His grip was firm but relief escaped him in our embrace. I buried my nose in his neck, breathing in deeply. He smelled of fresh leaves, the woods.

Someone coughed, bringing us back to our surroundings. We stepped away from each other, smiling awkwardly.

"I told you she could handle herself," Old Bob said.

I turned toward his proud smile. Stepping away from both boys, I moved to him, and he put his hand gently to my cheek. I could see through his smile, feel the grief, sadness... hollowness. Something wasn't right.

"What happened?" I asked.

Tears wet his cheeks and a soft sob escaped him. Without hesitation, I hugged him. This time his face buried in my shoulder. "I tried to save her," he whispered.

My stomach sank. "What?" I stammered, instinctively touching the silver butterfly on my chest. I knew before I heard her name who he meant, but I didn't want to believe it.

"Ellie," Tristan replied, putting a gentle hand on my shoulder.

I gulped and my eyes stung as I stared forward over Old Bob's shoulder at the tan fabric of my tent. It went blurry and no manner of blinking made it focus. My shallow breaths made the butterfly around my neck feel like a hundred pounds. My cheeks wet as silent tears rolled down them.

Not Ellie. I needed her...

Strong, warm arms surrounded us from behind. Both Tate and Tristan joined our hug. We stood in the middle of my tent, holding each other, letting our grief flow, but even with us knit tight together, her loss was like a gaping hole in the middle. It could never be filled.

"Am I interrupting something?" Derek stood at the entrance to my tent with the flap open, his gold eye almost looked amber from the angle of the light. Moving apart, we turned to him and all three men near me took a unison step back. The tension in the air spiked. They noticed his eyes. Great. I wasn't ready to breach that conversation yet, so I pretended I didn't notice and moved to a chair at the small table. I wiped my cheeks, motioning for them to sit.

"How did it happen?" I asked.

"Scourges," Old Bob replied. "Well, that's what we have come to call them. They are the beasts, human... but not."

Memories of the grey-skinned people with fangs and a gold eye flashed through my mind.

"Yes. I was chased by some but was lucky enough to be saved by Brian. That's how I ended up here."

"We've been concerned about the increase of these... scourges," Derek said, taking the last chair at the table. He watched Old Bob carefully, examining his face a little too long for comfort. My lip curled at the need to protect, but I pursed my lips. We didn't need a brawl right now.

"Increase? You've seen them before?" Tristan asked, still peering at Derek's eyes with unease.

"You haven't?"

We all shook our heads. "No. This is the first we have ever seen anything like them," Old Bob replied.

"Interesting."

"How long have you been seeing them?" Old Bob asked.

Brian entered the tent, not missing a beat before jumping into the conversation. I'm sure he had been snooping outside but just couldn't contain his curiosity anymore. "Years. We first heard of them when some others from a small camp about ten miles from here showed up. They had to leave due to constant attacks. Everyone but a few of them had been killed and their food supplies were taken. Here at our camp, our hunters used to only see them every once in a while, but sightings have increased even from our walls." He stood behind Derek, leaning on the thick wooden pole that held the center of the tent up. The room filled with silence a moment as my family surveyed him as well, no doubt seeing the resemblance in his eyes. Double great. My stomach hollowed, and I found my next few breaths hard to take. Old Bob managed to continue the conversation, buying me more time.

"Do they always travel in groups or have they ever been alone?"

"Groups. I have yet to see or hear about one that traveled alone. There is always one nearby. They hunt, attack, and kill."

"What are they?" I asked.

Derek shook his head. "Don't know. They look like they used to be human, but what made them the way they are? No one knows."

I watched Old Bob; his eyes glossed over in thought, probably reliving the traumatic event of Ellie's death. My eyes stung again. I dug my fingernails into my palm as I clenched my fists together. I had to keep my wits about me.

A change of energy in the room made me look to the others. Derek and Brian's tense bodies let me know they felt it too.

Derek looked to Old Bob. "I'm truly sorry for your loss. I wish there was something I could do."

Old Bob looked up. "There is." After clearing his throat, he said, "You can help me find them and kill them."

"Old Bob..." Tate pleaded.

Brian snorted. "Excuse me? Are you ser—? Wait, did you just say Bob?" He narrowed his eyes at Old Bob. "Robert Lewis..." – he sucked in a breath – "I thought you were dead."

Derek leaned forward. "Well, I'll be..." He chuckled. "I thought you looked familiar."

Old Bob pushed back his chair. "You both must be mistaken..."

"No, no, it's definitely you." Derek sat back, linking his hands on his lap. "You don't recognize us?"

Old Bob blinked at them. He fisted his hands, but not before I spotted them tremor.

Looking at Tate and Tristan, I verified that I was not the only one lost in the conversation. "What's going on?"

Old Bob stood. "Nothing."

"So, you're the man who kept Eden so in the dark," Brian said.

"What I did was to protect her! Protect all of them!" Old Bob's nostrils flared as he took a few steps toward Brian. The quiet warning growl rumbled through the tent and Old Bob halted. All eyes turned to me and I froze. Putting a hand to my throat, I felt the vibration. It was me.

Old Bob gaped his mouth and he jerked back a step. "What did you do to her?"

I stood. "What?" Nausea built within me at the look in his eyes as he looked at me. He was... disgusted.

"Look at you, Eden. It's like... like you're one of..."

"One of what?" I bit down on my lip to keep it from trembling. If he said what I thought he was going to say...

"One of them... the scourges."

I lunged forward, knocking over the chair. "Take that back!" Derek jumped in front of me, holding my arms.

"Eden! Breathe!"

Panting, I fisted my hands at my sides. Derek stood in my path to Old Bob with Brian slowly moving behind him. Narrowing my eyes at Old Bob over his shoulder, I said, "You have the audacity to call me that when you have lied to me? To us? Who are you, *Robert*? Why do Derek and Brian know you?"

Old Bob tensed, watching me. He glanced between Tate and Tristan pleading for their help. "I love you, Eden. Like my own child..."

"But I'm not your child! You're not my father!"

"Eden," Tate said quietly.

Old Bob's face dropped. He took an uneven step to his chair and sat. My heart fluttered with guilt, but my rage quickly trumped that. "Who are you?"

He sighed. "My full name is Robert Lewis. I was head of the guard within the city, a good friend of your parents." He paused, taking in a long breath. "Before the bombing, they had asked me to care for you if anything were to happen to them. I was part of the escape, and then when everyone died, that is exactly what I did."

"And you know Derek and Brian how?" I asked.

"I was a colonel in the Army, and Brian was my major," Derek said. "We worked closely with the president before Zane." I opened my mouth to speak, but Derek held up a hand. "That is all you need to know right now." Tate put a hand on my shoulder, and I squeezed my lips together in frustration. I wanted to hear it all, but I sat back and listened.

"Why didn't you tell us you knew our parents?"

"I don't know. I guess I felt it was safer. Again, everything I did... Ellie..."—he paused, swallowing hard—"Ellie and I did was to protect you. Because we love you." His sincerity was obvious. "We have a lot of information we could discuss, but right now I feel the most important thing is figuring out what these... scourges"—he gave me an apologetic look—"are and how to get rid of them."

"I just..." Feeling regret for my outburst, I closed my eyes. Losing Ellie was hard and we would never get her back. Even if he did keep information from us, I didn't want him gone. "Just... no more lies."

His face relaxed, dropping his head in relief a moment. He reached across the table, offering me his hand. I took it and he squeezed. "Promise."

Brian stood. "There are too many unknowns right now. It could be suicide going after them."

Wow. Right back to business. All right.

"Have you thought about tracking them? Trying to catch one and interrogating it?" Old Bob asked.

Derek nodded. "No, but we don't have the people to spare. It's dangerous. Most of our people aren't fighters. They do the best they can, but they wouldn't survive a mission like that. We don't know how many there are or what kind of resources they have."

"Is that why you have been training Eden? To have her become your... weapon?" Tristan asked.

The silence in the room became deafening. I couldn't look at any of them if there was the chance of rejection, so instead, I looked at the warped wood of my table. Old Bob's words, calling me a scourge, cut me. Wounded me more than I thought possible. Even if he regretted it, he had thought it, so I'm sure others did as well.

"No, we have been training Eden because she needs to learn how to control and live with what she is. We are best able to do that. Others wouldn't... understand."

"And, what is she?" Old Bob asked, his eyes burning into the side of my face. I continued to keep my gaze on the table. Memorizing every groove and crevice.

"That... is a story for another time. Just know, she is a survivor," Derek replied.

Tension coiled tighter within me. The way they spoke about me like I wasn't sitting right there, hearing everything they were saying. Like I was some kind of anomaly that no one has seen before. Squeezing my eyes and jaw shut, I focused on keeping my nerves at bay. My nose filled with the smell of wildflower. I turned to the tent flap; Brian's head moved in sync with mine. He also smelled her.

Sarah's head peeked into my tent. "Excuse me? I was just stopping by to grab Eden. I need to clean and rebandage her hand."

I stood quickly, grateful to escape the judgmental discussion and eyes. I pushed past Derek, following Sarah outside. Breathing in the fresh air and rolling my shoulders lifted a weight off me. Ash's strong body at my ankles helped steady me as tension rolled from my body. Sarah, who was much more perceptive than I originally thought, was wise to give me quiet and space as we walked to the medic tent.

Chapter 22

Eden

I sat on the same cot I always did when in the medic tent with Ash curled up next to me. My emotions had calmed and I was feeling very content, but the feelings from Old Bob's words and stares simmered within me, ready to boil over if irritated.

Sarah gathered supplies from the small cupboard next to my cot. She was quiet, but I watched her give Ash fleeting glances.

"You can pet him if you want." I smiled, scratching Ash behind his ears. He moved his head into my hand letting out a groan of pleasure. After touching the necklace Ellie gave me, petting Ash was the next best way to relax me.

Sarah watched us hesitantly. "So, he's a real wolf?"

I nodded as I stroked his head. "He's gentle. He would never hurt anyone unless they were a threat to someone he loves. I have had him since he was a pup."

"Interesting." She slowly moved her hand toward him. He leaned forward to sniff her, but she snapped it back quickly.

"It's OK. I promise he won't hurt you."

After she brought her hand back to Ash's nose, he smelled it, then gave her a quick lick. Giggling, she moved her hand to his head, giving him a good pat. She smiled and pulled her hand back to her lap. "Wow. He's amazing." She looked at Ash with admiration then turned back to gather more supplies.

She took my hand and unwrapped the old bandage. Her brown, silky ponytail fell over her shoulder. She was a natural beauty with a kind spirit. I could see why Brian liked her.

"So, I found something, but I am not sure what it means."

She glanced up from her work. "Oh? What did you find?"

"Well, after our last conversation, about the procedure. . ." She looked up at me, searching her memory of earlier that morning. She nodded, so I continued, "I searched Derek's tent and found some papers. There were drawings, but I'm not sure what they mean. Maybe you could help."

Her face paled. "You searched Derek's tent?" Her hands started to shake, and she quickly pulled them back to her lap. "You actually went into his tent? Without him knowing or asking him first?"

I nodded. "Yeah. I figured he wouldn't tell me anything, and do you really think he would allow me to search his tent, even if I asked? No, I had to take things into my own hands."

I could hear the fast pulse of her heart as she stood. She curled her arms into herself and paced next to my cot. Ash lifted his head watching her, a little whine escaping him. She was the one who said she was doing the best she could at keeping Jace alive, so I would think getting any information possible would be a good thing.

"Do you know what he would do if he found out you snuck into his tent and went through his things?" She stopped pacing and leaned on the back of her chair. She closed her eyes and pulled in some deep breaths.

"It's OK, Sarah. He won't find out." I kept my voice calm and set a gentle hand on hers. "Can you help me?"

Opening her eyes to look at me, she took a deep breath. "What exactly do you want me to do?"

"Do you have any paper? I'll draw what I saw and maybe you can make sense of it."

"I really like it here, Eden. I don't want Derek or Brian to find out I helped you." She handed me a paper and a pen.

I studied her as I took them. "I understand." I drew what I remembered. "I won't let them find out you helped me."

She waited patiently, hands and feet fidgeting. When I finished, she examined the picture intensely.

"Are you sure this is what you saw?" Her voice cracked.

"Yes." I described in more detail what I saw and she listened quietly.

When I finished, she sighed. "We heard of a procedure. It was just a rumor at the time, but now seeing this, maybe it was real."

"Do you know what it means?"

Her worried face met mine. "Eden, you need to understand that we don't have enough information about this. We don't know if it has been used and if it actually worked, or of side effects. There is so much risk."

"I understand. We don't know a lot, but what we do know is if we don't do anything, then he will die. If there is just a hint of possibility, then we need to try. Right?" I looked at her pleadingly.

She sighed. "These here are diagrams of DNA." She pointed to the ladder looking things. "It's what we are made up of, like a recipe. If something in our DNA is different or missing, then we, as a people, would be different." She paused, making sure I was following her. I nodded, so she continued, "This one is human, but this one looks like an animal of some kind. I am not sure what, but I don't think it matters."

"Human and animal DNA. That would explain the sketches of animals on the side of the paper."

"Yes, and this"—she pointed to the spider looking thing holding the two ladders of DNA together—"this is the virus."

"The virus."

"Yes. The rumor is that if you combine animal DNA with someone who is infected with the virus, then the two DNAs bond. They become immune to the virus, just like the animals are."

"Like a cure?"

"Maybe, but remember, it's a rumor. We can't just test on humans based on a rumor. It's unethical. We don't know the side effects. Nothing."

"Can you think of any possible side effects?"

She sputtered, "Well there are many, I mean, lifelong illness, death... becoming one of the creatures."

"A scourge?" I fidgeted with the pen in thought. I sure didn't want Jace to become one of them.

"Well, yeah, no, I don't know. That's the point, Eden. It's too risky. We just don't know what will happen." Her cheeks flushed with worry.

"True, but at this point, we don't have much choice. We either let him die or we try. Isn't it also unethical to just let someone die when there is a possible way to save them?"

"What about Derek?" I could smell the sweat that formed on her skin.

I tilted my head. "What about him?"

"If he finds out you did this without running it by him, he'll be furious. Like I said, I... I like it here."

"Like I said before. Leave Derek to me. He won't find out, and if he does, he won't know you had anything to do with it." I paused, watching her. "Why are you so afraid of him anyway? What has he done?"

"He is our leader."

"Yes, but that still doesn't explain why you are so afraid of him."

She sighed. "When everything was out of control, Derek came and put order back. He had to keep a tight control; otherwise, people would revolt. He doesn't let personal feelings and relationships get in the way of what needs to be done to protect his people."

Good to know.

"OK. I promise they will never know you helped me, but you have to promise one thing as well." She nodded. "You have to keep your emotions controlled when around Derek and Brian. If you don't, they will know you are guilty of something." If I could sense her so easily, so will they. I won't have to say anything about her helping me, she will give it away.

She nodded. After a moment she asked, "Who is Jacob to you?"

"What?"

"Who is he to you? Jacob?" I blinked at her. "He moans your name, Eden, so I know you know him."

I spoke carefully. "Jacob." She nods and I realize that they think Jace's name is Jacob. Why had he told them a different name? "I don't really know him that well." I paused and saw her surprise. "We were traveling together when he got sick. I went to get water, and he was taken. I was tracking him when I was found."

Her eyes grew wide. "So, you're from the city too?"

"No. It's a long story. I have lived in the woods my whole life with my family. We found Jace and his friends." I paused. "I'm not close with him, but I feel responsible for him. I can't just let him die if there is a possible way to save him."

"Wow," Sarah said, sitting back. "Well, I'm not sure how you are going to do it."

"I don't know, but I will figure it out." I smiled at her. "Thank you for the information."

"Of course."

She took my hand and finished cleaning and rewrapping my wound. As I watched her cleaning up the area, it dawned on me, she may try and tell Derek without me knowing, to protect herself.

When I stood, I narrowed my eyes at her. "One last thing." Her eyes grew when she looked at me, and she took a step back. "You may be scared of what Derek will do to you, but if I were you, I would be more scared of me. All I'm asking of you is your silence. If you do that, everything will be fine, but"—I paused for effect—"if you don't, you will have a visit from me. I may be young, but I'm not weak."

Her face blanched. "Your eyes," she whispered. "They glow, like Derek's and Brian's."

I nodded. "Yes, so just remember, your silence or you'll deal with me."

She bowed her head in agreement. A rush of power filled me, and I couldn't help but enjoy it. She turned to walk back to her desk. As Ash and I left the tent, I slipped an empty syringe into my pocket.

Chapter 23

Eden

Everyone was still in my tent, sitting around the table. Ignoring Brian's raised eyebrow as I passed him, I focused on calming the patter of my heart. I am sure he and Derek could hear it. When I passed Tristan's chair, he gently grabbed my hand.

"You all right?"

I nodded, giving him a closed-mouth smile. "Just tired."

The room had gone silent. When I looked up, all eyes were on us. Quickly, I pulled my hand away and cleared my throat. "You all done? I'd like to sleep." I didn't wait for replies as I moved directly to my cot and lay down.

"Of course," Derek responded, his eyes burning into the side of my face. "I think we have planned everything we can for now. Unfortunately, there are only two more cots in here and we don't have any extras, so I hope one of you is fine with sleeping on the ground."

"We'll manage. Thank you," Old Bob replied.

Derek and Brian quietly left the tent as I lay on my side, my back facing them, with Ash curled up at my feet.

Derek's voice rang through my head.

Sleep. We have much to discuss tomorrow.

Shaking off the invasion, I closed my eyes and was asleep before I learned who would sleep on the floor.

∽

Wetness slopped on my nose, again and again. Groaning, I fluttered my eyes open and saw Ash's nose touching mine, willing me awake.

"What is it?" My voice croaked. I moved to lift my head and it throbbed. "Argh." Rolling to my back, I pushed the heel of my hands into my eyes. Ash licked my arm, letting out an impatient whine. Rolling my head to the side, I looked at him. "What?"

Ash let out a bark then grabbed my sleeve, giving it a tug until I slowly sat up and set my feet to the ground. Resting my elbows on my knees, I let my head hang down and I yawned. I was alone; everyone must have risen early.

"No, please!"

My head whipped up at the woman's voice. Not just any woman, Sarah. Ash barked at me again.

That was when I heard the others. The hollers of angry people, mixed with the pleading cries of Sarah.

I was on my feet and out the door before I took my next breath. As I neared the clearing, I pushed through the people. Four men carried a stretcher. My stomach sank. Jace.

"No," I whispered.

Ash nudged my leg nervously, and I scanned the crowd for anyone I knew. Spotting Tate and Tristan, I pushed my way through the crowd to them.

"What's going on?"

"We are using the city boy as bait," Tate responded, giving me a wary look.

"Bait? Bait for what?" I screamed, my voice barely audible over the angry yelling of the crowd.

"The scourges," Tristan replied. "We want to see if we can capture one."

I shook my head, panic building within me. "No. This isn't right. You can't just sacrifice an innocent person…"

"Innocent?" Tristan scoffed. "Eden, he kidnapped you."

I froze. They had no idea. "You idiots. You didn't bother to ask me? I took him!" Turning away, I pushed back through the building crowd, not bothering to stop when I knocked over a woman.

"You didn't even bother telling us he was here!" Tristan yelled after me. I ignored him and ran to my tent.

Pushing the flap open, I charged into my tent. "I have to do something."

I wanted a better plan, but that wasn't going to be possible. I grabbed the syringe I had taken from the medic tent, sat on my cot, and looked to Ash. He set his head on my knee with a knowing look.

"It's going to hurt. You sure?" I asked him. His response was a quick lick to my hand.

I didn't have much time. Tuning out the angry calls of the crowd outside, I poked the needle into the thick skin over his shoulder blades and sucked out enough blood to fill the syringe. I had no idea how much I needed, so I filled the whole thing. I pulled out the needle and massaged the area. Ash panted happily.

"Thanks, buddy. Pray this works."

Wrapping the syringe into a small cloth from the washing table, I tucked it under my shirt sleeve and ran out of the tent. The crowd had progressed closer to the camp entrance, moving along with the cot. I picked up my pace, pushing and shoving people to the side as I moved through them. Tristan showed up at my side and put out his arm to stop me. His jealousy hit me like a wall.

"Eden, I know you may not agree..."

"I don't have time for this." I pushed past him.

Making it to the front of the crowd, I saw Jace, pale and weak, lying helplessly on the cot. His eyes were wide, or as wide as they could be, searching the crowd. He was looking for someone, probably me. The breeze picked up and hit my face. Fear filled my nose. Jace's fear and my instincts reacted. I needed to protect him. He moved his mouth, trying to speak, but nothing came out, or his voice was too weak to be heard over the screaming crowd.

Ash nudged my leg, and I looked down at him. "We have to do something, right buddy?" He nudged my leg again.

I took off toward his cot.

"Eden!" Brian yelled.

Ignoring him, I continued to the cot. I shoved one of the men aside and threw myself on him.

"Eden," Jace whispered. "What..."

I put my mouth to his ear. "Shhhh, just trust me. We don't have time. This may hurt."

After pulling the syringe from my sleeve, I stabbed it into his upper shoulder, injecting all of Ash's blood. He didn't even flinch; he was so weak. I pulled it out and shoved it back into my sleeve.

Strong arms pulled me from behind, but I clutched Jace's shoulders. "I'm sorry," I said, looking into his terrified, pale face. "I don't know if that will work, but I had to try."

Brian pulled me off him and Jace's cot was carried through the gate. His bright blue eyes twinkled from the light that streamed through the canopy of trees, and his mouth twitched in an attempt to smile, giving the hint of his single dimple on his right cheek. Closing my eyes, I looked away. The angry shouting continued as I pushed back through the crowd, only now some of the anger was directed at me. Grinding my teeth to stay composed, I pushed through the end of the crowd and met Sarah's wet eyes. She gave me the slightest of nods. She knew what I had done.

"Eden," Brian said.

I narrowed my eyes at him and stepped away, giving him my back as I headed toward my tent.

"I'm sorry. There was no other way," he said.

"There is always another way," I growled over my shoulder. Tate waited patiently for me at the first tent in the row, but I walked by him without a glance.

He followed me. "Eden. Stop."

Pivoting so fast I almost made a full circle, I met his eyes. "So, this was the big plan you guys thought of last night?"

"We didn't have any choice."

I snorted. "I'm sure if you thought hard enough you could have thought of something else." I turned and continued to my tent.

"Eden—"

Ignoring him, I reached my tent, whipped the flap to the side, and stomped in. Tristan and Old Bob sat at the table. My arms were tense at my sides with my hands fisted. I stopped at the table and looked between them.

"So, we sacrifice innocent, defenseless people now?"

They both blinked at me silently.

"Wow." I shook my head and took a step toward my cot.

"We thought he had taken you," Tristan said, and I froze.

"Well, he didn't; I took him. I was so angry with all of you that I decided to take things into my own hands. Jace and I were trying to track his friends before you got there." I paused. "We just had a few snags on the way."

Old Bob's eyes grew fire and he slowly stood. "You took a man we knew nothing about... a man from the city and... and ran off with him?"

I pursed my lips, not pulling my gaze from his, even if every instinct in my body told me to. "You underestimate me. All of you do."

"He could have killed you, Eden!" Old Bob yelled. "Did he hurt you?"

I laughed, raising my hands. "What? This is unbelievable. No! See. Just like this. You think that I can't defend myself. You taught me to fight, Old Bob. I'm strong, fast, smart. I can take care of myself. I'm eighteen, not eight."

Tristan stood slowly. "Eden, we know you are strong, smart, and fast. That's not the point."

"Really? What is the point then? That you all can protect me better than I can protect myself?"

Tate touched my arm, but I shoved it off.

"We don't want anything to happen to you," Tristan said.

"Well, things happen. You can't keep me locked up at the cabin my whole life." I closed my eyes and let out a long breath. "As much as you would have liked to. You can't keep the real world, real issues from me."

"Eden, we were worried," Old Bob said quietly. "I can't lose you too."

I opened my eyes looking at him and my heart broke. The pain from losing Ellie was written in every new wrinkle around his sad eyes. Her necklace hung around my neck like a heavy weight, a reminder of the love we all once had. Our life was simple, but it was love. "Oh my..." I whispered, sitting in a chair.

"What?" Tate sat next to me.

"It's my fault. Her death is my fault." My voice wavered and my chin wavered. I have never wanted to go back in time until this moment. I wish I could go back and never leave the cabin, then she would still be alive.

Old Bob moved around the table. "No, no, no, Eden, don't you think that." He knelt in front of me, gently taking my hands. "It was her time. As much as I miss her and I want her back, we all have a time." His eyes shimmered as he watched me.

I wrapped my arms around his neck, crying on his shoulder. "I'm so, so sorry."

"I'm sorry I lost her. She was the love of my life. I'll miss her every day, but right now, my only goal is to protect you, and I need to learn about the scourges to do that. I won't let them take anyone else I love."

I pushed away from him. "I get that, but you just sacrificed an innocent man. He has a family too. He isn't a bad person." Without responding, he dropped his eyes. "Please, all of you, don't underestimate me. I can handle myself." Old Bob nodded, squeezing my shoulder.

Derek stepped into the tent. "He is in position. You all ready for the watch?"

"The watch?" I asked.

"Yeah. We're watching him, and when we see the scourges coming, we'll capture one alive," Tristan replied.

"So, you all are still going to go through with this?" I don't know what I was hoping… maybe they would change their mind and bring him back?

No one looked me in the eye except for Derek. "Eden, he'll be dead soon from the virus anyway."

The thought of Jace being attacked while helplessly lying on the ground, the scourges ripping him apart, infuriated me. The fear and pain he would endure. "So what? That isn't a great way to die. Will you protect him? Save him if you can?"

"Why do you care so much about him?" Tristan snapped. The jealousy I smelled earlier still flowed in the air. I didn't even look at him; I couldn't trust myself if I faced him. I was too angry.

Old Bob put a hand on Tristan's shoulder. "I promise, Eden, if we can, we will protect him."

I knew that was the last thing on any of their minds, but it was pointless arguing. I walked back to my cot as they left. Unable to sit, I paced the length of the tent, hoping that the procedure worked. Ash watching me from the comfort of my blanket on the cot.

Chapter 24

Jace

I swallowed.

Shit that hurt!

My cheek twitched when I tried to wince, but my muscles were too heavy. I'm surprised I could still breathe despite the thirty-pound blanket lying on me.

My vision blurred and shook. Probably from the jostling of my cot as the men carried me further into the woods. My head pounded and my body ached. I wish I could move, but... that damned blanket.

The breeze hit my sweat-damp skin and a quiet groan escaped me. That felt so good. My body was on fire, but I couldn't move to cool off.

The damned blanket.

The spot where Eden pricked me on my shoulder ached. I closed my eyes and thought of her. I thought I was saved when I saw her.

When I felt her body cover me like a blanket, only it was more welcome than the current one on me.

Trust me. Her voice still whispered in my ears. If she had said that a few days ago, I would have laughed, but now, she was the only one I could trust and I barely knew her.

Grunting, I tried to pull my arm out from under the damned blanket, but it was no use. My body was too weak.

The world stilled when the men set my stretcher down under a group of pine trees. At least, they managed to get me in a shady area with the sun peeking through the branches around me, not on me. The small breeze still a relief on my scorching body.

"Here should be good," one of the men said. The others grunted in agreement.

Once the sound of my chauffeurs' footsteps disappeared, all I could hear was my own ragged breaths, birds singing, and the leaves chiming in the breeze. Trying to scan the area was hard given the heaviness of my pounding head. My eyes drooped and heavy walls within my mind grew. I tried to lift a finger, but nothing moved. I couldn't even twitch my cheek.

My mind's focus slipped in and out of darkness. Tensing my body, I worked to push the blanket off my sweat-soaked body. If I could just get that off, I would get better... I know it.

My exhaustion had won. Releasing the tension in my body, I sunk into the cot. My eyes closed and I moved into darkness.

☙

The tingling pulsed from every limb in my body. There wasn't one part of me that was free of the agony. I wanted to itch everywhere, but I was too weak, even to open my eyes.

The sounds around me were louder, more pronounced. It... hurt. I wanted to pull my hands up to cover my ears, but my arms wouldn't listen.

A small animal scurried on the ground near me and birds called from far away. The breeze hit me, and... was that a shiver? I wasn't overheated anymore, even under the heavy blanket.

My nose twitched at the smell of berries from a nearby bush, water from a stream, flowers from the bank of the stream, and food. Food from the camp. My stomach growled.

I urged my body to move, begged it, pleaded, but it wouldn't budge. The burning tingle continued to rage through me, and I screamed and thrashed inside the strong walls of my mind.

A twig snapped. My ears twitched, like actually twitched.

I pulled in a ragged breath, then another. I could hear a heartbeat, fast and steady. Someone was near. No, not just one, but two? Three? My blood pulsed through me, and my senses grew like the petals of a flower opening to greet the sun.

The tingling in my body dulled, and my breaths steadied out. They became sighs of relief.

My pursuers were closing in. I pushed myself to move, pounding the walls of my mind. My body was not yet fully mine, and the frustration built within me. The smell of birch and berries grew, filling my nose with every breath I took. I heard slow, shallow breaths. The heat from their bodies was so close I could feel it.

I pushed, screamed, and thrashed in my head until finally the walls cracked then crumbled. Relief engulfed me as I took my body back. The tingling evaporated and the heaviness lifted. I opened my eyes. After locking gazes with one of my hunters, without a second thought, I attacked.

Chapter 25

Eden

I paced in my tent for as long as I could, but the thought of Jace in the woods, defenseless, was too much. I had to go to him. Everyone was preoccupied from the excitement earlier that no one noticed me slip out of the gates, but I left Ash there just in case he needed to distract anyone.

Making my way into the woods, I used my nose to guide me. I spotted Jace. He lay on the cot, eyes closed and still, but his chest moved with a slow steadiness. I let out a small sigh; he was still alive.

Passing the others who crouched behind a large group of bushes, I went straight to him.

"Eden!" Tate hissed after me, but I ignored him. I ignored all their eyes burning into my back.

Eden! What do you think you're doing?

I ignored Brian's voice and reached out my hand to Jace. I was about to touch his cheek when his eyes shot open.

"Jace!"

He sat up so fast I fell back onto my ass, and he jumped over my shoulder onto the scourge behind me.

How did I miss that?

Shocked, I crouched, brushing off the dirt and turning toward the others. I was only met with wide, stunned eyes.

"We will do our best to protect him, Eden. We promise."

I scoffed. "Yeah right."

Ash snarled behind me as he bounded toward us.

Jace's grunts and the snarls from the scourge had me turning to him. He wasn't sick. Not one bit. He was on top of the scourge, pinning it to the ground by the throat. The scourge screamed, lashing out its hands trying to shove Jace off, but Jace was too strong.

"A little help here, Eden?" he rumbled.

I giggled. "It worked!"

"Seriously? Not now, Eden! Help me!"

Blinking, I shook my head, bringing me back to the gravity of the situation. I pulled out the small knife from my boot and moved toward Jace and the scourge. I bent down to stab it when Old Bob came running.

"No! Eden! Don't kill it!"

I looked up at the others coming out from their hiding spot. Jace grunted; he was tired. Turning the knife over, I used the handle and smacked the creature over the head, knocking it out. Jace slumped in relief.

"Jeepers. Took you long enough," he panted, falling back off the scourge.

I looked at him with a huge grin. He was alive.

His skin glowed, his body firm and muscular, and his hair long and shiny black. Jumping at him, I threw my arms around his neck, and he chuckled, slowly wrapping his arms around me. I giggled into his shoulder then moved back to look at him again when I noticed his eyes. One was gold, like mine; the other blue, his regular eye color. My smile faded. He looked like me, like the scourge.

"What did you do?" Derek growled, coming from the woods behind us.

We sat, embracing each other. I was slightly on Jace's lap, so I awkwardly slid off. My cheeks warmed at the weight of eyes on us, but I looked directly at Derek.

"I did what no one else would do."

"And what is that? What *exactly* did you do?" he repeated through clenched teeth. His eyes glowed with anger, and his dominance hit me so hard I almost dropped my head just from the sheer force.

"You know what I did. Don't ask silly questions. The big question is, if you knew about this, why didn't you try and save him earlier?"

Derek took a step forward, pointing a finger at me. "You have no idea what you're playing with, little girl."

I mirrored him, also taking a step forward. "I may not, but I do know that I'm not coward enough to let innocent people die when there is a cure!"

Jace put his hand on my shoulder. "Eden."

Glancing at the shocked crowd behind Derek, I took a step back. People from the camp had come out after hearing the commotion. Everyone stared in silent shock at the man who was almost dead not an hour ago and was now perfectly healthy.

"What did you do?" Old Bob whispered, examining Jace.

Derek didn't take his eyes off me. "She did something very dangerous that could have gone very wrong. We took her in, helped her, trained her, and she went behind our backs and did this."

I raised my eyebrows. "I guess I'm a little confused myself because all I know is that I saved Jace's life. I didn't hurt anyone, so why is it this huge deal?"

"You may not have hurt anyone, but like Derek said, you were lucky. This could have gone very bad. We don't have enough information on this kind of procedure. You took a very risky chance, risking us all," Brian said.

"How did you expect to learn anything new about it if you didn't try it? Just talking about it won't give you answers!"

"It's unethical!" Brian yelled. I could see Sarah look down behind him. Those were her same thoughts.

"I understood the risk, but I also understood if nothing was done, he would die anyway."

The air circulated aggression, and the growing crowd from the camp began to murmur. I took a step back at my sudden vulnerability. Jace's calming energy flowed behind me, uncoiling my shoulders, and I sighed.

"I would have told her it's all right," Jace said.

"But you didn't. She didn't ask you. She just acted. That's not OK," Derek snapped.

"You can't let them get away with this, Derek," Jon yelled from the crowd. "If she did this, think about what else she will do!" People yelled and nodded in agreement.

Derek's eyes were tight and fixed on me. He set his jaw. "Take them," he snapped, motioning to a few gunned men.

"What?" I shrieked. "This is crazy!" The crowd rumbled louder.

"You can't be trusted. We don't know what kind of side effects may happen to him, so we can't take a chance."

"Wait! Wait! There has to be another way," Tate pleaded to Derek, but he just pushed past him.

Men tied our hands with thick rope and guided us back into the camp. One man on each side, holding our arms. The murmuring crowd moved to the side to let us through.

I panted as the rage built within me. Rolling my neck, I cracked it, and when the man grabbed my arm, I bared my teeth and growled. "Don't. Touch. Me." He didn't hesitate before letting me go, taking a small step back.

"Relax, Eden," Jace whispered.

Grinding my teeth together, I focused on breathing through my anger. In through my nose, out through my mouth, just like Ellie taught me. Ellie. Thinking of her kind eyes and feeling the necklace around my neck soothed me. I opened my eyes, and through the crowd, I caught a glimpse of a worried pretty face, framed by long brown hair. Sarah. She stood to the side, quiet, watching us. The men grabbed my arm again, tugging me forward, so I lost sight of her. We were dragged to a large tent in the dead center of the camp that was surrounded by men with weapons. Their version of a prison.

Inside the tent were five large tree stumps. Each stump was about eight feet tall. They dragged us each to our own stump tying us to them, double-checking the knots before leaving.

I sighed. "Any ideas on how to get us out of this one?"

Jace smirked. "You tell me. You're the smart one."

I rolled my neck and shifted my shoulders to get into a better position before sliding down to sit. We sat quietly and awaited the news of what would happen to us.

Chapter 26

Tristan

I paced inside the tent, anger threatening to erupt from within me. My body ached from my taut muscles. She willingly helped him. She helped him. Every time I squeezed my eyes shut, all I saw was her throwing herself in his arms. Clenching my fists, I pushed my fingers into my hair and pulled. I needed to focus, to calm myself.

"You OK, Tristan?" Tate watched me with wary eyes. He sat on his cot, petting Ash. Since Eden was taken, Ash has been uneasy. Derek and Brian won't let him near her, or even let him sit outside her current prison, so he stayed in our tent.

I nodded. "Yeah. Just upset about... the situation."

Derek, Brian, and Old Bob entered the tent with Old Bob pleading on Eden's behalf.

"I hear what you're saying, but what she did was reckless. People could have been killed. I can't let something like this slide." Derek sat at the head of the table.

"So, what, you going to execute her?" I narrowed my eyes at Derek.

Derek met my eyes a moment, hollow and serious. Shit. They were going to execute her!

He let out a low growl. "What would you have me do?" He sat back, lacing his hands over his stomach, waiting for my reply.

My gaze never left his. His eyes, just like Eden's and now Jace's. He had to know something about this that he wasn't saying. "What did she do? Why does he now look like her, like…"

"Like?" Brian raised a bushy eyebrow.

"Like you. Both of you."

Brian stood taller but waited for Derek to take the lead. It was obvious who was in charge. Derek scratched his head. "We aren't talking about us right now. We are talking about what to do with Eden. Now, I could just do what I think is right, but I am discussing it with you, her family first. Out of respect."

He dodged the bullet, conveniently. I opened my mouth to push the topic, but Ash whined at me. Help Eden now, ask questions later. I gave him a pat on the head. He wouldn't let her get hurt. He would fight to the death for her. I should do the same. I can prove to her, to everyone that I'm worthy of her.

"Send them to hunt the scourge." Old Bob sat up straight, glancing between Derek and Brian. "You said before that you don't have the people to spare. So, use them. This way if they do perish"—he took a deep breath—"you won't be missing anyone vital to your camp."

Derek and Brian shared a look, their eyes locking a few moments too long. The look they shared was unnerving and almost intimate. Watching them felt like I was intruding on a private conversation.

Derek sat forward, running his fingers on the rough wood of the table. "How do we keep them from running? If we just let them loose with some orders, that doesn't mean they will follow through."

"I will go," I blurted out.

All eyes turned to me and Brian barked with laughter. "You would kill Jace yourself and run off with the girl, or try to at least. You don't fool any of us."

I looked down, avoiding everyone's eyes. I could feel my cheeks heating. Old Bob spoke, sparing me more embarrassment.

"Wait, he may be right. He can go and Tate and I will stay back, as collateral." Old Bob inched forward in his chair. "This way Tristan will be more inclined to keep them on track and bring them back... if they survive that is."

"Yes, and Eden won't risk losing me," Tate added.

"What?" My head snapped up. "I'm not letting you and Tate be insurance. That's crazy!"

"Why?" Derek smirked. "You planning something?"

"No. But..." I couldn't think of a good excuse that wouldn't be insulting.

"Fine. Tristan, you'll go with them to scout out where these creatures are. Brian"—he looked to his friend—"will go to keep *everyone* in line, making sure whatever information is found is delivered in full." He stood, heading for the flap of the tent.

"What about the scourge we captured?" Old Bob asked.

Derek looked at him. "We have it in custody. We'll see if we can question it." He studied Old Bob a moment before adding. "You may be present during the interrogation if you like."

"Thank you. I would."

"We will start in an hour. My tent." Without waiting for a response, both Derek and Brian left.

~

"So, you want to talk about it?" Tate asked quietly.

My stomach tightened. "Talk about what?" I gave Ash a good rub, avoiding his stare.

He chuckled. "Come on, Tristan. You don't think I haven't noticed how you look at her? Everyone has, for the past year."

"I'm sorry."

"What are you talking about?" Tate stood from his cot, facing me. "It's only natural, Tristan. I may be her brother, but I can still see she's a pretty girl. I would be nothing happier if she ended up with you." Resting his hand on my shoulder, he said, "You may have some competition though."

My brow furrowed at the reference to Jace. "He's not good for her," I growled.

Tate lowered his arm, sitting back onto his cot. "I can't just be against him when I don't know him. He didn't let anything happen to her when they were in the woods."

My jaw dropped. "Please tell me you are joking."

"Look. All I am saying is I can't hate him when I have no reason to. Listen, just go, protect her, be understanding, let it happen. You can't force it. She's stubborn, you know this. If you try and control her, she'll rebel, and it won't be in your favor."

Tate has always been kind and reasonable. *Always the voice of reason,* Ellie would say. I had a bad feeling he won't last long in this new world we were encountering.

"I get it. May the best man win, I guess."

∽

I walked through the lanes of tents monitoring the ways of the camp. Families each had a tent. If you were single, you were paired with others. Everyone worked, everyone got along, everyone followed the rules. It seemed too good to be true. The walk I took to calm my nerves did the opposite.

"Please. I just want to check her hand and check on him," a woman's voice came from a few tents ahead.

"I'm sorry, Sarah. It's too dangerous," a guard replied, blocking her way into the tent.

As I approached them, I noticed it was the tent they were holding Eden and Jace. "Excuse me, I can go in with her. I'll make sure nothing happens."

Sarah turned to look at me. She had a fresh pretty face. "You're one of her group, right?" I nodded, giving her a smile.

"I'm sorry, but that's not possible either. I can't just let you"—the guard nodded toward me—"go in when I don't know who you are." He adjusted his feet, proving he was not going to move.

I chuckled. "Trust me, I won't free them. Derek, Brian, and my father are planning their punishment right now. I'll be helping with it. Just let the lady in; she wants to do her job." I took a few steps toward the guard. I had about two inches and thirty pounds on him. He held a gun, but I was sure he rarely used it and never on an actual person. I could see what Derek meant by them not having the right people to capture the scourges.

The man looked uneasily between the woman and me. "Fine. Five minutes, no longer."

"Thank you," Sarah said, giving me a big grin of gratitude.

I nodded at her, holding my hand out for her to enter first. If I remember one thing Ellie taught me, it was to always be a gentleman.

Inside, Eden and Jace still had their hands tied, only they were tied around large nine-foot-tall tree stumps. They had managed to sit down, but the way their hands were tied made the position awkward. My shoulders tightened, and I pursed my lips at the sight of her so vulnerable. I dug my feet into the dirt to keep from running to her.

"Sarah." Eden was surprised, but when she saw me, her eyebrows shot up. "Tristan? What are you doing here?"

Jace quietly watched our interaction. I inspected him from side glances. He had a similar build to me, same height. He squinted up at me with a quick smile and nod, catching my eyes on him. I turned away without reciprocating his politeness. I could take him if I had to.

"Just helping Sarah."

"I wanted to check your hand," Sarah spoke quietly, dropping a shoulder bag down next to Eden. "And him." She nodded her head toward Jace.

"I want to thank you," Jace said to her from his post. "You made me as comfortable as I could have been." I wanted to gag at his politeness. No one was that polite.

Sarah smiled at him as she checked Eden's hand. "It's pretty well healed. I just wanted to make sure." She stood, walking over to Jace. "So, you did what we had discussed?" She spoke over her shoulder to Eden.

"Yes."

"And what was that?" I asked, looking between them. Sarah was in on her little plan?

"Nothing important," Eden replied. I opened my mouth to ask something else, but the look Eden gave me stopped me. Not now.

Sarah examined Jace, listened to his heart, felt his pulse, looked at his eyes. "Wow," she whispered.

"That pretty, huh?" Jace mused. I didn't keep from rolling my eyes.

"No. One is gold. Like the others."

I looked over Sarah's shoulder. When I looked back to Eden, she quickly lowered her eyes, almost ashamed. She had never been ashamed of them before. I stepped toward her and reached out to put a hand on her shoulder, but stopped midway, fisting it, then pulled it back to me. The last thing she probably wanted was my comfort. My need to make her safe and happy simmered within me. The thought of her here, tied up, Jace near, her new affection toward him, and now this new commonality between them was too much. I needed air or I would erupt. Without saying a word to her, I stormed from the tent.

Chapter 27

Eden

I tried to adjust my position, to relieve the pain in my shoulders and back. Groaning with frustration, I gave the stump a good kick. That didn't do anything but make my foot ache. I tugged my hands, trying to reach up and touch my necklace, but the rope wasn't long enough. Cursing, I kicked the stump again with my other foot. Now both feet ached.

"You OK over there, Spunky?" Jace smirked.

"Really? I saved your life and you're still calling me Spunky?"

He chuckled. "Just checking if you remembered how much you love it." He examined the area. "Any idea how to get out of here?"

"No. Brian and Derek are stubborn, and my family isn't strong enough to take them on."

"We are."

I snapped my head toward him, searching his face. His voice had been so quiet it was almost a whisper, but when we locked eyes, I knew he believed it.

"Now, now, don't get any crazy ideas." Old Bob popped his head into the tent.

I smiled at the familiar face. "Hi." I rolled my shoulders, releasing the tension.

Kneeling in front of me, he put a hand on my cheek and asked, "How you holding up?"

"Ah, you know. It's nothing fabulous, but it will do." I shifted, giving the illusion that I was more comfortable than I really was.

They both chuckled, but Old Bob's face turned serious in a blink.

"We need to talk."

"That's never good," Jace mumbled.

I widened my eyes at Old Bob. "If it's about what you just heard, we wouldn't be that stupid to try and take them on."

"No, no. It's not that, although I am glad to hear that."

"Then what?"

He took a deep breath. "The good thing is you guys won't be executed."

I gaped. "Executed? What the... that was really on the table?"

"Told you," Jace said.

I rolled my eyes at him, but I couldn't help chuckling.

Old Bob continued. "After some discussion, it was decided that you two will track and find the scourges. You'll find out where they live and any other information we can find."

"Seriously?" I could find them, but this was different. The scourges were relentless and who knows how many there were.

"How is this better than being executed?" Jace asked. "I mean, at least it would be quick rather than eaten alive. I prefer quick."

Old Bob held up his hands. "I know it's not ideal, but it was the only way. Tristan and Brian will go along as well."

"Tristan?" I asked. "Are you sure he is up for this? With, you know, us. Jace and me?"

"Yes." He paused, looking between us. "He has to make sure you stay on track and don't"—he paused—"run away together. Tate and I will stay here as insurance."

Jace laughed. "Run away... with her?"

I shot him a look, but he returned it with a wink. I rolled my eyes. "And Brian? Why is he going?"

"Well... to make sure Tristan is doing his job."

"So, they are sending pretty boy to make sure we do our job, and then scary man to make sure he does his. Typical," Jace said.

Brushing off Jace's comments, Old Bob continued, "Eden, it's also very important that you listen to Brian. You need to let him... help you."

"Help me?"

"Yes. To help you. With your... emotions, strength, and all the things you're going through." He kept his voice soft, trying to keep me calm. He turned to Jace. "It probably will be a good thing for you as well since you seem to have"—he searched for the correct word—"evolved."

Anger bubbled within me as I watched Old Bob. He was implying that I couldn't control myself. He has known me my whole life; how could he doubt me?

"Eden," Jace warned. "Look at me, Eden."

I held my gaze on Old Bob. My body tingled and my fingers twitched before fisting tightly. I set my jaw and narrowed my eyes. My rage was on the edge of pouring out.

"Eden!" Jace yelled, snapping my focus to him.

He panted, pulling at his ropes, but when he saw my attention was on him, he stopped. "Hey. OK, let's breathe. Take some deep breaths." He sucked in a long, slow breath of air before letting it out.

"What are you doing?" I asked him, amused.

He stopped, confused. "Ummm, helping calm you down?"

"Seriously?" Turning back to Old Bob, I said, "You both think I have an anger management issue?" I shook my head. "And next time you think you need to calm me down, let's think of a different way other than deep breaths. That's so... boring."

"Yeah, sure... but I could feel you. You were crazy angry. Like I haven't felt that much anger... ever."

"I'm angry, but I can handle it. Why don't *you* take a few deep breaths? You seem upset."

"Look, Eden," Old Bob continued before I could argue with him, "I understand you don't want help, but you're not the same as others. You never have been. We always kept it quiet because we didn't think it was important, but when I saw you the other day, when we arrived. I realized that you do need to learn how to harness it. Derek and Brian can help you. You just have to let them try."

"You're telling me that you have always thought I was... *different?*"

Old Bob closed his eyes. "I'm saying that you are special. You have always been special, and Ellie and I knew that. Your mother, she knew that and it's the reason she asked me to make sure nothing happened to you if anything ever happened to her."

He rarely, if ever, brought up my birth mother. I could feel his sincerity and see the truth behind his tired hazel eyes. He was doing this because he loved me. The least I could do was listen. "Yeah. Sure. I'll try."

"Good. Good," he said, squeezing my shoulders. "I'll see what I can do to get you both a bath. You leave tomorrow, so good to at least leave clean." He stood, smiling at us both.

Jace cleared his throat. "Any way you could see about us getting a little more comfortable as well? Not sure I can stay like this all night and walk normal tomorrow."

"Yeah. I'll see what I can do." Old Bob moved to the tent's entry. "Night."

Jace and I both nodded. "Night." I watched the flap fall and my stomach tightened. Old Bob was my family, my home. The thought of leaving him and Tate here was hard.

"What a nice guy," Jace said. "Hard to believe he kidnapped me not too long ago. And for the record, I think you're special too."

"Oh shush."

Jace's laughter filled the tent as I closed my eyes to rest.

Chapter 28

Jace

Being able to stretch out my neck and crack my back felt like heaven. We stepped out of the tent into the cool, bright morning. I pulled in a long breath of dewy air and smiled. Old Bob came through on his word and got both Eden and me a bath last night. Being the gentleman that I am, I let Eden go first, but that didn't mean I hurried up when it was my turn. My skin smelled like fresh roses from the soap. Any other time, I would have complained, but my clean, fresh smelling self never felt better.

Eden followed me out of the tent, doing her own stretches and groans of appreciation. Her apricot hair shone in the sunlight as it fell over her shoulders. She is the first girl I have met with that hair color, making it hard not to stare. Her eyes met mine, and I quickly looked away. I didn't want her to get the wrong idea. I had a few girlfriends growing up in the city, but it was hard work. I prefer keeping it light and fun. Eden didn't seem like the light and fun kind of girl, she was… a serious relationship kind of girl. I met one of those once, and she was scary. Not sure I wanted to try that again.

"Good morning. I hope your lodgings were sufficient." Derek strolled toward us with Brian and Sarah in tow. He smiled up at the morning sky and the breeze moved through his salt and pepper hair. The faint smell of wood smoke filled my nose and my stomach grumbled. The fish we had last night wasn't enough to satiate this growing boy.

I smiled. "I have been in better, but considering your situation"—I motioned to the woods and tents surrounding us—"it was fine."

He narrowed his eye. "You're a funny boy, aren't you?" I smirked in return.

Careful.

The voice rang through my head, making my heart pump. I kept my face stone, didn't want to look crazy, hearing voices in my head, but he gave me a knowing smile. Unsure of how that was possible, I made a note to ask Eden if she had that kind of… side effect.

"You two will be traveling with Brian and Tristan. They're going to make sure you do what you are tasked and you bring back *all* the information." Derek led us toward the entrance of the camp. Our display the day before had brought out the onlookers. We were the camp celebrities by the look of it. Scared, curious, and even some sympathetic eyes watched us.

I could sense Eden searching in the crowd. Probably for her brother, Old Bob, and the wolf. I hoped she wasn't looking for that guy, Tristan. He reminded me of a buddy I once had who had some security issues. Needless to say, we aren't friends anymore.

We arrived at the entrance. Tate and Tristan pushed through the crowd. Tate went straight to Eden, smiling, and gave her a big hug.

"What about Ash?" she asked.

"He'll stay with us." Derek turned to her. "It'll be safer for him."

"Safer? He's a wolf," she barked, glowering at Derek. My neck hairs tingled with the pull of dominance in the air... from them both.

He took a step toward her. "All right then. I don't want him to go. He'll be collateral, just like your brother and Old Bob. Better?"

Eden's rage was building, making it harder to breathe. Their eyes locked and she bared her teeth. Rolling my head in a circle, I fought the urge to bow down. Tate slowly moved to her and tugged slightly on her elbow. Reluctantly, she looked away and followed Tate to the entrance. I followed along behind them.

"You'll be fine. Just don't wander off and try to be a hero. Stay with the group," Tate told Eden. She nodded in understanding, but she didn't fool me. I could feel her defiance stirring under her surface. Defiance and sadness. She didn't want to leave them.

Old Bob pushed through the crowd, moving to Tristan. I stifled a low growl that built in my throat as Tristan stepped toward us. His blue eyes and blonde hair shone in the sunlight. He was handsome, and he loved Eden, but I know his type and it wasn't good for her.

"Here are your packs." Derek handed us backpacks. "They're filled with food, a blanket, a change of clothing, and water. This has to last you the whole trip, so portion it out carefully."

"And if we run out?" Eden asked.

"Then you'll be at the mercy of the woods."

Tristan and Brian moved next to us, packs loaded on their backs. I ignored Tristan's eyes on me, keeping my focus ahead to the trees outside the camp. I didn't need to start the trip off with a confrontation.

I got to the open gates when the sound of screeching had me whipping around and in a fighting position. I knew that sound, the scourge. It sent every nerve in my body on edge. My tense body relaxed when I saw three men dragging one of the scourges, hands tied behind its back and another rope around its neck. The smell of sweat filled the air, and I moved my hand to my nose. The crowd turned silent, watching the scourge with disgust and fear. Many clutched each other, jolting away at its every move.

"This is our guide," Brian stated, taking one of the ropes from the men. He glanced between Tristan and me, motioning to the remaining two ropes. "Care to join me?"

I cleared my throat, taking a rope from one of the men. "Do we expect this to pull us like a dog to its home?"

"When we get further into the woods, we'll let it loose and track it," Brian replied, rolling his eyes at my comment.

"And if it attacks us?"

"Then we kill it." Tristan gave me an intense gaze. Ugh, he was trying to be a hotshot. I really would hate to hurt him.

"There isn't going to be an issue with you two?" Derek came between us, sensing our silent power play.

I shook my head, still keeping my eyes locked with Tristan. "No. Not at all."

"Good, then you should be on your way."

I held the rope tightly as we left. Brian, Tristan, and I stayed near each other to keep the scourge in control, but as far as the ropes would go. My ears rang with the constant high-pitched screeching that echoed between the trees. When it would lunge toward one of us, the other two would pull back quickly. I slipped on the dewy wet ground too many times when I had to brace myself for a pull. My pants were already wet and covered with leaves. I quickly glanced back at Eden sadly walking behind us. Her emotions flowed thick through the air, anger and worry. Ash's howl echoed after us. I felt bad for her, but I was clean this morning. Clean and feeling great, now I was sweating with wet, mud-caked pants. Not to mention my aching shoulders from being tied up were now being pushed to the brink as I tugged at the scourge. She had every right to be sad, but that didn't mean I couldn't be annoyed with her.

After twenty minutes of dragging and dodging the scourge, I asked, "Why didn't we... put this thing in... a cage and drag it?" My shoulders ached and my arms shook from fatigue. Every time I had to lunge back to yank the scourge from attacking Brian or Tristan, my knees gave out. I feared when we stopped, if I had to run, my legs would collapse under me like paper, and I wouldn't be able to get up.

Brian stopped. "We don't have a cage," he panted. "I think we have gone far enough. We might as well set it loose." He let out a grunt as the scourge lashed out toward Tristan. "Eden, ready your bow. If it attacks, kill it. Understood?"

"Understood," we all muttered in unison. I begged for her to hurry. I don't think my arms can take much more.

Eden pulled out her bow, nocked in an arrow, and aimed at the scourge. She gave Brian a nod.

"Let's go."

We all dropped the ropes, and my arms fell in relief. As quickly as I could, I put a hand on my knife, preparing for anything, but with my feeble arms, I didn't think my fight would be much help.

The scourge stood, shocked almost that we released it. It looked between us, pondering if attacking was a good idea or not. It studied Eden too long, so I shuffled a step toward her, ignoring the burn through my legs. I would protect her if needed. After a few quick breaths, it turned and dashed into the woods, ropes flapping behind it. I let out a loud breath and fell to the ground. My hair and shirt dampened on the wet leaves and dirt. As I stared up through the twinkling green leaves of the trees, my entire body throbbed from the exhaustion I had put it through. I cursed myself for not staying in better shape.

"All right, now we track." Brian started forward after the scourge. "Be on alert. It could double back to us or there could be others."

I slowly turned over and groaned my way to a stand. The first few steps were the worst, but once my body warmed up, the pain numbed and I was able to get a good steady pace.

We followed Brian. Tristan moved up right next to Eden. I didn't want to start a fight over a girl I barely knew, so I sped up, passing them and taking a spot right behind Brian. He could be in charge of protecting her; I wanted to keep myself alive. I didn't need any distractions. Pushing down my pain and exhaustion, I continued on behind Brian through the thick woods.

Chapter 29

Eden

We trudged through the woods, following Brian's lead. Tristan stayed close to me, very attentive.

Ash had finally stopped howling, or we were so far that I couldn't hear him any longer. My heart hurt from the sound, but I know Tate would watch over him.

My foot hit a log. I threw my hands out as I fell forward, anticipating the wet, leafy ground only to be caught around the waist by Tristan.

"You OK?" he asked.

Shrugging out of his hold, I said, "Yeah."

The ground was still slippery from the overnight dew and the canopy of leaves made it hard for the sun to dry it up. The leaf and twig litter on the ground made it difficult for traction. Brian was keeping a quick pace, and even though I have been doing well with my conditioning, the awkward day and night sleeping while tied up left cramps throughout my body. Tightness in my thighs made it hard for me to stay upright when I slipped.

Brian jogged down a foothill, and when I followed, the heel of my foot caught a tree stump. Managing to lean back enough so I didn't fall forward, I landed on my behind and slid down the wet ground, soaking my pants in dew and mud. Tristan ran after me, grabbing my arm to yank me up before I could try to raise myself. Snapping my arm back, I brushed wet leaves off my pants.

He stepped back, hurt. "I was just trying to help."

I continued walking. "Yeah, well don't. If I fall, I'll get back up. I don't need you to rescue me."

"Eden."

"What?" I faced him.

"I'm just looking out for you."

"I don't need my brother to hover. All right? Remember, I can handle myself."

His eye widened and he took a small step back. "Brother?"

"Yeah, we may not be by blood, but you are my brother. I love you, Tristan, but I'm not five anymore. I can handle myself." I softened my voice. The hurt that flashed through his eyes gave me a twinge of guilt, but I knew him. If I wasn't direct, he wouldn't get it. I gave his arm a soft squeeze and continued on.

After some more time of sliding up and down small mounds and tree trunks, Brian shot up a hand to stop us.

Stop!

Jace looked pale with shock; he had gotten the same message. I stifled a giggle, remembering how I felt when getting used to the voices in my head. The only person who looked confused was Tristan.

"Why did you st—"

"Shhhh," I whispered. "Something is here."

Tristan glanced around. "I don't see anything."

Annoyed, I turned to him to tell him to be quiet once again when I saw it, a scourge flying through the air toward his back. I was too slow to push him out of the way before it landed on his shoulders. Tristan screamed out, in fear or pain I don't know, but they toppled to the ground. Grabbing my bow, I nocked in an arrow but stilled to watch the two roll in tangled limbs. Old Bob had taught Tristan to fight, and he was strong, so he could handle himself. I lowered my bow an inch but kept the arrow nocked in, just in case. Ropes from its limbs swung through the air, hitting the ground in loud thunks. It was the same scourge we had captured.

"Eden!" Jace called as he and Brian sprinted toward us. The light shone off the sharp knives in their hands.

I looked back at Tristan and the scourge rolling on the ground. The scourge, smarter than expected, tried to use the ropes to its advantage, twisting it around Tristan's body, trying to inhibit his movements. Tristan pushed, kicked, and rolled, trying to get out of its hold. My breath got a bit shallow, and I swallowed. Unsure of my decision, I lifted my bow again and aimed, but Jace moved into my view, his knife out and ready. When Tristan saw him, he rolled onto his back, placing the creature above him. Jace quickly stuck his knife into the side of the scourge's throat. Thick, black blood poured out over Tristan, and the scourge released him to grab at his throat. As he did so, Jace pulled him off Tristan, tossing him to the side. Tristan, covered in blood, sat up panting and turned to watch the scourge gap its mouth like a fish out of water. Tristan blanched and turned away, horror flashed in his eyes.

It was unnerving how human it seemed watching us, almost pleading for help. Tristan stood, moving next to us, as we all silently watched the life leave its familiar eyes.

Pulling the arrow from my bow with shaking hands, I turned and inspected Tristan. He held his side, but no blood other than a few scratches and bruises. Most of the blood that caked his body was from the scourge. I took a small step toward him, but he stepped away.

"Well, now what?" Tristan asked. "Our guide is dead."

Brian took a step toward the dead creature. "We do our best to find them on our own." Kneeling down, he slowly pulled the knife out of its neck. Thick blood gushed onto the ground, mixing with the wet mud to a dark burgundy. He stood, handing the knife back to Jace. "Open your senses. See if we can find anything left by them. Smells, prints, or even better, one of them." He turned to Tristan. "You OK?"

Tristan rubbed his neck and shoulder. "Yeah. I'll be fine." He looked to Jace. "Thank you." I could see the pride in his face falter. He hated the fact that Jace saved him; Jace only nodded in acceptance. I let out a small breath, relieved he didn't say one of his smart remarks.

Guilt built in my belly. I had just watched. I didn't think he would struggle as much as he did. He was always strong when fighting with Old Bob, so it was a shock when he was almost bested by a scourge. My insides dropped to a pool on the ground at the betrayal on his face when he glanced at me, then he turned around and walked into the woods.

Turning away, I followed Brian, swallowing down the lump in my throat, focusing on the hazy ground in front of me.

We walked until the rumbling of thunder rang in the distance, and the smell of a storm was in the wind. Brian stopped.

"We should stop and create a shelter if we can't find one."

Searching our surroundings, I noticed we were near the small cave where Jace and I had stayed. Before I could speak, Tristan spoke up from behind. "I know of a cave not too far off."

Jace and I turned to him.

"You do?" I asked.

Tristan kept his eyes on Brian. "Yeah. We found it when we were out searching for you. I think you were there too, were you not?"

I nodded.

"Yeah. We stayed in the same cave. This way," Jace said.

We arrived just as the first few sprinkles of rain started and the thunder rumbled louder. I let out a sigh of relief as we entered the cave. My clothes were damp and dirty from my clumsiness all morning. I wanted nothing more than to change into the clean pair Derek had put in my pack, but with the pouring rain, I decided against it. I would rather keep that pair clean for later.

"I am going to go rinse off," Tristan said walking out into the rain. He turned the corner for privacy. The thought of letting fresh rainwater wash over me was tempting, but I doubted he wanted my presence. My heart ached at the hurt in his face. He couldn't even look at me.

I walked as far into the cave as I could without being totally consumed by darkness and sat down, feeling the cool stone wall on my back. When my hand dropped, instead of being met by Ash's soft fur, it hit the hard stone. I yearned for my friend's warmth and security. I took the same hand and raised it to Ellie's necklace. Tears welled in my eyes at the feeling of her loss and now that I may be losing my friend, my brother.

"You all right?" Jace sat down next to me.

"Yeah."

As he studied me, I was relieved the darkness hid my lie.

"You just watched him. You didn't even try to help." He paused. "You sure you're OK?"

My throat constricted. "Yeah." I turned my face toward the deep darkness of the cave, hiding the tears threatening to escape.

Jace leaned a little closer, lowering his voice. "Eden, I know something is wrong. Maybe if you just tell me, we can figure it out together. It's not good to hold things inside like this."

Irritation at his pity built up inside me. I turned to him and snapped, "Why do you care?"

"What?"

Thankfully, I couldn't see his hurt face in the darkness, but his voice held unmistakable pain. "Why do you care?" I repeated.

The discomfort in his voice hardened. "I just want to make sure you are up to this. I mean, our lives... my life depends on if you are willing to step up and defend and fight for the people of your group. Today, it sure didn't look like that."

This time I couldn't keep the tears from slipping. They wet my cheeks, and I was thankful for the blanket of darkness. He was right, but... "You're just like them."

"What?"

I turned to him. "You're just like them. You don't think I can handle any of this."

"I never said that..."

"You didn't have to. It's implied in your words, the way you look at me."

The outline of his eyes widened. "Well, don't you think you know everything about everyone? I'm not sure where all of this is coming from. I didn't say anything like that, nor did I think that. I was just concerned about you and wanted to make sure everything was OK. You don't seem like yourself, but it seems that you're able to handle it on your own." He stood and walked away, his feet scuffing the rocky ground.

I groaned, pulling out the blanket from my pack to make a little bed. Tristan came back in, dripping wet, and left me alone, finding a spot near the opening of the cave to rest. I lay down and the sound of rain on the trees and the soft rumbling of thunder lulled me to sleep.

Chapter 30

Eden

The next morning, I woke before anyone else and crept outside for some fresh air. The woods smelled fresh and damp from the night of rain, and the cool breeze made the leaves sing, joining the song of the birds. I walked to the ravine that led down the stream. The crisp, cool water looked so inviting I almost slipped down the hill in anticipation. Crouching down, I washed my face and neck, letting out a sigh of pleasure as the mud and grime washed away. I fought the urge to slip into the stream and let the water roll over me, washing away the events from the day before. My stomach knotted at the memory of Tristan's betrayed look. I had never seen him look so hurt, but I didn't know what I could do or say to make it better.

Just then, a familiar feeling of contentment and happiness hit me. I jumped up to search the area, as my heart slowly increased to a fast pulse that warmed my skin. Ash. I smiled as anticipation built of seeing my best friend. I stepped through the shallow ice water downstream, careful not to slip on the stones. I neared him; the feeling grew along with my smile. I increased to a jog and let out a giggle, but when I rounded the bend in the stream, I stopped, my smile vanishing. At the top of the ravine staring down at me were two adult wolves and three pups. Frozen, we stared at each other, unsure of what the other would do. Their eyes, gold like Ash, didn't show anger or fear, but uncertainty.

I smiled. "It's all right. I won't hurt you." I spoke so quietly I hardly heard myself over the trickling water of the stream.

They tilted their heads in confusion, unsure if they understood me correctly or not.

A stick breaking echoed behind me, and I spun around. Tristan stood with an ashen face, his eyes glued on the wolves.

"Eden."

"It's OK, Tristan. Just go back to the cave."

"What? I'm not leaving you here with a pack of wolves to fend for yourself." He took another step toward me, pulling a growl from both adult wolves. Their eyes moved between Tristan and me unsure if he was a threat or not. Their pups cowered between their legs. The annoyance of Tristan's protectiveness resurfaced, and I glared back at him.

"Tristan! Listen to me, *please*! They will not hurt me, but they may hurt you, so for your safety, please *leave*."

Tristan shook his head, and I ground my teeth. Idiot.

"Eden, have some sense. They are not Ash. They are not wolves you raised from a pup. They're wild, and if you aren't careful, they will hurt *you*."

A growl started in my throat. "If you don't back down, I will make you."

Not paying me any attention, he kept his eyes on the wolves and slowly reached for his dagger. My hair almost whipped back when anxiety hit me along with the sound of their growls. I quickly looked at them, their hackles raised and muzzles twitching to show the tips of their fangs. The pups stepped back further so they were fully behind their parents.

"Tristan, don't do that. They will attack you."

Again, he ignored me, continuing for his dagger. When his hand brushed it, the male wolf jerked, letting out a snarl. Without a second thought, I bolted up the hill tackling Tristan. We both fell, rolling in the twig-and-needle-covered ground. Our grunts echoed through the morning breeze.

"What the blazes, Eden!" he barked, pushing me off him.

"I told you to back off!" I looked back and saw the wolves watching us, their hostility slightly calmer. I let out a breath of relief as the tension blew away.

"What in the world..." Brian's voice faded as he took in the situation. His eyes darted from the wolves to Tristan and me. "What's going on?"

"Eden's about to get herself killed that's what!" Tristan stood, brushing himself off.

"I told you already, they mean no harm. I was in the stream when they showed up. They have done nothing but watch me." I stepped in the path of the wolves just in case someone got the grand idea to try and attack again.

"They are not Ash, Eden!" Tristan yelled.

"I know! I heard you the first time."

"They were growling!" Tristan pointed at the wolves who were still monitoring the situation.

"Only because you were going for your knife!"

Brian sucked in a deep breath, putting up his hands. "All right, all right, let's relax." He continued to snap short glances toward the wolves but did well not to make any threatening movements toward them or me.

"Relax? No. This ends now," Tristan snapped. He grabbed my arm and pulled me toward the cave. "We are packing up and moving on. No more destructive actions. I told Tate and Old Bob nothing would happen to you." His grip was tight and demanding.

I tugged my arm back, but his fingers bruised into my upper arm. "Let go of me! I can handle myself!" His grip held tight.

I felt them coming; the wolves. They charged through the stream and were halfway up the hill by the time Tristan's grip loosened enough for me to turn around. Standing between the wolves and the others, I put up my hands and yelled.

"STOP!" My voice sounded like a predatorial snarl.

Immediately, the two wolves skidded to a halt. The sweet sounds of the morning woods were drowned out by the sound of my panting breath. They listened to me. I don't know how I did it, but they listened. I watched them with wide eyes, listening to their uncertain whimpers. They paced back and forth, watching and waiting for my command. I fisted my hands to keep them from shaking. My body trembled with a combination of excitement and power.

"What in tarnation?" Brian mumbled.

"What just happened?" Jace asked.

"You got me," Brian replied.

I smiled, taking a step toward the wolves. "I think I just made some friends." My voice was much stronger than I felt.

"Friends? Those *wolves* just tried to kill me!" Tristan yelled.

Narrowing my eyes at him, I said, "You, maybe"—I turned back to my new furry friends—"but not me. If you would keep your hands to yourself, then they wouldn't have attacked you." I felt a wave of embarrassment flow through the air, and without a word, he stormed back to the cave.

Brian stepped forward, his eyes still on the wolves behind me. "Eden, I don't..."

"Stop. I don't want to hear it." Smiling, I glanced back to the wolves who were turning to leave. "I had everything under control, so I don't need your opinions." Brushing past them, I headed back to the cave. For the first time in a while, I felt proud of myself.

Chapter 31

Jace

Brian took the lead tracking the scourges as best he could. As we moved through the woods, a squirrel scurried up a tree, stopped, and watched us. I locked gazes with its beady black eyes and started to reach out toward it. Its nose twitched as it tasted my scent in the air, but I halted halfway and pulled my hand back. What was I thinking? Shaking my head, I continued forward. I was becoming more comfortable with the woods and the inhabitants, but I wasn't as impulsive as Eden. What happened earlier was... downright crazy.

Shaking off my thoughts, I hollered to Brian, "So how you tracking the scourges right now anyway?"

Eden looked back at me. "It would have to be by smell since your hollering will either scare them off or invite them for a tussle."

"Ha. Ha. I don't notice much of a smell that could be tracked."

"That's because you're untrained," Brian replied.

"Untrained? What exactly am I to be training for?"

Brian laughed. "For yourself. You have new... talents that need to be learned."

I chuckled, sure, talents, that's a nice description of what was happening to me. I watched Eden's hair swish with her movements and took in a deep breath. Lavender and cedar floated from her trail; it was... relaxing. I pulled in another long stream of her scent, and she snapped her head back to me.

"You can keep your thoughts to yourself, please," she said quietly so the others didn't hear. "I already know what I smell like. I don't need your comments about it." She quickly stomped after the others.

Had I said that out loud? No, no I hadn't. "Hold up!" I jogged after her, stepping in her path. "Can you hear my thoughts?" Memories of Derek and Brian's voices in my mind came to me. Was that what I sounded like to her?

Watching me a moment, she closed her eyes. "Get out of my way, Jace."

"Not until you answer me. Can you hear my thoughts?"

She avoided my eyes, chewing on her cheek. I laughed. "Holy Hazelnuts! I'm going to have fun with this new... *talent*."

She scoffed, pushing past me, but her touch wasn't as rough as I expected. Lavender filled my nose and a tingle went up my spine.

No. I can't think that way.

"What new talent?" Tristan asked. He had paused to let Eden catch up.

Ignoring him, we walked past him, catching up with Brian. I pushed out my next thought.

Big idiotic birdbrain.

"Jace!" Eden snapped, causing me to let out a huge fit of laughter and do a little jig.

Brian stopped. "All right, you two. That's all fun, but you need to start to take this seriously. It can be used to your advantage."

Tristan jogged to catch up. "I'm confused. What are you talking about?"

"Don't worry about it, pretty boy," I said.

"Excuse me?" His face tightened in anger and he took a step toward me. I taunted him by wiggling my eyebrows.

"That's enough!" Brian bellowed. "There won't be any more of this bickering. We're here to do an important job. I don't need fighting between you all. I need you serious and alert." He turned to Tristan. "There are some things you won't understand because they don't pertain to you. It is just something you will need to deal with and not ask questions." He didn't let Tristan respond before he turned back to Eden and me. "You two. You will listen and learn. You *will* take it seriously." His eyes landed on me, then he turned to Eden. "And *you* will cool it. You have been very on edge lately, and you need to relax."

"Understood." Eden stared at her feet.

"Good," Brian said before he continued on. "I'm using all my senses to track the creatures. It takes a lot of concentration and it's exhausting. We'll rest in a bit, then I'll start your training."

We all followed to our resting place in silence. I had to pinch my fingers to keep from teasing Eden, but something about how Brian spoke made me realize he wasn't joking. I didn't think it was smart to test his authority, so I resumed my quiet walk, trailing behind everyone.

∽

"I won't do it. I'm sorry. I can't fight a girl by choice. Call me a gentleman, I guess, but I won't fight Eden."

"You're going to have to get over it. She's more capable than you think," Brian responded.

Looking over at Eden, I saw her standing with her arms crossed. A grateful look on her face at Brian's vote of confidence.

"All right then." Brian walked toward us. "If you won't fight her, then fight me."

I laughed. "Like that's a fair fight. You have much more training than I do, and you are..." I motioned to his muscular body. "Well, look at you!"

He smirked. "How about if I'm blindfolded? Would that be a fair fight?"

I thought about it a moment, tossing my head side to side. "I guess, yeah. That may be fair."

"Great. Let's begin." Brian pulled some fabric from his pocket and tightened it around his eyes.

Eden and Tristan moved out of our space, standing on opposite sides of us. I watched Brian position himself in the middle of a small clearing between a group of trees. I quietly stalked around him, careful not to step on any twigs, but the dry leaves made it hard not to make any noise. If I was able to surprise him from behind, I may have a chance. Stopping at his back, I sucked in a breath and charged. He swiftly twisted and put his arm out.

Smack!

I fell back onto the ground in surprise, rubbing my nose. "Crud..."

"No sitting around! Again!" Brian yelled.

Standing up, I wiped the blood that dripped from my nose. "All right then." I circled him again. This time I would try from the front since he expected me from behind. I rounded him the third time, then moved in quickly toward his front, swinging my arm out at his head. Brian crouched, moved his leg out, and swiped it under my feet. Flying up, I landed hard on my back. I wheezed, lying on the cold ground, my lungs begging for air. It felt like forever before my lungs filled again. I coughed. "This is crap! You can see through the blindfold."

"Really? You not man enough to lose with dignity?" Brian raised his blindfold on his forehead and crossed his arms. "I didn't cheat. I was using all my senses. You need to start harnessing yours, so you can fight me..." He smirked. "Well, have a better chance at it at least."

I laughed. "Right... Right. Harness my senses."

Eden stepped forward. "How do you plan to teach him? He can't even take you on blindfolded. It took me days before I started to understand."

Tristan stepped forward. "Yeah and even blindfolded she could dance around you."

Tristan's jab stung a little, but part of me knew that she probably could. I had a feeling that she was much more talented than we had seen. "Yeah, so"—I turned to Brian—"how do you plan to teach me?"

Brian pulled two more pieces of cloth from his pocket, dangling them in front of him with a smirk. "With these."

"Sorry?" I looked at him. "I'm not being blindfolded."

"Yes, you are. You and Eden both will be. Right now, I need you both to focus. Listen and feel your surroundings. It won't only help you in fighting, but also to really understand your capabilities and use them to your advantage. We will continue our trek, but both of you will wear these. It will force you to focus on your other senses."

"How do you expect us to follow you? We will slow everyone down. This isn't the time for all this," Eden said.

"Well, then, I expect you to really focus, so you don't slow us down."

My eyes met Eden's, and after a moment of defiance, she shrugged. "Fine."

"If she's in, I'm in."

Brian smiled. "Good. Get your eyes covered, and let's get going." He tossed the blindfolds at us.

Chapter 32

Eden

I stubbed my toe for the millionth time and cursed as I shook out my foot. "When is this supposed to start working? My body is getting sore from banging into everything." It was one thing fighting in one area blindfolded, but having to walk through the woods was much more difficult. Brian had to call Tristan forward because he kept trying to help me. Secretly, I wish he was guiding me. My toes do as well.

Jace chuckled behind me, and when I started to turn toward him, a firm grip grabbed my arm. "You have to try, Eden," Brian said.

"I am trying!" I yelled, yanking my arm away.

"No, you're not. You're so focused on not having your sight that it's taking all your energy. You need to use that energy and focus on your other senses. Use your hearing and scent. Focus on those, and you'll realize that you don't need your eyes." Brian's feet shuffled away.

"Really? That's your pep talk?" Frustration brewed within me, and I rolled my shoulders to shake it off. Standing still, I tried to listen to the sounds around me. The leaves sounded like chimes in the wind, and the songs of birds calling each other rang from all directions. My body released its tension at the calmness of the nature around me, and I let my head fall back. I smiled at the sun's warmth on my face.

Jace cleared his throat behind me. "Anytime you want to start walking would be good. We don't want to be left behind." The tension in my shoulders returned, and I let out an exaggerated sigh, starting after Brian.

I have heard you stumbling yourself, so shut up.

As you wish. I could feel humor flow from him as his voice radiated into my mind.

I focused hard on the sounds my feet made as I walked, the birds in the trees, and the breeze on the leaves all around us. After some time, I began noticing the sounds of the others' feet. Jace behind me and the other two up front. One set much louder than the others, not caring how many leaves and sticks he stomped on. I assumed that was Tristan since he would be the one that didn't realize how loud he was. If I could tell he was coming from this distance, it was no wonder he never killed anything when hunting.

"Let's stop here to rest," Brian said. "You two can take off the blindfolds."

I pulled off the cloth, squinting my eyes at the bright sun. Sitting down, I leaned on a large tree and let my throbbing legs stretch out in front of me.

"How are you doing?" Tristan sat down next to me.

Giving him a small smile, I said, "I'm OK. But I have learned one thing."

"Yeah? What's that?"

"You're the loudest walker I have ever heard."

Everyone chuckled... except Tristan.

"Yeah? How do you know it was me?"

"I assumed it was since we all are more sensitive to how loud we are. Jeepers, it was a joke." I tried to lighten the mood.

Jace tossed a twig toward Tristan. "Lighten up, dude. She didn't mean to make you feel bad."

Tristan's face softened a little. "Yeah, yeah. I know." He gave a forced chuckle. "So, I'm really that loud? Probably why I never get anything when I hunt."

I laughed. "That's exactly what I was thinking!" We all sat in awkward silence for a moment before Tristan stood.

"Well, I need to go... well, you know, I need to go." He walked off for privacy.

I kicked at some small rocks and twigs, avoiding conversation, when Brian came over, crouching down in front of Jace and me. "So, you seem to have noticed a change in your hearing, Eden?"

I nodded, picking at a twig.

"Good. It takes practice, but it will come. How about you, Jace?"

Jace sat forward. "I don't know. Maybe? I guess I had a hard time focusing on anything except not seeing."

Brian was agreeing with Jace when something near caught my attention. It wasn't a sound or a smell, but a feeling. Something wasn't right.

I jumped to my feet.

"Eden! Blazes!" Jace said, obviously startled at my quick movement.

"Something's wrong," I replied, staring after Tristan.

"What do you mean? What's wrong?" Brian asked, slowly standing. His eyes moved in the direction I stared at.

Staying focused on the woods in front of me, I slowly worked my way toward Tristan. "I don't know, but something isn't right."

A scourge. I could sense its urgency and agitation. Similar to what I felt the first time in the woods when I met them with the deer corpse. I searched the area for it, hearing its breathing, short and ragged. Loud thumping footsteps rustled through the leaves, sticks, and rocks. Tristan. He might as well yell out that he was there.

I crept in the direction Tristan was, but Brian grabbed my elbow.

I feel it too. Careful, go slowly.

Nodding, I moved again; Jace and Brian flanked me. We flicked our eyes around the woods, but none of us spotted the scourge. Tristan moved through the woods back toward us, oblivious to the danger that he was in.

I steadied my breath, trying to calm my racing heart, when movement caught my eye. The scourge. He was about the same height and build as Tristan but had dark, shaggy hair and ripped clothing. He spotted Tristan and froze.

No, no, no, no.

It crouched down in front of a bush, ready to attack Tristan when he walked by. I took off toward them.

"Tristan! Run!"

He looked at me with wide eyes but followed my gaze to the scourge coming at him. He managed to put his hands up just as the scourge tackled him. His grunt echoed through the trees. The scourge was on top of him, snarling and clawing. Tristan fended him off as best as he could, his arms straining to keep it away from his face, but the scourge's claws met their mark a few times.

When I reached him, I yanked the scourge off, tossing him behind me toward Jace and Brian. Tristan, startled and bleeding, could do nothing but lie there. Brian held the scourge while Jace knocked it unconscious with a large rock.

"You OK? Let me see." I pulled at his shirt to inspect his wounds, but he pushed my hands away, his cheeks blushed. He was embarrassed. Really? Last time I didn't do anything, he got mad, and now that I was trying to help, he got embarrassed.

"I'm fine." He sighed. "Eden, look at me." I looked at him, and he smiled at me. "I'm fine. It's just a scratch."

I nodded and reluctantly turned to the others who had laid the scourge on the ground. "What are we going to do with him?"

"We're going to use him. He'll lead us to the others," Brian said.

"What if he fights us? Doesn't want to lead us?" Tristan asked, holding his scratched side.

"He won't realize he's doing it. We'll leave him here and watch. When he wakes, we'll follow him."

I nodded. "I guess that could work." Glancing at Tristan's bloody hand, I said, "It's almost nightfall; he may not wake until morning."

Brian nodded. "Let's set up camp. I can help with your wounds, Tristan."

We found a small patch of heavy trees and bushes for cover, setting up our blankets where we could still see the creature, but be out of immediate sight.

"I'll take first watch," Jace said.

"Good. Eden, get some rest. Someone will wake you when it's your watch," Brian said, digging in his bag for supplies. Tristan rested with his back against a tree waiting for Brian's help.

Not complaining, I lay on my blanket under a large tree, trying to avoid as many twigs and rocks as possible, and quickly fell asleep.

Chapter 33

Jace

I yawned, rubbing my eyes. It was almost time for me to wake Brian. Growing up, I had read adventure books in which people say they will take watch, and it always sounded exciting, but this was definitely not. The fight to stay awake was a battle I never liked to lose.

Light footsteps had me turning back to where the others slept. Eden. Her apricot hair glowed in the moonlight, giving it a golden shade. She stretched and sat on the small stump next to me.

"It's not your turn. Brian's next. Why don't you sleep?" I eyed her as she watched the dark woods calmly.

"Can't."

Turning back to the woods, I looked out again to see nothing but the dark shapes of trees.

"What's the city like?" Eden asked.

"Umm..." Not sure what to tell her since I was never the most willing of citizens. "Strict."

"Strict?"

"Yeah." I sighed. "Zane, the president. He's an ass."

"You know him?" She looked over at me.

I nodded. "Unfortunately."

"Wow. Does everyone know him?"

I laughed at her naiveté. "No. If you're smart, then you try *not* to know him. He is a slimy man."

"Then, how do you?"

I pulled in a breath of cool, damp night air. How did this conversation turn to be about me? Wringing my hands, I looked back to make sure it was just us and saw Brian and Tristan still asleep on their blankets. I looked back at her. "My father."

She blinked. "Your father." I nodded slowly, watching her eyebrows rise. "And your father is..."

"Nobody." I looked forward again, clenching my jaw, but I felt the heaviness of her gaze on my face. Crap. I needed to learn to keep my mouth shut.

"Obviously, he's not a nobody if he knows the president enough to where you met him."

"Look, Eden"—I pinched the bridge of my nose—"my family life, it sucked. I really don't want to talk about it."

"All right." She looked forward again. "But just tell me who your father is?"

"Aghh," I hissed, then glanced back nervous I had woken the others. They both continued to sleep. "David. His name is David and he's"—she watches me expectedly—"he's the head of research in the city."

"Head of research?" Her whisper was so loud I swear the scourge stirred from where it lay.

"Shhhh! Keep it down. I don't like to advertise my lineage if I don't have to."

"Jace, you understand what this means, right?"

I opened my mouth to speak but closed it when I realized I had no idea what was going through her head. "Ah, no?"

She scooted her body to face me, leaned forward, and put her hand gently on my forearm. "It means we can go to the city together and tell them how to cure this whole thing, and all will be well with the world."

"You're joking, right?"

She shook her head.

"Eden." I rested my hand on top of hers, ignoring the warm sparks that moved through my fingers. "Don't take this the wrong way, but that is the most outrageous thing I have heard anyone say."

"Why? I mean, no one leaves the city because of the virus, and we aren't allowed in because of it, so why not tell them we have a solution?"

I let go of her hand and rubbed my face. Her heart was in the right place, but she didn't understand. Zane didn't work that way. "Because you don't know them. They are ruthless. They don't care who they hurt to get what they want."

"But what they want is a cure. We have that. We can fix it all." Her face was so beautiful and full of hope. I fisted my hand to keep from touching her cheek.

"I'm sorry, Eden. It just doesn't work that way."

"But Jace—"

"No, Eden." I stood. "Just drop it, all right? It's not an option." I closed my eyes at seeing her face drop in the moonlight. "I'm waking Brian. Get some rest, will you?" I walked away with a twinge of fear that she may not let this go so easily.

∽

Brian woke us shortly after I finally slept. The scourge had woken and stumbled away. Brian rushed us to get our things packed and get on the move. Next time I wouldn't volunteer to do watch first.

Stumbling through the dark woods, I grumbled at Brian's constant calls to *harness our senses*. I was too tired to harness anything. My stomach was still knotted from my talk with Eden. Telling her about my past plucked at the memories of the life I left behind and how much has changed since the night my friends and I were banished. Eden doesn't understand. Oh gosh. I can't imagine Eden being there. She is too innocent and will get herself killed.

My nose filled with the smell of sweaty body odor pulling me from my thoughts. Brian held out a hand, motioning us to stop.

They are here.

I crouched between Tristan and Brian, peering through the bushes. The knot in my stomach tightened at the sight of all the scourges. So many. Where did they all come from? Glancing at Eden, I saw her move next to Tristan. Maybe her idea of trying to work with the city wasn't such a bad idea.

Chapter 34

Eden

We sat low behind a group of bushes hidden within three tall Norway trees and watched the small group of creatures go about their day. They were dirty with greyish skin and one gold eye. They moved in a hunched-like posture with jerky movements as they caught the scents and sounds of other animals.

"This is crazy," I whispered. "There has to be a hundred of them. What do we do with a hundred scourges?"

"Can we kill them?" Tristan asked and all eyes slowly turned to him, brows furrowed. "What? It's a serious question. They're dangerous."

"Exactly. We can't just go in there and kill a hundred scourges; there are only four of us. Well three really since you're useless," Jace responded.

Tristan straightened himself, moving to take on Jace's jab.

"All right, relax you two," Brian said. "Jace is right. It would be suicide if we tried something like that. Our best bet is to return to camp and inform the others, then decide what to do."

"Just leave them all here?" Tristan asked.

"They aren't going anywhere. Look at them, they have a whole setup here. Little shelters, food, the works," Jace responded.

We continued to watch in silence for a few more moments, seeing how human, yet not, they were. They didn't talk much to each other but sat in companionable silence. They had small huts built from branches and leaves, but many just slept on piles of leaves under the bare sky. I soaked in as much information as I could until Brian finally spoke.

"OK, we should go." Leaving the putrid camp behind, we all followed him to our two-day walk back to the camp.

˜

We all walked in silence. Seeing the number of scourges made us more aware of the danger we were in wandering the woods. The conversation with Jace and watching the scourge made my body twitch. If only he would understand how much good we could do. I don't understand how anyone could turn someone away if they claim to have the cure.

I felt his eyes on me, and when I met them, he gave me a quick worried shake of his head. He knew what I was thinking.

No.

It has to work. They have to believe us.

It's not about believing, Eden. It's about not trusting them. You can't.

Frustrated, I increased my speed to stay near Brian. I could smell another storm in the air, and by looking at the dark billowing clouds and the wind that picked up, it was close. Brian raised his nose to the air, noticing it as well.

"We aren't going to make it to the cave," he said.

"Good thing I never changed my clothes," Jace said.

Tristan grunted at Jace and said, "Where we going to stay?"

A loud boom of thunder clapped right overhead, and we all ducked just as the rain started pattering down, slowly building up quickly into a deafening sheet. We were drenched in seconds.

"Find a group of trees! We can huddle there!" Brian yelled over the sound of the rain.

Following him, we all moved our packs to cover our heads, but it really did nothing to protect us from the rain. There was too much. I slipped and slid through the mud, grabbing trunks so I didn't fall. Brian stopped at a large group of northern trees that were close together. We all huddled close waiting for the rain to stop. My teeth chattered in the wet cold wind that blew memories of stormy nights at the cabin, snuggled under a blanket with Ellie by a hot crackling fire. My tears blended with raindrops, and I closed my eyes to imagine I was home.

Chapter 35

Tristan

"Where is she?" Brian yelled, kicking me awake.

I sat up from the cold, wet ground. My clothes were soaked and I had slept in a ball, trying to keep my warmth. The rain hadn't died down until the middle of the night.

"What?" Jace asked.

"Where is Eden?" Brian asked again.

Turning my stiff neck, I searched the area, not seeing any sign of her. "I don't know. Maybe she's doing a girl thing?" I stood, leaning back to crack my back. My stiff, wet pants scratched my skin. I should probably change them if I didn't want a rash, but from the look of my bag, the pair in there were just as wet.

"No. She left." Brian kicked some sticks around examining the ground. "Where would she go?"

Jace stilled and his face blanched. "Oh no."

"What?" I asked, taking a step toward him.

He rubbed a hand over his face and groaned. "She was asking questions the other night about the city."

I got into his face. "What kind of questions?"

"Just basic ones, but... but after I told her some things, she got this bright idea we should go there to tell them we may have a cure."

"What did you tell her? What is wrong with you?" Jace blanched and I took a step back, wary of my fisted hands.

"I told her no! I said it's not a good idea, but she's very... persistent."

Grabbing my sack, I started out, but Brian grabbed my arm. "Where are you going?"

"I'm going after her. She couldn't have gone far." Yanking my arm from his grip, I started toward the city walls.

"It's not a good idea!" Jace yelled.

I could hear Brian's feet sloshing through the mud as he followed me. A few moments later, I could hear Jace's. I didn't care how loud I stomped or if I attracted every scourge in the woods; I was livid. What was Eden thinking and how could Jace not have told us her brilliant plan earlier?

As we neared the tree edge, the ground became less muddy as the grass thickened. I increased my pace, trying to gain more ground. I couldn't let anything happen to her.

"Wait," Brian said from behind me. I ignored him and continued on, but he grabbed my arm and yanked me back forcefully. "I said wait!"

I pulled from his grip and lunged at him. I was really sick of him tugging me around. "What? We don't have time for this. We need to get to her!"

"You need to cool down."

Jace approached slowly and looked between us, guilt shone in his eyes. If anything happened to her, he would have to deal with me.

"We can't just march up to the city," Brian said, scratching his head in thought.

"Well, that's what she was going to do," Jace said quietly.

At least he had the good sense to look miserable, but I am not sure I bought it. "What?"

He sighed. "She said we should just go there and tell them we have a cure. She meant to literally knock on one of the doors." He rubbed his eyes with two fingers and let out a loud sigh. "The south entrance is the closest. We should try there." He brushed past us to lead the way.

"What exactly did she say she was going to do?" Brian asked.

"She wanted to find my father. She wanted to tell him and Zane that she knows the cure for the virus. She thinks they are good enough people to take her word for it and just let her go. I tried to tell her it doesn't work like that, but she's stubborn."

"If anything happens to—"

He spun around and faced me. "What? What are you going to do, pretty boy? I didn't ask for this to happen. I didn't think she would do this. Trust me, if I have anything to do with it, I won't let them hurt her." He turned and stormed forward, splashing up muck onto my already muddy pants.

Brian patted my shoulder to nudge me on. I kept my focus on not falling onto the muddy ground, clenching and unclenching my fists as I worked through my anger. We arrived at the tree line before the clearing and stopped. The grey metal city walls glowed in the morning light. The sight brought back memories from my early childhood. My father's green eyes smiling at me, proud. I had lost him, lost Ellie; I would not lose Eden too.

The south door was about a quarter mile down the wall, and there, standing in front of it, was Eden. Her hair glistened in the light as she talked to someone, someone in a full head covered mask.

Jace dropped his pack and took off, sprinting through the clearing right for her, calling her name.

"Don't, Tristan. It's too dangerous." Brian warned me as he took a step back into the thick of the woods, watching Jace and Eden helplessly.

"We can't just let them—"

"We have to!" he yelled. "They are on their own now."

I looked back at him before dropping my pack. Eden would never be on her own, and Jace wasn't going to be the only one coming to her rescue. My feet slipped and slid along the soaked grass, and I had to put my arms out to the sides to keep from falling. How had he run so fast?

Eden turned toward Jace as he approached. As I got closer, I heard Eden pleading with him and another person came to the door.

"Jace?" the person said.

They knew him? Maybe Old Bob was right, and he was planning on taking Eden from the start. He just wanted to manipulate her first. I picked up speed, and just as I was about to reach them, a loud blast echoed through the clearing, and pain shot through my stomach. I halted and fell to my knees.

"Tristan!" Eden screamed, running to me. She caught me as I fell forward, helping me to lay on the ground. "Tristan. No." She stared down at me with wet eyes.

Her beautiful eyes.

I coughed. "Eden."

"What did you do?!" Jace yelled at the man.

"He was running at us!"

Jace knelt beside me. "Tristan, just hold on. I'll get help." He turned back to the two men. "Get David. Now!"

Pain burned through my core as I took short, quick shallow breaths. I needed to breathe deep, but no matter how hard I willed myself, the air never filled me. I coughed, closing my eyes to the pain. Eden put her hands on my stomach, gentle but firm. I smiled. I had longed for Eden's touch. For a moment I forgot everything. I just stared into her eyes, relishing her hands on mine. Then her voice broke through my thoughts.

"Tristan. Stay with me." Her voice cracked, and she looked down at her hands. Following her eyes, I saw my blood painting them red.

"Jace?" A man's voice panted from the doorway.

"Help him! He needs help," Jace yelled.

"You know it doesn't wor—"

"I don't care how it works. David, get him!" Jace's voice was filled with authority. God, I hated him. I hated that he would do this to save me, for Eden.

Eden. I turned back to her and swallowed, still trying to fill my lungs with air. My throat was dry and scratchy. I coughed again. She still had her hands on my stomach, trying to stop the bleeding. Silent tears flowed freely and dripped onto her hands, washing away little bits of my blood. My vision faded in and out, just on the brink of darkness.

"Eden," I whispered.

"Yeah?" Her eyes looked to me expectantly, but they turned to the door when more masked men came. I didn't see what they had, but Eden's head shook, and she leaned over me.

"No!" I yelled. A small dart hit her in the neck. She met my eyes, whispering my name one more time before slumping over onto me.

"Eden?" I tried to jostle her, but my arms wouldn't move. My body throbbed and my vision tunneled. I managed to put my hand in Eden's soft hair, wetting it with my blood, before the darkness took over.

Chapter 36

Eden

I strained to lift my head, but it was so heavy and wouldn't budge. It throbbed too. Cracking open my eyes, I blinked to adjust my blurry vision and opened and closed my dry, prickly mouth.

"She's waking up," a woman said.

"Good," a man responded. "Get her some water."

Squinting, I looked around the room, trying to adjust to the bright light that shone right in my face. It wasn't the sun so we were inside somewhere, but the only place that had electricity was the city. I was in the city.

I lay on a small bed in the corner of a simple small room. Two of the four walls were windows, two metal. It was nothing like the cabin, how I longed for that.

I pulled my arms, but resistance around my wrists kept them at the bed. They were tied down with straps. My heart sped up; I was tied down.

A middle-aged man sat at a small table in the opposite corner. He scratched his light brown hair before patting out imaginary wrinkles in his grey suit.

"Eden, I'm so relieved to see you." His smile made my heart race more. I continued to tug my arms, the ties chafing my wrists. He held up a hand, motioning me to stop. "No don't. Just rest. You need it."

The woman came back with a cup of water, offering it to me, but I didn't immediately take it. I couldn't. Looking between her and the man, then down at my straps, I willed my heart to slow. The man chuckled. "Oh, of course. I'm sorry. Let me get those for you." He came to my side and untied me. The woman offered the cup to me again.

"Take it. You need it." He motioned toward the cup as he sat back down, his black, shiny shoes reflecting in the bright light.

I didn't wait any longer. I was too thirsty. I took the cup and drained it; the water soothed my prickly tongue and throat. Handing it back to the woman, I rasped, "More, please." She said nothing but nodded and left.

Sitting up, I examined myself. I was in a clean white gown. My hands were clean. Flashes of blood covering them came back to me. Tristan. Where was Tristan? Where was Jace?

"Where are my friends?" I coughed. Panic grew as images of Tristan bleeding out under my hands raced through my memory. "You shot him. How could you?" I narrowed my eyes at him. "Where is he? Did you bring him here?" I coughed again. Where was that water?

The man stood. "Now, now, Eden... let's not overreact." He held his hands in front of him.

"Not overreact? You shot him! He is my family!" I tried to stand, but I fell back as the coughing fit hit me. I rested my head on the wall. It throbbed so badly I closed my eyes, but when I did, all I saw was Tristan, helpless and covered in blood. His golden hair and kind hazel eyes, the feel of his warm safe body when he embraced me. I opened my eyes to reality, a small cage of a room.

The door opened and the woman returned with my water. "Sir?" she asked warily, staying near the door.

"It's all right," the man responded.

I took the glass of water from her, downing it as quickly as I could. It soothed my now itchy throat, subsiding my cough. She almost ran out of the room as I turned toward him. "I want to know where Tristan and Jace are."

His eyes dropped. "I'm sorry. There was nothing we could do. Tristan lost too much blood."

Air left my lungs, and it took a few blinks before I could take another breath. When I did, it sounded like a wheeze. Tristan was dead? No. He was strong; he should have survived. I sat up as tall as I could. "I will kill you."

The man sat back down, unthreatened by my words. "Eden, I know this is hard, but I need you to listen to me. Your safety is very important to me—"

"My safety? I came here to tell you I have the cure, so the walls can come down and people can live as they once did. But... but you shot him and drugged me. I'm in a... a cage!" I narrowed my eyes at the man. "You will pay."

He scratched his smooth chin, then said, "You mentioned you had a cure?"

"Yeah, but Jace was right. You are a slimy man. Zane... I presume?" I sat back, leaning on the cool metal wall.

"Jace." He chuckled. "Ahhh, Jace. So, you two..."

"Are friends." I sat forward so fast the room spun, and the water threatened to come back up. "If you hurt Jace, I will take this whole place down." I felt my lips twitch to show my teeth.

"Interesting." He leaned forward and rested his elbows on his knees. "Do you know who you are, Eden?" I blinked. "That's what I thought. Do you remember anything from life here?" He didn't wait for my reply. He looked down at his fingers as he spoke. "No, no. You were only a baby. You are special, Eden." He looked up at me. "You are what we call the Ferine survivor. The first and only survivor of the Fever... that we know of. So, when you say you have a cure. Yes. You do. It's you." His chuckle sent a ring of prickles up my spine.

Why didn't I listen to Jace?

"Where's Jace?" I swallowed, trying to wet my dry throat.

Zane sat back and motioned over his shoulder. His eyes watched me as I looked behind him and registered what was there. It was another room, identical to mine. The windows allowed us to see each other, but Jace was still asleep on the bed, his stomach moving slowly with each breath he took. The tension on my shoulders relaxed at the sight of him. He was still alive.

"Let me make one thing clear, Eden. You can't come into *my* city and make any demands. I am in control here." I stared back at his stone-cold grey eyes. They were so hollow you could get lost in them. "I thought you were dead but am pleased to see you are not." His smile crept along his face like a snake. A slimy snake. "You are the cure, Eden. I will use you to make what we need to survive."

"And if I refuse?"

He nodded his head like he expected this. "Then I will have to use Jace as... encouragement."

I felt the blood rush to my feet and the room swayed again. I don't know what encouragement he was referring to, but I didn't think it was good. Zane stood, brushing off his suit again as he walked to the door of my cage.

"I'll leave you to your thoughts, but... don't wait too long to decide. I would hate for our sweet Jace to get hurt." With his threat sitting in the thick air around me, he left.

I gazed over at Jace, still sleeping soundly, but a prisoner, like myself. Why didn't I listen?

Chapter 37

Eden

Two days. I have been in this cage for two days, but it feels like months. The only thing keeping me sane and grounded has been Jace. He's alive and jaunty as ever, twenty feet away behind two panes of glass. His voice invades my thoughts as I stare up at the crisp white ceiling.

Jaunty? You think I'm jaunty?

Chuckling, I glanced over at him. The glass was so clean it almost felt like there was nothing between us.

Stay out of my head!
But you make it so easy. You basically throw your thoughts at me.

He sat on the side of his bed, elbows resting on his knees, watching me. A smirk twitched at the corner of his mouth. His eyes were big and sparkly, his gold one more noticeable now that his hair was cut short. It was done the second day we were here, much to his dismay. I have spent every day insisting that he doesn't look like a child, which is his reasoning for having the long hair before. It was only appropriate that I keep him humble.

Babyface!

His roar of laughter caused LaRae, our torturer or what everyone here called a scientist, to almost fall off her chair. She stood quickly, brushing off her lab coat and looking between our cages. "What was that about?" She walked to the small hallway between our glass walls, looking right at Jace. "What's so funny?"

Jace strutted toward the glass, leaning on it. "Well, our golden girl over there thinks she's funny." He shrugged and looked toward me, his one blue eye sparkling.

I raised an eyebrow at him, still lying on my cot.

Golden girl?
You called me babyface.
You're an insecure boy.

LaRae turned toward me. "She didn't say anything? I didn't hear anything... I mean... I mean she hasn't said anything to anybody in two days."

Jace chuckled. "She talks to me all the time. I mean, All. The. Time. She's annoying really." He walked back to his bed. "I wake up daily, praying she'll just stay quiet for one day, but then nooooo, there she is. In my head." He poked his head with a finger.

I covered my face with my single blanket to hide my smile. He really was overdramatic at times, but I had come to really like him, trust him.

Oh please!

LaRae looked between the two of us. I avoided her eyes but felt her gaze on me. "Well, maybe you can tell her to please talk to me... talk to anyone. Zane isn't going to give her much more time and I fear for..."—she sucked in a raspy breath—"well for you, Jace. For you. It won't end well for you if she doesn't talk to me. To someone, anyone."

Her words wiped the smile from my face and put the dark pit back in my stomach. The reminder of Zane's threat hung over me like a blade – well, over Jace more like it. Whatever they had planned for Jace if I refused to talk wasn't good. They already killed Tristan, and I'm not sure what happened to Brian. Because I wanted to keep the camp as safe as possible, I hadn't mentioned him.

Remembering Tristan's blood on my hands makes it hard to swallow. Reaching up, I held the silver butterfly necklace in my hand. First Ellie, now Tristan. If anyone else I love is taken, I don't know if I will recover. I closed myself off, my mind, my senses, and pulled my body as far into the corner as I can. Sitting in my cage the last few days, I have mastered my ability to allow Jace into my thoughts but also to keep him out. I could feel him nudge me, but I ignored him.

"Eden!" His muffled voice and knock came at me through the glass. "Eden. Don't push me out. Please, look at me! Please!"

Keeping my face down, covered by my arms, I tucked into myself. I didn't know what to do. I couldn't let them hurt Jace, but I didn't want Zane to have any leverage for whatever he planned on doing. I didn't trust him. I couldn't live like this, so I tuned out the world, every sound, every scent, every feeling as I hid in the corner of my cage.

∽

I kept myself blocked off from the world for the next two days. I didn't leave my cot, didn't eat, didn't talk to anyone, not even Jace.

He watched me anxiously from his cage, frequently nudging at my psyche to get my attention, but I ignored him. He tried yelling at me, dancing, pretending to be sick and hurt, but I disregarded it all.

On the third day of silence, the dishes full of stale food piled up in the corner caused a wretched smell in my cage, but I did my best to ignore it. A man came to talk to LaRae. He was average height, middle aged, dressed in a suit, and had familiar facial features. Even with his greying temples, I could see it had been the same dark, shiny black as Jace and the bright blue eyes were the same.

David, Jace's father. He walked into Jace's cage and pulled up a single chair.

I glanced over at Jace to see his reaction. All I could see and feel was anger and annoyance. He sat on his cot, elbows on his knees leaning forward, ignoring David.

My ear twitched as I anticipated listening to their conversation through the glass. Some days I was thankful for hyper senses.

"What were you thinking?" David said.

"Thinking about what?" Jace continued to look down at his fingers. He was picking at a small piece of napkin from his last meal.

"Do you know how much trouble you put me in?"

"Put you in? You shoved me outside the walls! Banished me!"

"I had no choice, son!" The man's voice was so loud he almost sounded like he was in my cage.

Jace's eyes glowed and he fisted the napkin in his hand, crushing it, "Do. Not. Call. Me. Son. You lost that right when you discarded me like a piece of garbage!"

David's face fell. I almost felt sorry for him... almost.

"Jace, I did the best I could. If I hadn't done what I had, you would have been here. You would be dead."

Jace put his arms out to show his cage. "Well, I am here anyway."

"Yes... yes..." He lowered his eyes. "How is it you..."—he searched for his words—"that you have... I mean... what happened to your eyes?" His voice ended almost in a whisper.

I sat up, setting my feet on the ground, keeping my eyes on Jace. He focused on his father's face, not glancing at my movement. "Does it *scare* you, father?"

David just looked at him. "No... but it's the same as... her." He nodded his head toward me but kept his eyes on Jace. "What did she do to you?"

Jace growled.

Jace! Relax. He's your father.

I let the barriers of my mind down, but Jace didn't reply. He clenched his jaw, narrowing his eyes.

"She has a name. Eden. Don't you presume to think she did anything to me. She saved my life; that's more than you did."

"Saved you?" His father stood. "Look at you! You're an... an animal!"

David turned toward the door. With a burst of strength, Jace pinned him to the wall, holding him by the neck, their noses touching. "You know nothing!" His voice was deeper, almost unrecognizable. There was nothing there showing the funny boy I knew.

LaRae, who watched from the safety of the door, ran to her desk and picked up the phone. I was up, banging on my window. "Jace!" He didn't acknowledge me.

Jace! Stop! Relax!

I saw the tension in his shoulders slip, but his grip tightened. His father's mouth gaped open and shut trying to breathe; his face was red with a tinge of purple.

LaRae was now off the phone and rummaging through one of her cabinets, pulling out a gun. Panic ripped through me. I would not let her shoot him. Banging on the glass, I screamed, but what came out of my mouth was a roar. I continued to roar, trying to break his focus.

Jace! Please! They will kill you!

His face dropped at my voice in his head, glancing at me for a second before turning back to his suffocating father. As quickly as he grabbed him, he dropped him and stepped away. LaRae was at his cage door, panting and pointing the gun with shaking hands. David hunched over, rubbed his throat, and coughed. He bumped into LaRae as he backed toward the door.

"You're..." he croaked, "not my son. My son... would never do... that." He pushed LaRae out the door and locked it behind him.

Armed guards poured into the lab with their guns raised ready to shoot. They lowered their weapons when they took in the scene. Jace moved to the wall, resting his forehead on the metal, his back facing me as he breathed deeply.

Jace?

Nothing.

Jace?
Leave me alone.

The defeat in his voice made me want to break down the glass between us and hold him. I had never seen him so... helpless.

Babyface?

He turned toward me with a twinkle in his eyes.

Golden girl!

I smiled; he would be all right.

Chapter 38

Tristan

The bright light blinded me when I opened my eyes. Bringing my hands up to block it caused my stomach to throb, and I winced. "Ahhh..."

"Oh! Don't move." A petite blonde woman moved to my side, pulling the blanket away to inspect the bandage over my belly. "It looks all right, but you need to move slowly." She turned her bright green eyes to me and smiled. "How are you feeling otherwise?" She straightened the blanket over me.

"Ummm..." Shaking my head, I tried to focus on what she said. "All right, I guess."

Standing straight, she smiled, showing perfectly straight white teeth. She couldn't be much older than me. "Good. It was really touch and go there for a bit. I'm glad you've made it through the hard part." She walked over to a table against the wall and resumed sorting through papers.

I wiggled but stopped when pain shot through me. Taking a long breath, I croaked, "The worst part?"

"Yeah." She glanced back at me. "You were in pretty rough shape when you arrived. A bullet lodged in your belly, causing excessive bleeding, and you got blood poisoning, but luckily, we got it in time." She turned back to her work. "You have only been out for three days. I had expected longer, but it's a good sign you woke."

I cleared my throat. "Can I get some... water?"

"Oh! Of course!" She rushed to my bedside table and grabbed the pitcher and cup for water. "I'm sorry I didn't offer you before. You're probably totally thirsty." She put the full cup to my mouth, and I drank it all.

"Thanks."

"More?"

I shook my head. "What's your name?"

"Andy."

I raised my eyebrows. "Andy?"

"Yeah, it's short for Andromeda, but it's just easier to call me Andy." She chuckled. "My mom was a little... eccentric."

"Ahhh." It is all I can think of for a reply.

She turned to face me, leaning on the table with crossed arms. "As long as we are playing the question game, maybe you can answer a few for me."

"Sure."

"Name?"

She was straight to the point. I liked it.

"Tristan."

She nodded her head slightly, then grabbed a clipboard and pen to jot down notes.

"Age?"

"Twenty-three."

She looked at me, one eyebrow raised. "Really?"

"Ahhh... yeah. Why?"

Shaking her head, she looked back down at her clipboard. "Oh, nothing. Ok, how did you come here?"

I stayed silent. I didn't plan on coming here; it just happened when Eden decided to try and save the world. Eden. "The girl. There was a girl with me. Is she all right?"

"She's fine." She didn't take her eyes off the clipboard. "So how did you get here?"

I tightened my body, biting back the pain, and scooted myself up. After letting out a long breath, I narrowed my eyes back at her. "Where is she?"

"How did you get here?" She met my stare, and her eyes were fierce. She wasn't afraid of me.

"You get nothing until you tell me where the girl is."

She slammed the clipboard down and stomped over to her phone. Her eyes stabbed into mine as she held the phone to her ear. "Zane." She waited a moment. "He's awake." She slammed the phone down and stomped back to where her clipboard was. "Zane will be here to answer all your questions." She turned back to the work at her desk.

I waited as she kept busy, trying to move my arms again, and this time instead of feeling pain at my wound site, I felt it in my right arm. Looking down, I saw tubes tapped into my inner elbow that were attached to a tall metal stand holding bags of liquid. Using my other hand, I pulled at the tubes, but Andy's voice startled me to a halt.

"Don't touch that!" She rushed to check the tubes.

"What's this?"

"It helps keep you hydrated and the pain down." She stepped back, satisfied I hadn't pulled anything out of place. "Just sit still, will you? We don't need anything coming out. It could cause a lot of issues."

I leaned my head back on the wall, just as a tall man in a pristine suit strode in. "Andy," he said as he walked over to my bed and pulled up a chair. "Hello, Mr...." He held out his hand and Andy set the clipboard in it. He searched her notes. "Tristan." He smiled at me. "So, you came with our little superstar, Eden."

"Is she all right? Can I see her?"

"She's fine, fine. Stubborn, but fine." He smiled and looked back to the paper. "I see here Andy wasn't able to get some information. Maybe you will answer for me. "How did you get here?" His grey eyes bore right into mine and the look turned my blood to ice. There was something not right about him.

"Like I told Andy, I'm not answering any questions until I can see Eden."

Surveying me a moment, he sighed. "All right." He stood abruptly. "Andy, I think our new guest needs to be moved to the accommodations in the labs."

"Wait... what? Labs? Where's Eden?"

He dropped the clipboard on her desk and left the room as briskly as he came. I looked over to Andy, who watched me with worry. I dropped my head back onto the wall and squeezed my eyes shut, cursing Jace for putting crazy ideas into Eden's head.

Chapter 39

Eden

After the incident with Jace's father, I decided not to block him out. We needed each other.

I sat on the cot, calmly watching LaRae babble at me. She shook as she sat in the chair across from me. "Please, Eden, I don't want anything to happen to Jace, to either of you." She looked down at some documents in front of her. "Just let me take some blood. That's all I am asking at this time."

I cocked my head at her. "What for?"

She shook her head, startled at my response. It was the first time I had spoken to her. "Ummm, well, so I can..."—she looked at her papers—"umm... analyze it. See how it is different or the same as the previous subjects I have... worked with." She almost whispered those last words.

"Subjects?"

She closed her eyes for a brief second. "Yes. People like you... we call them... subjects."

"They don't have names?" I sat forward and she flinched.

"Well, yes... but. . ."

"But. . ."

"But if we keep their names, it will be harder for us to do our jobs since they will be more—"

"More . . .human?"

She blinked at me; regret flowed through her eyes. "Yes," she whispered.

I sat back. "So, why call me by my name? You won't get attached to me?"

"Well, you're... " she started, but her words hung in the air.

"I'm what?"

Awesome!

I scowled over at Jace, who was sitting in the chair right at the glass, watching us like we were some kind of entertainment. All he needed was a bowl of popcorn, and he would be set.

Shut up.

"Special." LaRae finished, glancing between us, curious still of our relationship. We hadn't told her of our ability to communicate, but I'm sure she has figured out there is something special about us.

Awe shucks, she called you special.

I rolled my eyes, turning back to LaRae. "So that's what is written on my paperwork? Special?"

"Well, no... it says Eden." She flipped through the papers, nodding in confirmation.

I sighed. "All right, take my blood." I put out my arm toward her.

She stared at me, mouth ajar. "Really? Ahh, all right. Hold on, I need to grab my equipment." She quickly shuffled out the door to gather her supplies.

Jace watched me, the humor in his face faded as he leaned on the glass.

You think that's a good idea?
It's just my blood.
Right, but it's not the same as others.

I nodded my head back and forth in contemplation.

We may learn something.

LaRae stumbled back into my cage, holding a bucket full of supplies. "All right, let's have you sit right here." She moved the chair to the little table and put on plastic gloves.

Avoiding Jace's eyes, I held out my arm.

"If you don't look, it doesn't hurt as much," LaRae mentioned as she wiped a cool, wet cotton pad on my arm and tapped the skin at the bend.

I looked toward Jace. His eyes linked with mine and everything around me silenced. All I could see and feel was him. His mouth twitched into a smirk, showing the single dimple on his left cheek, and bubbles in my stomach built. I hadn't noticed it until his hair was cut short, but it suits him. My cheeks warm, and I'm sure they are red.

"Little prick," LaRae says quietly.

The needle stung my arm for a second and I closed my eyes, breaking my link with Jace, but I still felt the tingle of his gaze on me. When the needle was pulled out, I opened my eyes again to see he had lain down on his cot and was looking up at his ceiling.

"There." LaRae put a bandage on the bleeding dot. "It should be good in a few minutes. Drink some water. That always helps after some blood loss." She stood and motioned to the pitcher and cup on the table before leaving my cage.

Taking a drink, I watched her put my blood in different machines to analyze it. I observed her face turn pale as she looked through the machine. She looked many times, scratching her head before picking up the phone to call someone.

It didn't take long for Jace's father, David, to arrive. He flew into the room out of breath and went right to the machine LaRae was looking in. She fidgeted and shuffled her feet next to him as he gazed at my blood for a long moment.

Jace stood and walked over to the glass to watch the scene with me. I sat on my cot but was itching with anticipation about what they saw. The memory of the drawings in Derek's tent flashed in my mind. The two ladders twisting together. I had no idea what it meant, but from Sarah's explanation, it had something to do with human blood, animal blood, and the Fever.

David stood and turned toward me. His eyes moved between me and Jace, then back to my blood. After wiping a hand down his face, he grabbed the small white gun that LaRae now kept out on her table and walked to my cage. Jace banged the glass, keeping his eyes on David.

"Don't touch her!" he yelled through the glass.

David ignored him as he walked through the door of my cage. LaRae grabbed his arm, "David—"

"It's fine, LaRae." He pulled his arm from her grip. "I'm just going to talk."

She watched him as he shut the door on her and sat down on the chair across from me. Jace paced back and forth in front of the glass, eyes focused on his father.

"Eden." David set the small gun next to him on the table.

"David."

We watched each other in silence. He worked at looking steady and confident, but fear poured out of every pore in his body. I could almost taste it in the air. He pressed his lips in a line, rubbing his fingers together nervously.

"Do you know what you are?" he asked.

I stared at him, keeping my face neutral, but my heart leapt. Every cell in my body screamed for him to tell me, but I remembered what Jace had told me. I just stared at him.

Jace stopped pacing and watched us through the glass. LaRae sat at her table, fidgeting with the cord of the phone. No doubt preparing to call for help.

"A chimera," he said.

Before I could stop myself, I furrowed my brow.

He smiled. "I can see by your reaction that you don't know what that is." He sat back, the look of power on his face. Crap. "Well, a chimera is a being who has DNA from two different organisms. You happen to have it from an animal and a human."

My brain worked hard to remember Sarah's words. She explained that DNA is what is in blood and makes living beings what they are. I sat up, "Ok, what of it?"

"Well..." – he clasped his hands together on his lap – "we have never actually seen one, not one that's like you."

"Like me?"

"More human than animal."

A twinge of insecurity hit me at his words. I was part animal. Animal. I knew there was something different about me, but an animal?

Don't let him get in your mind, Eden. You're fine.

"What do you want?" I asked.

"How did you make, Jace?"

Don't tell him. Let them squirm.
They will hurt you.
They can't. I'll be fine.

Jace started pacing again along the glass. I nodded slightly at him, turning back to David.

"Why? If you know what I am, you should know how to make me."

He tugged his earlobe and sighed. "It's not that simple. Just because we know what you are doesn't mean we know how to do it. But you do." He looked over at Jace with raised eyebrows.

Tell him nothing.

"And... why would you think I would help you?"

He scoffed. "Well, if you don't, then you know Jace will be... be hurt, maybe killed. And if he dies, I will make sure during your days here, you will wish you were dead as well." His voice was clipped and cold.

Jace smashed a hand into the glass with a snarl, and David jumped but didn't turn to look at him.

I cocked my head at him. "Why? You said it yourself, he's not your son anymore."

A brief flash of anguish moved over his face before he was able to steady it. "That"—he pointed a thick finger toward Jace—"may not fully be my son, but part of him is. He has his memories. As a father, I"—he dropped his hand—"I can't in good conscience let anything happen to him if I can help it."

Jace banged on the glass again, his muffled cry barely audible in my cage.

"So that's why you sent him out of the city... to die." I let the last two words hang in the air a moment before continuing. "Because you're a good father. Doing everything you can to save your son."

David's face reddened. "You know nothing about what happened. If I hadn't done that, he would have been a subject... a number, and he would be dead now. I did that with the hope...

the hope he would survive!" His voice broke and his eyes glistened. "I didn't know that he would turn into that!" He waved a hand toward Jace again.

I feel shame in the air, not from David but from Jace.

"Get out," I said quietly.

"Eden, lis—"

"GET OUT!" I lunged forward.

David jumped back, knocking over his chair. He took a moment to steady himself, then grabbed the gun in a shaking hand. He pointed it at me unsteadily and backed out of the cage.

I glanced over at Jace, who was still leaning on the glass, but his eyes were vacant. Hurt.

Don't listen to him. He doesn't understand.

Jace looked up at me.

Neither do I.

I sighed as I sat back on my cot.

Then we'll figure it out together.

He said nothing, only nodded.

Chapter 40

Jace

Leaning forward with my elbows on my knees, I gazed over at Eden on her bed. She slept so peacefully that it almost didn't seem like we were locked away in cages. Dropping my head, I ran my fingers through my thick, short hair. I hate that it was cut off, but it will grow back.

The door lock clicked and LaRae walked in with her nervous twitches. "Hey, Jace." She shuffled her feet forward, almost unsure if she was coming or going. "I just need to get some blood from you."

Dropping my hands, I looked up at her. "You already got Eden's. Why do you need mine?"

"We want to analyze it against Eden's. See how it compares."

I blinked. "We?"

She cleared her throat. "Yes, David... your father... and I."

Dropping my head again, I sucked in a breath. "He's not my father." I heaved myself up and sat at the chair next to the table, laying out my arm. "All right then. Take what you need."

As she prepared her supplies and drew my blood, I watched Eden, still asleep. I can't explain the feeling I got when my father went into her room with a gun. I was ready to take down the glass, rip him or anyone else that threatened her to shreds. I have never felt that before, about anyone.

"She's pretty." LaRae's voice pulled me from my thoughts. She put a bandage where the needle pricked me.

"Sorry?"

She smiled, nodding her head toward Eden. "Eden. She's pretty."

I blinked at her, then gave Eden a quick glance, still sleeping, "Yeah. Yeah, she is."

"Does she know?"

"Know what?"

Smirking, she gathered her supplies. "That you like her."

"Well, it doesn't matter, does it?"

She stopped at the door and turned. "Why?'

"Because I'm going to die." I didn't let myself blink as my eyes burned into hers.

"You don't think she..." – she shook her head – "she wouldn't let you die. Would she?"

I resumed my position, elbows on knees. "I hope she does."

"What? Why?" I can hear her heart increase; I still haven't adjusted to my hyper senses.

"Because if she lets me die, then I know she'll be all right. She won't become a subject. Poked, dissected, and discarded like a piece of trash." I smell the guilt flow from her, but I keep her eyes with mine. "That's more important to me than my own life. I want her safe."

Her eyes glistened and her chin began to tremble before she quickly looked away. "Right then." She sniffed, wiping her cheeks. "Well, drink water and rest." The lock of the door echoed in the silence of my cage.

When I glanced back at Eden, she was still lying on her bed, but staring right at me.

∽

I wake as the familiar smell of soap fills my nose, my father. I see him, talking to LaRae near her work table, but there is a third individual with him. Someone I had hoped I would never see again. Zane.

Zane towered over David and LaRae by a few feet. He adjusted his suit jacket before leaning in to look in the spectacles of the microscope. Both David and LaRae were visibly uncomfortable, twitching and rocking on their feet. Zane stepped back and turned to me. Locking eyes with mine, his mouth twitched as he walked toward me. David jumped up after him, obviously unsure of what he was doing as they both entered my room.

"Jace! My boy!" Zane's voice reeked of fake familiarity.

"Zane! The bane of my existence!" I gave an exaggerated, mocking gasp. "Hey! That rhymes! Zane, bane."

He chuckled softly, taking a seat in the chair. David hovered uneasily near the door, but I didn't give him any attention.

"What do you want?" I asked.

He leaned back, examining me, top to bottom. "Well, I was hoping you could help me convince our girl Eden to cooperate with a little experiment I wanted to try."

I bristled at his words. "*Our* girl?"

He chuckled again. "Yes, *our* girl. Eden is special. Has been since she was a baby. I never thought I would see her again, but thanks to you, here she is." His eyes twinkled as he watched my expression. My stomach dropped and the grip on my knee tightened. He thought I brought her here on purpose.

Looking away, I glanced through the glass at Eden. She sat, knees tucked into herself on her bed, watching our conversation. I didn't know if it was loud enough for her to hear, but like me, I'm sure she could feel our emotions. She was scared. I didn't like it when she was scared.

Why the long face, Eden? My stomach fluttered as she perked up at my voice in her head.

What's he saying? Her voice was desperate, nervous.

I gave her a small reassuring smile. *Nothing important. You don't have to worry.*

I turned back to Zane. "I won't help you."

"You do know what will happen if you don't. Correct?" He raised an eyebrow.

I looked down to examine my fingernails. "You will torture me and probably kill me slowly and painfully, blah blah or something like that." I looked back at him, seeing David's face blanch behind him. He always hated it when I never took Zane's authority seriously, but Zane was a bully. I don't like bullies.

"Interesting," Zane replied, looking over at Eden then back at me.

I stifled the growl of possession that built in my throat. I didn't like the way his eyes roamed over her.

"So, you don't care what happens to you?"

"Jace—" David said.

"No. If it protects her, then I'll do what I have to." I dropped my feet to the ground and sat forward, meeting Zane's eyes.

He looked down a moment, nodding his head in understanding. "Very well."

His hand moved so fast I didn't have time to register what happened. Then pain hit my ears from the loud gunshot that echoed through my room. I couldn't hear myself scream in anguish as I pushed my hands onto my thigh, trying to hold in blood.

Jace!

I looked over at Eden. She was screaming and banging on the glass, tears streaming down her face. That look hurt worse than my leg. I never wanted to see her like that. I moved my eyes back to Zane, who stood outside the glass with a look of disinterest. Bastard shot me.

David stood behind him, wringing his hands together with tear-stricken cheeks.

The ringing in my ears died down, and I now could hear Eden's screams and bangs on the glass. She fell to her knees, crying, "I'll do it! I'll do it!" She sobbed. "Just help him and I'll do it."

"No," I groaned out, trying to stand only to end up on my back on the floor.

Eden, no. I'll be OK.

I'm sorry. I can't watch you get hurt or possibly die. I can't lose anyone else.

Zane smiled in triumph. "Well, that wasn't as hard as I thought it would be." He adjusted the sleeves of his jacket. "Right then, LaRae, you may begin. Do what we discussed." I watched him stride out of the room.

LaRae and David rushed into my room, supplies in hand to help me. I turned my head to see Eden on the ground crying out my name before David gave me a shot and I blacked out.

Chapter 41

Eden

Squishing my face to the cool glass, I watched LaRae and David work on Jace's leg. My eyes were blurry and I clenched my jaw. The pop of the gunshot echoed in my head. I could still taste my fear and guilt when I had sat helplessly on the floor. It was just his leg; he would be fine.

Jace? Jace, you'll be OK. You have to be OK.

My eyes never left his unconscious body. David had injected him with a sedative immediately, so LaRae was able to pull the bullet out of his leg. She worked on him so confidently that I almost forgot how skittish and unsure she usually is. My legs turned numb under me as I watched, willing Jace to show any sign he was OK, but I told myself his lack of response was from the sedative.

LaRae sewed up the wound and bandaged it; then David helped her move him to his bed. After they cleaned up the pool of blood on the floor, David watched his sleeping son for a moment before locking the door. His eyes were rimmed red and tired.

Sitting up onto my knees, I banged the glass to get their attention. "Hey!" I yelled, unsure if they were able to hear me with their human ears.

LaRae saw me and paused before walking over to the door. "How is he? What happened?" I bombarded her with questions before she was fully inside.

Her eyes were tired as she looked at me. "He'll be fine. I got the bullet out. The bone isn't broken, so he'll just need time to heal."

"I need to see him. Please, let me go to him."

She stepped in front of me, blocking my path. "I'm sorry, I can't." Her eyes quickly darted to the far corners of the room before connecting back to mine.

The cameras. We were always being watched. I groaned.

"Please, LaRae, I said I would cooperate. I just need to see him, talk to him."

She bit her lip, examining my desperate face, then she moved close to me and whispered, "Midnight. Be ready."

She was out the door before I could respond. Turning back to the glass, I pulled up a chair to guard Jace as he slept.

༄

The click of the lock at my door startled me awake. Crap! I fell asleep. Jumping up, I knocked my chair to the ground.

"Come. You only have five minutes," LaRae whispered.

I was out the door behind her without hesitation. She unlocked the door to Jace's cage, and I almost knocked her over to get to him.

"Jace. Jace. Talk to me." I sat on the side of his bed and framed his face between my hands. "Jace."

His cheeks were warm and a good color. I could hear his steady heartbeat and breath. He was alive. I let out a long breath and the tension released throughout my body.

"He may not wake up. I gave him another sedative to help him sleep. I didn't want him agonizing in pain all night."

"Thank you."

Smoothing back his thick black hair, I stroked his right cheek where his dimple is, and his eyelids fluttered. "Jace?"

He managed to open his eyes and stared up at me. "Eden?"

"Yeah. It's me. Eden. How are you feeling?" I clutched his hand and leaned toward him.

"What are you doing here?"

Turning to LaRae, I said, "Grab him water, please." She moved right to his cup and pitcher, and I turned back to him. "I had to see you. See that you are all right."

His mouth twitched, and I saw the twinkle in his one blue eye. He would be OK. LaRae handed me the cup of water, and I helped him take a few sips.

"You like me," he drawled after he finished drinking, his voice sounding stronger already.

I rolled my eyes, but a chuckle escaped me. "Oh please."

His chest rumbled in soft laughter, but his stare quickly turned serious. "Why Eden? Why did you give in?"

My smile faded and I looked down at our clasped hands. His hands were warm, and he held mine tight. I felt secure, safe. "I couldn't watch them hurt you. I'm sorry. I just can't." I met his eyes. They were calm and understanding. "And they wouldn't just hurt you, they would kill you, and I can't let that happen."

"Eden."

"No, Jace. It's my choice. Please understand." I turned my head to look away, but he caught my chin, turned me to face him, and wiped a tear.

"I do. I understand." His voice was quiet as his thumb stroked my cheek. "I'm not going to lie. I'm happy they won't torture and kill me." He smirked and I chuckled. "But I don't like that they are going to use you."

"I'll be fine. I can handle it."

He tucked a strand of hair behind my ear. "Promise me something." He dropped his hand to take mine again. "Promise me that if it gets to be too much, you'll refuse. You'll tell them you're done. No matter what they say they will do to me."

I stayed silent and looked into his eyes, his beautiful eyes. The brightness was so striking against his dark hair and olive skin.

"Promise me, Eden."

"I promise," I whispered, but I vowed to myself that nothing will be too much.

"Eden, we have to go," LaRae whispered from the door.

My hand automatically clutched his harder in the anticipation of leaving him. Leaning down, I buried my face in the crook of his neck and drew in his fresh scent of spicy citrus. I wanted to pull it inside me and lock it away, so I could pull it out whenever I needed to feel him. Feel safe.

"Eden," LaRae whispered again.

Pulling away, I hid my tear-covered face and followed LaRae back to my cage. Once inside, I glanced through the glass at the dark shape of Jace on his bed. Putting a hand to my cheek, I remembered the feel of his fingers there moments ago.

Stop gawking at me and sleep.

Laughing, I lay down on my bed. *Whatever, you love it.*

You wish!
Night, babyface.
Sleep tight, Golden girl.

Chapter 42

Tristan

I was moved to a tiny room inside a lab. The two windowed walls let me watch Dr. Hahn, the doctor that was assigned to me, work in the lab. He checked on me frequently, which was annoying, but not as annoying as having to watch him bustle about all day.

Frustration built in me. I was now a prisoner, locked in a cell, not able to move without pain, and I didn't know if Eden was all right.

Dr. Hahn unlocked my door and entered my room. He fumbled with his bag of equipment while continuously brushing away his wild white hair. His too-large lab coat covered mismatched patterned clothes. Basically, he was a disaster.

"Morning there, Tristan." He dumped his supplies on the table. "Did you sleep all right?"

"Been better."

He smiled at me, and I felt bad being so cold toward him when he seemed like a nice enough guy. Nothing like that creep Zane or my last doctor, Andy, but my need to find Eden and get us out of here trumped any politeness Ellie and Old Bob had instilled in me.

"Well, let's take a look here. Yes, yes, a look."

He rubbed his gloved hands together like he just received a piece of his favorite cake and pulled down my blanket. The bandage on my gunshot wound was checked and changed daily, but whenever he pulled it off, I winced. I would have a hideous scar in my stomach.

"Looks good, looks good." He leaned in close and gently pushed around the wound. "Any of this hurt?"

"Of course it hurts."

"Yes, yes, but more than usual." He moved his head down low and turned his ear near my stomach.

"No. Not more than usual."

My stomach growled loudly, and he laughed as he stood. "Oh! Your stomach's telling me you're hungry!" He gave my arm a little pat before discarding the old bandages. "Everything looks great. Really great. I'll get it all cleaned and bandaged for you, then grab your breakfast. How does that sound?" He smiled at me, grabbing more supplies.

There was something about the way that he talked and looked that reminded me of Ellie. Not the idiotic way he repeated everything, but Ellie was always happy and positive. When we were young and would get hurt, she would always make us feel like we got a little stronger even if we cried. I set my head back, squeezing my eyes shut. Ellie. A piece of my heart was gone, and it will never be filled. I can't lose anyone else.

"Do you know of a girl here? Her name is Eden," I asked.

Dr. Hahn stilled for a brief second while putting the clean bandage on my wound. "Eden? Let me think, let me think. No, no, it doesn't ring a bell. Nope." He immediately focused again on his work.

"Is there any way you can look around for me? See if she's here and if she's OK?"

When he was finished, he stood and looked right at me. "Who is this Eden to you?"

"She's my..." I took a moment to think. What should I call her? She's more than a friend, but she's not my girlfriend. *Sister.* She had called me her brother. The words stung before they left my mouth. "She's my sister."

His eyes widened in surprise as he inspected my face. "Sister you say? Yes, yes. Sister." I ground my teeth every time he said the word. "Well..." – he gathered all his things and moved to the door – "let me see if I can find out something for you."

"Thank you, thank you so much." I winced at myself. I just repeated my words, and I really hoped his quirks were not rubbing off on me.

"Good. Good. Let me grab your breakfast." He smiled and left my room. My stomach fluttered at the new possibility that I may find Eden. Everything was going to be all right.

∽

I was sitting up doing core twists when Zane came into the lab. His eyes fixed on me the moment he walked in and never left me as he walked to my room. Dr. Hahn, more flustered than usual, unlocked the door and let Zane in.

"Tristan!"

I lay back, ignoring the subtle ache on my core. I had to get strong so I could get Eden out of here. Zane sat in the chair with meticulous care and crossed his legs. Lacing his fingers, he set them on his knee and met my eyes.

"So. How are you doing?"

"Fine."

"Dr. Hahn relayed some interesting information. He mentioned that you told him you are Eden's... brother. Is that right?" I glanced over his shoulder at Dr. Hahn, watching us through the window on the door nervously fidgeting his fingers.

"That's right." I looked back to Zane. "Where is she?"

"She's here."

A rush of anticipation hit me, and I tried to sit a little closer. "Is she all right? Can I see her?"

"No." He watched my face drop before continuing. "She's sick, unfortunately. The Fever. We have to keep her quarantined. You understand, don't you?"

"The Fever?"

My mind raced with the memory of having the Fever. I didn't wish that pain on anyone, especially Eden.

"How?"

He uncrossed his feet and stood. "I infected her."

"You what?" My voice was so loud that Zane actually winced.

"Yes. She is the Ferine survivor. She survived during our initial research. I needed to see if she can still... survive. It will help with the cure. She'll be a hero." He pulled the arms of his jacket down and buttoned it before looking back at me.

"You call her the Ferine survivor?"

"Yes, yes." Zane waved a disinterested hand in the air. "It wasn't my idea, but it stuck."

"You do realize that she isn't the only survivor, right? I am a survivor too."

"True, but you are part of the one percent who just naturally survives. Eden is in a league of her own. She was on the brink of death when something done in the research brought her back to life. I need to learn what that was, so we can make the survival rate much higher than one percent."

"And my blood can't tell you anything?"

He laughed. "Are you signing up to be a subject, Tristan?"

My blood froze at the thought. "No. I just don't understand why you can't find anything in a natural survivor that could help."

He watched me with a fake smile plastered to his face. "You're a smart young man, aren't you?" I didn't respond but kept my eyes on his. He sucked in a deep breath. "We have tried. There were a few natural survivors we worked with, but we came up with nothing. Eden, however, is special." He tilted his head. "But you already know that, don't you?"

I pursed my lips to keep my temper. "All right, so what exactly are you hoping to find?"

"A cure, of course."

"A cure." I scoffed. "You think you are going to be able to get a cure from Eden?"

"Well, yes. I know I will and wouldn't you like to resume to life before the virus?"

I blinked at him, searching my memory, not coming up with anything. I didn't remember life before.

He gave me a knowing smile. "Yes, yes. You would have been very young. Well, it was much more... pleasant than life now. The city walls can be down and people can move as they please. It will be glorious and Eden will be the reason that all can happen."

I clenched my jaw. He worked so hard to be convincing, but I could see through him. It wouldn't be that easy.

"Don't get mad at me. She agreed."

"That's a lie. She would never do that."

He chuckled. "People do many things they never think they will when there is enough... persuasion."

My stomach knotted. "What was the persuasion?" I spoke before I could stop myself. I didn't want to know, yet I did. The smile that crept on his face told me my answer before he said, "Jace."

My hands fisted the blanket, and I set my face to stone. Zane laughed. "Brother. Sure."

Dr. Hahn unlocked the door to let Zane out. He didn't look back as he left the lab.

I slammed my head back on my pillow and screamed.

Chapter 43

Eden

Twenty-seven!

Jace's voice was filled with excitement. We had created a game to fill our boring days called "How many times LaRae tugs at her earrings."

Liar!

Swear on my father's grave.

That's not reassuring.

I pulled up my blanket to warm me from my chills. My shaking had reduced, but it still came sporadically.

Feeling any better?

I look over at furrowed eyebrows. His eyes still sparkled, but with worry instead of humor.

I'll survive.

LaRae infected me two days ago. The fever was ramped yesterday but has died down today. She takes my temperature and what she calls "vitals" hourly, charting the numbers.

Twenty-eight.

Chuckling, I tried to shake my head, but it throbbed too much.

What time is it?

I watched him look over at the circular clock on the wall.

She should be in to see you anytime.

I pulled my legs into myself under the blanket to hold in my warmth and opened my eyes to the sound of the lock on the door. LaRae came in covered in her protective gear, face mask, gloves, and even a covering over her hair. She pushed her cart of supplies. "How are you feeling?" she asked quietly, concern etched around her eyes. I never realized how expressive eyes were until that was all I could see of someone's face.

"C-c-cold," I stuttered through shivers.

She felt my forehead and cheeks. "You're burning up." Grabbing the small device she called a thermometer, she moved it across my forehead. "102.4. Yup, you still have a fever." She handed me some pills and a cup of water. "Here, take these."

Slowly, I sat up, keeping the blanket draped over my shoulders, and took the pills. Looking up, I saw Jace, sitting on his bed, monitoring LaRae's every move. He had gotten better at pulling himself up with his arms to bring his legs over the side of his bed. LaRae made sure he was stocked up with pain meds to help him manage, but he refused to take them most of the time, said he wanted to be clearheaded in case I need him.

After swallowing the pills, I handed the empty cup back to her. "What do those do?"

"They should help lower your fever, and if you are having any pain, they help with that too." She smiled at me, holding my arm to take my blood pressure. Her anxiety and nervous twitches had dramatically reduced since I decided to cooperate.

I watched her work. Her brown hair framed a pleasant face with chocolate eyes. She must be near fifty, but I had never been good at telling ages. "You seem... happier."

She looked at me before writing down her numbers. "I'm just happy you decided to work with us."

"Why?" I pulled the blanket tighter around me.

"Because you could be the key to saving us all." She smiled at me and put her items away. "Doesn't that make you happy? You could be the one that saves us."

Staring at her, I'm unsure if she truly means this, or if it's some kind of propaganda. "I don't... trust Zane."

She froze. "I'm sorry?" I could smell the fear within her.

"Zane. I don't... trust him." My shivers are becoming so uncontrollable, it made it hard to speak. Darn, I thought they were getting better.

Staying silent, she finished writing some last notes before pushing the cart to the door. "Yes, well, he's not here. So, we don't need to worry about him at the moment." She opened the door and moved the cart out before her. "Rest, Eden. I'll be back in an hour."

Then she was gone, and I was left shivering and alone in my cage. I gazed across at Jace, and he gave me a small smile and a wave.

Better?
Not really.

His face faltered, but he held his smile.

Rest.

So, I do.

⁓

The stabbing pain in my stomach blew me out of bed. I heaved and heaved, but nothing came out. There was nothing to come out. I hadn't eaten in two days. Involuntary groans escaped me as my stomach tried to expel every drop of bile. The pain was so excruciating that I couldn't pull air into my empty lungs. I fell off my cot onto the floor, coughing, working to suck in a deep breath.

Eden?
Pain. Can't breathe.

The floor cooled my cheek as I lay on my side, trying to pull in as much air as my lungs would allow. After each pull, a stab of pain pushed it back out. Jace's screams and bangs on the glass were muffled, but my focus was completely on breathing. I had to breathe, but the pain. Oh, my, the pain.

The door to my cage opened and LaRae rushed to my side. "Eden?" Flipping me over, she examined my eyes with a light and felt my neck. "Eden, can you talk?"

Shaking my head, I gasped for more air. My wide eyes watched her terrified face as the blood drained from it and she ran out of my cage, not bothering to shut or lock the door.

Hang tight. She's calling someone.

The sound of Jace's voice in my head helped to soothe me. I focused on pulling in loud rasping breaths at a rhythm to help slow my heartbeat.

In, two three, out, two three.

LaRae rushed back into my cage and tried to prop me up, but I swung at her. It's more comfortable lying flat. My words turned to scratchy breaths; I couldn't speak. She continued to try and pull me up, so I pushed her away and kicked at her. My breathing rhythm faltered at my movement, so I closed my eyes to focus.

"Eden... Eden please." She tried to pull me up again, but I pushed her away. She fell. Hard. Her eyes watched me nervously as she scooted back toward the door.

Relax, Eden!

She was cowering near the door of my cage when an older man in a lab coat ran in. As he approached me, he slapped on a face mask but didn't bother with gloves.

"What did you do to her?" He knelt next to me, unafraid.

"Nothing! She just started acting like this moments ago." LaRae grabbed the cart from outside the door, pulling it inside.

The man firmly grabbed my head and examined my eyes, then moved to listen to my chest. "What did you give her?" Without waiting for LaRae to answer, he grabbed the clipboard and scanned it. "You gave her this medication?" He pointed to something on the paper.

"Well, yes." LaRae looked confused. "She has a fever."

My gasping increased with the pain. I pushed the man and heaved again, but still, nothing came out. Tears dripped from my eyes and I tried to curl into myself. I could hear Jace's pleas to let him out, but LaRae and the man ignored him.

"It's toxic to some animals," the man said to LaRae as he ran out of the cage to her cupboards. "I need to get her something to counteract it," he yelled back.

My already pumping heart skipped a beat at his words. *Animals.*

"Right, but..." – LaRae stood dumbfounded – "Eden is—" Her eyes widened. "Oh my..."

The man rushed back into the room with a pill and a cup of water. "Right. She isn't fully human, so she won't react the same way as humans to some medications. You need to be careful. Very, very careful."

I sat up with his support, giving him a questioning look, but his focus was fully on getting the pill into me. What did he mean, I wasn't fully human? He shoved the pill halfway down my throat and poured some water in. "Swallow."

Whatever pill he gave me acted fast and the pain lessened, making it easier to breathe. My lungs filled with fresh air, and I closed my eyes in relief. "Thank you," I whispered.

"Good, good." The man stood before he crouched down to help me up and to my bed. "Rest. Rest is good." He turned to LaRae, who had tears in her eyes as she watched me.

"I'm so sorry, Eden… I didn't think." She started to move toward me, but the man stopped her.

"It's fine, LaRae. Fine. Fine. Let her rest," he said quietly.

Before the door shut, I asked in the loudest voice I could muster, "What's your name?"

He smiled. "Dr. Hahn."

With the door shut and locked, I rolled over and faced Jace, still weak and cold. He was calm and watching me with worried eyes.

I'm an animal.

I watched his reaction to my words, but it wasn't as profound as I expected.

Aren't we all, aren't we all.

He smiled before I closed my eyes and slept.

Chapter 44

Jace

I sat on the side of my cot, lifting my leg up and down trying to stretch it. The pain had dramatically reduced over the past few days, but it still ached. A sheen of sweat glowed on my arms as I grunted through my exercises. Trying to keep the days busy was hard, especially when I had to watch Eden go through so much. My leg was nothing in comparison to what was happening to her.

Resting my leg, I looked up at her. She was lying on her cot snuggled under multiple blankets. She held out her necklace, examining the small silver butterfly.

Where did you get it?

She glanced over at me a moment before going back to inspecting it. Her face solemn.

Ellie.

I don't think she has ever mentioned Ellie before, but by the sound of her voice, I didn't think she wanted to talk about it.

Do you think they will come for me?

Who? I asked her, but I already knew who she meant. Her family.

Old Bob, Tate, Brian, Derek... all of them. Any of them.

I leaned forward with a sigh. They may try, but the chances of them getting in alive are little to none. Seeing her this way hurt. I rubbed a hand down my face and growled. She kept her eyes on the necklace.

I think they will want to, but they know that they don't have much chance of getting out alive.

She dropped the necklace and turned over to face the wall. With her back to me, she pulled up the blankets to her earlobes.

Yeah. You're probably right.
I will get you out, Eden.

She didn't respond and the walls of her mind went up. I hated it when she blocked me out. I looked over at LaRae. She was watching me. We locked eyes, and I felt she wasn't like Zane. She didn't like being here or doing any of this, but what choice did she have? I turned away as the frustration built within me. Letting out a scream, I punched my pillow, imagining it was Zane's cocky face.

Chapter 45

Eden

My fever disappeared two days ago, and I was feeling better. David had been talking to LaRae periodically through the day and both of them were noticeably agitated. Much more than I would expect since I survived their little experiment.

I looked over at Jace, who was struggling to stand from his bed. He sat upright with his legs over the side and his hands resting in the long metal crutches. He pulled himself up to standing, careful not to put any pressure on his injured leg.

You did it!

He tried not to grin too much, and my heart fluttered at the single dimple in his right cheek.

Of course, I did.

The smile on my face fell when Zane strode through the door. David and LaRae stood, dropping what they were doing to turn to him. Zane must have been the source of their anxiety.

Rising slowly, I sauntered to the window and leaned on it, never taking my eyes off Zane. He only showed up if he had a good reason, and usually, that involved me.

I leaned the side of my forehead into the glass to make it look like I was relaxing, but it really was so I could hear their muffled voices better. I wanted to hear what Zane had to say. Jace hobbled to the empty chair near the glass in his cage. He had the same idea, but it may be more difficult due to his injured leg.

Zane studied the paperwork LaRae gave him before speaking. "So nothing happened?"

LaRae shook her head. "No. Nothing of significance. She spiked a fever for two days, but that was about it. It reduced and she's fine now. Fever free."

Zane glanced at me before looking back to the papers. "Her blood didn't change?" I looked down at the bandage on my arm from when LaRae took my blood. The pinprick hole still throbbed from the needle.

"No," David replied.

Sighing impatiently, Zane dropped the papers on the table. "Do it again." He turned to walk out the door but stopped at David's words.

"I'm sorry . . .again?"

"Yes, again." Zane took one intimidating step toward David. "Infect. Her. Again."

"But—" LaRae protested but backed down when Zane turned his burning eyes toward her. She dropped her gaze to her feet. "Understood. Right away."

"Good." Zane adjusted his jacket and left the room. He gave me a side glance through the windows of the lab wall as he walked down the hall. When our eyes met, I saw nothing but emptiness.

Well, great.

Jace watched me as he rested his forehead on the glass. I could feel his unease, but I knew in my heart it was the only way.

Beats the other option.
Eden...
Stop, it will be fine. I'll survive.

Jace closed his eyes, but after a brief second, he banged the glass to get David and LaRae's attention. They looked over at him but ignored him to turn toward me.

David looked at LaRae. "You got this?" LaRae nodded, and she shuffled the papers together, putting them in a folder. "All right, good. I'll check back tomorrow." He left the lab, ignoring Jace's calls for attention.

Jace?

He ignored me.

Jace!

He ignored me again. He never ignored me, and it made me feel... rejected. He must have sensed my emotions because he dropped his head, then looked at me.

Eden, you don't need to do this. We can find another way.

His eyes were wide with desperation, but I shook my head.

You know Zane won't go for any other way except killing you. What would that get him?

I paused, blinking in thought at his comment, but then shook my head.

No. I won't risk it.
It's my life!
Right, and I can't lose you!

My cheeks warmed immediately and my words echoed in our minds. I looked away and slowly walked to my bed, keeping my face out of Jace's view. What I said was true. I couldn't lose him. I have lost too many people I love, and I won't lose anymore.

Eden?

His voice soft and caring.

Forget it.

I grabbed my necklace, rubbing my thumb over all the bumps and grooves of the butterfly. I wished Ellie was there to lean against and brush my hair. We could gossip about Jace, and she could give me advice. A sad smile grew on me as I lay down doing my best to avoid Jace's burning gaze. Keeping the necklace clutched in my hand, I stared up at the bright white ceiling.

For the record, I can't lose you either.

A tingling rushed through me at his words, and I had to count my breaths to calm my pounding heart. The bond we were building was strong, much stronger than I have ever felt outside of family.

LaRae entered my cage right when I decided to look over at him. Instead of watching me, he managed to move to his bed and lie down, his eyes staring up at his ceiling.

I turned back to LaRae. "Let's get this over with." Keeping my eyes away from the needle that pinched my skin, I felt the Fever infect me once again.

∽

The Fever didn't hit me as hard this time around, but my body was still weak. My legs gave out when I stood to get a glass of water. I grabbed the bedside table, knocking the chair over in the process. Closing my eyes, I focused on steadying the spinning room. Confident that I could stay upright, I pushed away and slowly walked to the table that had the pitcher of water.

The lock clicked and LaRae walked in. "Eden, let me—"

"Get out!" She froze, watching me hunch over and growl from deep in my throat. I took a step toward her. "I said GET OUT!" The thumping of her heart filled my ears and the smell of sweat and panic poured from her skin. I repeated, do not charge, do not charge. Every muscle in my body was tight as I fought the urge to protect my home. I needed her to leave so I could relax.

"All right. I'm leaving." She held her hands up and slowly backed out of the room.

Turning back to my water, I drank another cup. Then another. I've never felt this thirsty. My body shook with adrenaline.

Eden?

Pausing with the glass halfway to my mouth, I turned to the voice. Jace. He was in the cage across from me and his face was etched with concern. Ignoring him, I drank my water.

Eden... look at me.

His voice echoed in my mind again, but my body was weak. I didn't feel like talking, so I ignored him again and slowly made my way back to my bed and lay down. Pulling the blanket to my chin, I closed my eyes.

Eden, please.

I opened my eyes at the desperation in his voice and looked over at him. He sat on the side of his bed watching me. I smiled slightly before closing my eyes to sleep.

Chapter 46

Tristan

The cool water dripped down my face and I leaned over the sink, watching it slide down the drain. The pain in my belly had reduced to a subtle ache that hovered just below annoyance. Grabbing a towel, I dried my face and neck before leaning back to stretch. In the small mirror over the sink, I caught sight of my gold hair that had grown out to a pile of messy curls. I usually kept it short, but without Ellie and being on the move, I hadn't done anything with it.

Ellie.

Eden. Not knowing what was happening with her was driving me crazy.

Closing my eyes, I leaned on the sink again, grinding my teeth together. I kicked the base of the sink and screamed. My voice hit the metal walls and rang in my ears. I needed to get out of this prison.

Moving to the window, I leaned my shoulder on it and watched Dr. Hahn shuffle through papers on his messy table. I scanned the pile of papers and dirty mugs strewn about the table and floor. He had to be the most unorganized person I have ever met, even if I haven't met many people. I knocked on the window to grab his attention and motioned my hands like I was drinking. He quickly moved to a small corner table, picked up a mug, and filled it with steaming dark liquid. He has given me a mug of coffee every morning, and I have come to crave the warm richness of it.

Unlocking the door, he handed me the mug through the crack. "So sorry, so sorry. I didn't realize the time."

I took the mug, licking my lips in anticipation. "Not a problem, Hahn my man. Not. A. Problem."

He shut the door and headed back to his work as I sat and sipped the hot liquid. Before the rebellion bombing that pushed me, Tate, and Eden to the woods, my father would drink a mug of coffee every morning, sometimes two. I always loved the smell, and as I smelled my mug now, memories of my birth father came to me. Memories I had long forgotten. Including one memory I wished to forget forever, my father's hand in mine, turning cold as he died.

I drained the last bit of coffee just as Zane walked into the lab. The sight of him had me fisting the mug so tightly I thought it might crack. Dr. Hahn jumped up from his work, spilling some coffee on his already-stained white lab coat. The thickness of the glass inhibited me from hearing what Zane said to him, but he nodded and moved to my room, unlocking the door. Zane marched right in, turning to watch Dr. Hahn shut the door after him.

"Morning, Zane." I lifted my empty mug at him and gave him a closed-mouth, annoyed smile.

"Morning, Tristan. Enjoying your coffee?"

I gave Dr. Hahn a quick glance over his shoulder. He stood in his usual nervous flurry, wringing his hands as he watched us. "Very much so. Dr. Hahn is very kind to give me such a luxury every morning."

"Well, I'm glad he's being so... accommodating."

"What can I do for you, Zane?"

He examined his fingernails before speaking. "I would like you to give me some information."

"Information."

"Yes." He met my eyes, waiting patiently for my reply.

"About?"

"I need to know what Eden did to Jace."

"What? I have absolutely no idea."

"Really."

"Really, really." Crap, I did it again. Dr. Hahn *was* rubbing off on me.

"No idea. None at all." His eyes never left mine, and I found his stare unnerving. His eyes prickled along my face like a hundred spiders crawling, but I didn't look away. I wouldn't; it would show weakness, and I am not weak.

"No, I'm sorry. Honestly, I am. All I know is he was dying, almost dead, then the next morning – bam – he's alive and just like... well just like her."

He let out an annoyed sigh, rolling his head in a circle. I heard his neck crack, and I cringed.

"If it's not too much to ask, why do you need to know?"

He looked right back at me. "Because if I find out, I will have the cure to the Fever."

The blood rushed from my head to my feet, and I almost dropped the mug in my hand. "But you said that Eden had the Fever."

"I did. She did, but she recovered. No one recovers, except her."

My mouth went dry, and I wished there was a tad of coffee left in my mug. I trained my face to stay neutral at the knowledge Eden had survived even though my heart fluttered at the thought. I still had time to get her out. Save her. "What about Jace?"

He laughed, giving his head a small shake. "I don't want to risk him... yet. He's been very useful in getting Eden to comply."

I squeezed the mug again and pursed my lips. The way he talked about controlling Eden made the coffee in my stomach boil. "She's a lot stronger than you think." My words surprised both of us, but I kept my face serious and strong as his eyes traveled over it.

"Oh. I know. I'm counting on that. Why do you think I have kept you?" He stood and brushed off his suit jacket. "It was nice chatting, Tristan. Enjoy your coffee." Unable to respond, I watched Dr. Hahn unlock the door and Zane exit the lab. The coffee in my veins helped my adrenaline pump my heart and a cold sheen of sweat formed over me. I was being used. If Eden doesn't comply and Jace's use runs out, then it will be my turn. Crap.

Chapter 47

Eden

I cowered on top of my bed, tucked as far back into the corner as I could get. Small prickles of warmth covered my body, and I twitched and rolled my limbs and head to stop it, but it just continued persistently. My jaw hurt, hands hurt, everything hurt. The sounds and smells of everyone in the building filled my head, so I covered it with my arms, attempting to keep them out. Nothing worked. People continuously tried to invade my home even though I told them to leave. I screamed, lashed out, and threw things, but they still continued. A pile of items I had thrown lay on the floor in front of the door.

Growling low, I watched two people prepare to enter again. I rolled my shoulders, worked on taming the warm tingling sensation, and watched as they readied their small weapons that threw darts wherever they aimed. They have tried to use them before, but

I fought them off. I will do it again. Clenching my fists and rolling my back, I prepared for the invasion.

Relax, Eden. It's all right.

The voice moved through my head and I tugged at my hair to get it out. I don't need a distraction right now. I needed to protect my home. Protect myself.

Get out! Leave me alone!
Eden... look at me. Look through the glass.

Letting go of my hair, I lifted my head. Through two panes of glass stood a young man with short black hair. He leaned on metal sticks and favored a bandaged leg. Tilting my head, I searched my memory because there was something familiar about him. He smiled and a small ping deep in my stomach hit me.

It's me, Jace.

Jace. I know him. Our eyes met and his smile grew, showing one dimple on his right cheek.

Jace?

He nodded frantically, pushing himself against the glass. If he could walk through it, he would.

Yeah. It's me. Eden, you need to relax or they are going to sedate you.

At the sound of the lock, I snapped my head toward the door. Intruders. They were coming for me again. I jumped to my haunches and bared my teeth, ready to attack.

Eden, please! Just relax; don't attack them!
Quiet, Jace. They want to hurt me.
No, no, I won't let them.

As the humans entered my room, I glanced over at him. His voice had an honesty to it, and I wanted to believe him. So badly. My gaze sunk into his, and I felt he would do anything in his power to protect me. But... he was there, behind glass, and I was here. He may want to protect me, but he couldn't. I had to protect myself.

He flicked his eyes away for a second toward my door. "No!"

The sharp sting of a needle hit me in the neck, and I let out an echoing roar. Holding my hand to the needle, I looked up into Jace's face then blacked out.

Chapter 48

Jace

I clench my teeth at the sight of Eden lying unconscious. Her response to this round of Fever has not been typical. She is an... animal, literally. Lately she hasn't been blocking out her thoughts, so I hear and sense everything going through her, and it's not her. I grind my teeth together at the frustration. I need to help her.

LaRae and David approached her carefully in case the sedative didn't work. Everyone was always careful around her now. LaRae knelt next to her and went to work immediately. Since her metabolism has increased, the sedative wears off much faster.

"You take her vitals. I'll get her blood. We have five minutes," LaRae said. David didn't argue. He adjusted his face mask before he started his work.

As my adrenaline slowed, the throbbing pain in my leg returned. Using my crutches, I limped to the chair I had dragged near the glass. I sat, letting out a sigh at the relief to my leg, and watched Eden's still body be poked and probed. I should have kept my mouth shut that night in the woods and not told her anything about me or the city. I had given her hope that she could better the world, and now they were taking everything from her. Smashing my fist into the glass, I screamed.

LaRae and David stood and quickly left her cage when they finished. As they worked at the table, I knocked on the glass to get their attention. David looked over at me and my breath caught in my throat. I have committed to not calling him my father, but he had a certain look that brought back memories. Memories of when I was happy and life seemed easy, but I don't think it was ever easy for him. He just made it seem easy for me. My heart tightened at the thought, but it didn't change the fact that he discarded me, like trash.

"Come here." I motioned to him. Pausing, he watched me a moment, then came to my cage and LaRae followed.

"How is she?"

"She'll be fine. We haven't had time to analyze anything yet, so we don't know details, but her vitals were good," LaRae responded.

I nodded, looking down at my clasped hands. "I would like you to stop using her and use me instead."

Silence followed my request and they both blinked at me.

"Did you hear me?"

David cleared his throat. "Yes. Ummm... we heard you, but—"

"No but. I want you to leave her alone and use me."

"Jace"—LaRae's voice was quiet—"that would be difficult. We would have to start over with our baseline, with—"

"I don't care!" I glanced over at Eden, who was now starting to stir. "You have seen her. She's not"—I searched for the words—"not handling this well. I'm worried about her."

David took a step toward me. "We know you are, but—"

"I said no but!" I bellowed at them, trying to stand, but grimaced and sat back down as the pain shot through my leg.

"Jace, listen. If you take over, you may become like... like her," LaRae said. "Then neither of you will have your wits about you. Right now, you can protect her, but if you become like that, then you may not be able to. You do want to protect her, don't you?"

Scoffing, I looked away. "Low blow, low blow."

"This is serious. We don't know what's happening to her. Let us look at her blood and see if we see anything different. All right?" David said.

Looking back at Eden, I nodded. They knew exactly what to say to keep me from pushing too much. It was unnerving.

They left quietly and got back to work as I watched Eden move to her bed, scared and confused. Angry that I couldn't help her, I threw a crutch across the room but immediately regretted it since I had to drop to the ground and pull myself back to my cot, cursing under my breath.

∽

"Jace." LaRae tugged my arm, raising me from a deep sleep.

Opening my eyes, I adjusted to the light of my room. "How long did I sleep?" My voice cracked.

"Fourteen hours." She sat next to my bed and undressed my wound to inspect it.

"What?" I sat up too fast, making my empty stomach lurch. "How could I have?"

She didn't look up from working on my leg, but I could smell the guilt. "I... umm... I gave you something."

"I'm sorry?"

She sat back and sighed. "I gave you something."

I glanced over at Eden. She was safe, lying curled up on her bed sleeping. "Why would you do that?"

"I had to!" She looked at me with worried eyes. "You weren't sleeping. You are so consumed with keeping Eden safe that you aren't taking care of yourself. You had to sleep."

I searched her eyes for any unsaid reasons and didn't see any. "You're probably right."

She finished changing the dressings on my leg. "Nothing happened." She looked at me with a smile. "She has stayed the same. Nothing new or notable happened."

"Did you find anything in her blood?"

She opened her mouth to respond when a knock on the window made us both turn. Zane and David stood, watching us impatiently. "Enough chit chat. You have work to do," Zane said.

LaRae's entire body language changed. Her shoulders stiffened and her face turned taut. "Sorry. Have to go." She gathered her equipment and quickly left my room.

I watched them move to the table, talking quietly as they took turns looking into the microscope. Scooting myself over to the edge of the bed, I used my crutches and stood to move to the large window. Leaning on it, I looked between Eden and the scientists, trying to make out what they were saying, but they spoke just quietly enough for me not to hear, even with my ear to the window.

I started at the sight of Eden jerking awake and jumping off her bed with a snarl. Zane's eyebrows raised with surprise and interest, and he slowly walked over to her window. Eden growled, baring her teeth as he moved closer.

Eden, it's all right.

She stopped and looked toward me, but quickly turned back to Zane. He stopped just inches from the glass and smirked. A low growl rumbled in me at the sight, and I fought the urge to try and break the glass down to wipe the smirk off his face.

"This is how she is all the time?" he asked loud enough for me to hear.

"Yes," David said.

"How did she handle the second infection?"

LaRae stepped forward. "Better than the first time. Her fever only lasted a day. The only lingering effects are... what you see."

"Good. Infect her again. Let's see if she can handle a third time."

LaRae looked up. "Sir, I—"

I banged so hard on the glass I swear I heard a crack. Zane turned to me, unimpressed. "Do you have something to say?"

"Use me instead!"

Zane blinked. "I don't think I heard you right. What did you say?"

I opened my mouth, but David stepped between us. "He's not well. His leg. Just ignore him."

I banged on the glass harder. "No!"

"Right," Zane said before walking toward the door. "Anyway, you heard me. Infect her again. I need to be completely confident that she is immune. I want to see how many doses she can handle." Before leaving the room, he glanced at me, the smirk still a whisper on his face.

He had heard me, but he chose not to listen. He liked seeing Eden change, and he liked seeing me ache at watching her suffer.

After he left, I turned to both David and LaRae. "If you touch her with that virus, I will kill you both." They blanched and looked away. I had to figure out how to get us out of here.

Chapter 49

Tristan

Dr. Hahn inspected my wound, now just a thick pink scar. "Looks good, looks good." He smiled up at me. "We can leave the bandage off now. Give your skin some air." I pulled my shirt down and the feel of the fabric against my skin almost felt foreign. Dr. Hahn put his supplies away and headed toward the door.

"Do you think there is any way I can see Eden?"

He halted, keeping his back to me as he shuffled his feet nervously. "Oh. I don't know, I don't know."

"Please?"

He turned to meet my eyes before glancing around the lab. "I don't... I don't think Zane will agree." He moved a chunk of his wild white hair from his eyes.

Sliding off my cot, I took a few steps toward him. "Then can you get him? I will ask him myself."

The blood drained from his face. He swallowed and took a step back. "You will?"

"I have no choice. I need to see her. She's the whole reason I'm here."

He flicked his eyes around the room again. "Will you let me see what I can do? I will try. I will try."

Smiling, I held out my hand for a friendly handshake. "Thank you. Th—" I stopped myself this time before repeating the words. He took my hand, and I patted his shoulder with my free hand. "All I ask is you do your best."

"Sure. Sure. All right."

I watched him leave then bustle about with his papers and supplies, wondering how he would do it. It was a long shot at threatening to contact Zane, but the fear was so much more than I could imagine. A pang of guilt hit me at the situation I have put him in, but right now all that mattered was Eden and making sure she was safe.

৸

I was doing my workout when Dr. Hahn flew back into his lab, quickly coming to my door. He unlocked it and motioned for me to follow him.

"Quickly, quickly. We don't have a lot of time." Grabbing my arm, he dragged me from my small room and to the door of the lab. I don't know how he managed it, but I wasn't going to complain. My body tingled with anticipation of seeing Eden. Dr. Hahn peered out of the lab door before tugging me down the hall. For a little man, he sure moved fast.

We passed multiple labs, all exactly the same as his. Everything was transparent, windows everywhere, so no one could hide what they were doing. The only difference was in each small room of the other labs there were people. Sick people. Weak and deteriorating. Growing up in the woods, everyone got sick at times. Simple colds and what Ellie and Old Bob called the flu, but we were never like this.

My eyes met a girl. Her face was so dark and sunken that I almost thought she was dead, but the slight flick of her finger toward me told me she wasn't. Her attempt to wave. Everything around me darkened except the face of that innocent, sick child. She couldn't be more than fifteen. Dr. Hahn's yank of my arm broke my contact with her.

"Come, come. No time. No time."

I glanced back at the girl, but her eyes were closed, and I prayed that she was asleep and not dead.

My stomach tightened at the thought of Eden in that state. What was I walking into? If she looked like that, I don't think I would be able to control myself.

"What do these people have?" I asked.

Dr. Hahn glanced to the side as he scuttled forward. "The virus."

"But I thought there was no virus in the city. That's why there are the walls." He didn't respond, so I grabbed his shoulder and flipped him around. "Dr. Hahn. How did these people get the virus?"

His eyes focused on his shuffling feet. "This is a research facility. There is no virus outside, only in here."

"Right but... why would they come here?"

He looked at me and the regret that poured out of his eyes was so immense I don't know how I missed it before. It wasn't something he could just hide. "In the city... we have no jails. No homeless. No orphans. We have to use our resources carefully in order to survive."

I turned back to look at the door where the sick girl was. "So, you're saying, that girl"—I pointed toward her—"she is an orphan? So, you just infected her?"

He looked where I was pointing. "No. No. That's 56342. She was a thief."

I leaned over and rested my hands on my knees, realizing this was what Old Bob and Ellie were trying to protect us from. If we hadn't got out during the bombing, I might have ended up just like that girl. My stomach heaved, and I had to focus not to lose my lunch. "Do you know her name?"

He shook his head. "No. Once they are here, they are only numbers. It helps with... the job." He could see the disgust on my face, so he tried to add more to justify his actions. He needed to, so he could live with himself. "We don't just infect. We try to find a cure. That's why Eden is so important. She's the key."

I looked up at him and stood. "Take me to her."

Chapter 50

Jace

I looked toward the door and growled as I watched the pretty boy enter the lab. "Tristan."

Tristan's already fair skin was as white as a sheet and his blue eyes sparkled with fear as he watched Eden sleep. He hadn't noticed me, so I stood and crutched over to the window.

"Tristan!" I yelled, banging the glass.

He turned to me, licking the lips of his gaped mouth. It took a minute for his brain to register who I was, but when he did, he worked to change his face from fear to annoyance.

"Jace." He took a few steps toward my door.

Changing to a more comfortable position on the crutches, I looked past him to LaRae and pointed pleadingly at the door lock.

She looked toward the doctor who had helped Eden when she was sick, Dr. Hahn, with hesitation, but finally moved to Tristan's side and unlocked the door. "You can't leave your room. But you can talk from there with the door open."

I nodded.

"What are you doing here? I thought you were dead," I asked him, leaning on the doorframe. It was much more comfortable than leaning on the crutches. My armpits were getting bruised from the hard rubber on the metal.

"Dead? Yeah, I guess I thought that too." He glanced back to Eden. "I came to see Eden. Zane told me what they were doing to her." He turned back to me. "I had to beg, but Dr. Hahn finally got me to come see her."

I watched him for a moment. Something was different, but I couldn't quite pin what it was. He looked at Eden with the same love in his eyes, but there was something else there. Fear? Regret?

"Zane?" I asked.

"Yeah. He's ruthless, isn't he?"

"Isn't that the truth." We watched each other a moment in a silent conversation. We both had the same objective. Get Eden out. "She will be happy to see you. We were told you were dead."

"Who said that?"

"Who do you think?"

He looked back at Eden, ignoring my question. "Is she... all right?"

I followed his gaze to her sleeping back. "She's alive, but she's... struggling."

"Struggling?"

"Don't be upset if she doesn't recognize you right away. It's hard for her. Just know..." I looked at the desperation in his face, and I sighed. "Just know that she was really torn up when she thought you died. So, if she doesn't seem like it now, she does care about you." He nodded, then looked back at her. I could see the anticipation as he rubbed his fingers together. "Go. Go to the glass."

He took hesitant steps toward her cage, craning his neck as he tried to get a good look at her. I moved to the window that faced Eden to watch while LaRae quickly locked my door.

Eden?

Her back stirred and she slowly turned toward the glass. When she spotted Tristan, she sat up and set her feet on the ground. She looked past him to me before standing.

It's all right. He wanted to make sure you were OK.

She slowly made her way to the window where Tristan stood watching her. He put a hand on the glass and smiled. When she reached him, she looked to his hand then back to his face.

"Hey," he said quietly, but I knew she heard it.

She didn't respond but continued to scan him from top to bottom. I could feel her mind, a knotted bundle of memories, trying to untangle everything. This was why she was so on edge, constantly trying to remember who and what she knew.

"You look good," he said.

Her response was just to watch him. She tilted her head and examined every crevice in his body. They stood silently watching each other. I was impressed Tristan managed to keep his cool this long.

"Tristan, we must go. Go. Go. Now." Dr. Hahn looked nervously around to the neighboring labs and down the hallway.

Tristan rested his hand on the glass one last time and this time she met it. They stared at each other, their eyes linked and hands together.

"Bye," Tristan whispered, dropping his hand. He avoided my eyes as he walked back to Dr. Hahn, but I didn't miss the swipe of his finger catching the single tear on his cheek.

I looked over to Eden after they left. She was still at the glass looking after them but turned to me.

Who was that?

My heart sank for Tristan. She didn't remember him.

Tristan. He's your best friend.
Tristan?

She looked back at the door like she could still see him walking away, repeating his name in her mind. The knot was still there, but I started to see some unraveled strands. She calmly walked back to her cot and lay down with her back facing me. All I saw was the gold of her hair and the rising and falling of the blanket as her breathing steadied.

Yes. Yes. I think I remember him.

I rested my forehead on the glass and watched her sleep.

Chapter 51

Eden

The burning itch moved through my body like a flowing river. All my twitches and stretches gave no relief, but I learned that sleeping is the best medicine. My sleep was deep and long with recollections of my life and everyone I loved stirring through my dreams, so real I felt I was reliving them. Sometimes I woke with the taste of a memory still on my tongue or the smell in my nose.

When Tristan came to visit, a haze moved around him that blocked any recollection of him, but my mind worked to weave the haze back into the lines of thought. My mind was always working to put back the fractures of my past life into my new self.

I pulled all my furniture into the corner of my room next to my cot. Using my blankets, I created a safe den for myself. It was dark, cozy, and safe. I rarely left it now since all the humans want to do is stick me with needles and squeeze me. The den door faced Jace's cage, so I curled up in the corner to watch him and many times he was watching me.

Eden?

Jace's calm voice sang through my mind. For that second the burning in all my cells ceased. Closing my eyes, I breathed in the warm air of my den, content with my new self.

Yes?
What are you doing?

I spied him sitting on his chair as close to the window as possible, looking toward me. While looking at him, never letting my eyes leave his face, I crawled out of my den to the window and crouched. I broke eye contact with Jace and inspected what used to be my nails now much harder and pointier. The tips of my fingers had morphed into claws. Holding my hand up to show Jace, I expected to see disgust, but I saw guilt and regret.

Eden?
I have claws.

His forehead leaned on the window, watching me as I moved my fingers on the floor to hear the scratch on the tile. The burning tingle picked up, and I rolled my head and shoulders trying to tame it. It worked, for a moment. I went back to inspecting my new hands when Jace's voice rang through again, pulling my eyes toward him.

You all right?

I smiled and swung my hand out in front of me, pretending to scratch the glass.

They could be useful. I may not need my bow and arrow or dagger.

He smiled enough to show the dimple on his cheek, but his eyes didn't sparkle like they usually did.

What's wrong?
I'm so sorry, Eden.
For?

I cocked my head at him and he pursed his lips. He didn't respond, but I could feel it through the glass. He felt guilty that this was happening to me. He took responsibility for it.

Don't.

He raised his eyebrows and sat back.

Don't what?
Don't blame yourself. Don't feel guilty. I'm fine.

He leaned forward again and our eyes met. Locking gazes, we sat and watched each other for a long time. In his eyes there were a million unsaid words. Words I hoped that he would tell me someday.

I will. I promise.

I smiled before crawling back to my den, the only sound was the clicking of my claws on the floor.

Chapter 52

Jace

"GET OUT!!!" Eden's snarling growl blew me off my cot. I stood up so fast I forgot to grab my crutches, so I stumbled as quickly as I could to the window.

Eden was half out of her den, snarling and yelling at LaRae and another man who had entered her room. They wore masks, gloves, and padding under their lab coats, and of course, they carried tranquilizer guns.

"Leave her alone!" I bellowed and banged on the glass. Not even turning toward me at all, they continued toward her.

Eden panted furiously, baring her teeth. The claws were not the only new part of her, she now had longer canines. Her eyes held a combination of anger and fear, but I knew the anger would take over if she was pushed too far. I ground my teeth and pulled in a deep long breath as her fear and anxiety passed to me. Watching her body, my panting matched hers, and I let out a roar.

I banged on the glass again. "Just leave her be!" David moved to my glass, trying to grab my attention, but I ignored him.

I fell back when a thick rush of aggression hit me, and she flew from her den at the unknown man. Falling to my knees, I screamed, but all I could do was watch. Her claws were out and she swung but missed. I thought for sure she would be sedated. But instead of putting his gun up to sedate her, he gave her face a hard, backhand slap.

My vision turned red watching her hand move to her cheek. My body was tense and I panted through clenched teeth, turning my focus to the man who put his filthy hands on her.

"Jace," David warned, but I ignored him.

Fisting my hands, I punched the glass hard. Then I punched again and again until I heard it crack. My bruised knuckles were numb from pain, but I continued to punch it and the crack grew.

"Jace!" David moved to block my view, but my only focus was to protect Eden. I watched her face them with curled tight hands. She was getting ready to thrash out.

My knuckles split open and blood splashed onto the glass, but I didn't stop. I would never stop. I punched the cracked, blood-splattered glass until it shattered.

"Jace! No!" David yelled, diving to the side to protect himself from broken glass exploding out into the lab.

I charged out, injured leg or not, I was getting to Eden. The palms of my hands sliced open by the shattered glass as I crawled through it toward her. I pulled myself to stand on the corner of her room and hopped to her door, using the wall to keep me upright.

"Don't. You. Touch. Her." I looked directly into the man's eyes.

"There's another one?" he asked, nervously looking quickly to LaRae then back at me. He positioned himself with his back to the wall, so neither Eden nor I was at his back. Clutching his gun, he looked between Eden and me.

LaRae moved toward me slowly. "Jace. It's OK. We're not going to hurt her."

"He *hit* her."

Eden's panting slowed and she crouched, ready to fight if needed. I looked directly at her and held out my hand. "Eden... come here."

"Jace." David's warning came from behind me. He had moved closer but was clearly disheveled from dodging glass, and from the smell of blood, I didn't think his attempt was successful.

"No. I'm taking her and we are getting out. Now."

Eden stood and tilted her head at me. "Jace?"

Letting out a small relieved laugh, I said, "Yeah. It's me, Jace. Come on, let's get out of here." I continued to hold out my hand to her.

She took a step toward me, then looked over my shoulder. Her snarl startled me, and I dropped my hand just when the familiar sting of a tranquilizer dart hit my neck. Zane stood near the door, gun in hand.

"Too bad, Jace. Now I have to put you somewhere else. Somewhere away from Eden." Zane's words were like ice in my veins.

"Jace!" She growled and started toward me. I fell to my knees, watching her eyes move behind me, fixing on Zane, but he didn't move a muscle.

"Take her down," Zane said.

The man in Eden's cage pulled out his gun and shot Eden just as she reached me.

"No." I gasped, reaching out my fingers toward her.

The last thing I saw was Eden's beautiful face falling down next to mine.

Chapter 53

Eden

My eyes fluttered open to the blurry view out the window of my cage from the floor. My heart picked up a few beats as I watched two men drag Jace's limp body away. A growl grew from deep within my chest and my vision darkened, forming a silhouette around Jace's unconscious body. All I saw was him, and all I felt was rage.

The stinging prick in my arm turned the growl to a roar, and I flew up slapping away the needle. The man and LaRae both fell back, dropping their tools on the ground. Their eyes wide with fear, watching me slowly move to a crouch and face them.

"She's awake already?" the man said.

"Her metabolism must be much faster than we expected."

As they scooted toward the door, I looked back at Jace's body, now being pulled down the hallway. I looked at LaRae. "Don't let them take him." My voice edged on the brink of desperation.

She looked at me with helpless eyes. "I'm so sorry. I don't know if there is anything I can do."

The further away Jace got, the less in control I felt. The burning tingle that filled every cell in my body ramped up, and no matter how much I moved or focused, it didn't die down. I roared, partly due to the burning itch rolling through my body and partly from being ripped away from my anchor. Jace kept me grounded. I couldn't handle this change without him. My eyes moved between theirs as I scooted back to the door of my den, showing the tip of my fangs. My cheek still had the faint sting from the man's slap, and I fought the urge to put my hand to it.

"Eden?" LaRae asked.

"Get out."

The man, still hesitating near the door, said, "Just let us get some blood and vitals, and we will."

LaRae raised her hand to quiet him. "Just leave her be."

"What? This is crazy. How am I supposed to help you when you don't do what you're supposed to do? Just tranquilize her again, and we can get this over with!"

I snapped my eyes to him, stood, and slowly took a step forward. My hands instinctively curled, readying my claws. If he planned to shoot me again, I would attack. This time I wouldn't miss my mark.

Zane stepped into the doorway, pulling my focus to him.

"He's right," Zane said smoothly. "Oh, Eden… I have a friend here to see you, but if you don't listen, then he may have to leave… forever."

I tilted my head and grimaced at his condescending words. Dropping my eyes to his neck, I imagined what it would feel like to sink my fangs into his flesh. The taste of his blood I'm sure would be bitter, but worth it to watch the life escape his eyes.

"Eden, you need to cooperate," Zane said.

"Eden, can... I..." LaRae started.

"Only her." I nodded toward her and took a step back to my den. "I'll attack anyone else."

The strange man hissed and was about to ignore my threat, but I lunged forward with a snarl, snapping my teeth. The pop of them connecting echoed along the glass walls of my cage. He stepped back quickly, bumping into an annoyed Zane.

"Very well, LaRae, do your work." Zane pushed the man out of my cage.

I sat in the chair and focused on fighting my instinct to flinch away and retreat into myself. LaRae moved slowly and confidently, careful not to startle me. I was impressed she didn't flinch away from my claws as she prepared my arm for the blood draw.

"Where will they take him?" I whispered so no one heard.

LaRae didn't look up from her work. "I don't know, but I'll try and find out."

"Do you think Jace is serious?"

This time she did glance up at me, quickly, but not enough to cause notice from the others in the lab. "Serious? About what?"

"About getting me out."

She didn't respond right away but continued to work. When she finished collecting my blood, I immediately pulled my arm toward myself to smell and lick the wound but stopped when I felt eyes watching me. Zane's face was impassive as always, but David and the man showed... repulsion. Humiliation filled me, and I looked away. Sucking in a deep breath, I concentrated on replacing the humiliation with rage. Why should I be humiliated? They *made* me.

LaRae finished in silence, but as she wrote her notes, she whispered, keeping her eyes still on her paper. "He loves you. I think he'll do anything he can to keep you safe."

I watched her pack up her things while her words registered in my mind. *He loves you.* The others waited in the lab where Zane looked pleased that he got what he wanted.

"Will you help him?" I asked quickly before she left.

LaRae stopped, pretending to look in her bag for something when she whispered, "I'm beginning to think there isn't any other way."

Then she was gone and everyone was flaunting over the information she had written down. Exhausted, I retreated to the safety of my den to think about the boy who loves me.

Chapter 54

Tristan

Using the metal shelf that's bolted into the stone part of the wall, I pulled myself up repeatedly. My arms burned with fatigue, but I pushed them. Physical activity was all I had sitting here alone, the only person to talk to being Dr. Hahn. My grunts reverberated on the walls and the smell of my sweat filled my nose. Squeezing my eyes shut, I tried to rid the vision of Eden's eyes as she watched me from behind the glass. She was barely there. Jace had warned me, but I didn't expect to see her like an... animal.

I dropped down and quickly moved to my back and worked my abs. As I sat up and touched my elbows to my knees, I watched Dr. Hahn read his papers, writing furiously. That's all I ever saw him do when he was here. What was he working on?

When my abs burned and I couldn't breathe, I let myself lie on the cool tile floor. Spreading my hands and legs out, I stared up at the crisp bright ceiling. Jace was there with her. The thought was oddly reassuring, but I couldn't help the twinge of jealousy. I wanted to be the one that she leaned on. Growing up, it was always a split between Tate and me for who she ran to when she needed to talk. My arms were always open.

I shut my eyes and let out a long breath before heaving myself up to rinse off in the small corner shower. I was over six feet, so it was a tight fit, but it worked. I kept the water cool and let it stream over my body as memories of the night before I was shot came to me. We huddled in the pouring rain; Eden's face was tucked into my chest as I held my pack over our heads. I could smell the rose-scented soap in her hair and the electric shock from her hand on my stomach. But to her, I'm her brother. I yelled and punched the metal wall of the shower, and the loud reverberating clank hurt my ears. Leaning on the side with my head down, I let the water wash over me, trying to let the jealousy disappear down the drain.

"Tristan?" Dr. Hahn said from the doorway.

"I'm fine." I swiped a hand over the puffed pink scar of the gunshot on my stomach before turning off the water and stepping out with a towel around my waist. My stomach clenched when I met the hollow grey eyes of Zane.

"What do you want?" I pulled on a clean shirt.

"Oh, I just wanted to check in." He kept his hands clasped behind his back as he watched me.

"I'm fine." I pulled up some pants and hung the towel on the hook by the shower.

"I heard you went on a little trip yesterday."

I didn't take my eyes from him, but from my peripheral vision, I saw Dr. Hahn's nervous twitching. "So?"

"So? How did she seem?"

I fisted my hand to keep it from connecting with his jaw. His shallowness was infuriating. "Distant."

"Distant?"

"Yeah. She didn't even talk to me. If you knew her like I do, the girl doesn't shut up. Especially when she hasn't seen me in a while."

He smiled. "Must be hard knowing Jace is there with her and not you."

I pursed my lips and looked at my feet.

"I can change that, though."

"What?" My eyes snapped to his and a smile snaked across his face.

"I can put you where Jace is."

A flutter of triumph hit my chest, and I wanted to jump up and down. I could be the one for her to go to, not Jace. That's how it should be, but... "What's the catch?"

"Catch? No catch really, but if you could maybe try and get her to tell us how she made Jace. That would be helpful."

There it was. She wasn't cooperating, so they needed me to get her to. "What happened to Jace?"

"He became... a liability. I had to move him."

"So, he's alive."

He widened his eyes. "Of course, he's alive. What kind of man do you think I am?"

"Do you really want me to answer that?"

He gave me a knowing smile. "No. I suppose I don't. So. Do we have a deal?"

If Jace couldn't get her to, I don't know how much I could, but just the opportunity to see her daily was enough for me. "I can't promise anything."

"No, no. Of course not. Just do your best."

"Ok. Deal."

"Good! I'll make it happen today." Without hesitation, he pivoted and walked out of my room, and before I could blink, he was moving down the hallway.

I fisted my hands again, but this time, it was because I was giving myself a silent cheer instead of wanting to punch Zane's face.

Chapter 55

Jace

Groaning, I woke to cold, damp concrete on my cheek. I pushed myself up and winced at the new pain on my hands, now bruised and covered in dried blood. Blinking through blurry eyes, I examined my new surroundings. I was in a new cage, only this one wasn't as nice. There were no windows, only metal bars. It was an old prison cell. Since there were no longer prisons, they moved some to the basement of the labs many years ago for the more difficult subjects.

"Where am I?" My voice was dry and raspy.

"Oh, thank goodness. You're OK." David shuffled over to the bars, looking in at me. The bags under his eyes aged him, and I fought the urge to hug him.

"Why are you here?" I grumbled, sliding myself over to the small metal cot in the corner. Where were my crutches?

"I needed to make sure you're OK. You are my son."

I pulled myself onto the cot. "I'm not your son." My words clipped out through painful grunts.

"Whatever you may think, I still think of you as my son. I love you."

Too tired to argue, I rolled my eyes.

"Dr. Andrews," a man said as he moved to David's side, brushing his messy white hair from his eyes.

"Yes?" David responded.

The man cleared his throat nervously. "You wanted me to let you know when Zane was on his way."

David pushed back from the bars. "Yes. Of course. How much time?"

"Five minutes."

"Thank you, Dr. Hahn."

I jerked my head up at the name to get a better look at the man. It was the same wild-haired doctor that had helped Eden. Noticing my eyes on him, he smiled.

"Hello, hello, Jace. I'm—"

"Dr. Hahn."

He smiled broadly. "Yes."

David sighed loudly. "Well, I better be off before Zane gets here, but please, do me a favor." He paused, watching me. "Don't upset Zane. Right now, he's letting you live, so don't do anything to change that decision... all right?"

"Letting me live? You call this living?" I motioned my hands around the dark, damp cell. "It's the basement. I'll probably get bitten by mice in my sleep and die from infection. This isn't living."

David fisted his hands. "It's the best I could do! I have to go. Just please, I beg you. Don't piss him off, Jace."

I didn't respond as he left the room; his footsteps echoed against the stone walls. I looked back at Dr. Hahn. "You work in this room?"

He let out a nervous laugh. "No, no, but I have been assigned to you, so I'll come daily to check on you."

"Great."

Not only did he move me to the cells in the basement, but he was leaving me here alone most of the time. I let out a loud echoing snarl of frustration, startling Dr. Hahn into dropping his pen and paper. Smiling with satisfaction, I sat back and waited for Zane to arrive.

∽

I heard the footsteps before his slimy smile showed itself. I wanted to scratch it right off his face, but David's words repeated in my head. Don't upset Zane.

"Jace. How are the hands?" He stopped on the other side of the bars, giving my bruised bloody hands a quick look.

Unconsciously, I fisted them but winced at the pain. "Fine."

"Good. Now, your little... display earlier really had me thinking. You truly care for Eden, don't you?" He watched me, but I didn't respond. "I thought so. So, here's how it's going to be. You live down here, and if you're a good little boy, then you can see her. Now, if you begin to be more trouble. . . well then, you can't see her and who knows what else I'll have done to her."

I swallowed down the low rumbling growl threatening to burst from me as I stared into his dark hazel eyes

"What do you want with her?"

He smiled, "She's the key."

"The key?"

"Yes. The key. Once I figure out exactly how she created you, then I can make everyone immune and continue my mission to use the virus to control what's left of this burnt world."

I laughed. "You can't be serious." But watching his unchanging face, all smiles and determination, I widened my eyes. "You *are* serious. A plot to take over the world?"

"Of course, I am! After the war, our weak president wasn't strong enough to do what needed to be done. I had the virus created in order to help control the world, but there was a mishap." He paused, looking down at his unwrinkled hands.

"A mishap."

"Yes. Unfortunately, President Jacobs contracted a mysterious virus which spread quickly. A shame really."

"Yes. A shame," I said, watching Zane's cheek twitch.

I looked over at Dr. Hahn, who was trying to look busy with work, but I knew he was listening.

"Don't worry about him. He's been in on the plan this whole time, haven't you, Dr. Hahn." Zane didn't take his eyes from mine, but his voice pulled Dr. Hahn from his fake work.

"Yes." Dr. Hahn cleared his throat.

"Why are you telling me this?"

He gently picked at his jacket and said, "Oh I don't know, maybe just so I can see your reaction." I blinked, and he let out a loud laugh that crept up my spine. "Maybe so I can control you."

"Control me? And if I don't care what you do to me?"

"Well, I still have people you *love* under my thumb, now don't I? And I'm not just talking about Eden. Think of your father. It would be a shame if anything happened to him after everything he has done to keep you alive."

I pursed my lips. My hate for him boiled my blood, but right now I had to play by his game. "So, you created the virus. Everything that has happened, all the people that have died is because of *you*." He watched me with a look of satisfaction that chilled my bones. "How do you expect to travel to the rest of the remaining world? It's not easy these days."

"No. You're right, but I'll cross that bridge when I get to it, plus, I can't be giving away all my secrets now can I?" Zane gave me a satisfied look before he walked away. "Remember, Jace. Be a good boy!"

This time I didn't resist the growl from emerging, and I let it fill the room. Zane's laugh echoed after him until the sound of his footsteps disappeared. My head was dizzy, so I rested my forehead in my hands. Dropping to the ground, I pulled myself over to the small toilet, dragging my injured leg behind me, and vomited. The virus was man-made. Zane did all this in a crazy plot to take over the world. Or what was left of it.

I sat back and wiped my mouth. I don't know what is more disturbing. That Zane made the world the way it is, or that he may not let me live to tell anyone about it.

Chapter 56

Eden

I watched men replace the glass wall of Jace's cage after they cleaned the old shattered glass from the floor. I waited hopeful and crouched in the corner for him to return, but he never did. Just before I was about to retire to my den for the night, I saw a flash of movement enter the lab. I focused on the door. Someone came through. A face with gold curls and baby blue eyes, the face from my knotted dreams. Tristan's smile was wide when he saw me. The man that has been helping LaRae shoved him through the door of the cage, and he stumbled forward. My hands fisted lightly at the aggressive act, my claws pinching into my palms, but I relaxed when I watched Tristan stand and move to the window. We watched each other a moment before he put his hand on the glass. The tangled thoughts of my memories started to unwind and flashes of our life hit me. Running through the trees, jumping in the lake, hunting, fishing, and my favorite, telling stories by the fire. Tears welled in my eyes, but I didn't let them slip. I set my hand on the glass for just a second before retreating to my den.

～

The days passed by me like a blur, and I rarely left my den. Tristan did nothing but workout and watch me. The man that was helping LaRae was now here permanently, sent by Zane. I learned his name. Scott. I despised him. I involuntarily growled whenever a whiff of his soapy scent filled me.

I missed Jace. He was my constant in all this craziness, but now that he was gone, I had less control over my human side. Seeing Tristan every day was nice, but it was not the same. I cared for Tristan, but I needed Jace. I wanted to let the animal inside me take over; it would be so much easier.

"Eden?" LaRae hesitated in my doorway. "May I come in?"

"Oh, for the love of... just go in!" Scott fidgeted impatiently.

"Eden? Please respond."

Peeking my head out of my den, I gave her a small nod. When Scott started to follow, I snarled and lunged toward him.

"Just wait there," LaRae said forcefully, stopping him.

"Wait, you're listening to her? She's a prisoner!" He stomped his foot like a child and LaRae whipped around to face him.

"She is a patient, not a prisoner. You need to learn better interaction skills. You can't treat everyone like they are nothing but... but useless animals."

"Have you looked at her?" He motioned an open hand toward me. "She is an animal!"

I crawled out of my den and instantly relished the lack of fire that once inhabited my body. It was gone and replaced with something new. Confidence, loyalty, and indifference. I stood behind LaRae.

"What do animals do to their prey?" I asked him calmly, narrowing my eyes like he was a piece of juicy meat. I took a step toward him, passing LaRae, and I finally saw a flicker of fear pass over his face.

"What?"

"I said"—I paused dramatically—"what do animals do to their prey?" I was only ten feet from him now, and I could smell his anxiety.

"Eden," LaRae warned.

He licked his lips letting out a quick, quiet laugh trying to figure out if I'm serious or joking. "They... they kill them."

I smiled slowly, making sure to show my new elongated fangs, running my tongue along the new length of my canines. "Yes. You say I'm an animal. I say you're my prey. So, what do you think I'm going to do to you?"

He let out another nervous laugh. "What is this, LaRae? A joke?"

"Scott, I think you better leave," she said evenly. "I don't think Eden is joking."

He jolted his eyes from her to me, taking another step back. "If you hurt me..."

"What?" I crooned. "What will you do to me that you haven't already done?" I took another step toward him, holding out my hands to show him my thick sharp nails. "You have captured me, infected me with the virus over and over, taken the man I care for, and made me... this." I held out my arms and turned in a slow circle. I spotted Tristan, watching us with squinted eyes. I forgot his human ears wouldn't be able to make out our conversation. Probably a good thing since I don't think he would like what I have become.

"Whatever. You're crazy. You deal with this." He looked to LaRae and quickly retreated, slamming the door in my face.

Pushing up against the glass, I trailed one claw down it as I smiled at him. He tried to show no fear, but his smell gave him away. He reeked from terrified sweat.

"Eden," LaRae said. "That's enough."

Still smiling, I turned back to her. "That was fun. Think he'll want to come back in here?" I walked over to the chair.

She chuckled. "Knowing him? Probably." She took my vitals.

I turned back to watch Scott as I sat at the table. He was noticeably still shaken up and very angry. "Good. I can't wait to do that again."

⁂

"Infect her again!" Zane slammed his fist on the table, causing the half-full cup of water to splash to the floor.

"Yes sir, but—" LaRae shrank back as Zane towered over her. "Yes, sir." She bowed her head.

Zane leaned forward, putting his mouth right next to her ear. "And if I hear that you refused my order, you will be waving to me from the other side of that glass, Dr. Rammell." Her face blanched, and I growled at the scent of her fear.

With my eyes fixed on Zane, I slowly emerged from my den and crawled to the corner of the glass. Crouching, I inspected Tristan's cage first where he leaned on the window watching the show before I moved my gaze over to the others. Scott nervously tapped Zane's shoulder, motioning toward me.

"Sir, she's out."

Zane turned to me and his smile grew wide. "Oh, my. She's magnificent." He walked toward me slowly, and I cocked my head, gauging every step he made. "Beautiful! I think her eye sparkles even more gold. And are those... claws?" He looked down at my hands.

"She has fangs too."

"Fangs!" He smiled back at Scott before turning back to me.

I stood when he reached me, only the glass separated us, but I still sniffed the air to catch his scent. He's tall, but I know I'm faster, stronger, and smarter. Giving him a look from his head to his feet, I smiled. "You're weak."

He clapped with a bark of laughter. "She can still talk!"

"Of course, she can still talk, sir... that's not what I'm worried about." LaRae stepped to his side.

"What are you worried about then? She's perfect."

"Yes, she's healthy and strong and can talk, but she's... she's—"

"She's what?" Zane encouraged impatiently. I watched LaRae, curious how she would describe me, but it was Scott that spoke.

"Dangerous."

"I want her dangerous." Zane turned back to me and his smile grew.

"Unpredictable," LaRae finally said. "When she was first infected, everything happened as it usually does, then she was infected again, and it was less typical and her reaction changed her. She's less human now than she was before. The virus is making her more of an"—she gave me a quick, apologetic look—"animal."

I kept my gaze on Zane, inspecting him, memorizing his movements and every little wrinkle on his face. LaRae's words didn't anger me because they were true.

Zane met my eyes. "That's exactly how I want her to be."

"Right, sir, but she won't be controlled! She's still a person. A person with free will."

Zane's smile dropped and he narrowed in on LaRae. "You don't need to worry about the control. I'll deal with that."

"I don't understand what this has to do with finding a cure." LaRae wrung her hands together, but she wasn't backing down. Her strength was building, and I liked it.

"I want to know if she can withstand multiple doses of the virus. I also need to confirm what she gave Jace. Something doesn't add up."

"But, sir, Dr. Hahn—"

"I know what Dr. Hahn gave her! Animal blood!"

I tilted my head, watching Zane carefully as LaRae froze in shock.

"What?" she said. Zane rose a single eyebrow at her. "You mean... you know?"

"Of course, I know!"

"Then, what's the point of all this? I mean... you know the cure." LaRae took a step back, sucking in a breath. "All those people, their lives. How could you just let them all die?"

My laugh brought all their eyes to me.

"Is something funny?" Zane asked.

"If you already know that, then what do you think I did to Jace?"

"Animal blood?" Scott answered with an unsure tone.

I clapped slow and loud. "I wasn't sure your inferior human brains could figure that out." I hopped off the table and walked back to the glass. "All I did was give Jace animal blood. It's that simple."

Zane examined my face. "Is that so?" I nodded. "We will have to see about that."

They all jumped back when I let out a screeching roar, and I smiled as I moved my claws to the glass, clicking them at Zane. "Good luck with that."

"With what?" Zane asked me curiously.

"Well, using your human brain to control me." After seeing a flicker of uncertainty float through his eyes, I sauntered back to my den.

Chapter 57

Jace

"How are they feeling?" Dr. Hahn examined my hands, dabbing the cuts with a wet cloth. I gritted my teeth at the stinging ache of his touch. Every time I looked at them, they reminded me of how I didn't save Eden, so a little pain was good. I tried opening and fisting them and hissed.

"Better."

"It will take a little more time, more time. But I think you'll have a full recovery. Yup, a full one." He stood with his bag of items, opening the rolling bar door. "You haven't asked me any questions." He watched me as the door clicked back into place, separating us.

"Would you answer?"

He gave me the same steady incorrigible smile. "You never know."

"All right. How is she?"

"She's fine."

"Just fine?"

He shrugged. "Well as fine as she's going to be. She's alive, very alive."

Memories of Eden building her den and scurrying around like a scared rabbit have consumed me over the past few days. The ache in my heart to see her was always there, a persistent annoyance that wouldn't go away until we were near each other. I moved to the bars. "What's that mean? How is her..." – I searched for the word – "demeanor?"

Dr. Hahn set his bag on the table and turned to me. "Well, when you last saw her, she was what?"

"Scared, you could say. Scared of what was happening to her but also scared of others. Always ready for an attack."

He nodded his head in thought. "Well, that has changed a bit. Yup, it's changed."

Furrowing my brow, I tried to grasp the bars, but the bandages on my hands inhibited it. "Changed how?"

"She's not scared anymore. She's much more aware. . . very, very aware. And... oh, how would I call it... feisty?" He smiled again.

"Feisty?" He nodded, but I shook my head unbelieving. "I have to see her. Please take me to her. Something's wrong. Did they infect her again? I'll rip their throats out if that man touches her again."

Dr. Hahn approached my cell calmly. "All right, all right, relax. You've been fine the past few days, so I see no reason you can't see her."

My breathing ceased and I studied him. "What's the catch?"

"No catch, no catch, just a reward for your good behavior." The lines deepened around his grey eyes as he smiled, but the way he moved his hand through the wild white mane of his, I knew he was hiding something.

"I don't trust you."

"Well, I guess I wouldn't either if I was you, but it's the only way you can see her." He paused. "Your Eden."

The words warmed my heart. *My* Eden. I missed her, needed to see her, but I know Zane.

"And you want nothing from me?"

"Well, I guess it's not *nothing*, but it's nothing big. No, no, nothing big."

I laughed. "I knew it. So, what is it?"

"You need to convince Eden to tell us the truth about what she did to you."

My head was shaking before he even finished his sentence. "No way in hell I'll do that."

"Jace, just listen to me. Listen." He clasped his hands in praying motion, pleading with me.

"No! Did you really think I would sell out that easy?" I leaned as far forward through the bars as I could.

"I created her." I stepped back at his words, speechless. He nodded. "When she was just a child, a baby. It was me." He pulled up a chair and sat down, clasping his hands in front of him. "I was good friends with her mother. Kim and I... well, we knew each other a long time, even before the Fever hit. When she said she and Dan were putting Eden in the trials, I thought she had lost her marbles. Yes, yes, I did. I pleaded with them, but they were insistent. Very insistent." He paused, taking a few breaths before continuing. "When they first infected her, she responded like everyone else. She got the Fever, cough, weakness, the works. I couldn't stand seeing an innocent child suffer, so I snuck in at night and did my own experiment."

I watched him as he confessed, tasting his words in the air. He was telling the truth. I stayed silent and listened.

"I had infected animals before and none showed any symptoms but their white cells increased to fight off the Fever, so I figured I would try and inject her with animal blood, just to see if that helped. Usually, animal blood in high doses can be fatal to a human, but I used a small amount, very small, just to see if anything happened. It was a shot in the dark really, yup, a shot in the dark. But... well it worked. Within twenty-four hours, she was better, much, much better. But there was one defining characteristic of my interference."

"Her eye," I whispered.

He nodded. "Her eye. Kim knew something had been done but couldn't figure it out. When I told her, she panicked. Yes, yes, she panicked. We drew Eden's blood, and it was noticeable what had happened. The mending of two DNAs."

"So why didn't you tell Zane then and be done with this whole charade?"

He sighed. "You've seen Zane. Heard his... plan. He's always had such determination. So much so that he caused many of us to fear him, still does, yes, still does. Kim was fearful that Eden would become... well, I guess like she is now, a lab rat." He wrung his hands nervously, causing his knuckles to go white.

"Do you know who helped Zane create the virus? I mean, couldn't they have some idea how to cure it?" I watched his cheeks grow red, and he kept his eyes on the floor. "You. It was you!"

"And Kim." His words were so quiet a human wouldn't have heard him. "That's why she was so insistent on putting Eden in the trials. She wanted to try and fix things."

"Why not Tate?" I asked without thinking of the repercussions. They thought Tate was dead.

"You know Tate?"

"Of him." I coughed. "Eden mentioned him to me before." His eyes watched me a moment before accepting my answer.

"Tate was too old, yes too old. Nearly five. He wouldn't have understood since he couldn't go home at night. A baby was much easier, yes much easier."

I closed my eyes. This information will break her, break Tate as well. I hated having information that I couldn't let her know. I didn't want secrets from her, but I didn't have much of a choice at this point.

"You never tried to do it again? After Eden?"

"Oh, I did. Two men."

I startled. Hopefully, he didn't catch my reaction to that news.

Without looking at me, he continued. "They survived like Eden, but disappeared in the bombing along with Eden's parents, along with fifty or so citizens. I have tried after that, but none have turned out the same. No, no, never the same. I'm not sure why my new subjects are different. They are alive, but... not like you or Eden. No, no, not like you. They are savages. Very, very, savage."

Memories of the feral, grey-skinned scourges made my skin crawl. "What do you mean you still make them?"

"Look, Jace, you have to understand that everything I have done, I have done since my mistake of creating that wretched virus, is with the human race's best interest involved. Yes, yes, the best interest."

I stood and growled. "Just answer the question, Dr. Hahn!"

"After Eden... disappeared, Zane was obsessed with replicating her outcome. First, we used the orphans of all the people killed in the bombing, now... he uses delinquents or orphans if there are any, homeless, or people who break the law."

Memories of the night I broke into the labs to rescue my friend's sister hit me. Kids in cages, needles in their arms. I let out a snarl and Dr. Hahn flinched.

"Where are they now?" My voice echoed against the stone walls. "Are they dead?"

"No, no, they are... " He was shaking, from fear or regret I don't know, but he took a moment to gather himself before continuing. "They are in the woods. In the woods."

My stomach almost dropped out of me. "Scourges."

"I'm sorry?"

Limping to the bars, I leaned on them. "Scourges. It's what we named the creatures. I believe they are the creatures you created. Grey skin, one gold eye, wild, and violent."

Blood drained from his cheeks, and he swallowed hard. "You mean they survived?"

"Of course, they survived! What did you think, they would just lie down and die?"

He shook his head and stood. "I don't know... I don't know..." He pushed both hands through his white hair making it messier than usual. "I guess I didn't really think about what would happen to them, but I didn't think they would survive long. No, not survive."

I let out a derisive laugh. "Oh, well, they sure did. I'm sure Zane will be happy to know he has a little army of wild scourge children in the woods."

He looked at me again, dropping his hands. "Zane doesn't know."

"I'm sorry, what?"

"When they didn't turn out like Eden, he told me to... dispose of them, but... but I couldn't. I couldn't after everything we've done. Not in good conscience. How could I just kill children? No, no, no killing children." Tears welled in his eyes, and I watched him, wondering if he had children that he lost.

"Oh, that's perfect." I limped back to my chair and sat. "Just perfect." We sat silent for a moment before I asked him quietly. "Why are you telling me all this?"

Leaning forward, he rested his elbows on his knees and said, "Because there is so much you don't know. You think you do, but you don't, you don't.'"

I shook my head. "No, I may not know everything, but I do know that Zane is a psychopath, and I'll kill him for what he's done." I paused, examining him before continuing. "And you? Well, you may think you were doing what you thought was right, but you still made many... sketchy choices that have killed a lot of people, and still do."

"I did it for—"

"I know what you say you did it for, but if you want me to trust you, this probably wasn't the best story to tell me." My head spun with all the information he just gave me. He stood to leave, his face dropped and his lips were moving like he was talking to himself, but I heard nothing. He was almost out the door when I called to him. "Just tell me one more thing. Does my father, David, does he know all this?"

Dr. Hahn didn't say anything, but the distinct single nod pumped so much blood to my head I felt it may explode.

"Of course, he does," I said quietly before letting out a snarl, sending Dr. Hahn scurrying away.

Chapter 58

Tristan

I don't know what's worse, not being able to go talk to Eden or not being able to hear all the conversations that involved her. All I heard in my small room was the hum of the lights above. Eden was different, very different. She spent most of her days in her makeshift den but came out a few times to stretch and eat. Every now and then, I got her to look over at me, but it wasn't the same. She didn't have that sweet, fun sparkle she had growing up. The hole in my heart from Ellie's death was starting to rip larger at the thought that I would never be able to spend time with the Eden I knew and loved.

Eden hadn't left her den yet today, and I ached to see her. After my morning workout, LaRae arrived with Eden's plate of food. Before she passed my room, I knocked on the window and motioned for her to come to me. She looked over at Eden's cage where Eden's head poked out from her den watching her plate of food, before quickly coming to my door.

She typed in the code and unlocked the door. "What?"

"Let me bring it to her."

"What? That's not a good idea."

"No. It will be fine. She won't hurt me." I shrugged off her concern.

We both turned at the knocking from Eden's window. She was crouched as she watched us. Looking at LaRae, she gave her a small nod. Could she hear us?

"All right then. Come on. But no talk of this to anyone."

I nodded and followed her to Eden's door. She handed me the plate of sausage and maple syrup; the smell filled my nose and my stomach growled. Scott was in charge of my meals, but he was always conveniently late.

"There you go." She opened the door, moving to the side to let me in. "Just know, I won't shoot her if you piss her off. You're on her turf now. Understand?"

"Understood." I passed her, stepping into Eden's room, facing her. She stood only feet from me as the door clicked behind me.

She grabbed the plate of food and started shoving sausages into her mouth. My stomach growled again, and she paused, giving me a quick side glance, but instead of offering me one, she crouched and curled over her plate, finishing it all off. That's not Eden; Ellie always taught us to be generous.

When all the sausage was gone, she slid her fingers through the remaining syrup and licked them. She didn't look up at me until her plate looked as if there was no food on it, and she slid it across the floor toward the door. It just missed the side of my foot where I stood and waited. Our eyes met, and she didn't smile the way she used to when she saw me. She just turned and retreated to her den. I hesitated until she poked her head out and looked at me. "Well, come on then."

Shaking my head, I pulled in a deep breath, dropped to my knees, and entered her den. I blinked quickly until my eyes adjusted to the darkness. She was scooted all the way back to the far corner, a pillow at her back and a blanket crumpled around her. I moved to sit next to her with my back against the metal wall. No one spoke as she ran her eyes over my face, up into my hair, then down over my body. My throat restricted at the undivided attention, unsure of what she wanted.

"How are you?" she finally asked.

"Good." I cleared my throat. "Good."

She smiled and reached one of her claws out, gently trailing it along my arm. I shivered and pulled it from her reach, and she giggled.

"Scared?"

"No." It was the truth. I wasn't scared of her, but a little... unnerved maybe. I had seen her claws from a distance, but to see them up close was hard. Her hands once delicate were now... well, I don't know how to describe them, but they definitely weren't delicate anymore.

"Do you remember the last night we had at the cabin before... all this happened?" she asked.

I nodded, smiling at the card game Tate and I played, betting blueberries, then fighting with them. Eden and Ellie in their usual position on the couch, chatting quietly as Ellie brushed Eden's thick, long hair, the apricot gold shining in the firelight.

"I miss her."

I looked over at her at the sadness in her voice to see her holding the small silver butterfly necklace Ellie had given her. She had never taken it off. Maybe there was some of the old Eden in there still. "Me too." My throat was full and I swallowed down the lump.

"Do you think they will come for us?"

"No." She didn't seem surprised by my words. "I think they know it's too risky. If we are going to get out, we have to do it from in here."

She moved her hand and rested it on my shoulder, taking one of my blond curls on her finger and twirled it. "I miss him."

Any other person would think she was talking about Tate or maybe even Old Bob, but I knew she was thinking of Ash. "I'm sure he misses you too."

She smiled, lost in the memory of her and her furry friend as she moved her claws through my curls. A tingle moved throughout my body, and I rubbed my head along my shoulders. She gave me a knowing smile.

"I miss Jace." My stomach dropped at the name, and I ground my teeth. "I know you don't like him, but he's not a bad guy. He cares for me and has taken care of me."

"I should have been the one to do that."

Dropping her hand, she tilted her head, leaning forward. "You had your time, Tristan. Growing up you were always there. More than Tate even. If I got hurt, you came running. When I was mad, you were the one to talk reason into me. I love you for that, but... it's Jace's time now."

"What happened to him?"

She sat back. "He became too much for them to handle, so they moved him."

"Too much to handle? What did he do?"

"Broke through the glass to get to me."

I blinked at her passive face. "He broke through the glass." She nodded. "Can you... break through the glass?" She nodded again and I leaned forward. "Then why haven't you? We can get out of here!"

She smiled. "It's not that easy."

"What?"

"I can't just leave all these humans. They are weak. They need me."

Staring at her, I laughed. "You can't be serious." She just smiled back at me, never leaving my eyes. "Eden. Look what they did to you! They do this to innocent people, but those people aren't as lucky as you; they don't survive. None of them do."

"And that is why I can't leave. They need me to help them. Plus, I won't leave without Jace."

"Jace." I hissed out his name and set my head against the wall.

I felt her eyes roaming my face. "It almost broke me when I thought you were dead, but he kept me here. He always brought me back from my grief. And whatever they did to me... whatever this is. It's saved me. I'm better than I was before. Surer of myself."

"You would have become this way with age, Eden."

"Maybe. But that's not an option now, so we'll just have to deal with this." She reached her finger out and started playing with my curls again. "I love you, Tristan. I always have and always will, but as a... brother."

When she used that word, the pain wasn't there like it had been the first time. I don't know if it was the changes with her or maybe I have just come to terms with the idea. "I will always love you too. I will always try and protect you."

Her laugh reminded me of a cat we found as kids. We called him Mr. Tickler because his whiskers would tickle us when he rubbed on our legs. "I have a feeling I will be the one to protect you from now on."

I smiled. "Maybe." We sat in silence and I remembered Dr. Hahn's request. "Eden, what did you do to Jace?"

Her hand pulled away so fast I felt some strands of hair pluck from my scalp. "So that's why you're here."

"No, but they just thought maybe you would tell me. It's important."

She moved her face closer to mine. All the playfulness and peace gone. "I have already told them what I did, but their human brains are keeping them from seeing logic."

"What? What did you tell them?"

"It doesn't matter. They aren't listening, so I'll just... wait until they do."

"Eden."

She stretched. "I'm very tired, Tristan. Maybe we can have this conversation another time?"

I watched her curl up in the rumpled blanket with her back to me. She was done and no matter how much I pushed she wouldn't talk. "Yeah. Sure." I crawled out of her den and to the door where LaRae waited nervously.

"I was getting nervous. You probably shouldn't have gone in there."

Ignoring her, I dragged my feet back to my room. The hole in my heart was officially larger, and I have never wished so hard in my life to be able to go back to a time where it was whole.

Chapter 59

Eden

I was just finishing my morning stretches when Scott barged through the door of the lab bringing the smell of bacon and coffee with him. LaRae hadn't been in to give me breakfast yet, so my belly growled, and I licked my lips in anticipation of what it may be. I told her no more oatmeal, that I needed meat. Beef or pork, I didn't care, but no more of the bland grains. She had been bringing me sausages with maple syrup lately, and it was divine.

"Let's go, Eden!" Scott rapped on the glass door. "Zane wants you in the gym pronto."

Defiantly, I sat and slowly turned my gaze to him. "I haven't eaten yet."

"You can eat after. Come on, walk to the door." He held up a pair of metal cuffs, and I cocked my head.

"What do you expect to do with those?"

"Put them on you. What else?" He smirked.

Blinking at him, I rose fluidly. "Not a chance. I think I'll go back to bed. Let me know when LaRae shows up with my food." I walked to the entrance of my den when Scott rapped on the door again.

"If you go in there, I'll shoot you." He dangled the tranquilizer gun in front of the door.

I groaned inwardly at the familiar sight. After Jace's show and my previous outbursts, everyone that's near me carried one. Just in case I got "out of hand." What they don't know is, I'm much faster and could take it from their hands before they could pull the trigger. I held my head high knowing I could leave whenever I pleased, but right now, I wanted to be here.

"Sure. Try it." I entered my den.

I heard him scoff, but the smell of maple and sausage pulled me back out of my den. LaRae had arrived with my breakfast.

Moving faster than I usually did, I met her at the door with a large grin. "Sausage?"

She chuckled. "And maple syrup. I remembered your request from before."

Keeping my eyes on the plate, I quickly took it from her the second she poked it through the cracked door. I had one whole sausage chewed and swallowed before I made it to my corner and crouched.

"Ugh, she eats like an animal," Scott said.

Looking up at him, I snarled; a small piece of meat flew from my mouth almost making it to the glass, but it landed on the tiled floor. I made a reminder to lap that up later before turning back to my plate.

"Leave her be," LaRae said to him.

"She's supposed to be in the gym now."

Halfway through the plate, I looked up at him. "I said I would go after I had my breakfast! Stop your crying and grow some pants!"

He shot me an angry look, but I ignored him, going back to my food. I slathered a spicy sausage in the sticky sweet maple syrup and popped it in my mouth. My eyes closed at the beautiful pleasures dancing on my tongue.

Scott and LaRae waited patiently for me to finish my food and drink a whole lot of water. When I was ready, I stood by the door and knocked. Scott turned to me, and I held out my hands for the cuffs and winked. "Just because you were so patient."

He took a nervous step toward the door, then hesitated. "If you try anything I—"

"Will shoot you with the tranquilizer. Yes, yes I know."

He unlocked the door and put on the cuffs with no argument from me. As he checked to make sure they were locked tight, he hesitated at the sight of my claws, so I wiggled my fingers to give him a better look. "Nice, right? They are getting a little long, though. I may need to file them down some. What do you think?" I slid one along his forearm. "Yeah, I probably could cut skin pretty easily."

His face went white, and he swallowed hard. "Let's go." He pulled me toward the hall.

"Touchy, touchy."

Scott led me down the hallway. LaRae trailed behind. As we passed other labs, all eyes stopped to watch me. I gave as many people as I could a toothy grin, relishing the looks of horror that appeared on some of their faces. Some, surprisingly, showed curiosity and some... pity. I rumbled at being pitied. It's me who pities all of them when I decide to let loose.

We made it to the end of the long hallway, and Scott opened two glass doors that lead to a large open room. There was a black concrete track that curled the perimeter and blue mats in the middle. Zane waited for me on the mats with a large group of guards.

"There she is! We weren't sure if you were going to make it this morning." Zane gave Scott a poignant look. Scott kept his eyes on the ground, avoiding Zane's stare.

"My apologies." I gave my best smile. "I had to have my breakfast. I don't do much before I eat, sadly."

Laughing, he clapped his hands together and it echoed in the large room. "Well, *my* apologies for interrupting your breakfast. I'll have to be more thoughtful next time." He walked over to the line of guards. "So, these are my finest fighters. I would love for them to train you."

Before I spoke, I shoved my arms at Scott so he could unlock my cuffs. He gave Zane a quick look, and when he nodded, Scott unlocked them. I rubbed my wrists, strode over to Zane, pushed my feet into the mat hard, and jumped a little to get a feel of the give and take. "You sure you want them to train me? I bet I can train them."

A large man in the middle snickered, so I slowly moved to face him. Tension in the room rose as my face stopped an inch from his, and I gazed into his green eyes. His heart beat rapidly, and he gulped at my close inspection of him. I showed my fangs before putting my nose right to his throat. I sniffed. "Ahhh fresh."

"Excuse me?" His voice cracked.

Backing up, I smiled. "You smell fresh." I linked my hands behind my back. "What is it *you* would show me?"

He nervously licked his lips, looking to Zane, who nodded. "Well, uh how to disarm your opponent and kick their feet out from under them."

"Perfect! Show me!" I took a few steps back.

Everyone else moved off the mats to circle us, and he cleared his throat obviously unsure about teaching me. "All right, you grab your opponent here, pull forward, and swipe his feet from back to forward." He motioned to his wrist, pulling it toward himself, and then demonstrated swiping the feet.

"All right," I said, pretending I've never done this before, but all of Brian's and Old Bob's lessons came back to me quickly. I gently grabbed the man's wrist, pulled him forward with a quick hard yank that pulled a grunt from him, then swiped my leg out, hitting his back to front. He landed hard. I flipped him, and I pulled his arm to his back to keep control.

"Like that?" I whispered in his ear.

He coughed, trying to catch a breath. "Yeah."

Clapping echoed through the room as I pushed off the guard and stood. Zane headed toward me, face glowing with pride. "Wow! That was amazing!"

"Thank you."

"Can you do more?"

"Of course."

The next hour was spent with me taking down every one of the guards in every manner that Brian and Old Bob taught me. They all tried to outmaneuver me, but with my fast reflexes, strength, and heightened senses, I was not an equal match for any of them. Zane even had three of them fight me at one time. I still won and didn't break a sweat.

When all eight guards sat on the mat panting with exhaustion, I turned to Zane. "I think they've had enough. Maybe we try again tomorrow?"

He watched me with wide amazement. "Tomorrow, yes, but you won't be fighting them. I think we have established who's the best fighter in this situation."

After studying him a moment, I turned back to Scott and LaRae. "Sure. Whatever." I kept my tone unimpressed, not wanting to let on I was a little curious what he had up his sleeve. Plus, I liked feeling my new body and seeing what it could do. Rolling my shoulders, I reveled in the fresh feeling of working my muscles.

As Scott put the cuffs back on my wrists, he shook from fear and I smiled at him.

"Tomorrow then!" I hollered at them all as I follow Scott and LaRae back to my cage.

Chapter 60

Jace

I sat on the side of my cot extending and bending my leg. I had been walking on it for a week now and it felt good. I was able to walk and work the thigh muscle, but it still ached after a good workout. I didn't mind the pain, though; it reminded me I was alive.

I heard the pitter-patter of Dr. Hahn as he rushed down the hall to my cell in a frenzy. "Get up! We have to go!"

He hurried to unlock the door, motioning me from the ground where I was doing push-ups. My first thought was something happened to Eden and my throat constricted, but when he started mumbling about being late and Zane's punishment, I stopped at the door of my cell.

"Where are we going?"

"Th-the gym. Come! Come! They are waiting for you!" He tugged my arm, but I easily pulled it out of his grip.

"I'm sorry, buddy, but I'm going to need some more information than that."

He pressed two fingers to the bridge of his nose and took a deep, calming breath. "Zane is requesting you to the gym. You are to fight."

"Fight?" I stepped back.

"Yes, relax, not like that. No, no, not like that." He shook his head and wiped a hand over his frustrated face. "You are to spar. Train. With Eden. Yes, Eden."

"Train? With Eden?" I studied him skeptically. "Is this a trick? Because if it is, I will kill you." The thought of seeing Eden filled me with excitement. I could touch her, even if it was during a spar. My skin could still graze hers; I could be close enough to smell her lavender scent.

His head shook wildly. "No, no. I promise it's not a trick, but please. We need to go. They are waiting! Waiting!"

"All right. All right. Relax." I let him lead me out of the room and down the long, dark concrete hallway. We walked up five flights of stairs that led to another long hallway. As he led me toward two large glass doors, I glanced into the labs we passed. Not many faces turned to see us, but I saw subjects in the small rooms within, withered and weak. I turned back to Dr. Hahn's white hair bouncing before me as he nervously shuffled us into the large open room behind the glass doors.

Fresh air and lavender hit me before I saw her standing in the middle of the blue mats. Her apricot hair glowed in the bright light from the skylights that trailed along the ceiling. She held her cuffed hands in front of her body, but that's not what made me pause. She stood tall, back straight, and chin high. She smiled at me and the tips of fangs peaked out. Despite her confidence, her eyes were worried. Worried what I would think of her. I let a smile light up my face.

Jace!

Her voice danced through my head, and I closed my eyes to relish the sound. Continuing toward her, I put my hands on her cheeks when I reached her, resting my forehead on hers. "Eden," I whispered. "I have missed you so much."

She rubbed her head along mine and gave my cheek a little lick. I jerked back a tad at the sentiment but relaxed when I realized I didn't mind it, but rather... liked it. It was an act of claiming, and I wanted to be hers.

"I missed you too." She moved back, smiling big at me. Glancing down, I saw her fangs closer, longer, and sharper.

Scared?

Nothing about you scares me.

She flushed, and I rubbed my thumb along the pinkness of her cheek, fighting the urge to kiss her smooth skin.

"Well, isn't this sweet." My body tensed at Zane's sticky voice, and I glared over at him. "So, I brought you two here to fight, so I can see who's stronger."

Moving my eyes to him, I sidestepped between him and Eden. Working hard not to limp, I said, "What if I don't fight?"

Smirking, he looked me up and down before snapping his finger at a guard in the corner. The guard pointed the gun at me. "Then you die. Your choice."

Eden's cuffed hands moved to my arm pulling me back to her. "It's all right."

Looking down at the metal cuffs, I growled low. "Who's the lucky one that gets to unlock her?" I looked behind Eden to LaRae and the man that had slapped her. I let the growl grow as he took a hesitant step forward.

"No funny business or..."

"Let me guess, you have a tranquilizer gun?"

He froze and Eden and I roared with laughter.

I wiped my eyes. "What's your name?"

"Sss-cott." He watched us with fear dripping from him, arousing my more feral side. I took a step toward him, my eyes narrowed on his throat, and I saw him swallow hard.

"ENOUGH!" Zane bellowed, giving the man an impatient look. "Just unlock her, will you?"

I stepped aside and Scott moved quickly to unlock her cuffs. I smiled at his shaking hands, not giving him room to relax.

Once her hands were free, she gently rubbed her wrists. The red rings around them made my lip curl, but the mischievous look in her eyes kept me focused.

They don't know we can communicate.

Our eyes stayed locked as we circled each other, everyone else moved away to watch.

One request. Go easy on the leg. It's still healing.

I made a quick motion like I was going in for an attack that startled her, and we both laughed. This may be fun.

I don't want to disappoint, so maybe go easy on me?
I have a feeling that won't be difficult.
Come at me, I won't hurt you too much.

She winked, and I charged. Plowing into her belly with my shoulder, I wrapped my arms around her waist. She fell back but used the momentum to keep us rolling until she landed on top. My leg throbbed from my attack but feeling her was worth it. I could have grabbed her upper body with my legs, but being the gentleman I am, I let her grab my arm and twist me into submission.

Zane clapped, and by the smile on his face, he bought the whole charade. "Fantastic! Keep going!"

So, are you going to take me down every time or do I get to win at least once?

Her lack of response and wink told me she didn't plan on letting me win. I laughed when she charged me. Ducking, I tried to swipe under her feet, but she jumped over my leg with a flip, landing behind me, then swiped my feet out from under me before I could even turn around. If I wasn't trying to breathe, my jaw would have been on the floor.

"What the. . ." I coughed. "That's new."

She offered me a hand and pulled me up. "There are many things that are new about me." She swiped a claw along my cheek sweetly before pulling me forward to twist my arm behind me, then she pushed me down. "Yield?" she whispered in my ear.

A shiver went up my spine, and I nodded. "Yeah."

Releasing me, she backed up and continued to circle me.

"How does it feel to be beat by a girl?" a guard called from the back, nudging the guard next to him as they laughed.

Snapping my eyes at him, I opened my mouth to respond when Eden's musical voice filled the room. "I think I remember you from yesterday. Yeah, you were my first flip, right? Knocked the wind right out of you. How did that feel?" His face flushed red that quickly changed to purple as anger overflowed him. He cursed under his breath at her and I snarled, lunging forward.

Jace!

Eden's voice warned me, but I continued to stalk toward him anyway. Baring my teeth, I set my shoulders.

"Jace!"

Ignoring Zane's voice, I kept my eyes set on the cocky guard.

Jace, please!

"Guard!" Zane hollered behind me.

I heard the cock of a gun, then a tussle and grunt.

"Eden!" LaRae's voice pulled me from my rage, and I whipped around to see Eden across the room with a guard disarmed and on the ground.

"All guards! Take aim!" Zane yelled.

I froze as the doors opened and guards filed in, lining the walls of the room and taking aim at Eden and me. The tension in the room was so thick I'm sure Eden could cut it with her claws.

Jace, don't make any fast movements.
Same with you.

"Both of you will come back to the middle of the mat or you will meet your end here and now." Zane pointed his finger at the ground like he was lecturing a child.

I raised my hands slowly in surrender. "All right. Relax." I moved slowly back to the middle of the mat where Eden joined me. Glancing over her shoulder, I saw the guard lying on the ground with blood dripping from his face.

Dead?
He'll wish he was.

Zane positioned himself in front of us with his hands clasped behind his back. "Now, both of you will come here daily to train. If anything" – he narrowed his eyes at us – "I mean anything happens like this again. I will not hesitate to shoot you both down... dead."

"Wow, his words are so inspirational," I mumbled at her and she snickered, but with the way Zane's eyes stabbed into mine, I realized he would kill me without hesitation. "All right. Understood."

He turned to Eden who also agreed with a nod. "Good. Now, say your goodbyes." He turned and walked toward the door. We stood alone in the middle of the mat.

Stepping toward her, I took her hands. She looked into my eyes and smiled. "I miss you," she whispered, and I pulled her into a hug, wrapping my arms around her. Holding her as close as I could felt like home.

"I miss you too."

She pushed away to look me in the eye, but this time her smile was gone.

"What's wrong?"

"They don't believe me. I have told them, but they think I'm lying."

I studied her face. "Really? You told them?"

"Yes, but either he doesn't want to listen or he doesn't believe me."

"Zane!" I called to him, not taking my eyes from hers.

"Yes?" He stepped back toward us.

"She told you. She told you how I was made, but you don't believe her. Why?" I turned to face him but kept Eden's hand tight in mine.

He looked between us, trying to be one step ahead and figure out what I was up to. "Yes. Because we have tried that and it doesn't work." Dr. Hahn's confession comes to me, and I remember him saying he has been trying the animal blood for years, but what he creates are the scourges. So, Zane isn't lying, but neither is Eden. "All right. I don't have time for more of this."

I opened my mouth to speak but the pinprick in my arm caused me to freeze. Turning to Eden, I saw she had a dart in her neck as well. I gave her hand one last squeeze before we both fell.

Chapter 61

Tristan

The morning started out like any other. I woke, checked on Eden, who was still in her den, did a workout, showered, and waited patiently for Scott to bring me my breakfast. Scott came in but didn't have any food. He went right to Eden's room and started yelling for her. She ignored him until LaRae brought her food. When Eden was done, they cuffed her and walked her out of the lab. No one, not even Eden glanced at me. A few minutes after they left, a man stopped by with a bowl of oatmeal. My stomach was too hungry to complain, so I scarfed it down, then lay back down to wait for Eden to return.

I must have fallen asleep because when I opened my eyes, Eden, Scott, and LaRae were back where they usually were, and a plate of food was sitting on my floor, cold. I turned my head and had to swallow back down the oatmeal to keep it from coming back up. The room spun and my head throbbed. I managed to turn and look over to Eden's room. She was half out of her den, watching me. Finally, someone noticed me.

I focused hard to lift my arm and wave at her, but it felt like it had been belted down to the cot. Turning my eyes down, I saw that it wasn't, so why couldn't I move it? Eden stood, moving to her window watching me. Her eyes widened and she banged on the glass. LaRae and Scott looked at her then at me when she pointed. Scott ran to my door, but LaRae grabbed his arm just before he unlocked it. The only sound in my room was my own ragged breaths as they worked to pull in and let out air.

LaRae and Scott moved away and returned a few minutes later wearing suits that covered their entire bodies. I managed to turn my head and saw Eden still at the glass watching attentively. Worry written in her furrowed brow as she chewed her lip with her fangs.

The door clicked and Scott and LaRae walked in. "What's wrong, Tristan?" LaRae's voice sounded muffled through her suit.

I opened my dry mouth, but a cough escaped instead of words.

"Crap," Scott said.

LaRae came to my side and swiped a small handheld machine over my head. "102.7. How did this happen?"

It was the oatmeal, had to be the oatmeal. Since my voice didn't work, I lifted my thirty-pound finger and pointed toward the empty bowl.

LaRae's eyes followed my finger and she asked, "Did you bring him breakfast?"

"I thought you did!"

"Why would I? He's your responsibility!"

"Man," I managed to whisper out through the dryness of my mouth, but immediately coughed after.

"Get him water." LaRae motioned to the cup on the small table. Scott grabbed it and brought it to my mouth. I drank some, but most of it spilled down my chin. The passage of my throat to my stomach seemed constricted, only letting tiny amounts down. "I'll start an IV. We need to keep him hydrated."

"Maybe he'll survive. He is from the woods," Scott said.

LaRae's eyes moved over my clammy face. "Maybe."

I tried not to let them know how much my body hurt as they worked to make me comfortable. If my memory remembered anything, this was just the beginning. I didn't know if I could survive this again. Eden crouched next to her window, watching the whole time. I took comfort in the fact that she was here with me, here with me at my end.

Chapter 62

Eden

My nose touched the glass as I watched LaRae and Scott poke needles into Tristan and hang bags on metal stands next to him. I hadn't noticed anything wrong earlier when I saw him sleeping upon my return from my sparing session with Jace. I took a nap, but the smell of sweat whiffed through my den. Assuming Tristan was doing one of his many daily workouts, I was surprised when I saw him still sleeping. I knew something was wrong. He was pale, glossy, and his breaths were slow. He had tried to move but was unable to, except for one finger.

It reminded me of when I was infected with the Fever the first time, only he seemed much worse. The pain and heaviness were so intense I thought I would be pushed flat into my cot. I shook away a shiver from the memory and returned my focus to Tristan. He was alone now in his room, the peaceful look on his sleeping face was nothing but a mask. I knew what kind of pain he was feeling and my stomach knotted. I needed to help him.

I ran to my door and started smacking the glass, but stopped when LaRae clicked the lock open. "Is it the virus?"

"Yes." She stepped into my cage, shutting the door. "Eden, did you see who brought Tristan breakfast?"

I searched my memory; guilt hit me when I realized I hadn't paid much attention to him at all this morning. Not even a glance. I shook my head.

"Darn. All right. I need to make some calls."

"But—"

She put her hands on my shoulders, stopping my push for the door. "We are doing everything we can."

"No offense, LaRae, but your best hasn't done much." Her cheeks reddened at my stab of truth. "If he dies, I will let loose, and no one will be spared... not even you." My eyes met hers and I saw them fill with fear. I curled my hands, readying my claws to cut, and let out a quiet growl.

Dropping her hands, she swallowed. "I'm doing the best I can. Just... let me make some calls, all right?" She quickly retreated from my cage and I resumed my watch.

∽

My eyes stayed fixed on Tristan, but I could hear and feel LaRae and Scott running around in a tizzy, trying to figure out what had happened. I finally tipped my eyes from him when Scott started yelling into the phone.

"You have no authority to do that! He's *my* patient!" He pushed one hand into his brown hair as he listened. "What? Why?" His face dropped and color left his cheeks. "Fine." He slammed the phone down. Closing his eyes, he pinched the bridge of his nose.

"What? What happened?" LaRae asked.

"Apparently, it was an order from above."

"What? Why?"

Scott didn't respond, but when his eyes meet mine, I know who "above" meant. Zane. Since threatening Jace didn't work, he decided to use Tristan. My fist hit the glass so hard it shook my whole cage. I panted through clenched teeth, walking slowly to the door.

"Get me, Zane," I growled through the door. They both watched in fear. "Get. Me. ZANE!"

Scott nodded and he picked up the phone. I didn't wait to listen to his words because I went back to guarding Tristan.

Zane didn't take long to come, and the triumphant smile on his face as he entered into the lab tightened every muscle in my back. I would take this glass wall down, just as Jace had, if things went south. He wouldn't feel so triumphant then.

"Eden! I'm sorry to hear about your friend."

"Why? I told you what you wanted. It's not my fault, or his, that you don't want to listen."

"Don't want to listen? No, no, Eden. The problem is, we have been doing what you say you did, but it doesn't work."

"Of course, it works!" I slammed my fist into the glass again and Zane jumped back, the smile dropping from his face.

"Careful, Eden. I still have Jace I can use when this one... expires."

The word hit me like a brick. I thought I lost him before and knew how it felt. I can't lose him for real again. "He won't expire!"

"No? What are you going to do?"

I looked back to Tristan. He was watching us with glossy eyes, but I could see the faintest shake of his head. I knew he couldn't hear us, but he knows. He knows what we are discussing and he doesn't want it.

"Let me talk to him." I met Zane's hollow grey eyes and he nodded. Without a second to wait, I rushed to the door. LaRae unlocked it, and I pushed past her, rushing to Tristan's cage where Scott was about to unlock it.

"Does she need a suit?" he asked.

"I'm immune, you dingbat. Open the door!"

He didn't wait for Zane's approval but quickly unlocked and opened the door. Before I took my next breath, I was kneeling beside Tristan, the door clicking behind me.

"Tristan?" I took his hand, careful not to scratch him with a claw, seeing his cheek twitch with an attempt to smile. "It's all right. I know it's hard for you to speak." I remembered my blinking conversations I had with Jace in the camp. "I'm going to ask you a yes or no question. You blink once for yes and twice for no. All right?"

He blinked once. Yes.

I let out a long sigh. I know that it's a silly question I am asking, but it will change his whole life. He has a right to make his choice. "If I know how to cure you, do you want me to?"

He watched me a moment, his ice-blue eyes faded before he blinked once. Yes. I let out a long sigh, squeezing his hand.

"Good, good." I felt the slightest twitch of his hand in mine, and I looked up at him. He was moving his mouth, trying to speak.

"If... I"—he swallowed—"die—"

"No, no. That won't happen." I leaned in and smiled at him, but the wheels in my head turned.

"No... Eden... don't let... me... suffer. Kill... me," he finished, ignoring my words.

My mouth dried. "What? No. I can't." He didn't speak, but the look in his eyes meant everything. He doesn't want to live in pain or worse, and I understand, but how could I kill him? I let out all the air from my lungs. "All right." I could barely hear my own words. Resting my forehead on his chest, I breathed in his scent. Home. He smelled like home. The firelight on stormy nights, berry picking on cool mornings, card games, and laughter with Old Bob, Tate, and Ellie. If I had never left that day, would we be here?

I sat up, fighting the tears that threatened to spill out, and smiled. His eyes were closed and his breath steady. I stroked a claw along his sleeping face when the door clicked open. Giving his hand a quick squeeze, I stood and left his cage.

I waited to speak until I was in my own cage. Facing Zane with nothing between us, I imagined again what it would feel like to sink my fangs into his neck. Narrowing my eyes on his, I spoke with the strongest voice I could muster. "Get the blood."

"Good!" He clapped. I turned quickly before I lunged out and slashed him with a claw. That would have to wait.

Slowly walking to my window, I crouched and watched Tristan sleep. For the first time since I had changed to my new self, I was scared. Scared I was wrong and would have to kill my best friend, my brother.

Chapter 63

Jace

I haven't stopped smiling since I woke from my drug-induced slumber. Seeing Eden was a weight lifted off me. She was different, but I didn't care. Her changes didn't affect me the way they may have anyone else. They fit her.

"Oh no, no, no, no." Dr. Hahn shuffled into the room. His brow creased and his hair was more messy than usual. "Not good, not good."

I sat up, watching him wring his hands together. "What's up?"

"Something bad has happened. Very, very bad."

I walked to the bars of my cell. "What?" My body tightened in preparation for what he may say.

He looked at me. "Tristan has the virus. Oh, this is bad. Very, very bad. Bad. Bad."

I gripped the bar. How could that happen? "Does Eden know?"

"She's the one who noticed!" He paced. "Bad, bad. Very, very bad."

My heart sank. I saw how it affected her when she thought Tristan was dead, so I can only imagine what she's going through now. I should be there to help her through this. My grip tightened on the bars. "So, what's the plan?"

"Well, they are going to try the procedure."

My heart sank. "You have to tell her! Tell her what has happened!" If Tristan turns into a scourge, it will break her.

"I c... can't!" His voice cracked.

"What? Why?"

He stopped pacing. "If I say anything, then Zane will learn that I didn't dispose of all those people. He will know that you know what's happened."

I clenched my teeth. "This is not a time for you to be egotistical. If Tristan becomes a scourge, it will break Eden. Break her!" I pulled on the bars, stupidly thinking I could move them apart.

"I'm sorry. I'm sorry." Dr. Hahn avoided my eyes and hurried out of the room, leaving me with only the sound of the dripping walls to accompany my thoughts.

Chapter 64

Eden

I didn't take my eyes off Tristan the rest of the day yesterday. I watched as Scott went in, wearing his suit to inject him with the animal blood. When my eyes drooped, I slapped my cheeks to wake up. LaRae must have put something in my food because I woke this morning on the tiled floor, groggy. Lifting myself onto my hands, I shook my head trying to clear the fog.

"Eden?" LaRae's voice was distant, even though she stood just five feet from me. "We need to go."

"Tristan?" I stood, rolling my head in circles, stretching my arms. I looked over to his cage, but he wasn't there. I dug my claws into the tile before jumping to my feet.

"Just come."

"Where is he?"

"He's in the gym."

"The gym?" If he was there, then maybe it worked. She didn't bother cuffing me, knowing my eagerness to see Tristan was strong.

I followed her down the long hall, ignoring all the probing eyes. My focus was purely on getting to Tristan. Making sure he was all right. I bit my tongue and fisted my hands to stay in pace with LaRae and not bolt ahead. She walked much too slowly for my liking.

The first face I met when entering the gym was Jace. He lit up when he saw me and put his hands on my cheeks, keeping my eyes on him. I felt him sending me every ounce of patience he could give.

"Eden." Jace's voice was soft and I didn't have to look because I could smell him. The faintest scent of Tristan mixed with death. I closed my eyes and pulled in a deep ragged breath. "Eden, just breathe." Jace moved to be a barrier between me and the rest of the room. When I opened my eyes, I didn't stop the tears from slipping. "I'm sorry."

I failed Tristan. Just like I failed Ellie and led her to her death. They were both dead because of me.

When he stepped to the side, my eyes met Tristan's grey, vacant face in the middle of the mat, cuffed and tied to ropes held by two guards. One of his beautiful blue eyes had changed to gold, and he hissed at me. He was a scourge. With no air left in my lungs, I choked as I worked to suck in more, but the sound was like a sob. My hands shook, but Jace squeezed tighter to keep me from coming apart.

"Like I said before, we tried what you said you did, but it hasn't worked." Zane slowly walked toward us. "Will you now tell me what you did to Jace?"

I clenched Jace's hand, and I'm sure my claws ripped into his palm, but he didn't flinch. Moving my gaze to Zane, I narrowed my eyes. "I'm telling you the truth." I dropped my eyes to his throat, imagining sinking my fangs into it.

No. Not now.

Jace had seen it. He didn't say never, just not now. I licked my lips in anticipation before looking back into his hollow grey eyes.

"Pity. Take him away!" Zane motioned to the guards holding Tristan.

"Wait!" My voice echoed and I'm sure everyone heard the desperation in it. Zane looked at me quizzically. "Let me... let me say goodbye." I closed my eyes and dropped my hand from Jace's.

"Very well."

"Are you sure?" Jace asked.

I gave him a sad smile. "Yeah. There is something I have to do." He nodded and stepped back, trusting me. He always trusted me.

I fixated my eyes on Tristan's hunched and growling body. He watched me take my first step toward him and flashes of our life together hit me so fast I could barely breathe. We were laughing as we ran through the cabin's yard together playing tag.

Step two.

I was in the water of the nearby lake and Tristan jumped off the tire swing into the water.

Step three.

I huddled with him and Tate under a blanket as a storm raged over the cabin. They told me jokes to keep me from being too scared of the thunder.

Step four.

Our family sang me happy birthday in front of a plate of berries. Tristan was singing the loudest.

Step five. My last step.

Tristan lying on the cot, sick with the Fever, and making me promise to kill him if he suffered. *Kill me.*

I stopped. The only sounds in the gym were Tristan's rasping breaths and the guards' grunts as they kept the ropes taut. I fisted and relaxed my hands and met Tristan's eyes. Even though he was a scourge, there was a tiny bit of him left and that tiny bit spoke to me.

Kill me.

Pulling in a breath, I moved so quickly no one had time to react. The crack of his neck echoed, then the thud of his body hitting the mat, then nothing. The silence was so deafening I brought my hands to my ears and dropped to my knees. His eyes, smile, golden curls all rushed through me in a wash of fire. My body tightened and my head throbbed from the strain of keeping my feral side from letting loose. I let out the loudest scream I could manage.

"Eden." Jace's hand squeezed my shoulder and I turned into him, hiding my face in his chest. He wrapped his arms around me in a tight squeeze. Tristan was gone. Really gone, and I had killed him. I had to kill him because Zane didn't believe me. I squeezed my eyes tighter, trying to void Tristan's face from my mind. I didn't want to give Zane the satisfaction of knowing my full pain. Without making a sound, I composed myself, keeping my face hidden in Jace's chest until my heartbeat evened out. When I finally moved back, I met Jace's sad eyes.

You all right?
No. But I will be.

"I should probably thank you, Eden. You just rid me of a messy problem." Zane's voice dripped with condescendence. "But now... now I don't have much leverage."

I growled and Jace's hands tightened on my shoulders.

Not now, Eden.
He killed Tristan, and he will probably try and kill you.
Not. Now.

My eyes pinned to Jace's as we had our silent conversation, but I couldn't let Zane get away with this. "I'm sorry." I pushed Jace to the side and he flew across the mat. Turning to Zane, I grinned as his face lost all color and he took a step back. "You're a bastard. You killed my brother all because you are too arrogant to believe me, but I will not let you threaten anyone else I care about."

"Eden!" Jace called.

"Eden, please." Zane's voice held fear. It was the first time I had ever seen him scared since I arrived in the city, and it excited the predator within me.

I charged and a snarl ripped from my throat. Curling my claws, I was ready to slash him. I was just a few feet away when I was hit from the side. The force was so powerful we slid across the mat hitting Tristan's limp body.

I'm sorry, but now isn't the time.

Jace sat on my back, pinning me to the ground. I fought him, but my grief and position put me at a disadvantage.

"Why?" I rasped out.

"I'm sorry." I felt the regret and sorrow in his voice.

Please, just relax.

Jace let up just a touch to give me a chance to calm on my own, so I didn't fight. My face was level with Tristan's. His vacant eyes still open, watching me. I didn't want him to see me like this, even if he was dead.

"Well... Thank you, Jace," Zane said. I could hear him brushing off his jacket and the click of his shoes as they left the mat. "Guards. Drug her."

"Zane. She will—"

"Drug them both!"

The sting of the needle hit my arm. I reached out and took Tristan's still hand. He was still warm.

Go to her, Tristan. Go to Ellie. Find her and be happy.

Jace rolled to my side. We lay in a tangle of sedated and dead limbs on the middle of the mat. The last image I saw before I blacked out was Tristan smiling at me before he walked into the light.

Chapter 65

Jace

Even through my drug-induced sleep, guilt raged through me. The sound of her voice and the look on her face when I kept her from vengeance. She had to understand that I know this place better than her and I know Zane. There wasn't any way she was going to be able to attack him and come out alive. Even if she killed him.

I opened my eyes to the familiar crisp white ceiling. I was in my original cage across from Eden. Before turning to look, I closed my eyes and searched for her. I could feel her there and her walls were down. I gave her a small nudge.

Eden?

She didn't respond, but I felt her alert and listening. She had heard me.

I'm sorry.

After a thick moment of silence, her voice whispered through to me and the lump in my throat grew. I had hurt her, and I prayed she would forgive me.

Why?

I was protecting you.

Her edginess grew. She didn't want to be protected.

I don't—

Need my protection? I know, but I can't just let you commit suicide.

I finally turned to look into her cage, seeing nothing but her gold eye glowing within the darkness of her den. She was watching me, so I gave her a small smile.

I can't lose you, Eden.

She emerged from her den, slowly crawling to the window; her eyes stayed fixed to mine.

I can't lose you either.
I'm sorry.

I sat up and set my feet on the floor. Leaning forward, I rested my elbows on my knees and watched her. Her long apricot hair fell in thick waves past her shoulders, framing her high peach cheekbones and beautiful sparkly eyes.

Give me a warning next time. You tweaked something in my back.

She twisted her waist to show where it was sore, and I laughed.

Deal.

Smiling, we watched each other a moment, and I wished I had kissed her when I could because, in that moment, I wanted to more than anything. But then, her smile faded.

Do you think they really gave Tristan the animal blood?

Dr. Hahn's confession of creating the scourge reran in my mind, and I nodded.

Yes. Dr. Hahn told me he's been trying since he created you, but all he's been able to make are the scourges.
Dr. Hahn created me?
Yes.

She set her forehead on the glass, and I could see her jaw muscles working.

Then why didn't it work? With Tristan?

"Good! You both are awake!" Zane charged into the lab and stopped in the small hall between our cages. LaRae, Dr. Hahn, Scott, and David followed. "So, now that we are all together, let's try and work this out. LaRae and Scott, can you get the coms?" LaRae and Scott each went to the outside of our cages and hit a button. We didn't need the coms to hear them, but their human ears did. "All right. Eden, I have to say, I was a little surprised at your lack of reaction to Tristan."

"Trying to kill you wasn't enough of a reaction?" Eden said, sliding a claw along the glass right at the right height of his throat.

"Well" – he chuckled – "yes. That was exciting, but no. When you saw him, it's almost like you knew. You knew what he would become."

She dropped her hand and narrowed her eyes. "I knew it was possible, but I prayed it wouldn't happen."

"So you have seen them before. When the people become those... monsters."

"Yes. We have seen them in the woods."

Zane's eyebrows rose. "You have? Interesting."

Dr. Hahn fidgeted nervously as he watched his secret unfold.

"Yes. There are many," Eden said.

Zane sighed. "Many! Well, well." He paused a moment, the perfect picture of composure, but I could see the tautness of his shoulders. "Then, please tell me what you gave Jace, so this doesn't continue to happen."

I watched Eden examine Zane's face. She moved her eyes over his body from top to bottom, and I saw her imagining all the ways she could kill him. No doubt this was another reason Zane wanted to use the coms rather than take us out of our cages to have this conversation.

"I told you. I used animal blood."

"You saw what the animal blood created, so you must have done something different. THINK!" He leaned forward with his eyes on Eden's. His fear was non-existent with a two-inch piece of glass between them, but I remembered the terrified look on his face earlier when Eden almost let loose on him.

"I don't know! I gave him my wolf's blood. I don't know why Jace didn't turn into a scourge, but Tristan did. You all are the scientists; you figure it out!"

Zane stepped back. "A scourge?"

"It's what we call them in the woods," Eden replied.

Zane pivoted on one foot with his hands clasped behind his back to finally face Dr. Hahn. "Interesting." Dr. Hahn's eyes stay fixed to the ground. Sweat formed on his brow. He was terrified.

I stood and walked to my window. "That's not important now. What we need to figure out is what is different."

"Right," Zane said quietly, his eyes still daggers on Dr. Hahn's face. "Right." He turned to me.

"Dr. Hahn," I said, waiting for him to look at me. When he did, I asked, "What kind of animal blood did you use when you created Eden?"

He wiped a hand over his brow into his wild white hair. "Ahhh..." All eyes were on him, which didn't do much for his nervousness. "Let me think..."

"Today, Dr. Hahn!" Zane yelled.

"Yes. Yes. Sorry. I used strays for the blood. It was a secret, yes a secret, so I had to get the animal blood from strays."

"Like a cat? Or a dog?" Eden asked curiously. I could feel her need to learn about herself. Learn where she came from, what she was. Dr. Hahn nodded at her.

"All right. And, Eden" – Zane pulled her attention to him – "what animal did you use to turn Jace?"

"Ash. My wolf."

"Your wolf?" Zane's eyes widened, but Eden just watched him. "All right. And what did you use to change Tristan?" He directed his question back to Dr. Hahn.

"B... blood from the animal farm."

LaRae stepped forward. "I don't get it. They were all animals. Could it be the type of animal?"

"Maybe," Dr. Hahn replied, shuffling his feet. His face was lost in thought. When he got a moment of clarity, he pointed his finger at Eden. "Eden, your wolf. It's alive, yes?"

"Obviously. Why would I keep a dead wolf around?"

"Dr. Hahn?"

"Oh my. My, my, my. It can't be that simple? A simple, stupid mistake."

"What?"

"The stray I used on Eden; it was alive. Eden's wolf was alive, but all the blood I have been using for the past years has been from... dead animals."

Every set of eyes was on Dr. Hahn, and you could hear nothing, not even a breath. If it was that simple, all those people, innocent people died because of a stupid mistake and a power-hungry leader. I clenched my fists.

"You're kidding, right?" I asked.

"I'm afraid... not."

I leaned closer to the glass. "What about Derek and Brian?"

Zane's mouth set into an angry line as he studied Dr. Hahn, then he turned to look at me a moment. "Derek and Brian?"

"Yes." I glanced through the white faces of the scientists before landing back on Zane's angry eyes. "They helped Eden and me learn about ourselves. They are like us."

Zane pivoted with his hands clasped behind his back and focused in on Dr. Hahn. "So, there were more than just Eden?"

Dr. Hahn cleared his throat. "Y... yes, sir."

"All right then. Let's test your theory, Dr. Hahn." He turned back to me.

David stepped forward. "But, sir—"

"Dr. Hahn! Since you have trouble following orders, you will be one of the subjects. Then" – he pointed at the remaining three scientists – "eeny, meeny, miny, moe! LaRae! Congratulations. You will be the second." Zane brushed past them and out the door.

I watched the color drain from all their faces. LaRae put her hand on Eden's window to stay upright, and Scott brought her a chair just when she fell back.

"I'm sorry," Eden said.

"Yes... well... I suppose we better get working. Zane won't like it if we wait too long." David put a gentle hand on LaRae's shoulder. "Come. I will get you both set up in Dr. Hahn's lab." LaRae looked up at him with wet eyes. David helped her to stand, but the moment he let go of her, she swayed, so Scott grabbed her arm and led her out. Dr. Hahn looked at me with wide eyes, his mouth moved but no sounds came out. "Come, Dr. Hahn." David held out an arm. After a small smile, Dr. Hahn sniffed, then turned and followed David out of the lab.

Chapter 66

Eden

It would be a lie if I said I wanted them to succeed. A small part of me wanted Dr. Hahn and LaRae to end up like all the poor people they have tortured and killed over the years. Like Tristan. Even if I did like LaRae, she still killed people. Dr. Hahn was worse, experimenting on them. Creating monsters, the scourges. I had no sympathy for him.

Scott had come to inform us that they both were set up in their rooms and had been infected with the virus. When their symptoms start, they will inject them with animal blood from a live animal. Jace and I never responded. The air was thick and filled with sadness. Sadness for all the innocent lives that could have been spared over the years if not for a simple change that was made. Scott's attitude softened when he realized that everyone was dispensable to Zane. His hands shook as he busied himself with cleaning the lab and sorting papers, continuously pushing his hands through his short black hair every few minutes when he lost track of what he was doing.

After Scott left, we didn't see him again. He was replaced by a new scientist who didn't speak or even take the time to look at us. He brought plates of food, shoving them in the door, and left.

When he brought breakfast to us the next day, I attempted to catch his eyes, but he kept them fixed on anything but me. "How are LaRae and Dr. Hahn?" I asked him, but he moved about the room like he hadn't heard me. I snarled.

Maybe he's deaf.

Zane wouldn't allow that. He wouldn't be able to listen to orders then

The day went by slowly, very slowly. I stretched and did some exercises led by Jace from his cage, ate the food that was dropped off, and napped. My body itched for more exercise and to smell the fresh air. Closing my eyes, I imagined the sun on my face and the breeze moving through my hair, but when I opened them, it was just the bright light and ventilation.

We need to get out of here.

Jace stopped his leg raises and looked at me. *True, but we need a plan. I don't think now is the time.*

My head dropped, pursing my lips together. He was right. A voice of reason, just like Tate always was. My hand moved to the butterfly around my neck, and I crouched in the corner. Inspecting every groove and rounded tip as I ran my claws over it, I thought of Tate and Old Bob.

Do you think they are still alive?
I have no doubt.

I looked over at him sitting in the chair next to the window, leaning forward with his elbows on his knees and hands clasped. When our eyes met, he smiled and my heart fluttered at the dimple on his right cheek.

Maybe they can get us out.
Like I said before, it would be suicide for them to try and get in. We are better off trying to figure out a way out from here.

He was right. I dropped the butterfly, and it plopped onto my chest like a fifty-pound weight. A weight of all my memories of the life I once had. Groaning, I moved to my cot and lay down, giving Jace my back. I needed time to cool off and sleep helped. So, I slept.

S

I slept through the next day knowing that Jace would wake me if anything important happened. On the third day after LaRae and Dr. Hahn were infected, I was awakened by a loud banging. I slowly flipped over, staying snuggled under my covers, and saw Jace with his nose pushed into the glass watching whatever was making the noise.

Something is happening.

I stood and stretched before slowly walking over to the glass and leaning on it. Three men were setting up a rectangular black box. They moved the desk to the middle of us and had cords attached to it.

What's that?
A television.

I looked to Jace with wide eyes. Ellie and Old Bob had spoken about televisions before, and as a child, I wished every night I would get to see one. Now, I wished I hadn't wished so hard. This was not the situation I had imagined I would be in when I finally got to see one.

The screen flickered to light and the three men left. Jace and I silently watched an absent podium with a banner of the American flag hanging over it.

What's happening?

Jace didn't answer, but when I looked over at him, his face was almost green. He didn't turn away from the screen, so I looked back. After another moment, the door behind the podium opened and Zane emerged. He pulled out a piece of paper from his impeccable grey suit and set it on the podium. When he looked up and smiled, Jace and I both let out involuntary growls. It worked. Zane no longer had two hallow grey eyes, but only one. The other was replaced by gold. He had changed himself.

A crowd cheered and Zane held up his hands with a grin to calm them. "Citizens! I have tremendous news! We have found a cure!" The crowd cheered and the screen changed from Zane to people laughing, hugging, and some even crying. I drowned out all of Zane's propaganda words and my world went foggy.

Eden?

I turned to Jace, whose face still hadn't returned to his normal color. We looked at each other a moment, but the events of the past months rushed through me.

He doesn't need us anymore. You know what that means, right? We will be fine.

His words didn't match his face. He agreed. I paced the length of my room, thinking of any scenario where Zane would let us live, but I couldn't think of any. We knew too much; we knew what they did to others to get to this outcome. Yes, the people knew they were researching, but they didn't know the extent of what people went through here. If that got out, it could be catastrophic for Zane.

There's one thing I never told you, Eden. Something that Zane told me.

I could see the pain etched on his face and feel the regret from holding whatever it was secret from me. I watched him and waited.

The virus, it's man-made. Zane wanted it made.

That was not what I expected him to say at all. Tilting my head, I widened my eyes.

What?

That's not all... Your...

He closed his eyes.

Your mother and Dr. Hahn were the scientists that made it.

The world around me vanished into darkness. My claws pushed into my scalp as I squeezed my head, pricking my skin. I'm sure there will be blood. I screamed. How could that be true? How could my mother, the woman who Tate says loved us so much, create such a horrible thing and then use it on me?

Eden?

Jace's voice was distant. I put up the walls in my head and retreated to my den. I needed time and space to think things through, without Jace. I could feel him nudging me, begging me to respond, to look at him, anything, but I ignored him, curled up in the dark corner, and slept.

Chapter 67

Jace

It had been hours since she moved into her den. I called to her, but her walls were up, keeping me out. They were strong and didn't even crumble from my pleading nudges. The weight I had in my chest from holding that information was replaced with a heavier one from causing Eden so much pain. I never wanted to see her face look like that again—that is, if she ever spoke to me again.

I smacked a fist on the window and screamed. Looking at the faded scars on my hands, I thought of breaking through the glass again, but then what use would I be to her? Broken hands wouldn't be able to defend.

I kicked the glass, but it didn't have the same effect and only caused my wounded leg to throb. Pushing my hands through my hair, I closed my eyes and focused. I focused on Eden.

I'm sorry. So, so, sorry.

The words came back to me as they reverberated off her walls, and I snarled. Moving to the windowed door, I smacked that. Maybe it wasn't as thick as the wall, and I could get through with less damage to my body.

I halted my third smack in mid-air when I met my father's eyes watching me through the window. He was flustered and the crow's feet around his eyes aged him ten years. I stepped back as he unlocked the door.

"Come. We need to move fast. We don't have much time."

"What?"

He pulled me through the door. "Let's go! I'm getting you out of here."

Quickly moving to Eden's cage, he unlocked her door, but I grabbed his arm before he entered. "Wait. I better go. She isn't particularly fond of you." I pushed past him and entered. "Eden? It's me, Jace." She didn't respond, so I slowly moved to her den door and crouched. "Eden?" Peering inside, I found her curled up on a blanket in the farthest back corner. Her back was to me, and she didn't stir. "Eden." She twitched. She heard me this time. "Please, Eden. We have to go. We don't have much time."

She turned slowly and looked at me. "Jace?"

"Yeah. Come on. Please." I held out my hand to her with pleading eyes. "Come."

She sat up and stared. "Why didn't you tell me earlier?"

I sighed, dropping my hand. "Because I didn't want this to happen to you. I didn't want you to retreat into yourself and do something destructive that could get you killed." She watched me for a long moment, no urgency in her face.

"Jace! Come on!" David hissed from the door.

"Come on, Eden. You can hate me later, but right now we have to get out of here." I held out my hand to her again, and she hesitantly took it, careful not to poke me with her claws. Scooting back, I helped her to her feet.

"I don't hate you, Jace. It's not your fault what my mother did, but please don't keep anything from me again."

"I promise." I pushed her forward. "We have to go." We met David outside her cage.

He looked between us. "Good?" We both nodded. "Good. Let's go. LaRae and Dr. Hahn are waiting with a car."

"A car?" I asked. "Cars are restricted only for the highest officials to use."

"I am head of research." David led us down the hallway to the stairway. The labs were empty besides the dying subjects that hopefully now will be cured. There wasn't a soul in sight. "They are all at the rally. This was our only chance, and our window is small."

We moved swiftly down the staircase to the bottom floor, rushing outside to the car waiting for us. He opened the door and Eden and I slid in. LaRae and Dr. Hahn were both waiting inside. David slid in after us and knocked on the roof when the door was shut. The car jerked forward and Eden grabbed my hand tightly, her claws cutting into my skin.

You all right?
Yeah, just never been in a car before.

I watched her trying to keep a stoic face, but the tension showed in the corners of her eyes and forehead. I stifled a smirk; I don't think that would be the best way to gain her trust back.

It will be all right.

Keeping her eyes on the passing streets and buildings, she nodded. I turned to look at LaRae and Dr. Hahn. "So, it worked."

"It worked," LaRae said with a smile, her bright gold eye like a small light in the dark car. "I'm so thankful for all the help you two gave."

"Help?" Eden turned to her. "We didn't *give* help."

Her smile faltered. "Right. Of course. Nevertheless, I'm thankful."

"Me too, me too," Dr. Hahn said. His gold eye didn't quite fit his face with his wild, white hair framing it.

We rode the rest of the trip in silence, and I held Eden's hand tight, biting down at the pain from her claws. I would not flinch away in pain, even if they did break my skin.

When we reached the eastern wall door, everyone exited in a quick dither and Eden dropped my hand. I fought the urge to snatch it back and keep her close, but I didn't want to fight with her independent nature.

"All right, leave. Run. Don't come back," David said, pushing all four of us toward the door. His eyes met mine, and I felt his pain. The others hustled to the wall door, but we stood in silence, watching each other. He stepped forward and put his hands on my shoulders. I examined his face, every wrinkle, every grey hair he had flecked along his temples. He may have made some bad choices that I didn't understand, but I couldn't just stop loving him. No matter what I called him, father or not, he had been my by side most of my life. Now he would have no one.

Squeezing my shoulders, he smiled. "All right, my boy. Go. Be safe." He pushed me toward the others, but instead of going, I pulled him into a hug.

Closing my eyes, I imagined I was five again. My father holding me tight before sending me off to my first day of school. He said those same words then, *all right, my boy, go. Be safe.*

"I'm sorry I couldn't be what you wanted."

"No, no son. You have become more than I could have ever wanted." Sniffing, he pushed me back and smiled. "I love you."

"I love you too." I squeezed his arms before heading to the wall door.

I reached the door and Dr. Hahn opened it carefully, peering out. "All right. Let's go. Go, go."

LaRae and Eden followed after him. I stopped just before passing through the door and looked back to David. He held up a single hand, trying not to let his chin quiver. We gave each other a knowing nod. This would be the last time we ever saw each other. Sending him one last smile, I closed the door and ran after the others into the woods.

Chapter 68

Eden

The cool breeze hit me with the smell of dirt and evergreen. The sun shone on the green canopy of leaves over us like jewels. I smiled at the song of the birds and the scurry of the squirrels as we ran past them. Jace and I moved at the lead, both eager to get back to the camp.

We can't run the whole way.
But we can get as far as we can into dusk.
Eden, look.

Jace stopped and turned to look at LaRae and Dr. Hahn. He panted out a laugh. "I think we should rest."

LaRae was limping at a very slow jog, holding her side, and Dr. Hahn was further behind, barely able to stand. His face was so red and his breathing so ragged, I could hear it clearly where we stood. *I'm surprised neither has had a heart attack.*

"Please. Rest," LaRae said

Dropping my head back with a sigh, I groaned. "Yeah. All right." I walked to a few birch trees and set my hand on the moss-covered white bark. Resting my forehead on the trunk, I breathed in the sweet scent of home.

"How far... is this place?" Dr. Hahn gasped, collapsing against a large northern trunk.

Sliding down the birch to the cool dirt ground, I looked between him and LaRae. "We should get there tomorrow. There's a cave about halfway we would like to make it to tonight. It's safer. But you two will have to try and keep pace with us."

"Safer?" LaRae's eyes widened, and her green eye looked vibrant next to her new gold one.

"Yeah. The scourges are rampant. We don't want to get caught up with any of them if we can avoid it." I looked to Dr. Hahn, whose red face was blushed more from embarrassment, turning it purple.

"I'm sorry. So, so, sorry. I didn't know."

"Just leave it. What's done is done." I stood, brushing off my pants. "We need to get moving if we are to make it before dark." They both stood and started after us.

Jace and I slowed our pace, keeping at a fast walk. They managed better, but Dr. Hahn still straggled behind, breathing heavy.

"So, how long did it take for you to get used to your... new senses?" LaRae puffed behind us.

I glanced back at her before continuing ahead. "I guess I don't really know. I grew up this way. Jace may be able to answer that one better."

"Yeah, about a week for me to fully comprehend everything new, but to be honest, I'm still getting used to it." He smiled at her, and I looked away before my cheeks warmed. We were finally free, out in the woods. We could be together if we wanted, nothing was keeping us apart. The idea excited yet terrified me, and I don't terrify easily.

I looked up and Jace was giving me a questioning look, but I shook it off before passing him to continue on.

We made it to the cave just before the darkness completely took over. I have never been so happy to see the rock opening. Just like the trees, I slid my hand along the cool, hard surface and set my cheek to it. I was greeting my way through the woods. Closing my eyes, I stood in silence, listening to the drip of the water and the hoot of the owl in the trees. A warm, gentle hand slid along my back, and I tensed, opening my eyes.

"I'll sit on watch, all right? You rest." Jace kept his voice low, and when I turned to speak, he put a finger to his lips motioning for me to be quiet. LaRae and Dr. Hahn were already passed out on the rocky ground. I couldn't help but smile. Meeting Jace's eyes, we stood in silence, watching each other but, this time, not through glass. I could reach out and touch him if I wanted. When his eyes dropped to my lips, my stomach seized, and I stepped back, looking away.

"All right. Wake me when you want to switch," I whispered and slide down the wall.

"Sure."

I watched his back as he walked to the mouth of the cave and found the large boulder we usually sat on. Closing my eyes, I focused my mind to empty everything so I could sleep. It didn't take long.

※

With my chin resting in my hand, my eyes drooped shut. I caught myself before I tipped over. Jace had woken me only a few hours before dawn, but I was exhausted. The mental stress of the situation was taking a toll.

"Careful," Jace said as he walked up beside me.

"How are you awake? How are you not tired?"

He grinned. "Too excited to get back. I'm surprised at how much I enjoy living out here."

LaRae and Dr. Hahn pulled themselves up and limped out of the cave. Their disheveled hair and bags under their eyes told me they may have survived the virus, but living in the luxury-free woods could be their end.

"Any chance we can go a bit slower today? That wasn't the most comfortable bed." Dr. Hahn's wild hair stuck out in every direction.

"We can, but we just may not be able to make it there before dark comes. Maybe you will be better once you get moving," I said.

After scavenging some berries and water from the stream, we set off. I led and Jace held up the rear, not wanting Dr. Hahn to get too far behind. Everyone was so focused on the hike, pushing through bushes, stepping over logs, and not slipping on the motes that no one spoke. Jace didn't even try and speak to me in my head. A pit in my stomach formed when I thought of the night before. His eyes on mine and how they dropped to my lips. I panicked, froze. This was all new territory for me.

I was so preoccupied with my thoughts that I didn't hear the screech or smell of sweaty skin. "Eden!" Jace's voice pulled me from my thoughts, and I spun around.

Four scourge headed toward us. I tugged LaRae's arm and pushed her in front of me. "Run!" Her eyes widened, but she didn't hesitate, charging ahead.

I have nothing. No weapon.
Use your claws!

Smart, why didn't I think of that?

Jace picked up a thick branch, taking it out on two scourges. Dr. Hahn stumbled toward me, looking like he was about to cry. I pushed him after LaRae. "Run!" He kept moving forward, never looking back.

Curling my fingers, I charged the remaining two scourges. My training from both Old Bob and Brian flooded back through me and my arms and legs were a blur. I slashed and kicked each one, letting out all of my pent-up rage from the last few months, and before Jace had taken down his two, mine were dead. I stalked over to help him as he knocked one to the ground, then turned back to attack the other. I grabbed the one from the ground as it stood, and in one swift movement, broke its neck. Jace wavered a second to watch me, but then turned again hitting the last scourge on the head with his stick. It fell to the ground, still.

"That was impressive," he said, and I tried not to look too proud of myself as I wiped my bloody claws onto my pants.

A twig snapped, and we both whipped around. Jace held up the branch ready for anything. Standing just behind a few trees were the most beautiful ice-blue eyes and curly blond hair. "Tate!" I bounded toward his stunned face, but as I got closer, he opened his arms to let me in. We collided with so much force that he fell back onto the leaf-infested ground. I buried my nose in his neck and breathed in his rosy citrus scent.

We had made it just short of the camp. They must have heard the fighting or seen LaRae and Dr. Hahn.

"Eden?"

I turned to see Old Bob approach us. Sniffing, I stood and moved to him, not caring that my cheeks were soaked with tears. He pulled me toward him, giving my claws a quick glance before his burly arms completely covering me, and I relaxed. He saw what I have become, and he didn't push me away. I let all the tension from the last few months free. I was safe. Safe in my father's arms. He tried to push me back, but I refused, holding him close. His warmth, his smell, was home.

"What happened?" Tate asked.

"Oh. It's a very long story," Jace said.

"Is Tristan with you?" Old Bob said into my hair and I stilled. Tristan. I would have to tell them what happened, and they will hate me for it. I killed him.

Stop. That's not true.

I stepped back but kept Old Bob's hands in mine. When I met his eyes, I didn't have to say a word. He knew.

"No," he whispered. "How?"

I opened my mouth, but nothing came out. I couldn't say the words. Jace's hand touched my arm. "That is part of the story. Let's talk about it over dinner?"

Old Bob tore his eyes from mine and looked to Jace. "Yes, of course." He put his arm around my shoulder, pulling me close. Tate's eyes roamed my face, down to my claws, but he also didn't balk at me. Relief flowed through me; they accepted me for what I have become.

A loud bark rang from the camp and my heart leapt. "Ash!" I took a step forward, then spotted his grey fur springing toward me. He jumped into my arms, and I buried my face in his thick mane. "Oh, Ash. I missed you." Moving back, I smiled into his gold eyes. He licked me, then turned to Jace who knelt next to us.

"Hey, buddy." He scratched behind his ears and Ash groaned with pleasure. Jace smiled at me, but I quickly looked away and stood feeling my cheeks warm. Ash stayed so close he was leaning on my leg as we moved.

Little one?

Brian and Derek emerged from the crowd and surveyed us. Brian pulled Jace into a one-armed hug. "Jace! Eden!"

"Hey, Brian," Jace smirked.

Grabbing Old Bob and Tate's hands with Ash at my heels, we pushed through the growing crowd. Most people were smiling and greeting us as we passed, all curious how we escaped the city, but some watched us nervously.

It looks like you have a lot to tell us.

Derek's voice rang through my mind. He watched LaRae and Dr. Hahn as they followed us to his tent with wide nervous eyes.

You have no idea.

Chapter 69

Jace

We sat around the table in Derek's tent with fresh food on our plates, and my heart was happy. I haven't known these people long, but in that short time, they have wormed their way into my heart to become like family. Eden, Dr. Hahn, LaRae, and I told our stories of what happened and everyone listened with eager ears. Jon had joined as the people's voice and ears, whatever that meant. Everyone inspected Eden's new claws and her longer fangs with curiosity, but no one dared make her feel like a monster. I could feel that fear within her, but I insisted that it would be all right, and it was.

"So, the walls are open?" Jon asked.

"That was going to be the next step once everyone was given the cure," LaRae said.

"And by cure you mean, becoming like... you all." Jon waved a hand toward all of us.

"That's right," LaRae said.

Jon scoffed, shaking his head. "No way I would do that."

Derek sat back and ran a hand through his greying hair. "Wow. So, this could all be over." Everyone sat stunned at the possibility that life may return to somewhat normal. "Zane." He shook his head. "I knew he was a slimy bastard, but to have created the virus himself? That's a new low."

"Why would he do that?" Tate asked.

Old Bob sat forward. "He never agreed with President Jacobs. He thought he was weak. After the war, resources were so low, Zane was pushing Jacobs to try and take control of resources, both in the north and south. Jacobs was insistent on working peacefully with both sides."

"Even though communication was non-existent, Zane still insisted on world power. That must be why he went behind Jacobs's back to create the virus. He wanted to give him a reason to attack our neighbors," Derek said.

"What happened to Jacobs?" Eden asked.

The room rushed with sadness. "He died from the virus. That's when Zane made his move to take control," Derek replied.

Dr. Hahn wiped a single tear away. "I'm so very sorry. I wish... I wish I could go back and—"

"Nothing we can do now about it," Brian said but pursed his lips. "Just tell us one thing, Dr. Hahn. Why? Why did you create it?"

"I... I was scared. Zane... threatened me. My family. I didn't have much choice."

"And my mother?" Eden asked.

"What? Mom?" Tate said.

"The same... Zane, he threatened Tate and your father. She was just doing what she thought was protecting you, but later regretted it."

"That's why she planned the bombing," Old Bob added.

"What?" Tate said again. "Our mother created the virus *and* planned the rebel bombing?"

"There is a lot you can learn about your mother." Old Bob gave Tate's shoulder a squeeze.

I looked to Eden who had been avoiding my eyes ever since that moment in the cave. I could sense her fear. I just needed a moment alone with her to let her know that I understood, and I wasn't going to push her. It was all on her terms.

"Should others, who want to, go and get the cure as well?" Jon asked. He sat forward with intent grey eyes on LaRae. They had a similarity to Zane's, only Jon's weren't hollow.

"No, no." Dr. Hahn sat forward. Since the escape, he had become much twitchier, making it hard for him to focus or do simple tasks such as eat. "I believe that since you have lived out here, you have built up an immunity. If you haven't caught it already, then you should be fine. Yes, fine, fine."

Brian sat forward and looked to both the scientists. "So, you have the same... side effects as all of us?" He motioned to him, Derek, Eden, and me.

"Yes." LaRae smiled. "It's very... new."

He laughed. "I bet it is."

Dr. Hahn looked between Derek, Brian, and Old Bob. His face dropped, and he brought up a shaky hand to his mouth. "My, my, I didn't... I didn't realize." He pointed between them. "Robert Sewell." Old Bob smiled. "Derek Robins." Derek gave him a single nod. "Brian Jacobs." Brian smiled. "I... I changed you."

"Yes, you did. I was wondering if you would recognize us," Derek said, giving the nervous scientist a friendly smile.

"We... we thought you were... dead. Yes, dead. That is until Jace mentioned you the other day to Zane."

"That was the plan," Brian said, turning to Jace. "So, Zane knows we are alive?"

"I'm afraid so," LaRae replied.

"Well, this could get interesting," Brian said.

"How so?" Tate asked.

"Well, we didn't leave Zane on the best of terms." Derek shared a smirk with Brian. "Who knows what his next play will be. We just need to be on alert."

"He doesn't know a lot of us are alive. It could be a rude awakening for him," Old Bob said before taking a long sip of his tea.

"Well good thing we have you then, Robert." Derek smiled. A lot must have happened on their end as well when we were gone. The tension that was felt before we left wasn't there, replaced with more of a mutual respect and understanding.

"So you knew nothing of what was done to you? What about the pictures in your tent?" Eden asked Derek.

His cheek twitched. "Ah, yes. I would rather not think about you breaking into my tent." Their eyes locked but didn't hold anger only humor. Everyone was fine, so all was well. "And, no. We didn't know what was done to us." He looked to Dr. Hahn, then back to Eden. "When the bombing happened, we took the chance to run. I grabbed those papers as we ran from the lab. I didn't have time for questions or analyzing anything."

Dr. Hahn sat forward. "So that's where those papers went." He scratched his head with a chuckle then looked to Eden. "No. I didn't disclose what I was doing. I had to make sure what I did to you wasn't a fluke, but I didn't want to chance them fighting it as well. Turns out, it wasn't a fluke." He frowned. "Even though I wasn't able to replicate it after that due to—"

"It could have happened to the best of us," LaRae said, putting a reassuring hand on his. He gave her a sad smile. She turned to the others. "I'm sure you all are very curious about life since you... escaped."

I sat back and watched the conversation of old comrades catching up on the last eighteen years. Glancing over at Eden, I smiled to see her reunited with Ash. She slowly pet his head as it rested on her lap. Her cheeks turned rosy with my eyes on them, but I didn't look away.

Can we talk?

Her hand stilled and she swallowed. So many emotions flowed through her, but the biggest was fear. She was scared of me... of us.

Eden... It's all right. I get—

She stood so quickly her chair tipped and everyone turned to her. She cleared her throat. "I... I need some air."

"Sure." Old Bob started to stand. "Do you want company?" I put my hand on his shoulder shaking my head.

"I'll go. You stay and talk. There's a lot to get caught up on." He nodded, then turned back to the others.

I followed Eden out of the tent. She was already halfway down the row of tents by the time I made it outside. I jogged to reach her side but didn't speak. We walked in silence a moment until we reached the small clearing that we used for our training.

"Eden."

She turned quickly to face me, keeping her eyes down. "I'm sorry. I just don't..."

I chuckled and she looked at me confused. "Eden. Relax. I get it."

"You do?"

"Yeah, of course, I do." I stepped forward, keeping my hands at my sides. I wanted so badly to touch her, but I didn't want to scare her away. "We have just been through something major. Life changing. You have changed; heck, I have changed more than I ever expected." I sighed looking at how the sun hit her hair, making it shimmer. "Let's just take it slow, all right? Let it happen... naturally."

She swallowed again, watching me. "Really?"

"Yes really. God, Eden. Did you think I wanted to marry you or something?" I laughed again when her eyes went wide. "No. I don't want to marry you. I mean... not now... I mean." I needed to shut up. "Let's just take it slow, all right?"

She let out a long sigh and smiled. "Thank you."

"You don't need to thank me, Eden, but maybe next time just... talk to me?" I gave her arm a little nudge, and she giggled. The tips of her fangs peeked out as she smiled. I was so happy the Eden I met wasn't fully lost to the new one. Her confidence was still there—she was still Eden.

"There you are." Tate walked up to us. "Everything all right?" He looked between us with a knowing look.

"Yeah." Eden smiled and pulled his arm to her, resting her head on his shoulder. "Come. Let's go for a walk." He held her hand, feeling her claws with interest before placing it back on his arm. I didn't breathe, waiting for him to say something, but he didn't.

"Sure." Tate smiled at her.

I watched them slowly walk away, arm in arm, reminiscing about their life, about what happened. I could almost see the relief and love flowing off Eden and just that alone was enough. Seeing her happy and safe was enough.

Chapter 70

Eden

Ash was curled up with me on the cot, and I stroked his sleeping head. He hadn't left my side since I returned. I loved him, but these cots weren't made for a human and a wolf. I had woken to the sounds of the camp and the sun warming the fabric of the tent walls. Laughter sounded from a nearby tent, and I smiled at the feeling of home. It wasn't the cabin, but it was a home. Ash and I were alone as Tate, Old Bob, and Jace left to their assigned jobs as guards. The past few days have been all about planning and getting back to normal. Guards were increased in the fear that Zane may send people to bring us back, but so far, nothing has been seen except some scourges scrounging for food.

LaRae and Dr. Hahn have made themselves at home with Sarah in the clinic. Dr. Hahn's nervous twitches have slowly relaxed, and with the lack of constant threats from leadership, they may completely disappear over time.

After my talk with Jace, we have returned to normal. Teasing each other, which of course means him driving me crazy, but his beautiful eyes and single dimple still make my heart skip. I know he knows it, but I'm thankful he is giving me space to figure everything out.

"Eden?" Sarah peeked her head through the tent flap. I sat up, meeting her eyes. "Eden. You need to come. Something—"

I was on my feet moving toward her with Ash at my heels. "What happened?" I pushed past her, heading toward the medic tent.

Her short legs worked fast to catch up with me. "It's... It's—"

"Who!" I turned to her and she stepped back, scared. Sighing, I closed my eyes taking a long breath. Turning, I started again toward the tent. Images of Tristan shot, then Tristan sick, then Tristan dead flashed through me. I couldn't lose anyone else I love.

She grabbed my arm to a halt before I entered the tent. "Here." She handed me a face mask.

Slowly taking it, I looked at her. "What's going on?"

"Just put it on. We need to be careful." She put one over her face and entered the tent.

The elastic of the mask tugged at my ears, and I immediately hated it. After making sure it covered my nose and chin, I followed her. Lying on two cots were LaRae and Dr. Hahn. They glistened with sweat and wheezed with every breath.

Sarah stood next to LaRae's cot, and I slowly approached. "I don't understand. They have the cure."

Sarah nodded. "Yes, but viruses morph. They have the cure for the original virus. It cured them of the virus they were injected with. It's been eighteen years since that virus, so the one that's out here is most likely different. They must have now come down with the one out here." She put a cool cloth on LaRae's brow. I could see her body relax into her cot at the cooling sensation. I remembered the overwhelming fire that burned through me, the heaviness, and the throbs.

"Then why don't I get it?" The thought of going through the Fever again made me cringe.

"You lived in the woods your whole life. Your body has built up some immunity. Now, I'm sure you could still get it, but chances are much less."

"Jace?" My heart froze at the thought.

"Again, unsure. Since Jace contracted the virus when he was in the woods and given blood from Ash, who has lived in the woods his whole life, he may be more resistant to it, but like you, there is a chance he could get sick as well. "

I turned back to LaRae. Her eyes fluttered open and her finger lifted ever so lightly. Pulling up a chair next to her, I took her hand.

"Run."

"What?"

LaRae swallowed and I could hear her dry tongue slide across the roof of her mouth. "You run."

I met Sarah's eyes. "Do the others know?" She nodded.

"Get them, please."

She left the tent, and I turned back to LaRae.

"Why should I run?" I squeezed her hand gently, trying to pass any strength I had on to her.

"Zane... won't give up. You need to... Get far away."

Her words sent a chill through me. *Zane won't give up.* I ran my tongue over my pointy fangs and imagined sliding them into his throat. The same image I have had over and over. I should have killed him when I had the chance.

"She's right," Derek said from the tent flap, pulling me from my vision. He entered with everyone in tow. Jace and Tate came to stand near me while Old Bob stayed by Derek, and Brian held Sarah's hand. "You and Jace need to go. If people start getting sick, he will want you." He adjusted his mask, which seemed almost too small for his large head.

"What about you two?" I looked at Derek and Brian. "Zane now knows you are alive. Won't he come for you?"

"Probably, but we can take care of ourselves. Plus, we have some unfinished business with him," Derek said.

Gently releasing LaRae's hand, I stood. "Why shouldn't I just fight? I mean. I am stronger now. Faster."

"It's suicide, Eden. You are stronger and faster, but they have weapons that can take you down in a second." Jace touched my arm. I looked to him and then back to LaRae.

"We could go back, try and help the people who get sick."

"What? Why?" Tate yelled. "After everything they did to you!"

"Because Tate! You didn't see them. All those innocent people whose lives are gone because of Zane. Now people trusted him, got his cure, and may still get sick. Maybe we can help."

"No, no, no, no, Eden. Stop. You don't have to save the world."

"But—"

"No!" Jace moved in front of me. "You can't always be the savior, Eden. You have to let others do their job. They have scientists. They will figure it out."

"They didn't for eighteen years!"

"It was a simple overlook. That doesn't mean it's going to happen again." He lowered his face level with mine, peering into my eyes.

Please. I can't lose you. Remember?

I let out a frustrated sigh. "I just got back." The hole in my heart started to grow more. The thought of leaving them again made me ache already.

"I know, but it's the only way," Derek said.

"I'm going with you." Tate stepped toward me. "I just got you back, and we are safer together." I reached out and squeezed his hand.

"I agree. If you both go, then I go too," Old Bob said. The hole filled just a tiny bit knowing they would be with me. There were only two spaces left, spaces only Ellie and Tristan could fill.

"Where will we go? Since the war, there isn't anything left?" I asked.

"We don't really know that. No one has ever explored. We might as well go see. The four of us," Old Bob replied.

"Five," I corrected, looking down at Ash.

"Five." Old Bob laughed, giving Ash an apologetic pat on the head.

"Well, you better pack. You don't want to take too much time," Derek said.

I looked down at LaRae, who watched our conversation with slitted eyes. Her cheek twitched as I reached down to squeeze her hand again. "Thank you." She gave me a long blink back. We watched each other a moment, a silent goodbye. We both knew that this may be the last time we would see each other. I glanced at Dr. Hahn. He was sleeping as peacefully as he could. Sighing, I exited the tent after the others.

∽

"Remember everything we taught you," Brian said as he set the pack on my back. "And stay focused."

"Got it." I faced him and he smiled down at me, the grey flecks of his scruffy chin catching in the sunlight. "Thank you."

"Ah, no. Don't thank me." He squeezed my shoulder. "Show me. Be safe."

I nodded and moved into him, wrapping my arms around his thick neck. "I'll see you again." He tightened his arms around me.

"I hope so."

But I didn't hope, I knew. I would see them all again. When, I don't know, but I would.

After giving Derek and Sarah both goodbye hugs, I turned to my family. With everyone ready, packs on their backs, even Ash, we set off into the unknown. For the first hour of walking, I clutched my butterfly necklace, feeling the spirits of Ellie and Tristan walking with us. Even though we were no longer living in the cabin, we were together. Wherever they were was home.

Thank you

This is only the beginning of Eden's story. I hope you fell in love with Eden and Jace as much as I did when I was writing them.

Thank you for taking the time to read my first novel in a world filled with amazing stories. I am honored you picked up my book.

Authors wouldn't exist without readers, so thank you for making me an author.

I would greatly appreciate your review on this book, since that is the best social proof a book can have.

Acknowledgments

There are so many people to thank for the development of this novel. First, my grandmother, Elizabeth Harri. She was my first reader and always had positive things to say about my six-year-old writing.

Thank you to my friends, Melissa Williams, Katie Ginivan, Vanessa Barnes, and Anna Lynch. You all helped me so much in the creation and flow of this story. It wouldn't be what it is today without all of your help.

Thank you, thank you, thank you to Katie Chambers at Beacon Point LLC for your expert editing. You not only edited my work, but you made me a better writer with all of your help and insight. My book went to you as a caterpillar and came out a butterfly. I will be forever thankful.

Thank you to Ellen Bitterman, my proofreader. Your sharp eye and positive nature helped me get my book over the last hill before publication.

Thank you to my parents who always kept my path open so I could be whatever I wanted. To my brother, you will get a signed first edition. Don't worry.

To my husband, thank you for encouraging me and letting me make this dream a reality. Now you get to read your fourth book!

To my daughters, you have thrown my life upside down with both your wild spirits, but I wouldn't have it any other way. I love you both to the moon and back.

Last, but not least. Thank you to my dog, GCH CH Chrisan Playing for the Ashes, 'Ash' You are my inspiration for Ash in the book. If it wasn't for you, the seed of Eden's story would not have bloomed on our walk in the woods. Thank you, buddy.

About the Author

At a young age, C. J. Singh was enraptured with books and the art of storytelling. She would write little stores about animals for her grandma to read. As she got older, she enjoyed reading fantasy, romance, and thrillers in between studying for tests for her master's in education. Longing for a real-life adventure outside the pages of these books, she traveled around the world, learning about other cultures and ways of life. To date, she has been to twelve countries. While out on one of her adventures—walking her dog, Ash, in the woods—she got the idea to write about a girl living in the woods with her pet, Ash. She tested out her ideas by telling short made-up bedtime stories to her daughter. Eventually, she decided to embark on one of her greatest adventures: writing this book. She may have just been destined to be an author; after all, she shares a birthday with her favorite author, Beatrix Potter—how cool is that?

Made in the USA
Las Vegas, NV
22 February 2021